# EVIE GRACE

# *The Lace Maiden*

arrow books

1 3 5 7 9 10 8 6 4 2

Arrow Books
20 Vauxhall Bridge Road
London SW1V 2SA

Arrow Books is part of the Penguin Random House group of companies whose addresses can be found at global.penguinrandomhouse.com.

First published in Great Britain by Arrow Books in 2020

www.penguin.co.uk

A CIP catalogue record for this book is available from the British Library

ISBN 9781787464407

Typeset in 10.75/13.5 pt Palatino
by Integra Software Services Pvt. Ltd, Pondicherry

Printed and bound in Great Britain by Clays Ltd, Elcograf S.p.A.

*To my family and friends*

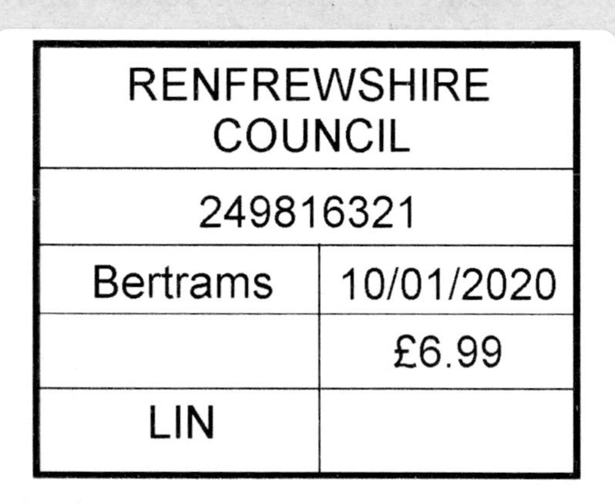

# *Acknowledgements*

I should like to thank Laura and everyone at MBA Literary Agents, and Cass and the team at Penguin Random House UK for their enthusiasm and support for The Smuggler's Daughters series.

# Chapter One

## *Under Cover of Darkness*

**Deal, August 1811**

The sea was running up the beach as it had on the night Ma died. Blades of lightning tore rents in the dark sky and illuminated the black canvas sails and painted keels of the Deal luggers and galley punts hovering in the Downs. The rain seeped through Louisa's oilskins and seawater rushed over the tops of her boots, taking her by the ankles and dragging her down the steep slope towards the foaming breakers.

Winnie threw her the end of the pony's rope. Twisting it around her hand, Louisa hauled herself back to safety and stood on the stones beside the pony, the white star between his eyes covered with blacking.

'You need to be more careful. The gobblers are watching us!' Winnie's voice was drowned out by a crash of thunder that echoed from the sandhills to South Foreland.

'I'm sorry.' Louisa was aware she should have known better, being the eldest of the Lennicker daughters. She was nineteen to Winnie's seventeen.

'They're looking in our direction.' Fourteen-year-old Grace huddled closer to her sisters while the Revenue men looked on.

'What can they do? There are five of them to at least two hundred and fifty of us,' Louisa said lightly. The loose association between the Deal families was based on trust, an undefined code of honour. They might fight amongst themselves from time to time, but when they were running goods, bringing them over from Gravelines and Dunkirk, unloading them on the beaches and carrying them inland to be hidden or sold, they worked together, united against the Revenue.

Her heart pounded with a heady mixture of excitement, anticipation and fear, as the pony fidgeted and tossed his head.

The plans had been made and the conditions were perfect: an oppressively hot August day had turned into a stormy night, the moon obscured by heavy cloud. But the bad weather hadn't been enough to keep the gobblers away, and the wind kept dimming the lanterns and blowing out the fire that the women were looking after at the top of the shingle beach.

The Riding officers came closer, then stopped.

'They won't get through tonight,' Louisa heard one of them say. 'The cutter, *Pride*, is armed and waiting to intercept them, and the Waterguard are on patrol.'

'I don't like the sound of that,' Winnie whispered.

'Ah, good evening, ladies. What brings you out on a night like this?' one of the officers asked. 'Let me guess,' he went on, his voice laced with sarcasm. 'You are taking the air.'

'We're collecting lugworms for bait – they creep out from between the stones under the cover of darkness.' Louisa noticed how he glanced towards his fellow officers for guidance.

'You should know better – she's having you on, Officer Chase,' one chuckled. 'Lugworms are dug up from their burrows in the sand at low tide. You have much to learn of our adversaries' ways, coming from the country as you do.'

'Don't keep ragging him – he's doing his best.' Louisa recognised the speaker as Tom Lawrence who had given up ropemaking to join the Revenue many years before. He'd made a few enemies of former friends and acquaintances in his role as a Riding officer, employed to intercept the free traders as they carried contraband inland, having evaded the Revenue cruisers looking out for them at sea. 'It's been a pleasure as always, ladies, but we have work to do.'

They rode their horses a little further along the shore and waited, their hats pulled down, shading their faces as the rain began to ease and the fire above them started to smoke then burn with a fierce flame, thanks to a few armfuls of dry straw.

First the *Whimbrel* came in, grinding her keel on to the shingle. Master Jason Witherall, who was better known as Marlin – short for marlinspike – and the captain of the giant three-masted lugger, forty feet long and seven feet wide, set his crew to unloading her straight away, removing goods from her open deck. Soon after, came the *Good Intent*, a second lugger owned by the Rattlers, the gang run by One Eye Feasey. Then came the *Spindrift*, a single-masted galley punt, laid low in the water by her hefty cargo and taking two attempts to beach, then several smaller luggers or cats, including the Lennickers' boat, the *Pamela*.

'Where's the *Pride*?' Winnie asked. 'There's no sign of her.'

'She can't get near the beach in these conditions without ending up as matchwood.' Louisa kept her eye on the Riding officers who, perhaps put off by the armoury of guns on the luggers and galley punt, continued to look on as the men relieved the boats of their cargo. 'There's Pa and Billy.'

Protected by batsmen armed with staves, Mr Lennicker and their lodger were lowering tubs, bales and trunks from the *Pamela* on to the shore. The tub carriers – labourers whom Pa had hired from their uncle's market garden – took on the rib-crushing task of carrying two casks each, one on their chest, one across their shoulders. The duffers, the men who carried the tea, grabbed the dollops or bags of it and removed them from the beach to find somewhere dry where they could divide the spoils and hide them in their slops for the long walk to London. The horses and carts, hooves and wheels muffled with rags, were made ready to stash the remaining goods in various hiding places.

Many of the townspeople of Deal and others living in the outlying villages joined in as they and their families had done for generations, starting out as owlers, smuggling wool to France, then continuing in the lucrative free trade, taking advantage of the Kent coast's proximity to Northern France and the plentiful landing places.

They imported goods such as tea, gin and leather under the noses of the Revenue officers and Customs men, evading the taxes imposed by the government for paying towards the war against Napoleon, duties that they would willingly have paid, Louisa thought, if they'd been fair and reasonable.

Grace held on to the pony while Louisa helped Winnie strap several oilskin-wrapped packs of what she hoped was a fine haul of lace, gloves and silk to his back. With luck, it would bring them a tidy sum when they came to sell it. The fact that it was illegal to bring such luxury items over from France lent them a precious rarity in a time of war. 'Hurry,' Winnie urged. 'You're all fingers and thumbs.'

'It's because her mind's elsewhere,' Grace teased, glancing over at Master Witherall.

'It isn't,' Louisa said firmly. 'Rumour has it that he's promised to Miss Hibben.'

'Margaret from the bakery in Middle Street? Oh, that's a pity.' Grace sounded crestfallen. 'Then there's no chance for any of us.'

'Not with Marlin. He's never taken any notice of us anyway.'

'Will you please make haste?' Winnie said. 'The sooner we're away from here, the better.'

'I know. I know.' Louisa was checking the fastenings when Officer Chase suddenly raised his pistol and fired off a shot. Men yelled and women screamed, the horses started, and the pony they'd borrowed galloped away.

'Run after him, Grace.' Louisa panicked, thinking of their money vanishing into the darkness. 'Why did you let him go?' she grumbled when her sister returned a few minutes later with the pony at her side.

'I couldn't hold on to him,' she said contritely. 'I thought he was going to tear my arms out.'

A volley of musket fire rang out from one of the luggers and a group of batsmen began cursing and waving their staves at the Riding officers who – apparently deciding that discretion was the better part of valour – turned to ride away, but before they had travelled any distance, a lieutenant and his guard arrived.

Eyeing their glinting sabres, Louisa wasn't sure whether to make a quick departure or stay – either way, they were in danger of being arrested. She heard Winnie muttering the Lord's prayer for deliverance as the soldiers marched down towards them, stopping beside the *Whimbrel* where the figure of Marlin's father stepped up to greet them.

'May I offer you a little cognac?' he asked.

'Do you really think I'm that wet behind the ears?' the lieutenant said. 'It's a heinous crime to bribe one of His Majesty's loyal servants, as well as being against the law to import French brandy.'

'I thought it a gen'rous offer to warm the cockles of your heart. I'm sorry that you and your honourable men 'ave been called out unnecessarily on such a miserable night.' Mr Witherall looked in the direction of the Riding officers who had come back, apparently reassured by the presence of the militia. Officer Chase had dismounted and broached one of the barrels with a gimlet. He grimaced as he tasted its contents.

'That's far too strong for you, my lad,' Mr Witherall said cheerfully.

'My Inspector will be here in a minute – you won't be laughing then, I tell you.'

'My old friend, Nick Chase, I 'ardly recognised you.'

'You know this man?' the lieutenant asked the officer.

'I know them all by name and nature,' he responded. 'You've never met such a band of villains. They must be arrested forthwith, every one of them.'

'On what charge?' the lieutenant asked.

'Use your eyes, sir.'

'Not being able to see in the dark, I'm finding it impossible to tell one from the other. I suggest we wait until first light.'

'That's no good – they'll be long gone by then.' Louisa's heart began to flutter like the wings of a panicked sparrow as Officer Chase turned to them. 'Take these ladies into custody at the very least.'

'You know we're forbidden to rummage persons of the fairer sex.'

'They've been loading this pony with run goods right under our noses.'

'Ladies, does this creature belong to you?' the lieutenant said, addressing them.

'No, sir. It has nothing to do with us.' Louisa trembled as the memory of another night flashed through her mind.

She had been carrying Grace in her arms when she, Winnie and their mother had been confronted by one of the Riding officers. Winnie, who'd been complaining of being too hot, had fallen silent and hidden behind Ma's skirts while Louisa had hugged Grace tightly.

'That's the roliest-poliest babe I've ever seen,' he'd said. 'Surely your children will boil in this heat, missus? I beg you to remove the outer layers of their clothing on this warm summer's eve.'

Louisa's instinct had been to run, but Ma was as cool as a cucumber.

'If you have the best interests of my daughters at heart, you will let us go forth so I can remedy the situation – I will not undress them in front of all and sundry,' she had said in the same King's English that she had taught her daughters to speak, liking to maintain her standards. She had been beautiful, tall and slender, and to look at her, many people, including the Riding officer, made the mistake of thinking that she was like a piece of willow, easily bent and swayed from her purpose, when in fact she was as straight and strong as a sweet chestnut. He had had no choice but to let her go, leaving her free to sell the lace that they were carrying, wrapped around their waists, to the draper on another day.

'We found the poor thing on the beach,' Grace said, bringing her back to the present. Her face in the guard's lantern was a picture of innocence. 'All I can think of is returning it to its rightful owner.' If the lieutenant noticed how the blacking was coming off on Grace's hand as she stroked the pony's head, he didn't say.

Another uniformed man on horseback came and halted beside them: Inspector of Riding Officers.

'You sent for me?' He yawned. 'Why have you dragged me from my warm bed?'

Officer Chase sounded petulant when he described the operation and the fact that the militia wouldn't assist in bringing a stop to it so they could arrest the free traders and seize the contraband.

All the time, the men continued unloading and the crowd dispersing, the duffers trudging away wearing coats over their slops, their brows beaded with sweat, and the tub carriers struggling up the beach, taking three steps forward and sliding two steps back.

The rain stopped, and the fresh salt air filled with the sweet scent of tobacco and smoke as the tension grew: between Officer Chase and his superior; the Riding officers and the militia; those upholding the law and the boatmen.

Deciding to slip away while those responsible for maintaining order were preoccupied, Louisa reached out for Winnie's hand.

'Let's go,' she whispered, and the three of them walked the pony along the beach as their father, shrouded in his sou'wester and oilskins, left Billy transferring the last of the goods from the *Pamela*. Instead of joining his daughters, he diverted to where One Eye's gang were fighting each other as they unloaded the *Good Intent*.

Alarmed, Louisa insisted that she and her sisters follow him.

'What's he up to?' Winnie asked. 'He'll land himself in trouble one of these days.'

'I'm going to find out. You two, wait here.' Before Louisa could investigate, their father came back, dragging a sledge loaded with boxes and a couple of tubs.

'What are you doing?' she hissed. 'They don't belong to you.'

'Finders keepers.' He grinned. 'The Rattlers are too busy having a punch-up to notice.'

'But they'll find out. Oh. Leave it. Please. For all our sakes,' Louisa begged as he continued to drag the goods away. 'They'll have your guts for garters.'

'Don't fuss, my dear. Old lady luck is smilin' down on me tonight. I thought the cutter was goin' to 'ave us, but then the *Whimbrel* bore down on 'er and she backed off. Once we were past 'er, she didn't dare follow – only the Deal boatmen are bold enow to land in this kind of surf. Now, don't 'ang about. Take what you 'ave to the usual place – Mr Trice's agent will be waitin' for you at the Three Kings with his post-chaise. Keep your eyes and ears open.'

'Come with us,' Louisa said.

'You've done this kind of thing many times before – you don't need my 'elp.'

'I'm asking so I can keep my eye on you.'

'Much as I'm grateful for your concern, I don't need you mitherin' me. Run along now.'

Louisa and her sisters followed him up the beach, whence his figure merged with the shadows of the night and disappeared altogether.

As they walked uphill to Kingsdown, then turned northwards towards Walmer, Louisa recalled how Ma had used to go out without them, slipping out on what she described as an 'errand of mercy', while Pa went fishing. She would be left alone with Winnie and Grace, praying that the gobblers wouldn't catch their mother and that the notorious Goodwin Sands – the monstrous expanse of ever-changing sandbank and swatches nine miles wide and four miles offshore – wouldn't entrap their father as they had Marlin's grandfather many years before when he'd given up his life to save the captain and crew of a sinking ship.

To distract her sisters and make the time pass more quickly, she would tell them stories.

'Do you remember the legend of the lace?' she said softly.

'Our parents' story.' She thought Grace was smiling as she went on, 'How once upon a time, a fisherman fell helplessly in love with a girl from the woods and fields.'

'He asked for her hand in marriage and she said yes,' Winnie joined in. 'And then she wove him a fishing net.'

'He went out on his boat and cast the net into the sea,' Louisa said. 'When he pulled it up again, he'd caught a strange web of seaweed, woven into a beautiful pattern of flowers and sea creatures. He gave it to the girl and on the very same day, he was called up to war. Crying her eyes out, she sat on the shore to wait for him, unpicking the web. When she found out how to make the pattern, she worked it with bobbins and silk, and that's how the first lace was made.'

'Ma never made lace,' Winnie pointed out.

'I know – and Pa was never called up to fight—'

'He's volunteered for the Sea Fencibles,' Winnie cut in.

'It's just a fable, a legend like I said.'

'I will continue to think of it as true, no matter what you say, Winnie.' Grace pulled the pony to a halt and they took turns in removing a few lengths of lace from one of the packs and wrapping them around their waists and thighs beneath their petticoats. Safe in the knowledge that they couldn't be searched, Louisa stuffed a few handkerchiefs and pairs of gloves inside her bodice for good measure before they moved on again.

'You're waddling like a duck,' Grace giggled.

'Whist!' Winnie said sternly, and they went on their way in silence, travelling through Walmer and eventually reaching the road into Deal. Having hurried past the castle to avoid any unsavoury characters who might be lurking in the shadows of its great walls, they left the barracks and signalling tower behind them.

'Watch out for Jacks and thieves,' Winnie warned as a pair of sailors on shore-leave emerged swaggering from a doorway, fighting over a coat.

'They think they're such dapper fellows in those flouncy shirts,' Louisa chuckled, realising that they were almost home and dry.

'The fashions of yesteryear,' Grace added as one snatched the coat and ran, closely followed by his drunken friend.

They carried on to the Three Kings Hotel, where Winnie and Grace waited with the pony while Louisa went to find Mr Trice's agent who was ready and waiting. They loaded the run goods into his post-chaise by lantern light before he set off for London, an eleven-hour journey if he chose to travel the toll road connecting Deal to Sandwich, longer if he took the back routes to avoid detection.

Louisa breathed a sigh of relief.

'We've done it,' Winnie said.

'And the gobblers didn't arrest us,' Grace added.

'Farmer George has missed out on his taxes again,' Louisa said, amused, 'not that he needs the money. He can't spend it – he's gone mad.'

'The Prince Regent will want his dues to pay for his extravagances, though,' Winnie observed.

'We'd better stop cotchering. We've still got to return the pony back before we can go home.' Louisa glanced back at the hotel where a light was shining in one of the windows. 'Do you remember Admiral Nelson's visit to Deal, Grace? You could only have been four or five.'

'He stayed here, didn't he?'

'Lady Hamilton was staying at the same time. Ma was furious, considering it an unforgivable scandal. I don't think his heroism at Trafalgar went any way to make up for it – in her eyes, at least,' Winnie said.

'How can you say that? Don't you remember the way Ma wept when the *Victory* came sailing past with Nelson's body? Every ship in the Downs lowered their pennants and ensigns to half-mast.'

Winnie changed the subject. 'I hope all is well with Pa. I can't think what possessed him to take what wasn't his to take.'

Their father's actions worried Louisa too. You didn't steal another man's goods, least of all from One Eye. She had no doubt that when he found out, he would make his feelings clear, and she didn't like to think of how he might go about it. Men who had crossed him in the past had had a way of disappearing, their bodies turning up months later, washed up on the beach.

They returned the pony to the meadow behind the mill where they'd borrowed him from the Brockmans, or more strictly from Abel, the oldest son, whose main occupation was breeding and breaking horses for riding and driving. He was always advertising in the newspaper, offering the services of his stallion to cover mares at half a guinea a leap and a shilling to the man.

The pony rolled in a muddy patch, snatching at mouthfuls of grass at the same time.

'You greedy pig,' Grace said fondly as she hung the bridle and rope on the gatepost. 'I expect we'll see you again soon.'

'I'm sure we will,' Louisa agreed, and they waddled home to Deal where the houses in Cockle Swamp Alley were in darkness, their exteriors belying the activity going on behind closed doors.

'Our neighbours will have the Revenue on to us at this rate,' Winnie said as shouting and laughter rang out over the sound of rolling barrels and slamming doors. 'Hurry,' she went on as Louisa slipped the key into the doorlock of the Lennickers' cottage.

'There's no need to panic – they'll be abed by now.' Louisa pushed the door open and stepped inside, closely followed by Winnie and Grace, who closed the door behind them. Louisa headed into the parlour where the flame of a candle flickered feebly from the mantelpiece, illuminating the limewashed walls, the woven rug on the floor, and the furniture, of which Louisa had always thought there was too much.

'Pa? Are you home?' she called gently.

'He isn't back yet – his boots aren't in the hall,' Grace observed.

'Billy?' Louisa was answered by a muffled snore that seemed to be coming from behind the wall beside the fireplace.

'That's him,' Grace said.

'Where are you?' Winnie asked. 'Show yourself.'

There was another snore, louder this time. Louisa darted towards the fireplace, picked up the candlestick and opened the panel in the wall. Billy, a young man the same age as Louisa, was slumped inside the hiding hole, fast asleep and stinking of drink. She held the candle to his face, illuminating his freckles, fine head of curly red hair and prominent ears. She gave him a prod, but he didn't stir.

'He's in his cups,' Winnie said, stating the obvious. 'We should put him to bed before Pa finds him. He won't like seeing him like this. He's not merely tipsy – he's ape-drunk.'

'I don't think we can move him,' Louisa said. 'We'll leave him here with the panel propped open and a bucket in case he casts up his accounts. Don't worry about him, Winnie.'

'He's going to have a sore head in the morning.'

'Maybe it'll teach him a lesson. If he isn't careful, he'll end up as one of One Eye's regulars, nothing but a pickled elbow-crooker.'

Winnie lit more candles, Grace fetched a bucket from the hang, and Louisa propped the panel ajar with the poker from the fireplace. Billy continued to snore as the three sisters helped each other to unwrap the lace from around their waists and thighs, and Louisa retrieved the other odds and ends from inside her bodice.

As she folded the goods and placed them in the secret drawer that Pa had had made to fit beneath the oak tabletop, she caught sight of her reflection in the mirror on the wall. Tall and slender with blue eyes and a few freckles across her nose, she took after her mother, even wearing her long dark brown hair in the same way, in a chignon with loose curls framing her face, while Winnie was half a head shorter with honey-blonde hair that fell in waves, naturally crimped. Grace, whom Louisa secretly envied for her thick, ebony locks, had yet to grow to her full height.

She had just closed the drawer when she heard Pa stomping through the hall.

'Quickly,' she whispered, and the three sisters left the parlour, closing the door on a sleeping Billy. 'It's good to see you're back safe and sound.' She took Pa's coat and hung it on the hook in the hall. He took off his boots and they retreated to the kitchen.

'You've packed everythin' away?' he asked.

She nodded.

'You didn't 'ave any more trouble with the Ridin' officers?'

'No. How about you?'

'My business is done,' he said, smiling as he rubbed his hands together, warming them over the fire that Winnie was coaxing back to life. 'That was a successful run – we should make a tidy sum out of it. We 'ave a lot to thank old Boneyparte for.'

'And much to hate him for,' Winnie pointed out.

'Where do you think we'd be without war and taxes?' Pa said, raising one bushy eyebrow. 'I tell you we'd never 'ave a sixpence to scratch with. Is there any of that fruit cake left, or 'as Billy eaten it all? Where is the boy anyway?'

'He's asleep,' Louisa said quickly, thinking that Billy might have recovered by the morning.

'There's some cake, and pease pudding as well,' Winnie said, and soon, they were sitting at the kitchen table, eating leftovers and supping small beer, as Pa regaled them with tales of the free traders' adventures from yesteryear.

'There was an occasion when the Revenue men forced the *Whimbrel* on to the beach. They were about to remove the goods – wine, baccy and playin' cards, if I remember rightly – when we rallied a huge mob from the town to come and 'elp us. The Revenue backed off and we carried on unloadin' unmolested.' Pa grinned as he wiped crumbs from his mouth. 'They didn't 'ave time to send for the militia to back 'em up.

'It was after that when I did a run with One Eye. It was back in the day when we were on speakin' terms and we got wind that the Revenue were followin' us up near Kingsdown.'

'What did you do?' Winnie asked.

'We came across a house set back from the road and went and knocked on the door. The gentleman answered it and we pushed past 'im, and up the stairs. We went into the first room we came to and blow me down, the wife was in bed. When she saw us, she shrieked and 'ollered, but when we told 'er all we wanted was to 'ide our goods under 'er mattress, she shut right up.

'They turned out to be most 'ospitable, letting us stay until dawn – in return for some wine, somethin' the gentleman was most partial to.'

A little bribery went a long way, Louisa thought when she finally retired to bed. She had no doubt that the Inspector of Riding Officers would find a cask of genever or cognac on his doorstep that morning.

# Chapter Two

## *A Father's Advice to his Daughters*

By the time she had risen from her bed, Pa had gone out fishing with Billy who had somehow, Billy must have managed to pull himself together despite the state he'd been in the night before.

Louisa and her sisters went to shop at the market, then returned via the beach where some of the boatmen were looking out to sea, watching for vessels in distress. Smoker Edwards was leaning against a capstan, while Mr Witherall and Terrier Roper perched on tubs in the sunshine at the top of the slope. Mrs Edwards was pegging out her laundry – it flapped about in a blustery wind.

'It's a right airy day today,' she said, smiling as the Lennickers stopped to pass the time of day. 'When the wind's pipin' from the west, it brings the merchantmen into the Downs. The sailors are easy pickin's for His Majesty's service – I've seen them out there today with a frigate and a tender.'

Louisa looked out to sea where the line of golden sand marking the Goodwin Sands was clearly visible, exposed by the low tide.

Several of the other boatmen's wives were occupied on the shore: Mrs Roper was watching her younger children who were playing with crab carapaces, seaweed and driftwood that had been washed up by the previous night's storm. Louisa didn't envy her – she had twelve sons and daughters, ranging in age from two to twenty-two. There had been one more, a boy who'd died by drowning when Louisa had been about eight years old.

'We can all eat well tonight,' Mrs Witherall commented as she sorted rods of willow cut from the osier beds inland, dried and then soaked, ready to make new lobster pots. 'What are you making for Mr Lennicker's supper?'

'Boiled fowl in oyster sauce,' Winnie said, showing her the contents of her basket. 'It's a special treat.'

'I wish God had blessed me with a daughter,' she said wistfully. 'Alas, He gave me four sons who have all flown the nest, apart from my Jason who is out all hours with his crew and their precious boat. He slept for an hour, then took the lugger out again – he said they were taking a pilot and some mail out to one of the brigs in the Downs.' She paused as the men's voices carried on the wind.

'It's my 'umble opinion that women and fish may be treated much the same.'

'Ha, you think you're a wag, but I can see your wife waggin' 'er finger at you.'

'Mr Witherall, I 'eard that. You'll be singin' for your supper tonight,' his wife called.

Mr Witherall – unwisely, Louisa thought – carried on. 'It takes gentle persuasion and 'andlin'.'

'You won't get your 'ands on me, talkin' like that.'

'Danglin' shiny items like gold and diamonds in front of 'em brings 'em in close for the catch. That's 'ow I caught you, isn't it, my dear one?'

'I should 'ave darted away when I knew you was anglin' for me.' Mrs Witherall grinned. 'Go 'ome – I 'ave a few chores for you, but you would rather the 'ouse fell down around our ears than leave off idlin'.'

The Lennickers wished her good day, but before they left the beach, Mr Witherall called Louisa aside.

'I'm sorry to 'old you up, but I need to ask you somethin',' he said, nodding towards her sisters who waited nearby. 'I tried to catch Righteous before 'e went out this mornin', but I missed 'im. There's a rumour goin' round ...'

Louisa knew what he was referring to and she could hardly meet his eye.

'So it's true? Oh, you don't have to say anythin'. Anyway, I wanted to warn 'im that what 'e's done has roused One Eye into a fair old fury. I'd suggest that 'e gives 'im a wide berth for a while, or – even better – makes amends. Will you speak to 'im when you see 'im?'

'Of course.'

'I'm sorry if I'm scarin' you, but this is your father's fault. 'E and One Eye used to be friends of sorts, but recently, they've been arguin' over goods that 'ave gone missin' and the alleged theft of a last of herrin', and accusin' each other of cheatin' at cards. It's bad enow 'avin' to watch your back because of the Revenue – we don't want to 'ave to be lookin' out for our fellow free traders as well.'

'Thank you, Mr Witherall. I'll let him know.' Louisa walked back to her sisters.

'What did he want?' Winnie asked.

'Nothing,' Louisa responded.

'It didn't look like nothing,' Grace said.

'He gave me a message for Pa, that's all. Let's go home.'

With that, they returned to Compass Cottage where Winnie prepared the oysters, fresh from Whitstable. She washed them and took off their beards, while Louisa found the other ingredients to make the sauce: anchovy liquor; lemon; mace; butter and flour. Grace plucked and boiled the chicken they'd bought.

Winnie and Grace were still in the kitchen while Louisa was sweeping the floor in the hall, when their father came back to the house later that afternoon.

'I'm relieved to see you're still in one piece,' Louisa said, greeting him as he removed his oilskins and boots. His hands were covered in silvery fish-scales and he smelled of the sea.

'Not that again.' His smile didn't quite touch his eyes. 'I've told you, there's no need to fret about it. If I see somethin' goin' beggin', I take it.'

'Mr Witherall asked me to warn you about One Eye,' she said, keeping her voice low.

'I can 'andle 'im. 'E's a bully and 'e deserves everythin' 'e gets,' he said bitterly.

'I don't know why you're so at odds with him.'

'And there's no need for you to know, my dear Louisa. All will be well. Trust me.' He tipped his head slightly to one side, his eyes twinkling with humour. 'You do trust your old pa, don't you?'

Not wanting to hurt his feelings, she said that she did, and she pushed the kitchen door open for him so he wouldn't leave the doorknob covered in scales.

Later, he retired to the herring hang – Louisa could hear him singing sea shanties, 'The Saucy Sailor Boy' and 'Hanging Johnny', at the top of his bellows.

Wiping her hands on her apron, she went to answer a knock at the front door.

'Aunt Mary, Cousin Beth, what a lovely surprise,' she exclaimed, finding them on the doorstep. 'It's been such a long time.'

Pa's singing stopped.

'Good day, Louisa.' Her aunt, a matronly figure in a blue dress and straw bonnet, stepped in front of Louisa's cousin who was struggling to carry a wicker basket. 'I've come to have words with your father.'

'He isn't here.' Louisa caught sight of him out of the corner of her eye, shaking his head frantically before disappearing back through the doorway at the end of the hall, where his slops were making a puddle on the floor. 'May I take a message?'

'Where is he?'

'Out fishing.'

'That's odd – the *Pamela* is hauled up on the beach and Master Fleet assured me that I would find him here.'

'Then he must have business elsewhere,' Louisa said quickly. It wasn't a complete lie – he was dealing with the day's catch.

'You'll invite us in for refreshments then. We have been on our feet for quite long enough.' Aunt Mary turned to Beth who was wearing a grey bonnet and matching dress, with a pink redingcote over the top. 'Hurry inside, my dear. One doesn't feel safe on these streets any more, thanks to all the strangers who've set up home here. Old Boney has much to answer for.'

'Although the war is a mixed blessing for those who are in trade,' Louisa said.

At the word 'trade', Aunt Mary winced. 'The Laxtons are but a few acres short of being able to live on the rental income from their estate, just as Sir Flinders does,' she said haughtily.

'My mother considers us part of the landed gentry,' Beth cut in with an apologetic smile. She was two years older than Louisa, her appearance and manner far more refined.

'One should always aim high – you've all seen what happens when you don't.'

It was a dig at the Lennickers, Louisa realised, glancing up at the framed silhouette of her mother on the wall. Ma's side of the family had built up their income and property by growing food for a town that had become increasingly hungry, due to the War of American Independence, followed by the wars against France. There was little love lost between her father and the Laxtons, her mother's family considering that she had married down, yet it had been a happy marriage and Pa had grieved deeply when – after eighteen years together – she had been seized by a deadly pneumonia and died in her devoted husband's arms.

Although it had been three years before, a wave of grief washed through Louisa's heart as she showed their visitors into the kitchen where her sisters looked up from the table, needles and thread at hand.

'Your mother, God rest her soul, always kept the parlour for best,' Aunt Mary complained.

'Ah, we haven't been able to use it for the damp – it only takes a spring tide and an easterly wind, and it's flooded.' The kitchen with its stone floor, rush mat, timber beams and whitewashed walls was perfectly acceptable for receiving callers in Louisa's opinion, especially those who arrived unannounced.

'It's high time your father moved out of Deal – there is a house near us in Sholden available for rent.' Aunt Mary stared at the slab of seasoned driftwood that served as a mantel over the fireplace, as if she was checking for dust. She wouldn't find any – Louisa had cleaned it the other day, rearranging the brass candlesticks and the pot of wooden shuttles and gauges for mending nets.

'It would bring me much joy to have my cousins as neighbours,' Beth said.

'I'll tell him.' Louisa knew full well that he'd never leave the town where he'd been born and bred. 'Winnie, pull up a chair for Aunt Mary. Grace, please make us some tea.'

Winnie snipped her thread and slid her needlework underneath a roll of linen, then fetched two chairs from the inglenook. Before Aunt Mary sat down, she moved up behind Grace and stared over her shoulder.

'Oh, let me see … Is it a garment of some kind?'

'You could say that, Aunt Mary,' Grace replied. 'It's slops for the duffers.'

'I beg your pardon!' Her fingers were on her necklace, her eyes wide with shock, but Louisa couldn't help feeling that she was merely pearl clutching.

'Not really. Of course it isn't,' Grace backtracked. 'I'm making a pattern for a bustle. Mr Gigg has the most beautiful pale green muslin in his shop, and Pa has said that if I'm a dutiful daughter, he'll buy it for me to make a gown.'

'Then he is spoiling you,' their aunt said sternly.

'The tea, Grace, if you will,' Louisa reminded her. She cleared the table and replaced all trace of her sisters' sewing with the best china: the blue and white cups and saucers, and tea plates, most of which were sadly chipped. 'Aunt Mary, Beth, do sit down.'

At her mother's request, Beth handed Louisa the basket. She peeked under the cloth that lay across the top, revealing Aunt Mary's gift of fresh tomatoes, carrots, runner beans and a small joint of pork wrapped in paper.

'It's very kind of you,' she smiled. 'We must give you something to take home in return.'

'A little tea – some souchong, if you have it – would be most acceptable.'

Winnie glanced at Louisa who was thinking the same: their aunt had some nerve.

'I'm afraid that we are almost out of tea. We can offer you some bloaters – that's all that we have.'

'Well, that does surprise me, Louisa. Mr Laxton's men were late for work this morning, so I was under the impression ... Oh, never mind.'

They took their places at the table while Louisa found some bread and cheese, and slices of fruitcake, trimming off the mould before serving it, and Grace measured out the tea leaves from the caddy into the pot, then added hot water. Leaving it to steep, she fetched a parcel of fish from the hang and placed it in front of their aunt.

'I'm sure I can smell brandy,' Aunt Mary said. 'Anyone would think that your father has turned to drink.'

It was no use denying it. The aroma of French cognac was overwhelming: even the all-pervading smell of smoke and fish couldn't mask it.

'Our lodger partakes of a little spirit now and again.'

'For medicinal purposes,' Winnie added brightly. Louisa wanted to giggle. Grace had turned her face away, pretending to look out of the window.

'I don't know what he was thinking of, taking in any old Jack Tar off the streets and giving him a home and an apprenticeship. I don't suppose Master Fleet pays any rent.'

'Billy helps Pa on the boat in return for his keep.' Louisa didn't know why she was trying to justify her father's kindness – it was none of her business. Billy was a neighbour's son – his father had gone away to sea a few weeks after Billy was born and was never heard of again. His mother was forced to scratch a living, selling fish. She bought bloaters from the Lennickers, and knowing that Mrs Fleet was always short, Ma would slip her the broken ones as extra. In return, Mrs Fleet would come and help Ma mend the nets and they would sit by the fire, sharing gossip while the girls chattered and sewed, or chopped vegetables for the pot, and Billy went out fishing with their father. When he was orphaned at fourteen by his mother's untimely death, Mr and Mrs Lennicker had taken him in.

'How is my uncle?' she asked, changing the subject.

'Mr Laxton is quite well,' Aunt Mary said. 'He works very hard, making a living from honest means—'

'That tea must be ready by now,' Louisa interrupted.

'I'll pour,' Grace said, at which there was a thump and the sound of a door creaking.

Aunt Mary was on her feet and out of the kitchen in a shot, intercepting Pa on his way along the hall.

'There you are, Robert,' she said, being one of the few people who used his given name rather than his nick-name of Righteous. 'It's no use – you can't keep hiding from me,' she added as she came back into the room, sending him ahead of her with her arms held out each side as if she was driving a wayward bullock into its pen. He turned, coughing and rubbing his red-rimmed eyes.

'It's the smoke,' he muttered. 'What can I do for you, Mary?'

'I'd like you to take notice of what I have to say for once. That's all I ask.'

'Go on.' Pa pulled a clay pipe from his pocket.

'It's about the girls. It worries me that you allow them to walk the streets unchaperoned, to come and go, and do as they please.'

'I don't understand.' He pressed a pinch of baccy from his leather pouch into the bowl.

'You know very well what I'm talking about – they are left to run riot. Cuthbert saw Grace walking alone the other day when he was supervising deliveries.'

'She was running an errand.' Pa gave Grace a look, meaning, *I'll be having a word with you later, young lady.*

'It isn't right – there are some unsavoury characters about and the men in Deal can't be relied upon to behave like gentlemen. Don't smirk like that, Robert. The moral welfare of your daughters is no laughing matter. I come, not to interfere, but to keep my promise to my sister-in-law, to advise or chastise whenever I see fit. Tell me this – how are dear Louisa, Winnie and Grace to find suitable husbands with their reputations under scrutiny?'

Pa chewed on the end of his pipe, then removed it from his mouth to speak.

'Much as I appreciate your concern, I'm 'ead of this 'ouse'old and what I say goes. I trust my daughters to keep theirselves out of trouble.' He beamed suddenly. 'I'm glad to see you – and you, Beth, but I reckon it's time you were gettin' back – you don't want to leave it too late with all these unruly Jacks and soldiers about, waitin' to pounce and steal a woman's virtue straight off the street.'

'Oh, you are insufferable as always,' Aunt Mary said crossly. 'Come along, Beth. We are done here. Don't forget the bloaters! And I'll have my basket back, Louisa.'

After they'd gone, Pa started to laugh.

'I thought I was goin' to end up smoked if I stayed in the 'ang any longer.'

'You always seem well-preserved, but today, you look even more so,' Grace chuckled. 'Your face is the same colour as the chimney sweep's boy.'

'Then I must wash before dinner. What wittles do we 'ave?'

'It's your favourite, cooked just like Ma used to make it,' Winnie said happily. 'It's ready to eat.'

'Thank you, my dears. I shall 'ave it early because I'm goin' out tonight.'

'Fishing or hovelling?' Louisa asked, referring to the work of the Deal boatmen who cruised around the Sands, assisting vessels that were passing by or anchored in the Downs. They would ferry letters and pilots, anchors and ropes, and retrieve crews and cargoes from shipwrecks for salvage money.

'I'm 'avin' a drink with some of my old friends and acquaintances. Don't you worry – I shan't be late.'

Louisa was concerned, though, knowing what her father had done and having listened to Mr Witherall's warning.

'I'd rather you didn't go,' she said, but he wasn't listening.

'Far be it from me to tell anyone 'ow to bring up their daughters … I'm no expert, merely a father who loves 'is girls more than 'e ever thought 'e could. From the very first cry, I lost my 'eart to each one of you, which is why I 'ate to scold you for goin' against me.' He stared at Grace who bowed her head. 'I don't like to think of you cooped up in the 'ouse all day, like Beth, always tied to her mother's apron strings. She's turnin' out to be a right timid flower.'

He cleared his throat. 'Much as it pains me to admit it, what your aunt said 'as some truth in it, though – there are some ruffians about. Oh, I wish your ma was 'ere … She always knew what to say and 'ow to say it, but she isn't, so I'll do my best.

'If a stranger of the male persuasion should approach you, you should turn and walk away, findin' safety in a crowd. If 'e should persist in 'is attentions, then you know what to do …?' Mr Lennicker paused, his complexion scarlet beneath the grime as he waited for their answer.

'I have absolutely no idea,' Winnie said.

'Call for help?' Louisa suggested.

'Do tell us, Pa,' Grace urged.

'You kick 'em where it 'urts. In the nether parts. And you scream as loud as your lungs will allow it.'

There was a moment of silence. Pa looked so serious that Louisa wanted to laugh. Not wishing to hurt his feelings, she stared at the ragged hem on her dress, but when she heard Grace gulp, she couldn't hold back, and soon they were all laughing together.

They were still chuckling when Billy came home.

After they had eaten, Pa dressed in his Sunday best – a rather shabby navy tailcoat over a shirt with a collar that rose almost level with his cheekbones, a silk cravat and a pair of snug pantaloons. He put on his shoes and round hat.

'Will I do?' he said, smiling.

'Oh. You will indeed,' Grace teased. 'You are quite the macaroni.'

Pa went out first, then Billy, leaving the sisters to their work. Winnie stayed in the kitchen and the house began to fill with the scent of burning sugar. Grace returned to her sewing, bringing her box and materials into the parlour, while Louisa fetched a bucket of fresh water and put it down beside the barrels that their father had rolled out from their hiding places earlier. One had been concealed in the hang, the others in the space under the staircase.

'You're slopping it all over the floor,' Grace grumbled. 'You're making a right mingle mangle.'

'You can mop up later, Grace,' Winnie said, carrying a pan in with her, holding it by its handles, her hands wrapped in cloth.

'Why should I have to do it? Louisa should've been more careful.'

Ignoring Grace's protest, Louisa glanced into the pan where the bubbles in the deep golden syrup came roiling to the surface, popping and releasing tiny bursts of steam.

'That needs to be darker,' she said. 'And don't forget to add the fat so it doesn't set hard this time.'

Winnie went away and while Louisa was waiting, she blew the dust from Ma's prized possessions that they kept on the shelf beside the fireplace. Their mother had taught them to read and write, and understand the basics of arithmetic, and some of the boatmen had sent their sons to her for lessons, Master Witherall and his brothers included. They were the only family on the beach to have any books: a gilt-edged bible, a volume on botany and a treatise on painting in watercolour.

Winnie returned.

'I hope you're going to tell me that it passes muster this time.' She showed Louisa the liquid caramel again.

'It's perfect, thank you. Now to work.' Louisa drew the curtain across the window and lit candles, then she and Winnie started letting down the cognac, mixing the caramel with water, and pouring it into one of the barrels. Winnie stepped back to allow Louisa to drop their set of glass beads inside and wait to see which one floated to the surface, indicating the strength of the diluted spirit.

'That's about right now,' she said, debating whether or not they could risk diluting it further.

'That'll suit the English taste,' Winnie said. 'Nobody will buy it if it's any weaker.'

'You're right,' Louisa said. 'Grace, why on earth did you mention the duffers in front of Aunt Mary? You know how she disapproves.'

'I couldn't help it – I wanted to see the look on her face.' Grace laid out the last piece of the slops she'd made for the men who carried the tea inland from the beach: the linen crown to go with the waistcoat, bustle and thigh pieces, each with pockets that could be packed with a goodly amount of tea.

'She wasn't happy,' Winnie giggled. 'Oh dear.'

'She is appalled by the very mention of free trade, yet more than willing to accept the spoils from it.' Louisa froze at the sound of fists pounding at the door. 'Did you hear that?' She knew as soon as she'd said it that it was a stupid question.

# Chapter Three

## *Cockle Swamp Alley and the Rattling Cat*

'We're done for,' Winnie exclaimed, hastily pouring the remaining caramel into the barrel on the floor and giving it a stir as Grace blew out the candles, throwing them into darkness. With the curtains closed and the door locked, there was a chance that their unwanted callers would assume nobody was at home and go on their way, but within seconds there was a loud thud, followed by an explosion of splintering wood.

'Hide everything,' Louisa whispered. 'I'll waylay them.'

She hurried out into the hall to find a young man in a dark riding coat, light buckskins and top boots, standing hat in one hand and lantern in the other on the doorstep, the door wide open and the latch torn away from the jamb. Moving towards him until she could make out his features, his high cheekbones, square jaw and his short hair combed forward and glinting gold in the flickering flame, her fleeting sense of relief that it wasn't the Revenue was quickly replaced with a sense of impending doom.

'What is it, Master Witherall?' She hardly dared ask, guessing from their neighbour's expression that he was bearing bad news.

'Miss Lennicker, summon your sisters and come quickly. Your father lies injured at the Rattlin' Cat.' He tugged at the reins looped over his arm as his gleaming black steed stamped impatiently, its iron shoe showering the cobbles with tiny orange sparks. 'I'm on my way to fetch Doctor Audley. Don't stand there gawpin' – there's no time to waste.' He put on his hat, turned and vaulted on to his horse, swinging it round as though on a sixpence and sending it off down the alley towards town at a spanking trot.

'You heard him, Louisa.' She was aware of Grace draping a shawl across her shoulders before Winnie pushed her out of the door and dragged it up behind them as well as she could. Hitching up her skirts and petticoats as she came to her senses, Louisa tore along Cockle Swamp Alley, turning left on to Beach Street and passing the dark shadows of the capstans, sheds and boats that lined the steeply sloping shingle shore.

Her bellows ached and her mind raced as she and her sisters dodged the people loitering along the street, making the most of the balmy August evening, so different from the night before: soldiers, sailors, their wives and fancy women. She couldn't help thinking that Master Witherall had been mistaken. The Rattling Cat was the last place that their father would choose to visit after what he'd done. One Eye, the landlord, would hardly give him a warm welcome. What's more, the tavern was well known as one of the haunts of the fabled Fey Lady, the spirit of a young woman, veiled and dressed in white. Louisa had often heard their father remind Billy about her, advising him to keep his wits about him and not stay out drinking late at night, because there was no telling what she might do to him.

'Why on earth,' she gasped as they arrived at the tavern, 'has Pa gone to the Rattlers' rondy?'

'We'll find out soon enough,' Winnie said. 'He will be fine, I'm certain of it. He'll have cut his finger or slipped on a sprat.'

As they pushed through the crowd gathered outside the Rattling Cat, Louisa noticed that Grace was crying.

'You're a temptin' article, my love.' One of the Jacks in a blue broadcloth jacket and petticoat breeches stepped in front of Louisa, leering drunkenly.

Shoving him aside, she ran up the steps to where Billy was holding the door open.

'Where is he?' she asked.

''E's over yonder.' He pointed in the direction of the bar. 'Let the misses through!'

The audience made way and, assaulted by the stench of stale ale and debauchery, along with the acrid scent of gunpowder, Louisa found herself like an actress, centre-stage with her sisters, playing out the final act of a tragedy where her father lay moaning on the floor in the arms of a buxom middle-aged woman. She wore a wig, powder and beauty spot, and a dress the same colour as the creeping stain in the sawdust as the blood slowly dripped through the pad of cloth that she was holding against the shoulder of her father.

'You must press harder,' Louisa cried out, falling to her knees beside them.

'You shouldn't be 'ere,' Pa muttered gruffly as her sisters joined her. 'You shouldn't 'ave to see this. Where's the doctor?'

'He's on his way.' At least, she hoped so, she thought, looking up at One Eye Feasey who was leaning against the counter, a pistol in his hand. He stared back, his good eye oddly marbled, the other covered with a patch. Like Nelson, she'd heard him brag before, but that's where any resemblance to England's hero ended. Greasy locks of grey hair stuck out from under his cloth bandanna, and the sleeves of his scruffy brown linen shirt were rolled up to reveal tattoos of an anchor on one arm and a mermaid on the other.

'You shot him!' Louisa glanced wildly around her. Nobody moved. Even the cats on the counter – three of them – sat as still as statues. 'Somebody, fetch the constable, the army ... do something.'

A young man, swaying and belching, stepped forward. 'Constable Pocket at yer disposal. My apologies for bein' a trifle disguised, but I weren't expectin' no trouble tonight.'

'Give the young ladies the full and true version of events,' One Eye said. 'There's an 'alf anker in it for you.'

Looking sheepish, the constable cleared his throat and began to weave a tale.

'There's been a terr'ble accident. As far as I'm given to understand ... I mean, so far as I understand it, Mr Lennicker entered the inn by way of the back door, armed with a pistol and demandin' to speak privately with Mrs Stickles 'ere, but she was unavailable, bein' employed servin' be'ind the bar. Mr Feasey told 'im to go 'ome, but Mr Lennicker forced 'is way past, and bein' keen to disarm 'im, there bein' a large number of his loyal patrons present, Mr Feasey took the pistol from 'im. As 'e did so, it went off, 'itting Mr Lennicker in the arm.'

'If I 'adn't got it off 'im, who knows what would 'ave 'appened.' One Eye stopped speaking as one of the cats, the bones rattling on its collar, made a leap from the bar on to his shoulder where it settled, just before Louisa caught the sound of horses' hooves and voices outside.

'Is that how it was, Pa?' Louisa asked, and he took a sharp intake of breath, his expression etched with fear and pain.

'Don't strain yourself – it can wait,' Winnie said as Louisa turned to Mrs Stickles whom she knew was a woman of ill-repute.

'Is that the truth of it?'

She nodded, keeping her eyes fixed on One Eye as she hugged their father to her bosom. Louisa couldn't help noticing that her dress was trimmed with a piece of the finest French lace she'd seen in a long while – from Chantilly, she guessed.

'Out of regard for the long association I've 'ad with Righteous 'ere, I'll give 'im a room for the night,' One Eye offered, at which Pa reached out and gripped Louisa's hand.

'Not that. 'E'll 'ave me poisoned to death.'

'It's all right. You're coming home with us,' she said, looking up to find Master Witherall and Doctor Audley struggling through the crowd which had swelled with a number of new arrivals, the gossip already having spread through the narrow streets and alleyways of Deal.

'Louisa,' she heard Winnie say beside her. 'Where's Billy?'

'I don't know,' she said, slightly exasperated. 'He was here a few minutes ago.'

'Mr Lennicker, the Misses Lennicker,' Doctor Audley said as he joined them. 'Master Witherall has apprised me of the situation.'

'My father has expressed a wish to return home.' Louisa stood up to make way for the physician who had attended their mother during her last hours. 'Can he be moved?'

'I'll administer a dose of laudanum, then some of these fine gentlemen will transport him to his house. Mr Feasey, we require a stretcher.' The doctor, who was in his early thirties and wearing a smart maroon coat and dark pantaloons, opened his bag.

Having waited for him to administer the medicine, Master Witherall, his father and two other men slid Mr Lennicker on to an old door they'd dragged in from outside. They tied him down with a length of rope.

'Mrs Stickles, you will come with me this time.' Pa's eyes were wide and beseeching as the woman hesitated, her cheeks streaked with tears. Apparently riven with indecision, she looked towards One Eye.

'May I?' she whispered.

'If you step through that door, you'll 'ave no work and no bed to come back to when this partic'lar gen'leman goes aloft.'

'I'm dyin'.' Droplets of perspiration trickled down Mr Lennicker's grey forehead and dripped from the tip of his nose. His grizzled hair and beard, which he'd groomed so thoroughly before he'd gone out that evening, were tousled and his cravat undone.

'Don't take any notice of him.' Louisa stared at One Eye as her father began to sob – she'd never seen a grown man cry before. 'He isn't worth listening to – he isn't a doctor.'

'I can't 'elp it – my dear girl, I can feel the life ebbin' from my body.'

'Pull yourself together – you aren't going to die. You should have listened to me and stayed at home,' she said sharply, and a ghost of a smile crossed his lips.

'You sound just like your mother …' With difficulty, he turned to face Mrs Stickles. 'Oh Molly, my love, I done a lot of promisin' in the past, all of which came to nothin'. This time it will be different.'

'Love?' Louisa exclaimed, glancing towards her sisters.

'He's delirious. He doesn't know what he's talking about,' Winnie said, her eyes filled with confusion. 'That must be it.'

'She isn't your love, Righteous,' One Eye said scathingly. Rumour had it that he'd had his men pull teeth out of the heads of people who'd crossed him, then had them made up into a false set which was why his teeth were all different shades and sizes. 'She'll go with anyone for a measure o' gin and a ha'penny.'

'Take. That. Back.' Pa strained against the rope, but to no avail.

'I 'ave to stay 'ere, Robert. You shouldn't 'ave come, knowin' my situation. I 'ave ties, responsibilities … There isn't just me to consider, as well you know. Do what the doctor tells you and you'll soon be up and about. Till we meet again, my darlin' …' A distraught Mrs Stickles followed the stretcher as the bearers carried it to the door, while Louisa tried to make sense of the shocking revelation that their father appeared to have been carrying on with a lady of pleasure.

Back at the house, the men struggled to get the patient up the narrow staircase to the first floor and then into his room, where they helped him into bed.

Louisa asked Grace to give them a tot of brandy for their trouble before turfing them out. She wanted to thank Master Witherall, but having wished Mr Lennicker a rapid recovery, he had already retreated to fetch his horse which he'd left at the tavern.

The sisters turned their attention to tending their father. Doctor Audley instructed Winnie to cut away his jacket and shirt.

'The injury is more serious than I thought,' he said when Winnie had put the scithers down.

'It was an accident,' Mr Lennicker maintained, keeping to the constable's version of events. Whatever the truth was, Louisa guessed that he was scared of what One Eye might do next, and was protecting her and her sisters as well as himself.

'Be that as it may, I do wonder what possessed you to get involved with Mr Feasey and his gang of rogues.'

'I 'ave my reasons, Doctor. Now, what can you do for me?'

Louisa suspected that it would be very little, recalling how he'd prescribed saltwater for Ma to drink. No sooner had Winnie poured it into her mouth than she had taken her last breath, but Pa had been strangely comforted, knowing she'd died with the taste of old briny on her lips.

'The wound must be cleaned with vinegar and dressed, and I will give you laudanum again for the pain,' Doctor Audley said. 'Rest is essential.'

Louisa and Grace left Winnie with Pa and the doctor – she could be relied on not to cry out or swoon at the sight of blood.

'Stoke the fire, please,' Louisa said, thinking to keep Grace occupied. They'd already had one burning in the grate to make the caramel earlier that evening, but the flames had died out, leaving a few embers visible beneath the blackened logs. Louisa poured water from a bucket into the copper pot.

Soon, great walms were rising in the boiling water in the pot over the fire, but according to Winnie when she joined them in the kitchen, there was no need for it.

'Pa's asleep now and the doctor's coming back in the morning. The lead's lodged deep in his shoulder and he refuses to have the surgeon come to look at it.'

'Then we must persuade him,' Grace said.

'You know what he's like – he's a stubborn so-and-so,' Winnie pointed out tearfully.

'Did the doctor say anything else?' Louisa asked.

'He said – aside to me as he was leaving – that with a wound of this sort, there is a high chance of gangrene setting in.'

'What's that?' Grace cut in. 'I've never heard of it before.'

Winnie opened her mouth to explain, but closed it again when Louisa shook her head.

'Let's not worry about that now,' Winnie said. 'What did he think he was doing going to the Rattling Cat with a loaded pistol, especially after walking off with their run goods? And why did he speak so fondly to that dreadful woman?'

'She's nothing but a whore.' Grace took the pot off the fire and relit the candle which had gone out, leaving a whiff of tallow-scented smoke hanging in the air.

'What do you know about it?' Louisa asked.

'Mrs Stickles works in the kitchen, baking pies and cakes. On occasion, she serves behind the bar and Isaiah told me that the rest of the time, she's on her back with any old Jack for a bit of pin money.'

'You've been talking to One Eye's son?' Louisa glanced towards Winnie who raised her eyebrows. 'How come?'

'It was ages ago – I ran an errand for Pa, delivering snuff to Mr Gigg, the draper. On my way back along the beach, Isaiah saw me and called me over to offer me a drink. I didn't think there'd be anything wrong in accepting, because I was almost faint from the heat, and it was only a small beer, and more than likely watered down beforehand.'

'You know Pa doesn't want us associating with the Feaseys—' Louisa began, but Winnie interrupted, 'Leave her alone – this isn't the time.'

'I know. I'm sorry.' They had other, more pressing worries, like what Billy would do while Pa was bedbound and unable to skipper the *Pamela* when she went out fishing and hovelling. Where was Billy, for that matter?

What if the worst came to the worst and their father succumbed to his injury? Louisa didn't like to think of it, deciding she would try to recall the past rather than dwell on an uncertain future.

She remembered the day when he'd brought back the puzzle box. Her father had raised the alarm, having heard shots being fired from a vessel in the Downs. The *Vivid*, a merchant brig with two square-rigged masts, had lost both anchors and was being blown towards the Sands which were exposed by a spring tide. Louisa could have been only ten years old when she and her sisters had watched the luggers launch from the beach that morning. Pa had joined the Witheralls on the *Whimbrel* to make up her crew of seven men and a boy, while One Eye had gone out with his son and the Rattlers on the *Good Intent*.

Built for speed and strength, the luggers had cut through the water, racing each other to reach the stricken ship. In those days, it had been in the spirit of camaraderie and friendly competition, the crews of both boats sharing in the spoils: the reward for saving the *Vivid* and towing her back to safety along with payment for delivering two new anchors.

When Pa had returned home that night, he had greeted Ma with a kiss, then turned to Louisa and her sisters, keeping his hands behind his back.

'Guess what I have for you,' he'd said.

'A kitten?' Grace had said hopefully.

'No. How about you, Winnie? What do you think it is? What would a master mariner and captain of a merchant ship give an 'umble boatman for savin' 'is life?'

'A gold ring?' Winnie had suggested.

'No. Louisa?'

'Something special,' she'd said, and her heart had swelled with pride when he'd told her she was quite right. Grinning, he'd made a show of revealing his prize: a wooden box veneered with a pattern of mother-of-pearl. 'Shall we see what's inside?' He'd carried it into the parlour and placed it on the table.

'One of you had better open it,' he'd said.

Grace had had a turn, and then Winnie, but without success. Pa had pushed the box towards Louisa and she had picked it up and given it a gentle shake. She'd tried lifting the lid, tipping it upside down and tapping at the sides, to no avail. But then she'd caught sight of the slight irregularity in the panels on the front. She'd slid the centre panel up, revealing a lock, but where was the key?

'You're almost there.' Pa had encouraged her to keep going when she was all for giving up, and then she'd found the secret compartment at the base and taken out the key. She'd turned the key in the lock and the lid had opened, revealing a cache of coins: shillings, sixpences and thrupenny bits.

'It's treasure,' she'd said, showing her sisters.

'We'll count it out.' Pa had sat at the table and divided the money into three stacks: one for Louisa, one for Winnie and one for Grace. 'Spend it wisely, my children.'

'Oh no, they must save it for a rainy day,' Ma had interjected, and she had found each of them a pot in which to put their money. The puzzle box had been given pride of place on the shelf next to their mother's books in the parlour.

Wishing she could turn back time, Louisa took some broth up to her father who turned his nose up at it, saying he'd prefer some cold beef which she duly supplied, but when she went back to collect the tray, he'd barely touched that either.

Later, when they had settled down for the evening, she gazed at her sisters who seemed preoccupied, caught up in their own thoughts, Grace squinting in the candlelight as she darned a sock, and Winnie unravelling a gansey, winding the springy wool into a ball.

Even if their father made a full recovery – something she had to believe would happen, despite the sickening sense of doubt deep in the pit of her stomach – she felt that the attempt on his life had, like a heavy hand on the tiller or a rapid alteration in the wind, set the Lennickers on a changed course.

'I've been telling him, he's the worst kind of patient, stubborn and cantankerous,' Winnie said fondly as Louisa returned to her father's room early the next morning, having tried to sleep for an hour or two.

'Which just goes to prove I've got a bit o' fight left in me,' he said. 'Reg'lar application of saltwater on this wound and I'll be as right as rain in a couple of weeks.'

'Have you thought any more about sending for the surgeon?'

'I wouldn't let 'im near me with a bargepole – One Eye pays 'im a retainer.'

'There must be somebody else – in Sandwich or Dover, perhaps?'

'Louisa, I know you mean well, but I won't be chopped about. I'm placin' my trust in the power of old briny as I've always done. And as soon as I'm on my feet, I'll be after that –' he cursed aloud '– old rogue. I'll see 'im strung up if that's the last thing I do.'

Noticing that the curtains were still drawn even though it had been light for some while, Louisa walked across to open them.

'Leave 'em,' Pa shouted.

'A little sunshine is good for keeping the spirits up.'

'No ...' His head sank back into his pillow.

She did as she was bid, stepping back as Billy put his head around the door.

''Ow are you, sir?'

'I've been worse,' Pa said.

'Will we be takin' the *Pamela* out today?'

'Mr Lennicker isn't going anywhere,' Winnie interjected.

'I'm under the thumb as you can see,' Pa grumbled lightly. 'I think it's best that you stay ashore and do some chores. We won't be missin' much – we didn't catch a lot yesterday, only a few stink-alives and herrin'.'

'Thank you.' Billy excused himself and disappeared. A door slammed behind him.

''Ow many times 'ave I l'arned that boy to close a door quietly?'

'Hundreds,' Louisa smiled, but, recalling the doctor's comment about the risk of gangrene, her fears for Pa's health grew.

'Have you found out what happened last night?' she asked Winnie when they went downstairs briefly to eat.

'Each time I question him about it, he comes over all peculiar as if he's about to fall into a faint. I reckon it's deliberate – he's hiding something.'

'I expect he'll tell us eventually. What was that fuss about the window?'

'One of the cats from the inn was outside looking in when I went to draw the curtains earlier,' Winnie whispered. 'I threw the pisspot at it, but it wouldn't go away.'

'Is it still there?'

'Pa's too afraid to find out, and to be honest, I feel the same. Oh Louisa, you know what it means – it's a bad omen.'

'Let's wait and see what the doctor says.' She wasn't about to give up hope, just because one of the Feaseys' cats had made an appearance, but she felt uneasy all the same, and her sense of dread grew when One Eye himself turned up on their doorstep.

'How's ol' Righteous?' he asked.

'It's nothing to do with you.' Louisa tried to push the damaged door shut, but he had his foot in the way. 'Leave him alone.'

'You'll give 'im a message from me.' This was a statement of fact, not a request. 'If I 'ear anyone badmouthin' the Feaseys, there'll be strife. I used to have a lot o' respect for Righteous, and 'is father and grandfather before 'im who would go out in a storm even when others didn't dare.

'We were bosom friends until he broke 'is engagement to my sister all them years ago. I could see why 'e did it, your mother being partic'larly beautiful and 'im being a young man with 'is own mind and an 'eart that couldn't be tamed.'

'I don't believe you.'

'That's up to you, miss.' One Eye shrugged. 'Anyway, when the prospect of makin' our fortunes came up, we called a truce and went into business, along with the Witheralls and other willin' folk who live along the spit. Up till your ma passed away, I could rely on the Lennickers to do their part.' He leaned towards her until she could smell his foul breath and see the spittle on his beard. 'Don't go all pouty on me. You know very well what I'm referrin' to.' Her skin crawled as he continued, 'The honourable trade that's been pursued by the Cinque Ports men for 'undreds of years in return for our services, aidin' the defence of the realm.

'Your father is truly Righteous by name, but not by nature. Sometimes 'e claimed a few ankers fell overboard, or 'e miscounted the number of bales of silk, or on one occasion, before 'e was widowed, 'e forgot 'e 'ad a wife waitin' for 'im at 'ome. Then the other night, he committed an unforgivable sin: 'e took goods that didn't belong to 'im. Or perhaps I'm speaking ill of the dead ...?'

'He's living and breathing, no thanks to you. You have some gall, calling here after what you did to him last night.'

'You 'eard what the constable said – it was self-defence. Remember the proverb: Hear no evil, see no evil, speak no evil. Follow my advice and nothin' evil will befall you.'

'I'm not scared of you, Mr Feasey,' she said, fear shuddering through her bones. 'Go away.'

'Well, it's been a pleasure to talk to you.'

He grinned as the milkmaid walked past, weighted down with her yoke and buckets, and crying out, 'Milk below, milk below.'

'Good day,' One Eye said. As soon as he'd removed his foot, Louisa heaved the door shut in his face.

Doctor Audley arrived shortly afterwards.

'You don't 'ave to wait around on my be'alf,' Pa said as she and Winnie ushered the physician into his room. 'Winnie will stay. You get on with your work, or we'll all starve.' He forced a smile, and Louisa smiled back. There couldn't be much wrong with him, if he was still jesting with her. He knew very well that they didn't need to scrimp on food – their income from the free trade was the icing on the cake.

Louisa made her way to the draper's in Walmer, carrying her wares in a basket, covered with a red-and-white check cloth and half a dozen candles. The bell rang as she entered the shop, bringing Mr Gigg's son to her assistance. He showed her past the counter into a private room, saying his father would be with her shortly.

Mr Gigg joined her a little while later. He was in his sixties, older than Pa, his eyes set like currants in a pale, suety face.

'I'm sorry to keep you waiting. The ladies must have their linens and calicoes or the world will fall apart.'

She couldn't help feeling envious of the wives and daughters of the rich who had the luxury of spare time and money to go shopping, and she didn't like the way that the draper, whom she had known for many years, never addressed her by her name. Although she was a familiar face to her buyers, she might as well have been anonymous, all the better to keep their consciences clear.

'You have come for the green muslin – your sisters were admiring it the other day.'

'No, sir. I've brought you your recent order.' Out of habit, she glanced quickly around the room to check that nobody was watching, before extracting the goods from her basket and laying them out on the table: seven lengths of black Chantilly lace.

Having mopped his brow, Mr Gigg put on a pair of gloves and picked the first piece up, holding it up to the light before putting it back down again, and poring over it with his quizzing glass. It was part of the act, Louisa remembered, playing along.

'There are flaws,' he announced. 'Here … and here …'

'I can't see them,' she said.

'Ah, I have the eyesight of a much younger man.'

And the wallet of a niggard, she thought wryly.

'This is the best lace from the Continent, far superior to that which is brought from Honiton to London. A young lady of the ton would give anything to lay her hands on it.'

'I'll let you have the muslin – enough to make three dresses – in return.'

'Mr Gigg, I can buy muslin anywhere. The lace is like gold dust and far more expensive.' Her mother would work out the value using the old-fashioned method of counting how many coins it took to cover each piece of fabric, but Louisa preferred to haggle.

The draper stared at her, his head slightly to one side.

The art of business being to hold one's nerve, Louisa began to fold the lace. 'I have other customers who'll be delighted to take this off my hands for twice the price.'

'The muslin and five pounds in banknotes. Fair exchange is no robbery.'

'If that's the case, why do I feel like I'm being robbed?' She refused the muslin – her youngest sister wouldn't be seen dead walking around Deal with her and Winnie in matching gowns, looking like the Three Graces. 'I will have the money, seven pounds in coins, not banknotes.' A metal coin held its value, while a banknote was merely a promise on paper – easily broken or forged.

'You drive a hard bargain, miss,' he said, eventually giving in and fetching the money from his safe. He counted it out and she transferred it into her purse.

Having stopped to buy a tonic from the apothecary on the way, she returned home to find Mrs Witherall and Mrs Edwards gossiping in the kitchen.

'Our neighbours have kindly dropped in to see if there's anything they can do,' Grace said, rolling her eyes.

'We're very sorry to 'ear about Mr Lennicker,' Mrs Witherall said.

'I've brought 'im some barley water – it does wonders for my 'usband's bowels, especially if you add it to a little currant jelly.'

'I find it works better added to milk,' Mrs Witherall opined.

'Thank you for the advice,' Louisa said. 'There's much truth in the adage that wisdom comes with age.'

'Let's 'ave less of the "age", my dear.' Mrs Witherall smiled at Louisa's discomfiture. 'I for one don't need to be reminded that I'm not as young as I was. Isn't that right, Mrs Edwards?'

'I think you must speak for yourself.' Mrs Edwards was about thirty-five, fifteen years younger than Mrs Witherall. Both wore caps, dark dresses and grubby aprons, clothing suitable for domestic duties and running errands for their husbands.

'Grace, you haven't done your chores – the pavement hasn't been swept,' Louisa said pointedly.

'I'm sorry,' Mrs Witherall said. 'You 'ave an invalid to look after. We must get out from under your feet. Come along, Elsie.'

Grace saw the neighbours out, then she accompanied Louisa upstairs.

'I thought they would never leave.'

'They were sitting there as though they had all the time in the world,' Louisa agreed, 'but they mean well.'

'I know,' Grace said.

Louisa told Pa of her dealings with Mr Gigg, much to his amusement, but a few minutes later, he closed his eyes, exhausted.

The doctor called every morning for another three days, but despite his efforts, the wound began to fester and gangrene set in. On the fourth day, he bled the patient, and with the gravest of expressions, bade Louisa and her sisters farewell.

They abandoned their daily duties for their father's bedside. Grace sewed by candlelight, any thought of economy being thrown aside by Pa's wish to leave the curtains closed. Louisa sat with a pestle and mortar containing a few partially crushed rose leaves, watching Winnie mop their father's brow and pour a spoonful of tincture from a small brown bottle.

'I don't want no more of that stuff – it puts me in a fog.' He pushed the spoon away. 'There are things that must be said before ...'

'Oh Pa ...' Louisa breathed.

'I'm a simple man, always 'ave been. A boatman's life and the love of a good woman 'as always been enow for me ... and the affection I 'ave for my daughters.'

'You should rest,' Winnie said sternly as he strove to sit himself up, his eyes wide with effort and agitation.

'I must – I must speak,' he muttered. 'When my father passed, I 'ad the comfort of 'earing 'is last words. "She's done for me," that's what 'e said, if I remember rightly. "She's done for me." 'E meant the sea, old briny. A huge wave caught the lugger, tippin' us all out as she beached. I 'auled me ol' man out, but it was too late – 'e went aloft within the hour.'

Louisa noticed a tear trickling down Grace's cheek as their father struggled to continue, 'There are things you should know, and others best left unsaid.' He paused again, seeming to lose his thread. Louisa turned briefly to Winnie who shook her head. Pa's health was failing rapidly now.

'Firstly, there's our share from the last run we did, and a couple of the others before that – manage it wisely, and it'll last you a fair time. With Billy's 'elp and the use of the boat, you'll be able to make a tidy amount out of fishin' and the like. As for this 'ouse, the plot and the rest of my worldly goods, I leave them to be divided among my daughters in equal measure.'

His breathing came in short, sharp gasps. 'You will tell One Eye that I will do for 'im, one way or another. 'E threatened to break 'is silence – I couldn't 'ave that. I 'ave wronged you, my beloved daughters, and many besides. I'm a sinful, wicked man.' He tugged at the coverlet with both hands, his knuckles blanching, as though he was trying to cling on to life.

'Many years ago, your mother and I were goin' through a stormy patch when I made a terrible mistake, turnin' to another woman for comfort.'

'That woman, you mean?' Winnie exclaimed.

He nodded.

'Poor Ma,' Grace murmured.

'I make no excuse for it. I loved your mother.'

'And now?' Louisa asked.

'When I lost her, I was beside myself with grief. Molly 'elped me through it. Tell 'er to come to me – I 'ave to make amends ...'

Suddenly, he lay back, pale and trembling. It was more than enough for one day, more than enough for all of them.

Louisa took a step back. It was unnerving, disturbing and shocking – she'd always thought of the sea as his mistress.

'What shall we do?' she asked, having drawn her sisters on to the landing.

'I don't know,' Grace sighed.

'I don't want her here,' Winnie said quickly.

'You would deny him his dying wish?' Louisa whispered.

'I need time ...'

'Winnie, there is no time. I don't like this any more than you do, but if we make the wrong decision, I fear it will haunt us for ever.'

'What about Ma? She'll be turning in her grave,' Winnie said. 'He worshipped her – he still does. How could he have taken another into his heart?'

'Perhaps he refrained from taking a second wife out of respect for our feelings,' Louisa suggested.

'How long has he been carrying on with her behind our backs?' Grace asked.

'It doesn't matter now. I don't care for Mrs Stickles in the slightest, but if her presence gives our father some peace, then we should fetch her. Billy can go.' Louisa couldn't bring herself to return to the Rattling Cat after their visit from One Eye.

'I don't like it.' Winnie stood with her hands on her hips. 'I won't stand for it.'

'I agree with Louisa. I'll find Billy.' Grace began to make her way downstairs, and Winnie went into the bedroom she shared with Louisa to compose herself. Louisa returned to her father's bedside, and within the half-hour, Billy had brought Mrs Stickles to the house.

Sending her sisters to wait in the kitchen, Louisa greeted her in the hallway.

'I'm ever so grateful for this kindness, Miss Lennicker.' Mrs Stickles took a handkerchief from her pocket and blew her nose.

'I do it for my father, not for you,' Louisa said bitterly.

'Is he terr'ble bad?' Mrs Stickles' eyes were swollen as if she'd been crying.

Louisa nodded, then showed her to their father's room, following her broad haunches as she squeezed her way up the staircase. Her dress was made from a dark green brocade, edged with lace and bearing the patina of stains that comes from several weeks of regular wear, and her boots, although constructed from quality leather, were decidedly down at heel.

'Oh, my dear woman.' Pa's eyes lit up when he saw her.

'Don't trouble yourself to speak on my account, my darlin',' Mrs Stickles murmured, reaching out for his hand.

'Just a few words,' Pa mumbled. 'I've rescued many a ship in distress, taken the crew to safety when all seemed 'opeless, yet I weren't never brave enow to look after my loved ones, my own flesh and blood—'

'You don't know what you're sayin',' Mrs Stickles said quickly.

'I'm sorry, my love …' He grimaced with pain and fell silent, his breath rattling in his throat like the shingle rolling with the waves on the beach.

Louisa couldn't take any more. As the scene blurred in front of her, she turned and fled – straight into the arms of a well-fed, middle-aged gentleman.

'Reverend North!' she exclaimed.

'The door was open, so I let myself in.' He released her and removed his Canterbury cap to reveal his sparse powdered hair. 'It was a most fortuitous occurrence as I seem to have prevented you falling headlong down the stairs. I've heard of your father's parlous state – he is abed?'

'You can't go in,' she said, panicking. 'He isn't decent.'

'I've attended many of the sick and dying in this parish, and at my time of life, there can't be anything I haven't seen before.' Pushing past her, he entered the sickroom to find Mr Lennicker in bed in the arms of his paramour with his face pressed into her bosom. Louisa's yelp of horror brought her sisters rushing back upstairs.

'What is it?' Winnie shouted. 'Has he gone?'

Everyone stopped and stared as Mrs Stickles looked up, her face contorted with grief.

'My poor darlin'. 'E's on 'is way out.'

Winnie fetched Billy in from the garden where he was having a smoke, and Reverend North said a prayer, and they watched Mr Lennicker take his last gasp in the middle of the afternoon – at the turn of the tide, Louisa noticed when she opened the window to let his soul fly free, while the black cat stalked away across the rooftops.

# Chapter Four

## *Going to Hell in a Handbasket*

'To think that 'e passed away on dry land, not out on old briny after the life 'e led,' Billy commented as Grace broke into howls of lamentation. Mrs Stickles, having pressed her lips to Pa's forehead one last time, made her way out without saying a word, and the vicar left shortly afterwards, having advised them to arrange the funeral in haste, the weather being inclement for watching over a body. There would be no inquest, the story of the accident being confirmed by multiple witnesses.

Louisa and Grace helped Winnie wash and dress their father, comb his hair and wrap him in a woollen winding sheet. One of the carpenters at the boatyard brought round a coffin and helped Billy lift him into it. Before Billy nailed down the lid, Winnie placed her locket with a curl of Ma's hair into Pa's hand and Louisa removed the coins that she'd deployed to keep his eyes closed, thinking she had better use for them on Earth than he would have in Heaven.

Later, Grace arranged the lilies that Aunt Mary had brought with her when offering her condolences and warning them not to attend the funeral out of consideration for their delicate feminine constitutions.

'I have no intention of letting him go alone.' Louisa wrapped a piece of crape around her bonnet the following day and put on the black dress she had inherited from her mother, in readiness.

'I'm coming with you,' Grace said.

'You'll walk with us, won't you, Billy?' Winnie asked.

'I would be at your side if I could.' He looked pale but proud. 'It's an honour to be one of Mr Lennicker's bearers – 'e was like a father to me – but times 'ave altered, and it's occurred to me that you won't want me livin' 'ere any longer.'

Louisa frowned.

'It's never crossed my mind that you should leave us, unless you want to.' If Billy left, they'd have to find another tenant – before him, they'd had a soldier housed with them, but Mrs Lennicker had asked him to leave, finding that his presence put a crimp in their activities. 'We still have the *Pamela* – she'll need a new skipper.' She glanced at her sisters, both of whom nodded.

'It's what Pa would have wanted,' Winnie said, choking back a sob.

'It's what he intended,' Grace confirmed.

'Then I'm the 'appiest …' Billy's voice faded. 'Well, I would be, if things were different.'

'It's all right,' Louisa said as the carriages drew up outside the house. She had hired them from the Brockmans at the mill: one for the coffin and one for the bearers, each pulled by two Belgian blacks with ostrich plumes, even though it was only a short walk to St George's, the chapel of ease where their father would be laid to rest.

'How can we afford this grandeur?' Winnie whispered as they walked arm in arm with Grace behind the cortège.

'Remember what Pa talked about before he passed?' Louisa said.

'Oh yes.' Winnie's step lightened a little.

'We'll have to pay for the ringing of the knell, for the vicar, the carpenter, and stonemason. Our father …' Louisa stifled a sob '… was a hero of the seas and a loving family man … No matter what else he's done, he deserves a decent funeral.'

'Look at all these people who've turned out for him,' Grace marvelled as they reached St George's, where the Witheralls, Terrier Roper and his sons, and many other Deal boatmen had put down their sails and oars for half a day to pay their respects. The Brockmans, the smiths, coopers and sailmakers, and her father's friends from the boatyard were all present. The Feaseys and Mrs Stickles were conspicuous by their absence.

'Dear Misses Lennicker.' The Reverend North, wearing a cassock and surplice, greeted them at the door. 'My deepest and most humble condolences. Mr Lennicker was a kind and generous man, a gentleman at heart. There's been many a time when I've expressed my gratitude for the Communion wine that comes my way, and I hope that you'll continue the family tradition in his memory.'

Louisa could only surmise that her father's offerings to the church were his way of salving his conscience over his infrequent attendance. He'd always maintained that there was only so much praying one could do when there were nets to mend.

'It's a shame that those in greatest need of God's help don't come.' The vicar surveyed his flock. 'I would urge you to pray and follow an honest path through life, knowing that I'm always here to welcome you and your sisters back into the fold.'

As far as Louisa knew, there was nothing in the Bible against smuggling, and having thanked him for his advice, she attended the service with Winnie and Grace, but remained inside for the committal. Only Billy, their uncle, the vicar and sexton were present at the burial in the walled graveyard behind the chapel.

'I don't see why we can't go and see him put in the ground,' Grace said softly as they waited.

'You know very well why,' Winnie said. 'You've heard the story of Adam and Eve, and how Eve succumbed to temptation.'

'All she did was eat an apple,' Grace protested.

'And in doing so, she committed a sin. As sisters of Eve, the church considers us to be sinful too.' Winnie frowned. 'At least, I think that's how it works.'

After a while, Billy came to collect them.

'It's done. Reverend North is on 'is way back to St Leonard's and Mr Laxton's asked me to convey 'is apologies for not stoppin', because 'e 'as an urgent appointment in Kingsdown.' He offered Winnie his arm and walked with her, while Louisa walked with Grace.

Having reached the end of St George's Passage and crossed into Oak Street, they heard the sound of a commotion that grew louder as they approached Beach Street.

'Hark,' Winnie exclaimed. 'The Frenchies are on their way! Grace, remember what it said in the pamphlet – don't faint or scream.'

'I don't think it can be Napoleon,' Grace said as Louisa tried to recall the instructions they'd received a few months before, including plans for their escape and how to ready the beacons with wood for fires at night, and hay and water to make smoke during the day.

She hurried ahead of the rest of the party, afraid of what she might find: hundreds of barges laden with soldiers about to land on the Kent coast, or a ship in distress? But there were the usual two hundred or so vessels assembled in the Downs, nothing out of the ordinary.

'Billy! The Misses Lennicker!' Mr Witherall hastened up to meet them at the top of the beach, his hair once golden, lightened through with grey, his eyes blue, much like his son's but deeply creased at the corners, and his complexion weathered by the sun and wind. 'The *Pamela* – she's gorn.'

'How? She was 'ere this mornin'!' Billy exclaimed.

'Not Pa's beautiful boat . . .' Winnie turned to catch Grace as she fell into a faint, and Billy helped to hold her up.

'Someone must have seen 'er,' he said.

'Everyone was at the chapel, payin' their respects.'

'Except for you know who.' Louisa felt sick.

'We don't know that they took 'er,' Mr Witherall said.

'I do, but I'll never prove it. One Eye will have paid his men off or frightened them into silence.'

'Louisa, be careful what you say,' Winnie warned.

'I will speak my mind – I'm not afraid.'

'You should be, miss. I can see your mother in you, my girl – don't you even think about takin' matters into your own 'ands,' Mr Witherall said quietly. 'Jason and the crew 'ave taken the *Whimbrel* out to look for the *Pamela*. All is not lost.'

A little unnerved that he could apparently read her mind, she retreated to the house. Winnie and Billy followed, carrying Grace inside where they revived her with a breath of hartshorn and a tot of brandy.

'They'll have taken her down Romney way and hauled her up somewhere in the marshes.' Louisa returned to the subject of the missing boat. 'Or they'll have scuppered her on the Sands, or taken her to France or—'

'Mr Witherall's right – you can't go around accusin' people,' Billy broke in.

'They've taken her, I know they have, and the proof will come when we see her again, re-caulked, altered and her name painted over with another. Dear Lord, what are we going to do without her?'

'There's still the run goods, Pa's legacy to us,' Grace mumbled, emerging from her stupor. 'We can sell them and buy another boat. It won't be the same, but …'

'… needs must,' Winnie finished for her. 'Billy, you'll still be able to go out fishing. Louisa, we don't have to get our hands dirty any more. We are released from any obligation to follow in our parents' footsteps. Oh, this is a blessing in disguise. We'll be free from any ties to the honourable trade.'

Louisa frowned.

'I don't mean it's good that the *Pamela*'s gone. I shall miss her,' Winnie went on. 'I've never been comfortable about breaking the law. We've been fortunate so far, but I can't help feeling that one day our luck will run out. I'm sure I speak for us all when I say I have no fancy for being strung up on the three-legged mare, or taking a journey across the high seas, never to return.'

'Whatever happens in the future, our involvement isn't over yet,' Louisa said sternly, not appreciating her sister's talk of hanging and transportation. 'Tonight, we have work to do.'

The rain poured and the owls screeched from the overhanging yews, as they crept along the isolated path to St Leonard's, the parish church proper, with Grace's lantern lighting the way and the other sitting in the handcart.

'I don't like it,' Grace muttered. 'We'll die of the frights like Slicer did.'

Louisa smiled. 'The ghost was just a story put about to stop people snooping in places they weren't wanted.' Slicer had been on the fringes of the Rattlers' gang, but his death – rather than being anything to do with the smugglers –

had been down to an assignation with his mistress's cuckolded husband and a cudgel much like the one Billy was carrying, feinting at the shadows as he walked.

Grace didn't seem convinced.

'The Fey Lady's been seen on the cliffs at Kingsdown, in churchyards and cellars, and at the Rattling Cat,' she said. 'She comes out at night, dressed in white from top to toe, and some say she has a strange glow about her.'

'I've seen 'er at one of the upstairs windows at the tavern,' Billy said, 'and I wasn't the slightest bit castaway at the time.'

'What did you have to go and say that for?' Louisa grumbled.

'Because it's true.'

'Told you so,' Grace said.

'One Eye says 'e's made a pact with the Fey Lady, offerin' 'er protection in return for 'er workin' on the Rattlers' behalf, hauntin' their hidin' 'oles and frightenin' other free traders and the Revenue away.'

'Thanks for giving us the frights,' Winnie said.

'We'll be all right if we keep together,' Billy reassured her.

'Billy, didn't I hear Pa telling you to oil those wheels the other day?' Winnie pushed the handcart along, its wheels squeaking like a tormented mouse.

'I didn't get around to it,' he said, apologetically.

'Cover the lantern.' Louisa pulled her sou'wester down over her ears as they reached the lychgate. 'There's someone inside the church.' A light flickered behind one of the stained-glass windows, then went out. A door opened, and a figure appeared. Louisa shrank back, and the four of them huddled together, hardly daring to breathe as the vicar stumbled past them and away.

'If he wrote shorter sermons, he wouldn't need to stay out so late,' Grace observed when his footsteps had faded into the murk. She uncovered the lantern again as they tiptoed along the perimeter of the churchyard, the gravestones – old and new – looming up in front of them. 'We should have borrowed one of the ponies – I can't carry a tub by myself.'

Ignoring her complaint, Louisa halted beside the tomb where Pa had hidden the goods. It was the length and breadth of a man, and up to her waist in height, and she knew the inscription etched in the mossy slab on the top off by heart: *Here lieth Michael Kent, a mariner of Deal, gone aloft on this day 17th March 1702.* She felt guilty for disturbing the dead, but it had to be done for the benefit of the living.

'The lantern, Grace.' Louisa snatched it from her.

'Our sister's bravado seems to have deserted her,' Grace said wryly.

'I'm not scared,' Louisa affirmed as she gazed at the fresh set of footprints in the mud alongside the end panel of the tomb.

'As the eldest, you should do the honours,' Billy whispered.

'Mind the skellingtons,' Grace warned.

'Go on, Louisa, if you're in such a hurry – open it,' Winnie said.

Having handed the lantern to Billy, Louisa wiped her palms on her dress, then squatted down to heave the smooth slab aside, revealing a dark hole through which a man of small stature might slip. Billy handed the lantern back as if it was a hot potato.

The tremoring light revealed the glint of a coin – a ha'penny – from the moist earth, and beyond, a scooped-out hollow with signs of a recent visitation, and plenty large enough to take a goodly number of tubs, bales and boxes.

With one hand over her mouth to stifle the odour of rat and stale beer, and the incongruous scent of rosewater,

Louisa crawled into the hole. A skull lay on the ground a few feet below her, its eye sockets staring straight at her from the splintered remnants of a wooden coffin. Stifling a scream, she moved on, sliding down into the hollow where she shone the light in every direction. All she could see were the boundaries of the pit, lined with stone and brick.

'Can you see it?' Winnie called.

'There's nothing to see. I don't understand.' Pa wouldn't have sent them on a fool's errand, but Louisa feared someone else had made a fool of them. As she stood up, she bumped her head, sending a shower of stones scuttering across the earthen floor. Taking a step to one side, she fell backwards through a gap in the wall, her landing broken by a mound of soft sheets. The lantern glass cracked, and the light went out.

'Billy, it's you who should be here looking, because you know where it's hidden,' she shouted, fighting to disentangle herself from the musty shrouds. 'Get yourself down here this minute.'

She heard him stumble into the first chamber.

'Where are you? I can't see a –' he swore '– thing down 'ere.'

'Follow the sound of my voice – and mind the drop.'

'You're in the right place,' he said, joining her, his hot, sticky hand finding hers in the darkness. 'I 'elped carry goods up 'ere from the beach. But where is everythin'? There were tubs – more than fifty of 'em by my reckonin', and at least the same number of boxes of other items; bandannas, baccy ...'

'Who else knew it was here?'

'A goodly few. I don't know 'ow many times I suggested that Mr Lennicker should move it on, but then you couldn't tell 'im anythin'. 'E always thought 'e knew best.'

'I saw my father removing goods that weren't his, the other night.' Her blood ran cold. 'And now the Rattlers have got it in for us.'

Billy didn't deny the possibility. 'They 'ave their own 'idin' places, but it's no use askin' me where they are – if you don't know nothin', you can't 'ave it forced out of you.'

'This is a disaster.' She wished she'd come up here before, having had some idea of how the land lay. 'What are we going to do?'

'I don't rightly know,' he said.

'What exactly did happen at the Rattling Cat? You haven't told us ...'

'There isn't nothin' you don't already know. Mr Lennicker turned up, with his barkin' iron in 'is 'and. 'E said somethin' One Eye didn't like. Then One Eye said somethin' Mr Lennicker didn't like. 'E was threatenin' to tell you and your sisters about some scandal to make your father look bad.'

'Scandal? Was it to do with Mrs Stickles?'

'I don't know anythin' about it,' Billy said quickly. 'All I know is that they argued a bit more before One Eye grabbed 'is piece from where 'e keeps it under the counter and fired at 'im.'

Louisa's forehead tightened. 'I thought Pa's pistol went off when One Eye tried to get it off him.'

'Then that's the way it went,' Billy stammered.

'Why are you lying for him?' Louisa said, dismayed. 'It was murder, not self-defence.'

'I shouldn't 'ave told you. One Eye threatened to crush me underfoot like a mankie pea if I blabbed. Louisa, 'e'll kill me if he finds out. Please don't say anythin'. In the end, it don't make no difference who did what.'

'Of course it does. One Eye must be brought to justice.'

'There's no chance of that – everyone in Deal is in 'is pocket.'

'I'll think of another way then – I'm going to give him as good as he gave,' she avowed. 'I'll see him suffer.'

'You aren't thinkin' of doin' away with 'im? You can't 'ardly bring yourself to kill a spider.'

'No, but there has to be some way of—'

'It's done now. Best leave it.' Mild-mannered Billy sounded unusually snappish. 'You promise me you won't repeat what I told you to anyone, or I'm a dead man.'

'I'll keep my silence – you have my word. But I will have vengeance, one way or another.'

'I should sleep on it. Don't do somethin' you'll come to regret – it isn't worth it. One Eye won't show you any mercy.'

Louisa turned sharply as a faint phosphorescence flickered into her vision and instantaneously disappeared. 'Did you see that?'

'No, but I can 'ear footsteps.' Billy grabbed her hand again. 'It's the Fey Lady. We 'ave to get out of 'ere.'

Although her heart was pounding fit to burst, she kept her head.

'Spirits don't have footsteps.' Nor did they wear rosewater, Louisa thought, detecting the scent she'd identified previously. Had One Eye employed the ethereal being to spy on them, or merely scare them? If the former, she was worried, especially for Billy.

'I'm not waitin' to find out. Louisa, run for your life!'

They scrambled back up on to the ledge and into the first chamber, then emerged into the churchyard, gulping breaths of fresh air. Billy quickly slid the panel back across the end of the tomb.

'It's gone. They've taken every merciful thing,' Louisa said flatly.

'Are you all right, Billy?' Winnie asked. 'You're trembling like a brawn jelly.'

'He thought he saw a ghost,' Louisa explained.

'I did,' he countered. 'You saw it too! Let's go 'ome. There's nothin' else to be done 'ere.'

Having collected the handcart, they hurried back down the Tar path in silence.

'Pa must have had other assets stashed away somewhere,' Winnie said eventually. 'We just have to find them.'

Louisa agreed, but she had her doubts, and when she retired to bed, she couldn't sleep for grief and worry – and anger, whenever she heard the rumble of a barrel overhead. The Rattlers were rolling them along the valley formed by the intersections of the roofs of the adjacent houses in Cockle Swamp Alley, part of a hidden pathway leading from the Rattling Cat to an attic belonging to a gang member, a Mr Bodkin.

Knowing that it was the Lennickers' goods being spirited away only added insult to injury. The last thing she'd expected was to be left in this position: landed – out of the blue – with the role of head of the household without any obvious means of supporting herself and her sisters.

The next morning, she threw a shawl over her shoulders and slipped out before the others were up and about. The inn was closed, but when she rang the bell – salvaged from a wreck and appropriated by the Feaseys – she heard the locks being undone and the latches slipped across before One Eye's son opened the door. His dog, a rough-coated black longdog bred for coursing, was at his side, its lips wrapped around a bloody marrowbone.

'Miss Lennicker?' Isaiah frowned. He was a couple of years older than her, handsome in a rugged, unkempt kind of way, with curly hair the colour of jet, and dark brown eyes.

'I'm here to see your father.'

'You'd better come in then,' he grunted.

Noting that he was in a state of undress, wearing a shirt, a torn brown waistcoat, pantaloons, and no shoes, Louisa stepped across the threshold and entered the bar, carefully skirting the dog which remained glued to its master's side.

'It's all right – 'e won't bite unless I tell 'im to. Pa, there's somebody to see you.'

The hairs on the back of her neck stood on end as she surveyed the scene: despite the fresh sawdust scattered across the flagstones, she could still see Pa in the arms of Mrs Stickles, and the stain spreading over the floor.

'Who is it?' One Eye stepped through the gap in the counter. 'Oh, it's you. What do you want?'

Louisa didn't feel quite as brave as she had when she left the house, her mouth running dry as she started to speak.

'You need somethin' to wet your whistle,' One Eye said. 'Molly, come and get the lady a sup of ale.'

'No, no thank you,' Louisa said quickly. 'I'm not stopping.'

'It's on the 'ouse. I'm a gen'rous man,' he added as Mrs Stickles appeared behind the bar, her face partly hidden by a veil attached to her cap.

'Mornin',' she muttered while pouring a tankard of ale from one of the barrels. She handed it to One Eye, who gave it to Louisa. She took a sip – for courage.

'You may observe that our Molly has met with a little accident,' One Eye said slyly.

'Clumsy clodpole that I am, I walked into a door.' Mrs Stickles' smile didn't reach her eyes, one of which was bruised and bloodshot. 'Is that all for now, sir? I'm a little be'ind with the puddin's.'

'You make sure they're ready, or there'll be hell to pay. Men get jittery when they 'ave to wait for their wittles.'

'Oh, I know ... Don't I just know it?' Bowing her head, Mrs Stickles scurried away and One Eye turned on his son.

'Don't just stand there, you useless good-for-nothin',' he said, and Isaiah retreated with the dog. 'What is it, Miss Lennicker?'

As she gripped the tankard to stop her hands shaking, she fancied she could hear her mother's voice, whispering, 'Keep your chin up and shoulders straight.'

'You're a liar and a cheat,' she blurted out. 'You should be tried and hanged for what you did to my father. It was no accident!'

'I know you're upset, my dear, but you really shouldn't go around makin' false accusations against a respectable member of the community. I've done nothin' wrong. Take ten or twenty witnesses and they'll all say the same.' He grinned. 'My conscience – if I 'ad one – would be clear.'

'You took my father's life and now you've stolen his boat and goods, items that rightly belong to me and my sisters. It's all we have.' Instantly, she regretted playing for his sympathy.

'Righteous shouldn't 'ave taken what wasn't 'is to take – when we did the last run, 'e done me over good and proper.'

She couldn't deny what she had seen.

'Let me enlighten you – your father was in debt. Bringing up daughters costs a pretty penny, especially when you 'ave three or four of them, but that's not my affair. 'E stole from me, then when I decided to tell everyone the truth about 'im and 'is morals, 'e didn't like it.

'Your father wasn't the brightest button in the box, whereas Mrs Lennicker, 'aving an 'ead for business, took to the honourable trade like a duck to water. Now that you've said your piece, go and make yourself scarce. I 'ave better things to do than listen to your fantastical delusions.' He walked over to the door to open it for her. 'As I've warned you before ... watch your back, miss.'

Once outside, Louisa picked up her skirts and ran home to find Billy waiting for her on the doorstep in his sea boots and hat, his arms folded across his chest, his cheeks scarlet with ire.

'I know where you've been – I followed you! Louisa, how could you? You promised me you wouldn't say nothin'. If you were a man, I'd call you out.' His eyes flashed, not with anger, but tears, a sight that pierced Louisa through the heart. In doing what she thought was right, she'd done Billy a terrible wrong.

'I'm sorry,' she muttered, but she knew it would never be enough.

He pushed past her and stormed off towards the beach.

'Where are you going?' she called after him.

'Out!' he yelled back. 'As far away from 'ere as I can get.'

He didn't get far. As he turned the corner, she heard him screeching, 'No! Get your 'ands off me!'

'Who's that, singing like a banshee?' She turned as she heard Grace's voice.

'It's Billy,' Winnie exclaimed. 'He's in trouble.'

'I wish Pa was here – he'd know what to do,' Grace said.

'I'm going after him,' Winnie said. 'Whatever they're doing to him, we have to stop them ...'

Louisa tried to tell her to keep away, but Winnie wouldn't have it. All Louisa could do was accompany her and Grace to the beach, where two of One Eye's men were stripping the shirt from Billy's back, as a growing crowd egged them on, and a pair of soldiers stood idly by. Billy writhed and kicked.

'Punch 'im,' one of the men shouted.

'You do it,' said the other, whom Louisa recognised as Awful Doins – one of the Rattlers' spotsmen – from the weedy tone of his voice.

'I can't, or I'll 'ave to let 'im go.'

Awful Doins dropped Billy's shirt, screwed his eyes up tight, aimed a swipe at him and missed.

'For goodness' sake, let me do it,' the other man – Lawless – said, letting Billy go.

Billy made to run for it, only for Lawless to trip him up so he landed flat on his face in front of One Eye himself, who had made his way down from the inn with Isaiah and the dog at his side.

'Pick 'im up,' he growled.

Awful Doins and Lawless stood him up. Dazed and defeated, Billy could only wait to meet his fate.

'Paint it on, then,' One Eye went on. 'Where's the tar?'

'Here.' Isaiah handed Lawless a bucket of pine tar and a brush.

'Oh no ...' Winnie covered her face with her hands. 'I can't look.'

'Leave him alone.' Louisa stepped forward, only to be met with One Eye's harsh stare.

'No,' Grace whispered, taking her hand and pulling her back.

'This is my fault,' Louisa said quietly, turning to her sisters. 'Billy told me what he saw the night our father was shot – I went to confront One Eye over it. He's a murderer.'

They looked at her, eyes wide with shock and pain.

'How can I ever forgive you?' Winnie began to cry. 'Look what they're doing to him.'

'You can't blame Louisa for it – it's One Eye's fault.' Grace winced as Billy groaned in anguish.

Lawless continued to slap the warm tar on to his skin, and Awful Doins hung a sign around his neck, reading 'Traitor'. A bucket of feathers was passed around the crowd, and as One Eye's men drove Billy ahead of them, people threw feathers at him. They covered his torso and bony arms, and stuck to his face, making him sneeze.

The crowd laughed and roared and pointed their fingers.

''E looks like an 'alf-plucked pullet,' Louisa heard one say.

'That's what 'appens when you cross One Eye and the Rattlers,' another said, in awe.

They paraded him from one end of Deal to the other, bringing the bakers, bankers, boatbuilders, boot makers and shopkeepers to their doors to watch. When they were done with him, they let him go, stumbling into Winnie's arms.

'Come home with us,' Winnie said.

'I can't – I've never been so 'oomiliated in my life,' he muttered. 'I'll never show my face 'ere again.'

'Don't be silly.' Winnie tried to pick a feather off his cheek.

'Ouch,' he exclaimed.

'Come home and we'll get you cleaned up. Ignore these people – they should be at work.'

'I'm sorry.' Louisa shrank back as he looked her straight in the eye.

'I've been thinkin' about the footsteps we 'eard last night. It could 'ave been somebody spyin' for One Eye. 'E knew we'd go up there to fetch the goods. 'E didn't know I'd blab, but 'e must 'ave known that I 'ad before you went to see 'im. I'm not sayin' I can forgive you ...'

It was enough for the time being.

'Thank you,' she said, and they returned home where Grace picked off as many feathers as she could, and Winnie spent ages scrubbing Billy's skin with soap, sand and water, until he glowed like a beacon fire.

'This stuff doesn't come off easily. I hate the Rattlers, every single one of them. I hate that we have to earn money this way,' Winnie said. 'I hate how we have to creep about in the dark, looking over our shoulders.'

''Ave a care!' Billy yelped. 'You're pullin' my 'air out.'

'I'm trying to be careful, but …' Winnie returned to the subject of the gangs and the honourable trade. 'We have to stop before we come to grief, and this is as good a time as any. If we could just buy another boat, we could make our living out of fishing and taking in a little sewing. I don't want much – a happy home with you and my sisters.'

'With food to fill our bellies,' Billy added.

'And beautiful gowns like the ones that the Misses Flinders wear,' Grace joined in.

'That might be a stretch too far,' Louisa smiled.

'So, we are all in agreement?' Winnie said.

'There's still some lace and cognac to sell,' Louisa pointed out. 'We have to find the money for a new boat as well. I'm not sure where it's going to come from.'

'After that, then?' Winnie insisted. 'Promise me that we'll stop.'

'I can't promise anything.' Louisa had already broken her word that day – she didn't want to make a habit of it, but she felt bad for her middle sister who had a conscience that was more easily pricked than hers and Grace's. 'Let's take one step at a time.'

With her father's murder, her dislike of the Feaseys had turned to a passionate hatred. She recalled the day when Isaiah, who must have been about fifteen at the time, had rounded up the younger children on the beach to recount the tale of the Fey Lady that haunted the cellars and alleyways of the town.

'It's a story,' one of the boys had said as Grace had stood with her face buried in Louisa's skirts. 'It's hogwash.'

'I can prove it,' Isaiah said, his eyes dark with evil. 'An acquaintance of Mr Jackson – you know 'im.'

'Mr Jackson's a boatman,' one of the Roper boys had piped up.

'Anyway, 'e broke into the cellar at the Rattlin' Cat – when my father dragged 'is dead body up the steps, 'e said 'is eyes were fixed wide open like 'e'd seen a ghost.'

'What did the coroner say?' Louisa had asked. 'There must have been an inquest.'

'I don't know. I don't remember. I was only a little lad.'

'So you can't prove the existence of this ghost,' she mocked, even though a shiver of fear ran down her spine as he glared at her.

'There's more. 'E wasn't the only victim.' He pulled an object from his shirt pocket and threw it at Louisa.

She caught it and immediately let it go.

Isaiah laughed. 'That comes from a pile of bones we found lyin' in one of the underground passageways leading out of the cellar: whoever it was 'ad gone down there when 'e wasn't supposed to, and nobody found 'im until it was too late … Who knows what the ghost did to 'im? The bones are gnawed right through.'

'That one isn't,' Louisa challenged.

'I took the best lookin' one, not wanting to disturb anyone's peace of mind more than I 'ave to. Somebody needs to l'arn you that girls are supposed to keep their mouths shut.'

She had turned and walked away, taking her sisters with her.

The sight of Winnie cutting Billy a piece of bread from the loaf on the kitchen table brought Louisa back to the present. Not knowing what to do next, she pulled out their father's old ledger from the dresser and placed it on the table. On opening it, the sight of his chaotic notes and her mother's copperplate handwriting stirred her grief anew.

He had scrawled summaries of the catches he'd made, and the proceeds of his hovelling activities.

The *Charlotte*, towed into Dover for repairs – fee for services rendered, paid in full.

Salvaged from the cutter, *Fenella*, seventeen yards of sail, five lengths of rope and a quantity of copper. Paid, with a half share going to Mr Witherall.

She found other loose sheets of paper: notes of fishing grounds with the marks included; lists of goods obtained, bought and sold, some well-thumbed and watermarked. There were invoices: bills from the greengrocer, butcher and ropemaker; a threatening letter regarding an amount Pa owed for 'services rendered', whatever they were; a note screeved on behalf of Mrs Stickles requesting the settlement of her regular monthly account for an outrageously high sum.

How could he have been so besotted that he'd pay out that kind of money? It seemed that he'd got himself and his daughters – she had no doubt that his creditors would soon be arriving on their doorstep in droves – into a pretty pickle. She couldn't help thinking they would be going to hell in a handbasket.

# Chapter Five

## *Beggars Can't Be Choosers*

For two weeks, Louisa was torn between grieving for her father and worrying about how they were going to make a living and pay back the money owed. Every day, she was on tenterhooks, expecting a knock on the door.

On the morning of the last day of August, Billy left the house early, rousing the alley's occupants as he fell out of the front door. Louisa looked out to see him fallen arsey yarsey over a leather bucket, and several silvery mackerel spread across the cobbles.

'Some buffoon left this on the doorstep,' he grumbled.

'If you'd been half awake, you wouldn't have tripped over it,' she scolded. 'Where were you last night?'

'I 'ad a few at the Waterman's Arms.'

'I thought as much. I heard you staggering through the door well after midnight. Billy, I wish you wouldn't drink. You can't possibly defend yourself when you're in your cups.'

'You can't tell me what to do. You aren't my keeper. Oh, I'm sorry. I'm not myself.' He began to pick up the fish.

'I'll do it – it's my turn to sweep the pavement,' Louisa said, taking pity on him and wishing she hadn't spoken harshly. 'You go on.'

'Take care,' he said. 'Don't let your sisters out of your sight.'

'I won't, but you don't think ...?'

'I dunno what to think, except we must stick together and find a way to make a livin'. If I 'ad a choice, I wouldn't show my face again after what One Eye's men did to me. I'm goin' to 'ave the life teased out of me by the likes of Marlin and his crew. I'll be back later – today, tomorrer or in a few days' time, dependin' on what I'm offered.'

Realising that he wasn't coping very well, she wished him luck and watched him go, his face scratched, his red hair sticking up in a cowlick, his trousers torn and his usual swagger having disappeared, before she collected up the fish. The mackerel were fresh, their eyes still bright as if they'd only just been pulled out of the sea, but she hesitated. Were they a present from some kind soul or was there a more sinister reason for the offering?

Having taken the bucket inside and collected the broom from the kitchen, she'd begun to sweep the cobbles when a phaeton pulled by a pair of dapple greys came flying around the corner at speed, its showy wheels narrowly missing the side of the house. With a clattering of hooves and much shouting, it came to a halt.

Her heart sank as a skinny gentleman in his forties, dressed mainly in black and carrying a short cane and case, got out and came hurrying towards her.

'Miss Lennicker, what an uncommon delight.' He doffed his tall hat, revealing strands of chestnut hair swept across in a vain attempt to hide his balding nob.

'Mr Trice,' she said stiffly while he looked her up and down, as though he was a dealer assessing a horse. His eyes were dark and small, and his cravat gave the impression of a white throat, like a weasel's.

'I have business to discuss with you.'

'You'd better come inside,' she said. He pushed his way past her and went into the parlour where he took a seat, having flicked away some imaginary dust with a silk handkerchief. Unsure why he'd assumed that he was entitled to barge into their home without a by-your-leave, and force his presence on her unaccompanied, she offered him a drink.

'No, thank you.' He checked his gold pocket watch. 'It is in vain that I try to inculcate my clerks that time is money. Allow me to express my sympathy for Mr Lennicker's sad demise – I saw news of it in the papers at my club last night. There's no need to state your gratitude out of convention and politeness.' He raised one hand slightly as though to check her. 'I will move on without further ado to the reason for my visit.'

She had met him several times before – normally, he sent one of his clerks to collect the monies due to him. Occasionally, he'd called on her father in person with a bodyguard at his side, presumably to protect him should anyone try to make off with the money he had been paid that day.

'I shall speak slowly and plainly, knowing that young ladies have neither the education nor the inclination to make sense of the complex legal terminology used by the learned members of my profession.'

He wasn't only an attorney-at-law, Louisa recalled, bristling at his condescension. He was also steward to several of the landed gentry, agent for various foreign merchants, and administrator for many a privateer.

'Anyway, to put this succinctly,' he droned on, 'Mr Lennicker owes me money – his payments to the merchants for goods, and my commission plus interest for the past nine months.'

'Owed,' she corrected him.

'Ah, you are more astute than I had reckoned with. A deceased person may not carry his debt with him – he leaves it behind for his creditors to claim what they are due from his estate.'

'He had nothing left,' Louisa said coldly, wishing that the objectionable Mr Trice would get up and leave.

'There's always something – I just have to find it. Your father was in debt to the tune of—'

When he named the figure, Louisa gasped.

'We aren't talking of pin money, such as young ladies are used to receiving from their fathers or husbands. Gentlemen like Mr Lennicker and their investors have made huge fortunes out of the trade.'

'My family is comfortably off, no more than that. My father had no money – even his boat has gone.'

'Ah, that may be so, but there is still the profit due to me from the last two runs he made, along with five ankers of cognac.'

'Those goods were lost, presumed stolen.'

'That's all rather convenient, isn't it?'

'It's the truth,' she said firmly.

'Let's say that you're right and the goods have been misappropriated by persons known or unknown, your father had other assets.' Mr Trice looked around the room, floor to ceiling, and wall by wall. 'This house is part of his estate.'

'He has left it to his daughters, sir.'

'He may only leave the residue to his issue after his creditors have been paid. The house will be sold to release the capital, not that it will make much, being in such an undesirable position close to the beach where common families live cheek by jowl.'

'You would make us homeless?' Louisa hissed, incensed as much by his opinion of their neighbourhood as the idea that he'd sell the roof over their heads.

'Although this is allowable according to the letter of the law, please don't assume that I relish the thought of it.'

'I wish to see proof of these debts, Mr Trice.'

'I can have one of my clerks provide you with copies of the evidence – for a fee, of course. Every word uttered, every note screeved, and every breath taken is fully chargeable.'

What good would it do? she thought. A man of his resources could easily have a record created.

'You find me a reasonable man, and moderately patient. I can afford to give you some time to find the means to pay me and the other creditors back.'

'I'm very grateful, but it's only delaying the inevitable,' she said through gritted teeth.

'I have a suggestion …' Having pulled a handkerchief from his pocket and wiped the silver ferrule on his cane, he stared at her neck, making her wish she'd put on her lace. Leaning towards her, he made his offer.

'I could loan you the monies. You learned the tricks of the trade from your mother; your knowledge of the finer goods from Alençon and Chantilly, along with your manners and demeanour, allow you to sell to the moneyed ladies of the gentry. You're perfectly placed to pay off the debts and go on to make your fortune.' He sat back, waiting for her reaction.

'You hesitate,' he said.

'How do I know I can trust you?'

'Ah, you can't trust anyone in this game – only your instincts.'

All her instincts were telling her to stay away from this man whose breath stank of mint and scallions, but it felt like the only way out.

'Will you prepare a contract?' she said eventually.

'Of course. It will include the terms on which we have agreed, along with a clause explaining that if the terms cannot be met, I shall be entitled to claim ... goods in kind. You are in possession of a most valuable asset, something more precious than money, and just as easily lost.'

'I don't understand,' she stammered.

'You are being disingenuous. My clerk, Mr Mellors, will call on you tomorrow, bringing the loan in the form of a promissory note from my bank in Dover.'

'I will have it in coins.' She recalled what Pa used to say, that when a bank folded, which they often did, the money wasn't worth the paper it was written on.

'That's rather inconvenient, Miss Lennicker.'

'I won't change my mind.'

'Then I will make sure my clerk has deep pockets, and a method of defending himself – Deal is a godforsaken town where the streets are ruled by villains. I shan't take up any more of your time.'

She stood up, hardly able to bear his presence any longer, at which, without asking permission, he took her hand and raised it to his lips.

'I look forward to continuing our discourse.' He pressed his mouth to her skin before releasing her and stepping back. 'I'll see myself out. Good day.'

When he had gone, she paced the tiny parlour, like a caged lioness in a travelling menagerie. Out of desperation, she had settled on a way of keeping the roof over their heads, but at the risk of losing her maidenhead to Mr Trice.

Trying not to think about it, she returned to sweeping the pavement.

'Mornin', Louisa.' Mrs Witherall stopped with her basket of shopping to ask her how she was. 'Everyone's thinkin' of you and your sisters, and Billy, of course.'

At yet another reminder of what they had lost, tears sprang to Louisa's eyes. Thanking their neighbour for her kindness, she turned and bolted inside, finding her sisters in the kitchen.

'You're crying,' Winnie said. 'What did the old weasel say to you?'

'Oh, it wasn't him that upset me. No, I've agreed to borrow some capital so we can replace the *Pamela*.'

'That's wonderful news. I've been praying for something good to happen, and it has. Billy will be able to go out fishing again.'

'There's more to it than that,' Louisa confessed. 'Mr Trice wants us to run goods – lace, silk and kid gloves – using our network of contacts and our feminine wiles to sell them for the high return they bring. There's no way we can pay him back peddling fish. You know that, Winnie,' she went on, noticing how her smile had changed to an expression of doubt.

'You should have spoken to me, Grace and Billy first.'

'He wanted a decision – I used my initiative.' Hurt that Winnie should question her judgement when she was trying to do her best for them, Louisa changed the subject. 'Will you come with me to the beach for some fresh air?'

'I'll stay here with Grace, thank you,' Winnie said in a small act of rebellion, making Louisa feel sadder than ever as she put on her boots and headed to the capstan grounds. Despite Billy's warning, she didn't feel unsafe going alone on this occasion. There were plenty of people about, too many potential witnesses for One Eye and his gang to try anything.

Smoker Edwards, Mr Witherall and Terrier Roper were in their usual places. It was painful, looking out for Pa and not finding him there in his customary spot. Pausing to gather her thoughts, Louisa searched the shingle for pieces of rope or driftwood, anything she could use or sell. She collected a little sea kale for dinner and picked a single stem of Queen Anne's lace for its umbrella of white flowers.

As she wandered, she heard the men gossiping worse than the women did, although they'd never go so far as to admit it.

'It's over twenty years since I saw the luggers go up in flames ...' she heard Smoker say as she gradually made her way towards them. 'I've never seen anythin' like it.'

'I remember it well – it was in the January. We were waitin' for 'em – the Light Dragoons, but they sent the 38th Foot from Canterbury with 'em, and we 'ad no 'ope of defendin' our property.' Mr Witherall chewed on the end of his pipe.

'The townsfolk – God bless 'em – refused to give the soldiers a bed for the night. Even One Eye wouldn't serve 'em,' Terrier said.

'Pitt was Warden and Prime Minister then, so 'e should 'ave known better,' Smoker added. 'It was all done on the basis of a lie anyway: 'e was goin' to stop our trade because we were violent towards the Revenue men.'

'There were a few shenanigans,' Terrier pointed out.

'That's true, but 'is plan didn't work, did it?' Mr Witherall said. ''Avin' been roused to a fury, we were even more determined to continue our work. It didn't take us long to get back to makin' a livin', and an honest one at that.'

'That's right,' Terrier chuckled.

'A penny for 'em, miss,' Mr Witherall said. 'Oh, I shouldn't 'ave asked. You'll be thinkin' of your dear father. I miss 'im too.'

'It isn't the same without Righteous,' Terrier added. ''E was one o' the finest.'

'As a mark of respect and knowin' 'ow your father would 'ave wanted me to 'elp 'is daughters and Master Fleet, I've come up with an idea. Billy's a good lad, but 'e's young for his age and still l'arnin' the ways of the sea. I 'ope you don't think I'm interferin', but I've consulted with the men and worked out that I can give 'im a share in the *Whimbrel*. 'E can pay me back out of 'is earnings as 'e goes along.'

When she told him that they were buying a boat to replace the *Pamela*, his bushy brows shot up and quivered aloft.

'Your father must have 'ad a little more tucked away than 'e made out.'

She didn't mention Mr Trice's loan – he didn't need to know the Lennickers' business.

'Billy will be skipper, but what about a crew? 'Mr Witherall continued. 'You'll need at least another couple of 'ands. I'll 'ave a word with Jason to see what we can do.'

'There's no need for you to go to any trouble—'

'We're all friends 'ere,' he cut in. 'Take it from me, don't go tryin' to do everythin' by yourself. You 'ave nothin' to prove. I've told you, let my boy 'elp you out – I know of a boat that's comin' up for sale. She's rough around the edges, but with an overhaul, she'll be perfect for a bit o' fishin' and provisionin'. Jason will cast 'is eye over 'er for you …'

'As I said, I'm very grateful but Billy knows about boats—'

'That's as maybe, but 'e 'asn't got a clue when it comes to negotiatin' a purchase. Let Jason look after it – that way, you won't get taken advantage of. Louisa, you must see the sense of it. Take my boy with you. If two 'eads are better than one, then three 'eads – well, you can't go wrong, can you?'

She smiled briefly at the way he kept calling Marlin – a grown man – his boy.

'I'll make arrangements for you to view it – Jason will call on you when he's back.'

'Have you seen Billy today?' she asked, having thanked him.

''E's gone out – there was a space for 'im on the *Whimbrel*. A little advice – keep away from the Feaseys and stick with us Witheralls. That way, we can keep you safe. With a good boat, an 'alf-decent crew and a followin' wind, you'll do well. I'm only trying to 'elp, miss, not tell you what to do. Righteous would have done the same for me, if it had been the other way around.'

Mr Witherall didn't waste any time, making Louisa wonder if he was on a commission. As soon as the *Whimbrel* returned that day, Jason and Billy arrived together at Compass Cottage to take her and her sisters to view Mr Jackson's boat.

'Good afternoon, ladies.' Jason removed his cap and held it crushed in one hand, rumpling his blond hair with the other. He looked weary with grey shadows under his bright blue eyes, and fresh grazes across his knuckles. 'Let's make 'aste – I 'ave other fish to fry.' He stopped abruptly as though regretting his rudeness. 'I'm truly sorry for startin' out on the wrong foot. Your father was kind to me – and brave. He saved my bacon on more than one occasion.'

'You don't 'ave to come with us, Marlin,' Billy said.

'I promised my father I'd take a look at her for you, so that's what I'm going to do.'

''E was out all night,' Billy told them. 'Came back to drop off 'is spoils, then went out again all day. 'E's a true 'ero.'

'An East Indiaman slipped her moorings and started drifting towards the Sands – although they tried, the anchor wouldn't bite, and she struck the bank and sank very quickly. At great risk to ourselves, we managed to save the captain and crew, her mainmast and some of her cargo.' Although marvelling at his courage, Louisa didn't appreciate his bragging. 'Shall we go?'

'I must fetch my gloves.' Grace disappeared upstairs for a few minutes, while the rest of them waited, looking at each other.

'Make haste,' Louisa called, and she reappeared, having changed her bonnet as well.

'I like to look my best, that's all.' Grace blushed at Louisa's enquiring stare. 'Ma always said we should keep up appearances.'

'We're only goin' down to the beach.' Jason scratched his head. 'It betwattles me the way young ladies like to dress up.'

Laughing as though trying to impress him, Billy admitted to sharing the same sentiment, much to Louisa's annoyance – and Winnie's, she guessed, from the expression on her face. Jason and Billy set out at quite a pace while the sisters strolled together in their wake.

'Most of the young ladies in Deal think Jason's more sightly than a Greek god,' Grace commented.

'What do you know of Greek gods?' Louisa asked scathingly.

'Only that they must be very handsome.'

'Hush now,' Winnie said. 'His ears will be burning. Anyway, he and Margaret Hibben are definitely engaged. I reckon they'll be married by Michaelmas.'

Louisa felt envious of Miss Hibben's good fortune. Although Jason was a neighbour and they'd grown up on the beach together, he was two years older than her, and she didn't know him well. By reputation, he was a decent, hard-working lad who, although respectful, kept his distance, confirming Winnie's view that the Lennicker sisters were of no consequence to him.

Not only was he a Deal boatman, he was a Sea Fencible like Pa had been, a member of a regiment of volunteers, called to defend their king and country should Napoleon invade England. They were drilled and ready to fight as soon as the French army set sail, although they resented the idea of having to leave their other, more profitable activities.

'It's horrid to think old Boney is watching us,' she said as they caught up with the men.

'How can he do that?' Jason was derisive.

'Through his telescopes – they're said to be so sharp that he can count the stones in the walls of Dover Castle.'

'I don't know where you heard that one,' he laughed. 'There's no telescope that powerful – it's a lie, propaganda put about by the Frenchies.'

She felt a little foolish as they walked on to the beach, passing the *Whimbrel*, a clinker-built lugger, the forepeak of her deck covered over to make a small cabin where four men could sleep side by side when they needed to, and armed with eleven three-pounders, thanks to the war. Her name was painted on each side of her bow.

Beyond a row of other vessels, they met with Mr Jackson, an elderly man bowed almost double like a broken mast.

'It was a rum do,' he said. ''Tis a shame nothin' could be done.'

Louisa wasn't sure what he meant – whether he was sorry that their father couldn't have been saved, or that One Eye couldn't be brought to trial, or that he regretted the loss of the *Pamela*.

''Ere she is.' He limped across the shingle to the nearest boat beached high and dry on the stones. Her name – the *Curlew* – was written in peeling paint on her side and there were boards missing from her barnacle-encrusted hull.

'She looks past 'er prime, but with a little love and attention …' Mr Jackson grinned – he had no teeth.

'She looks worn out,' Billy said.

'She has a dipping lug, the same as the *Pamela*,' Jason said. 'You go out on one tack, then dip for the way back. The design with the mizzen mast stepped well aft means there's plenty of space to work amidships. She's small but easy to handle, perfect for the fishin' trips your father used to go on. It wouldn't take much to make her seaworthy again. How much do you want for her?'

Louisa frowned – she hadn't expected him to take over the negotiations on her behalf.

Mr Jackson mentioned a sum that matched what she wanted to pay.

'That's far too much for a leaky old sieve,' Jason cut in before she could say anything.

'I'll take a little less for 'er, although it pains my poor old 'eart to do so. Ten per cent, seein' she'd be going to a good 'ome where she'd be brought back to 'er former glory.' Mr Jackson had a tear in his eye when he turned to Louisa and her sisters. 'What do you say, ladies?'

Louisa reached out and touched the *Curlew*'s weathered timbers – they were smooth and warm in the sun.

'You could say she has character,' she smiled. 'What about you, Billy? You'll be skipper.'

'She's full of 'oles,' he sighed.

'If you want something seaworthy in a hurry, this is your chance,' Jason said. 'There are waitin' lists at all the boatyards – you could be stranded for months.'

Louisa wanted the boat, barnacles and all – only she understood exactly how far Pa had sunk them into debt. Only she knew the terms of Mr Trice's loan.

'Winnie? Grace? What do you think?' she asked.

Grace wrinkled her nose.

'There's another one for sale at the boatyard,' Jason said. 'Black Dog told me about her the other day.'

'I'll have nothing to do with it – I'm not lining the Feaseys' pockets,' Louisa said.

'I agree with you, but I thought I should mention it – in case you wanted the *Pamela* back.'

'You think it's her?' The thought of retrieving the Lennickers' boat tugged at her heartstrings.

'Everyone knows it's her.'

'Oh Louisa, we must buy her back.' Blinking hard, Grace picked up an empty wilk-shell and rolled it about in the palms of her hands, apparently not caring that she might soil her gloves.

'One Eye will charge you for the boat – just the shell, then you'll have to pay for everythin' else: sails, mast, tiller ... on top. Before you know it, you'll be payin' double the original price,' Jason said.

'Please – it's what Pa would have wanted,' Grace began again.

'I'm sorry – we can't let our hearts rule our heads.' Louisa felt guilty knowing that their father would have paid anything to have her back, but their mother would have put her foot down. 'This is about making the most of our money.'

'You sound like Ma,' Winnie said quietly.

'My father has someone lined up to do the repairs on this one,' Jason said. 'Terrier's son, Mark, is gettin' shackled soon – he needs the money to set up home.'

Louisa didn't know what to do – it was a lot of money to spend in one go and she was afraid of making a mistake, but they needed a boat. She thought of the bills piling up and the moist imprint of Mr Trice's lips, hot and slug-like, on her skin. She had to have a way of paying him off, and soon.

'We'll have her, Mr Jackson,' she decided. 'I'll bring the money tomorrow.'

'I'll sleep easy tonight, knowin' the ol' lady's goin' to a good 'ome.' Smiling and nodding, Mr Jackson shook Jason's hand, and the deal was done. 'The Rattlers showed some int'rest in 'er, but I told One Eye to sling 'is 'ook. You know 'e killed a good friend of mine? He lured him into the inn and knocked him on the head, then claimed he'd died of fright, but I know better. I've had this rage burning in my breast ever since, but my dear wife has finally persuaded me to let it go. I'm goin' to enjoy my retirement, for as long as it lasts. Good day, ladies and gen'lemen.'

Having wished him a good day in return, they set off for home.

'Miss Lennicker, may I have a moment of your time?' Jason said.

'Yes, of course.' She bit her lip as they dropped back behind the others, wondering what else he could possibly have to say to her. 'I thought you were in a hurry.'

'I am, but this is important – Billy's a good lad. He's a hard worker, but sometimes ... he drinks a bit too much and doesn't take life that seriously. What I'm tryin' to say is that it would behove you to keep him in line, like your father used to.'

'I'm grateful for the advice, but it's entirely unwarranted.'

'You don't like bein' told what to do, do you?'

'I rely on my own judgement,' she said, affronted by his impertinence.

'I was tryin' to be helpful, but it seems I needn't have bothered.' He bowed his head slightly before walking away, leaving Louisa to catch up with Billy and her sisters.

'I've accepted a share in the *Whimbrel*,' Billy said.

'You won't be able to skipper the *Curlew* then?' Winnie sounded disappointed.

'Of course I will. Lots of people 'ave shares in more than one boat, if you're offerin' me a share, that is.'

'We can't do it without you,' Louisa said. 'There'll be one share for you, one for the boat, one for the tackle, and one for me and my sisters.'

'You mean you're goin' to take up fishin'? Oh no. No way. We'll 'ave to find a crew.'

'That won't work,' Louisa said decisively. 'There won't be enough profit in it for us if we do that. It isn't like we'll own the *Curlew* outright, not straight away.'

'You'll 'ave to go out every day, rain or shine. Winnie, tell your sister she can't do this – it's madness.'

'You know what she's like – it's impossible to change her mind once it's made up.' Winnie smiled. 'Anyway, she's right – we have to do this ourselves. The sooner we pay off the debt, the sooner we can settle for a quieter life.'

'I always 'ad you down as the sensible one. What about you, Grace?'

'It isn't uncommon for women to go out provisioning the ships in the Downs,' she said. 'I don't see anything wrong in it.'

'Thank you,' Louisa said, glad to have her support. 'We have to be prepared to do whatever's necessary to get the Lennickers' finances back on an even keel – as Pa would have called it. We're going to pay back what we owe and make our living. If we're blessed with making our fortune on the journey, we'll buy some land and retire from the sea.'

'The world will be our oyster,' Grace smiled.

'We're going to prove ourselves to the rest: the Witheralls and Ropers.' She was still stinging from Jason's comment. 'And one day we'll get back what we're owed, and more from the Rattlers. The Lennickers will have justice, one way or another. Billy, say that you'll accept a quarter share.'

'I'll be 'appy to. If you were a man, Louisa, I'd spit on it,' he said. They had reached the cottage and he followed the sisters inside. 'What's for supper? I'm starvin'.'

'There's mackerel,' Winnie said.

'Oh no, they didn't seem too fresh to me,' Louisa said quickly.

'They're fine.' Winnie frowned. 'I had a look at them earlier.'

'We should feed them to the gulls.' Louisa didn't want to use them even as bait.

'Waste not, want not,' Winnie went on.

'We don't know where they came from ...'

'Some kindly neighbour dropped them off for us,' Winnie said.

'Or someone up to no good. What if someone's trying to poison us?'

'For goodness' sake,' Billy said, staring at her. 'I'm startin' to think the birds are flown.'

'You were out on the beach today – didn't you think to ask who'd left them?' Winnie said.

'I should 'ave done, but it slipped my mind. I'll go and ask around. I won't be long.' Billy made to leave the house, but as he stepped into the alley, he spun round and headed back inside, slamming the door behind him, his face oyster white beneath the freckles.

'It's the gangers,' he hissed. He had documents exempting him from being 'volunteered' for the Royal Navy, but in these dark times, he couldn't rely on them.

'Quickly! Hide!' Winnie grabbed him by the arm and almost dragged him up the stairs, while Louisa pressed her back against the door and waited, hardly able to breathe as she listened for the sound of footsteps. Over the beat of an approaching drum and shouting, she heard women's cries, begging the officers not to take their men.

When the dreaded knock came, Louisa was forced to step aside and let the officer and his men into the house where, ignoring her entreaties, they searched up and down.

'There are no men here, sir,' she kept saying as Grace and Winnie looked on, arm in arm. 'My father passed away very recently.'

'According to the landlord of the Rattling Cat, you have a lodger, though, a Mr Billy Fleet,' the officer said.

'He moved out months ago,' Louisa stated.

'I see.' He called his gang together and sent them back out on to the street, having confirmed that Louisa's story held water. 'Good night, ladies.'

Louisa closed the door on them, heaving a sigh of relief, and later when the streets were quiet again, she and Winnie went upstairs, moved the bed in Pa's old room aside and slid the panel away to reveal Billy's hiding place behind the false wall abutting the staircase. Thanks to her mother, Pa had had the house extended and a few 'useful' alterations made.

Billy emerged, blinking and complaining of sore knees.

'I thought my poor rumblin' belly was goin' to give me away,' he chuckled.

'I've heated up the leftovers from yesterday and cooked a few potatoes to go with it. You won't go out tonight, will you?' Winnie said, her voice soft like a mother talking to a child – or, Louisa thought with a jolt of recognition, a young woman speaking to her lover.

Billy shook his head.

'Then I'm very glad.' Winnie smiled.

Louisa was glad too, but she couldn't shake off the sense of something being out of the ordinary as the four of them spent the rest of the evening in welcome peace and quiet. Billy and Winnie had always been close, so perhaps it shouldn't have been a surprise to her that they'd turned to each other for consolation over Pa's death. She pushed it to the back of her mind, letting her thoughts drift. What if the press gang returned and found Billy next time? Without him, they'd have no skipper, their investment in the *Curlew* would be worthless, and Mr Trice would be after her. She imagined the press gang rounding up Jason, then pulled herself up. There was no reason why that should bother her, no reason at all.

# Chapter Six

## *A Sea Change*

Having warned Billy to look out for the gangers in case they were still in town, Louisa watched him walk along the alley towards the beach early the next morning, ready to join the *Whimbrel*'s crew. All she could do was wait, hoping that Mr Trice would be true to his word. It wasn't long before a young, well-dressed gentleman arrived on their doorstep.

'Good day, miss.' He almost dropped his hat as he swept it from his head. 'Mr Mellors. May I come in? I have been instructed to carry out Mr Trice's orders in a suitably furtive manner.'

'Do come in,' she said, noticing how he glanced warily behind him before stepping inside. She closed the door and showed him into the kitchen, aware that Winnie and Grace were working in the parlour, continuing with the letting down of the rest of the Lennickers' cognac, diluting it to reduce its strength.

'This is for you.' He pulled two bulky bags of coins from under his coat and placed them on the table, then retrieved some paperwork from his pocket, along with a pen and inkwell. 'Mr Trice requires your signature.'

'I'll check the amount first, thank you,' she said, and she sat down and counted out the money, which was exactly as she and Mr Trice had agreed. She signed the papers and Mr Mellors went on his way.

'Those coins are dazzling to the eyes,' Winnie said, joining Louisa as she returned to marvel at the unfamiliar sight of riches beyond her imagination. Even with Pa having made money from the trade and from salvaging, she'd never seen so many guineas at once.

'I have to keep reminding myself that it doesn't belong to us,' Louisa said. 'Don't say a word to anyone about it – I'm going to pay for the boat, then put the rest away for the repairs and anything else we need.'

'Where will you hide it?' Grace said, wandering into the kitchen.

'I have an idea,' Louisa said. 'It involves more sewing ...'

'You've said yourself that we shouldn't spend all day indoors grieving,' Grace said. 'I was hoping to buy that muslin Pa promised me, though – it sounds selfish, but I'd make it into a dress and whenever I wore it, it would remind me of him.'

'Things are different now and we're going to have to cut our cloth, so to speak. You can come with me while I go and see Mr Jackson, Winnie as well. In the meantime, I'm going to wrap the balance in oilskins and—'

'Put it inside Pa's old mattress,' Winnie suggested.

'That's the first place a thief would look.' Louisa managed to raise a small smile.

'In the hiding hole upstairs?' Grace said.

'What about the privy? Don't mock my ideas, Louisa,' Winnie said.

'It's too obvious. We'll put it in the herring hang under the woodchips – it won't be there for long, because we're going to sew the coins into the hems of our father's slops and hang them back in the wardrobe. Nobody will ever guess.'

'Oh Louisa, you aren't just a pretty face,' Grace said. 'But all that needlework. Do we have to?'

'We have to do whatever's necessary to keep our heads above water.'

'Will we be going to the Waterman's Arms tonight?' Grace flung her arms around her neck. 'Please say we are.'

'Stop. You're half strangling me,' Louisa chuckled.

'It's wrong to go out when we've only recently buried our father,' Winnie admonished them. 'The likes of the Misses Flinders wouldn't be seen out dancing while they were in mourning, and besides, these are dangerous times.'

'Oh Winnie, it wouldn't hurt, would it?' Grace straightened and stepped away. 'Pa wouldn't have wanted us to be sad, not for long anyway. I mean, I am …' Louisa looked up at her – her lip wobbled.

'We know,' she said softly.

'What would Pa say … have said?' Grace asked.

'That life has to go on,' Louisa replied. It would do them all good to have something to take their minds off their predicament, she thought. 'Winnie, won't you reconsider? I don't want the Rattlers to think we're hiding ourselves away because of what they've done. It's true that we don't have much to celebrate, but we don't have to stay out all night, just an hour or two.' Both her sisters looked pale from sorrow and exhaustion. They weren't eating properly, surviving on a diet of bloaters and bread to save money.

'I'll go for Grace's sake,' Winnie said eventually, 'but I shall wear crape on my bonnet and black gloves.'

Louisa went out with her sisters to pay Mr Jackson for the boat, doing her best to give the impression that everything was normal as she walked along, weighed down with a bag of coins hidden under her shawl. They arranged for Master Roper to make a start on the repairs. When she asked when the *Curlew* would be seaworthy, all he could say was that she would be ready when she was ready, and Louisa had to be content with that. She knew from experience that a boatman couldn't be rushed.

They returned home to get ready for the dance.

Louisa wore her plain ivory muslin gown, Winnie dressed in dark brown with a dash of black, and Grace complained about having to put on her Sunday best, a garish blue and white hand-me-down that had belonged to Louisa, then Winnie. Grace had altered it, raising the waistline and taking some of the weight from the skirt.

'We won't stay late. Billy, are you coming with us?' Winnie called.

'I'm on my way.' He ran down the stairs in a black shirt with ruffles, and dark pantaloons. 'Will I do?' he said, collecting his boots.

'You'll do very nicely,' Winnie said. 'All the young ladies will fall for you.'

'I know I'm not a swell of the first stare, but I'd be very 'appy if just one took a shine to me.'

'Hurry, or it will be over before we get there,' Grace urged before suddenly falling silent.

Louisa felt sorry for her, her conscience pricked by guilt at the prospect of snatching a few hours of happiness while Pa lay cold in the ground.

When they arrived at the Waterman's Arms on Beach Street, the dancing was already underway, a band of fiddlers and pipers playing outside. Some of the boatmen's wives were sitting on benches, watching while their husbands drank at the bar.

Mrs Witherall beckoned them over. 'I've saved you a seat. I'm glad to see you out and about again. What a shame Righteous didn't live to see his daughters all dressed up today – you have grown into three beauties.' Louisa wondered if Mrs Witherall was already a little foxed, an empty glass in her hand.

'Thank you, but I should like to dance,' Grace said.

'I shall stay here,' Winnie decided, so it was left to Louisa to dance with her younger sister. They took to the floor and danced a riotous jig, while a barrel-shaped gentleman with a bird's nest of a beard belted out the order of the steps. She couldn't see One Eye or any of his gang, but she did notice Jason with Miss Hibben, leaning down and whispering into her ear. He was easily the most handsome man present – she envied Margaret who looked cool and graceful in an eye-catching Romanesque gown, bought perhaps in anticipation of her wedding day.

'Louisa, you aren't concentrating. Either that, or you have two left feet.'

'I'm sorry, Grace. I was miles away.'

They danced another jig before Louisa retreated to sit with Mrs Witherall and Winnie, her eyes on Grace as she partnered Billy, then three of the Roper girls.

'Don't forget to ask if you need anything,' Mrs Witherall said.

'Everyone's being very kind,' she responded.

'Who will look after us, if we don't look after our own?'

'Excuse me, Miss Lennicker.'

She looked up to find Abel Brockman in front of her.

'I apologise for not havin' spoken to you before,' he said, 'but I wanted to say how sorry I am for your loss and let you know that the arrangement with the Lennickers carries on the same as before when Righteous was alive. That's if you're intendin' to continue in the trade.'

'Of course she is,' Mrs Witherall said. 'It's in her blood.'

Abel smiled and walked away, leaving her wondering if she really could take her father's place and become a free trader in her own right. It was all very well selling a little French lace now and again like Ma had done, but did she have the confidence to survive – and thrive – in that line of work?

As she gazed at the swirl of people who were laughing and talking, dancing and tapping out the rhythms of the music, she thought she heard her mother's voice, urging her on. 'You can do anything you wish, Louisa. All you have to do is believe …'

When the dancing was over, a feverish peace settled over the town of Deal. Louisa kept busy, not knowing how long it would be before they took on the *Curlew*. In the meantime, they still had to support themselves and make plans for their first run without their father.

A few days later, they walked over to Limepit Acres to call on their uncle and aunt.

'I wish we didn't have to throw ourselves on their mercy,' Louisa said.

'This is a business opportunity for Uncle Cuthbert. At least, that's how I shall present it to him, so you and Grace must keep your mouths shut while I speak.'

A terrible grunting and squealing greeted them as they arrived at the farm. Somebody was killing a pig, and Louisa was grateful when the maid let them in to the kitchen where their aunt was giving instructions to the cook.

'Oh, it's you. To what do we owe the pleasure of this unannounced visit?'

'We wanted to thank you in person for the flowers you sent for our father's grave.' Louisa's stomach growled when she saw the leg of lamb adorned with sprigs of rosemary on the table.

'It was very thoughtful of you,' Winnie enjoined.

'My consideration for others has often been remarked upon. Oh, I'm forgetting my manners. You've walked some distance.' Aunt Mary stared at the mud on their boots and skirts with distaste. 'Take off your shoes.' She turned to the maid. 'Bring some refreshment for my nieces.'

'Yes, ma'am.' The maid curtseyed and Louisa smiled to herself as she slipped off her boots. Talk about pretensions of grandeur – the Laxtons lived in a different world.

'And let Beth know her cousins are here.'

The distant tinkling of a pianoforte stopped soon after the maid had left the kitchen, and the Lennickers followed their aunt through the house to the parlour. Grace and Winnie sat down on the chaise while Aunt Mary took a chair beside the fireplace where a copper log basket with brass feet gleamed beside a screen decorated with a fine painting of a galleon.

'I'm sorry for interrupting you,' Louisa said, sitting near the window next to her cousin who gave her a brief smile. Beth wore a pale pink muslin gown, the waistline higher than her natural waist as was the fashion. Although it lent her an air of grace, it was entirely impractical for work. Louisa smiled to herself. Like the fox in the fable, she was beguiling herself that the grapes were sour – out of envy for her cousin's good fortune.

'I'm glad for the excuse – Ma would have me play all day, if she could.' Beth turned to her mother. 'May we invite my cousins to stay for dinner? I should like to go walking with them this afternoon.'

'That's very kind,' Louisa said quickly. 'We'd love to.'

'Are you sure you aren't otherwise engaged?' their aunt enquired.

'Quite sure,' Winnie said.

'Then you must stay,' Aunt Mary said grudgingly. 'I won't accompany you in taking the air – Louisa seems to have taken more than enough of it, judging by her rude complexion. May I remind you not to stray from the farm, Beth. We can't have you gallivanting about the countryside now that you're engaged—'

Louisa noticed how her sisters sat up, all agog.

'We'd have congratulated you on this news, if we'd known,' she said, smiling. 'Who is the lucky gentleman?'

'It's Beth who should count herself lucky.' Aunt Mary could hardly contain her delight. 'Mr George Norris, our neighbour, has pledged his hand in marriage. It's no mean feat on your cousin's part that she has, by virtue of her modest appearance and quietness of manner, managed to attract the attention of one of the few remaining bachelors in this county, for there are very few eligible suitors left in the shires, the rest having paid for their commissions in the army, in return for the honour of defending the realm.'

'I don't believe we are acquainted with him,' Louisa said, looking towards her sisters.

'Beth will tell you all about him while you're out walking,' Aunt Mary said.

Their cousin wore a coat, a short spencer made from silk, and a bonnet embellished with feathers, and her mother insisted she wear pattens to protect her kid boots, when they went out strolling through the cornfields where Mr Laxton's labourers – and the Lennickers' tub carriers – were gleaning the last of the barley in the early September sunshine.

As they passed them, they touched their caps before going on with their work.

'I've never noticed before, but all three of them have crooked fingers on the same hand,' Louisa observed.

'They didn't want to be impressed,' Beth explained. 'Neither the navy nor militia will take them.'

'You mean that they hurt themselves deliberately?' Winnie said, and Beth nodded.

'Then they are cowards.' Louisa thought of the boatmen setting out to save lives in the worst of storms.

'Somebody has to be left to work on the land, or there'd be no food. It doesn't grow by itself,' Beth said, and Louisa changed the subject.

'Do tell us about Mr Norris,' she said.

'Will we be introduced to him soon?' Grace asked. 'I can't wait to meet him.'

'He's very busy,' Beth responded. 'Not only does he run his estate, he's a magistrate and Master of Foxhounds. Oh dear, I don't know what else to say. I barely know him, only by sight as he rides around the countryside with the hunt, damaging my father's gates and crops. Towards the end of last season, the hounds chased a fox into our kitchen where it was killed. Mr Norris presented my mother with the brush by way of an apology. Since then, he's called three or four times, bearing gifts of beef and mutton.

'Oh dear, he isn't what I imagined my husband would be. He has a florid countenance and portly figure, and he's more than twice our age. It isn't fair that men can choose and women only refuse, but if I had been bold enough to turn him down, my mother would have disowned me.'

'Can you get out of it?' Grace said, her eyes wide with horror.

'You must break the engagement immediately,' Louisa added.

'How can I? If I back out, my reputation will be in the mire. No, I must look on the bright side – I'll have my own establishment, servants … children … I won't have my mother breathing down my neck. Oh, I'm sorry, I forget myself … I'm sure you wish your mother was still here to guide you.'

'Have you set a date for the wedding?' Winnie asked.

'Not yet. The longer I can put it off, the longer I'll have to get used to the idea. I envy you your freedom, being able to come and go as you please, but don't worry about me, my dear cousins – my mother says I should be feeling sorry for you. What chance have you got of making a match like mine?'

Very little, Louisa hoped, but she said no more on the matter.

Having dined with the Laxtons on gritty carrots and meat that melted in the mouth, with bread and butter pudding for dessert, and having listened to Aunt Mary's comprehensive plans for the wedding, Louisa broached the reason for their visit with their uncle.

'As you know, Deal is a hungry place and a lively trade has come with the war, and I was wondering if you'd consider delivering a regular amount of produce every week for my sisters and I to sell, the profit to be divided between us?' She was aware that her aunt's mouth had dropped open and her knife was quivering above her plate. 'I don't ask this as a favour, but as a financial arrangement.'

'Oh no,' Aunt Mary interjected, recovering her wits. 'Your father was always most diligent in reminding us of his ability to care for his wife and daughters and give them every comfort that money could afford.' She was being sarcastic, Louisa realised. Beth glanced away, embarrassed, and her uncle scratched his chin. 'Surely, he has left you adequately provided for?'

Louisa gave her the story of how the *Pamela* had been stolen.

'Master Fleet can't go out fishing until the new boat's ready. Due to this unfortunate turn of events, my sisters and I require another way of making a living.'

'This is a terrible state of affairs, but we aren't in a position to help,' Aunt Mary said.

'Don't be too hasty, Mrs Laxton,' Uncle Cuthbert cut in. 'I think we can, out of respect for my sister's memory. One of the men will bring a selection of whatever fruit and veg is available, every week. You'll sell it, then pay back the cost of the produce plus fifty per cent of your profit.'

'I would prefer twenty-five per cent,' Louisa said quickly.

'I'm sure you would, but that's the deal. I can't be seen to favour you over my regulars.'

'Then thank you. I'd be delighted to accept.' She could always renegotiate the small matter of percentages later.

'You have saved our lives, Uncle,' Grace piped up. 'We won't have to give up our chastity to the highest paying Jack. Ouch!' She looked pained as well she might, Louisa thought angrily. 'What did you do that for?'

'Our sister is young,' she said quickly. 'She doesn't think before she speaks.'

'Clearly not,' Aunt Mary said, before sending Beth to her room and giving Grace a right royal telling-off. 'Out of charity, your uncle will keep to his word, but I don't want to see you anywhere near Limepit Acres again.'

'May we call on our cousin?' Louisa asked.

'No, you may not.' Aunt Mary called for the maid and told her to see them out.

'Oh Grace, what are we going to do with you?' Winnie said as they made their way along the lane, the shadows long and the sun beginning to disappear behind the hill.

'I told you to let me do the talking,' Louisa added, smarting less with shame than with annoyance that Grace had almost wrecked the deal with their uncle.

'I don't know why Aunt Mary makes out that she's so prim and proper – as soon as she was with child, she told our uncle to go and find himself another woman in the village. According to Pa, that's why she only had Beth. She wouldn't let her husband anywhere near her again.'

'Pa wouldn't have told you that,' Louisa said, 'and you certainly shouldn't go around repeating it.'

'I overheard him talking to Mr Witherall about it one day. He thought I was too young to understand,' Grace continued matter-of-factly. 'I keep it all in my head, never knowing when it might come in useful. I'm telling the truth.'

'One should be honest as a general rule, but there are occasions when a little tact is required,' Winnie tried to explain to Grace as Louisa walked ahead, turning off at the crossroads and following the bishop's finger in the direction of Upper Walmer.

'Where are we going?' Winnie called.

'The long way – I thought we'd kill two birds with one stone and pay a visit to Mundel Manor while we're here. I've used all the rose leaves up and need some more. I'm sure Sir Flinders won't notice if we acquire a few from his rose garden.'

They continued walking along the lanes towards the Flinders' estate as dusk fell, bringing bats flitting through the air. Louisa pulled her bonnet down, having a horror of the creatures getting tangled in her hair.

'I can hear music,' Winnie said as they passed the gatehouse guarding the entrance to the long drive. 'The Flinders are entertaining – our invitation must have gone missing.'

'Perhaps we'll be asked one day,' Grace said hopefully, looking into the distance where the baronet's manor house was ablaze with light.

Louisa laughed dryly. 'That'll never happen.'

'It will, if we make our fortune,' Grace said.

'It's wrong for common people like us to have ambition,' Winnie whispered.

'There's nothing improper in it,' Louisa countered. 'All this about knowing our place is merely a way of keeping us down. The Flinders are old money, but there are plenty of self-made men out there now. I don't think you'll find they had any scruples about bettering themselves.' Using some loose stones as makeshift steps, Louisa climbed up the wall beyond the gatehouse, swung herself over and landed on the other side. Her sisters followed, and they made their way through the thicket to the formal gardens beyond.

'We shouldn't be here,' Winnie said.

'It's late,' Louisa told her as they skirted the low box hedge and stopped behind a topiary statue. 'The gardener will have hung up his hoe by now.' She glanced from the rose bushes, the petals from the season's last flush of blooms scattered across the lawn like snow, to the rear of the house where the long French doors were wide open. She caught snippets of laughter and conversation floating on the autumnal breeze as she watched the elegant ladies and gentlemen, some of them officers in their regimental uniforms, milling about, and then she saw the familiar figure of Mr Trice, a nauseating reminder of the arrangement she'd entered into.

'Why would they begrudge us a few leaves when they have that many?' Grace said.

Louisa crawled along the edge of the lawn. When she looked over her shoulder, only Grace was with her, Winnie having lost her nerve. She and Grace tore handfuls of leaves off the rose bushes and stuffed them into the pouches at their waists.

'Take the blooms as well – we can always find a use for them.'

Suddenly, she heard the call of an owl: the sisters' coded warning.

'Down.' She dropped to the ground and lay flat in the rose bed alongside Grace with her shawl across their faces, as two officers came striding rapidly in their direction.

'Show yourselves.' One of the officers used the tip of his sabre to move the shawl aside. 'What have we here?' he said, as Louisa felt the cold steel against her skin. The more she tried to still her trembling, the worse it became. 'Ah, I see,' the officer said eventually, before calling back to his fellow. 'There's nothing to worry about – it's only a fox.'

'Then you must shoot it,' came a lady's voice.

'Or set the dogs on it,' said another.

'It's gone now, but your brother will see that it's dealt with tomorrow. I have no appetite for ruining our celebration, Honora.' Having given Louisa a quick smile, he withdrew his sabre, turned and walked away. As soon as they were out of earshot, Louisa and Grace fled back to where Winnie was waiting for them.

'I thought they'd caught you,' Winnie breathed.

'We were in luck – the officer took pity on us and let us go. At least we have what we came for – the roses in town look as if they've been attacked by a plague of locusts.' Louisa sucked a thorn from her finger and spat it out. They had had a narrow escape, but overall it had been a successful day.

*

Their uncle sent the first supply of provisions the following day, and Louisa and her sisters sold them from the handcart on market days: Tuesdays and Saturdays. During the next few weeks while Master Roper – between carousing and courting – worked on the *Curlew*, they managed to make ends meet, eking out the money they'd made from selling the run goods and the rent they received from Billy.

But the herring hang stood unused, and their supply of run goods dwindled.

When the butcher, having run out of patience, turned up on their doorstep armed with a cleaver, Louisa paid him out of the amount she'd kept back to pay their uncle. All she could do was pray that Mr Trice would stay away and that the boat would soon be ready.

# Chapter Seven

## *Befriend the Stranger: Deal's motto*

On a quiet morning in early November, three months after their father's demise, Master Roper pronounced that the *Curlew* was ready.

'As near as makes no odds,' he said as Louisa, her sisters and Billy stood with him on the shore, admiring her.

'She's turned out to be quite a beauty,' Billy said.

'She's lovely,' Louisa agreed, breathing in the smell of fresh paint and pine tar.

'I can't wait to take her out,' Billy went on.

'I wouldn't go today.' Dressed in his longshore toggery, Terrier was in his usual spot, leaning against a capstan with one eye on the shipping. 'The weather's on the turn, but you should know that, Master Fleet.' He gestured towards the horizon. A pale sun was rising into a sky streaked with a few wisps of cloud, and the men-o'-war, their masts and gun ports clearly visible, were floating on a sea as flat as a millpond. Many of the boats were out, but a few remained beached. 'What do you say, son?'

'It wouldn't hurt to go a little way. It isn't as if you're plannin' to take 'er to France, is it?' Master Roper said.

'What do you think, Billy?' Louisa asked, wishing she had Pa to advise her.

'We won't go far,' he said.

'It's a pleasure trip, eh?' Terrier said.

'We're going fishing,' Winnie joined in.

'All o' you? Grace too? Oh no, that isn't right. Trim your sails and listen to what I 'ave to say! Righteous wouldn't 'ave allowed this. He 'ad brine for blood, but you ladies, let's make no bones about it – you're landlubbers through and through. Stay at 'ome and 'ave Master Fleet's supper ready an' waitin' for 'im. I'll crew for you – I 'ave a fancy for bein' ship's boy for a day.'

'You're most kind, but no thank you,' Louisa said firmly. 'Billy will look after us.'

'That's all very well, but will the sea look after you? She's a capricious mistress.' He fell silent, a shadow crossing his face, and Louisa recalled how he'd lost a child overboard. 'Conditions are perfect now, but I'm tellin' you, it's the calm before the storm.'

'I've been fishin' with Mr Lennicker for many years – I know the ropes. And I'm no fair-weather sailor neither, 'avin' been out on the *Whimbrel* for the last few weeks – I could almost sail that lugger single'anded,' Billy bragged. 'Fetch oilskins, provisions and blankets, Louisa. Winnie, we need the buckets from Mr Lennicker's hut. Grace, you can help me drag the nets over.'

Within the hour, they were ready for a day at sea.

'I feel like some old fisherwoman in this smock, my boots are like lead weights, and the sou'wester – it's ruining my hair,' Grace grumbled as they loaded the empty buckets on board.

'I don't like it,' Terrier said as Billy began to help them into the *Curlew*.

'We'll be back before you know it. Ladies, 'old on tight. Terrier, will you do the honours?'

Terrier grudgingly agreed, moving to the bow as Billy jumped in. Louisa glanced across at Grace and Winnie and smiled reassuringly as their knuckles turned white on the gunwales. The sea was thirty yards below them and the *Curlew* was ready for launching.

'Let 'er go!' Billy shouted and Terrier released the rope. The *Curlew* began to move stern-first down the slope over the rollers, picking up speed until it felt like she was flying.

Suddenly, she hit the water with a huge bang. Louisa gasped, Grace shrieked, and Winnie held on for dear life as the *Curlew* settled, her timbers creaking. Billy took up an oar to push them clear of a breaking wave before it could send them back on to the beach.

'Winnie, take 'old of this. Grace, that's for you.' He nodded towards one of the buckets. 'Louisa, you're in charge of the tiller. I'll rig the sails then I'll l'arn you three 'ow to do it.'

'Aye, aye.' Winnie was smiling. 'This reminds me of when we used to go out on the *Pamela*.'

It had been a very long time ago, Louisa thought sadly, taking the helm. Many moons had come and gone since they had gone out with their father as little girls, to watch him put out the nets and fight to sit on his knee while he smoked a pipe and waited to pull in the catch.

There had been one particularly magical moment when he had made himself a seat in the stern, covering it with an oilskin cloth. He'd sat down with Louisa on his knee, looking down like a queen at her sisters who were having to wait their turn. The *Pamela* had bobbed up and down as tiny waves topped with lace broke against her hull, and the sun shone from a cloudless sky.

They had already been along the coast to the sandhills where Pa had dug up two tubs from a mound of sand marked with a broken stick. They had returned to sea and brought in one catch – buckets filled with salt and herring lined the *Pamela*'s deck – and Pa was waiting to pull in the nets a second time. Later, they would go home where Ma would be looking out for them.

Everything had been perfect until a Revenue cruiser came into view, appearing from behind a row of merchant ships moored in the deep water.

'Pa, look out,' Louisa had said, thinking of the tubs.

'It's all right, my dears,' he said as the crew lowered a jollyboat from the side of the cruiser. 'Watch and l'arn.' A pair of officers rowed towards them, and although Louisa's heart was hammering, Pa seemed remarkably calm as they came close and dropped their oars.

'Good day, sir,' the senior officer said.

'It's a lovely day indeed,' Pa confirmed.

'Where are your papers?'

'I have them here. Winnie, they're in the chest.'

Winnie, who could have been only seven at the time, fetched the papers, a big smile on her face at having been given an important job to do.

'Thank you, miss,' the officer said, handing them back.

'I'd welcome you aboard, but there's nothin' of interest 'ere for you fellows,' Pa said. 'I 'ave some baccy for my own use, that's all.'

'What about the tubs?' Winnie suddenly blurted out.

Pa gave a wry chuckle. 'Ah, the tubs. We have no tubs on board, my dear. You must be mistaken. What do you say, Louisa?'

'I haven't seen any tubs,' she said, boldly staring the officer in the eyes.

'Pull in your nets,' the officer ordered.

Her knees weak, Louisa slipped down from Pa's lap. Pa stood up, then picked up little Grace and placed her on his seat.

'Stay there – we don't want you goin' overboard, do we?' he said, and Grace, who was four, grinned at having been given Pa's spot. Louisa watched him pull in the nets, bringing another haul of fish flapping and gasping on to the deck. It wasn't what the Revenue officers had been hoping for because they soon turned and rowed away.

'Where are the tubs, Pa?' Louisa whispered when they had gone.

'They're 'ere, 'idin' in plain sight,' he said, his eyes glinting with amusement as he lifted Grace up high in the air and plonked her down, giggling, on the boards.

'Ah, I've got it.' Louisa knelt and picked up the corner of the oilskin. 'Found them,' she sang out.

'Whist, my dear,' he said, and she felt a little ashamed for forgetting herself, but she wasn't as upset as Winnie who cried all the way home, even though Pa said that it didn't matter what she'd said about the tubs, because all had turned out well.

A sudden splash, a wave breaking against the *Curlew*'s bow, brought Louisa back to the present.

'Get bailin',' Billy ordered when Grace hesitated.

'Why is there so much water comin' in?' She picked up the bucket and started scooping it out. 'Ugh, my boots are leaking.'

'You can never make a boat completely watertight – there's always some bailin' to be done.'

The clouds began to billow across the sky, letting through only the briefest glimpses of the sun, and a light wind caught hold of the rust-red canvases of the *Curlew*'s lugsail and mizzen.

'That's it: every stitch of canvas set. Louisa, keep your eyes peeled for shippin', and remember the marks for the fishin' ground,' Billy shouted as the boat gently rose and dipped, slicing a path through the sea, like scissors cutting through blue broadcloth. Louisa's spirits started to soar as she began to believe that they could make a success of their new venture.

Spotting a Revenue cruiser, she moved the tiller, swinging the *Curlew* hard round – too hard, from the look on Billy's face.

'You've got to be gentle with 'er. Treat 'er roughly and she'll be mean back.'

'You have to say, "Aye", Louisa,' Winnie said.

'Aye.' Louisa couldn't help smiling as she set the *Curlew* on a new course. Looking back at the town, she could see the muddle of houses built along the beach, some with distinctive red Dutch roofs, others tiled or thatched, and many with wooden balconies and verandas. The Three Kings Hotel and the shacks thrown up along the shingle by the families who'd followed their men to the barracks, not knowing what else to do, began to shrink into the distance. To the south, she could see a small boat like the *Curlew*, provisioning a merchant ship against the backdrop of the white cliffs, while to the north, she could see the sandhills and then Ramsgate.

'We're missin' the mark,' Billy said.

'Are we?' Louisa said guiltily. He gave her the three marks again and she brought them into line before holding the tiller steady so that he and Winnie could shoot the net, feeding it out into the water, making sure it didn't fold on itself or snag on the boat. Watching the cork floats bobbing around on the surface, Louisa waited for Billy to lower the lugsail, leaving the mast bare, but for the halyard and burton. The sea was becoming increasingly choppy and the *Curlew* kept turning in the freshening wind, aiming north-east as if she had a mind of her own. Grace was sick over the side.

'Somebody 'asn't found 'er sea legs yet,' Billy observed.

'I'm dying,' Grace groaned. 'I wish I was one of the Misses Flinders who'll never have any reason to go to sea … Or Margaret who will soon be married.'

'She'll still have to cook and clean, and sew,' Louisa said.

'Jason can afford a maid, can't he?' Winnie said. 'He mightn't dress like a dandy, but he isn't short of a few bob. Rumour has it that he's buying one of the merchants' houses on Dolphin Street.'

'We should pull the net in and make for 'ome.' Billy seemed subdued, Louisa thought. 'Winnie, give me an 'and. Grace, you as well.'

They began to drag the net through the water and back on to the boat, bringing up a few dabs and codlings, shellfish and seaweed.

'It doesn't look much,' Billy said. 'I remember one time when we 'ad to cut our gear away because the weight of mackerel would 'ave sent us under.'

As they pulled together, a gust of wind turned the *Curlew* broadside and the net snagged.

'Louisa, turn 'er,' Billy shouted.

'I can't,' she shouted back. 'The tiller's locked.'

Billy swore. 'It must be the net – I'll 'ave to unhook it.' He leaned over the side and started to tug at it, but to no avail. 'I'll cut it – I don't like to, but what choice do I 'ave?' Reluctantly, Louisa handed him a knife from the box at her feet and watched him slice the net away, pulling what was left of it into the boat. 'Mr Lennicker would 'ave a fit.'

'It's a bit of bad luck. It could have happened to anyone.' Louisa thought of Jason, doubting that he would have let the net catch if it had been him in Billy's place, but she was being unfair, she decided.

Billy rigged the lugsail for the trip back.

'It's the wrong side of the mast,' Louisa pointed out.

He lowered the sail completely again, and Grace and Winnie hauled it aft and forth before hooking the halyard to the other side of the mast, ready for the journey back into a much livelier wind and – Louisa tried not to look – a much bigger sea.

'There's quite a swell on, but it's nothing to worry about,' Billy kept saying as the wind gathered strength and the *Curlew*'s canvas billowed, driving her away from the coast under a darkening sky. Grace swapped places with Louisa who dealt with the few fish they'd managed to retrieve, covering her oilskin with gore and scales as she tipped the guts into the sea, turning the water crimson and attracting the seagulls that came wheeling in, following in the *Curlew*'s wake.

'Grace, keep 'er straight,' Billy shouted as he fought to trim the canvas to slow the *Curlew*'s relentless progress in the wrong direction. 'Steer 'er into the wind. You keep lettin' 'er turn. Oh, you're worse than useless.'

'You do it then, if you're so clever,' Grace yelled back, her eyes flashing with annoyance.

'Stick with it, Grace,' Louisa said.

'Hey, I'm skipper – I give the orders. Winnie, you take the tiller. Grace, get bailin' again.'

Winnie pushed and pulled at the tiller.

'It won't budge,' she said as they drifted, and the terrifying roar of breakers surged into Louisa's consciousness.

'Billy,' she screamed. 'We're too close to the Sands.'

'We're nowhere near 'em,' he called back, his voice calm as he continued to battle with the canvas, but Louisa knew him too well, as did Winnie who cried out in panic, 'I don't want to die.'

'We aren't goin' to die,' Billy shouted as the *Curlew* ran on, swept up in the angry embrace of the wind and pitching in the choppy water. With a snap and splintering of wood, the mast broke near the base, and the weight of the wet canvas still attached, dragged it into the water. Billy grabbed the knife again and sawed it away while Louisa picked up the oar and began to paddle, but they were still drifting. It was growing colder, the longer they stayed out.

Tears stung her eyes as the wind howled, moving them ever closer to the sandbank until the *Curlew* nudged the sand, coming to rest with a jolt. Louisa leapt to her feet, trying to shove the boat away with the oar.

'She's grounded, good and proper,' she yelled, as Billy tried to push her off with his feet over the side, his face red and the sinews of his neck knotted with effort. 'We're stuck.'

'I can't swim,' Winnie whimpered.

'I'm sure you can, if you put your mind to it.' Billy was shivering. 'We 'aven't got no way of raisin' an alarm.'

'Of course we have. Scream and holler as if your life depends on it!' Louisa yelled until her throat was hoarse, but nobody came. All she could hear was her sisters crying, the whistle of the wind and the waves crashing down over their heads, bringing a fresh rush of water each time. It had reached the gunwales and no amount of bailing could save them now. Louisa held Grace in her arms, while Billy and Winnie huddled together, waist-deep in water.

All hope drained out of her when she spotted the blackened ribs of an old wreck a few feet from them, disappearing into the rising tide. But just as she thought they were facing the end on the giant ship-gobbler of the Goodwin Sands, she caught sight of another vessel.

'Look!' she exclaimed.

'We're over 'ere,' Billy bellowed.

For a heart-stopping moment, she thought they had missed them, but then the crew of the lugger manned their oars and rowed towards them, heaving-to alongside the *Curlew*. Louisa looked up, peering through her sodden tresses, to where a figure shrouded in oilskins stood staring down at her. He removed his sou'wester and ran one hand through his blond hair.

'Jason,' she murmured.

'We've found the *Curlew*,' he shouted, and his crew let up a cheer. 'Here are the dunderheads who would take a boat they don't know, out on a day like this!'

Frozen to the bone, Louisa wasn't sure how the crew of the *Whimbrel* managed to take them off the *Curlew*, then float the boat so she could be towed back to Deal through the fearsome wind. All she did know was that she'd made a terrible mistake – an unforgivable one – in encouraging Billy to launch their boat that morning. She didn't need Jason to tell her so – she could see it in his eyes whenever he glanced in her direction: his expression one of seething anger that she had put everyone's lives at risk. And then she recalled how his grandfather had died on the Sands, and how today's rescue must have brought it all back. It felt like the longest journey she'd ever made.

When they had hauled the *Curlew* and the *Whimbrel* up the beach, Jason's crew took their catch, the codlings and dabs, for their trouble. The remaining section of the *Curlew*'s mast was carried off, never to be seen again, and the last Louisa saw of her canvas was it being rolled up and stowed amidships in the lugger, as Jason held her hand to help her out. She stood on the shingle, wanting to thank him, but not knowing what to say.

'What are you waitin' for?' Jason said sharply. 'Go back to your cookin' and sewin'.'

She opened her mouth to speak, but he turned and walked away, leaving her mortified. How would she ever bring herself to face him again?

She shuddered to think what would have happened if he hadn't taken the lugger out to find them, the shallow-keeled vessel being one of the few that could live in the treacherous Goodwins. She dreamt that night of being swaddled by the Sands, suffocated as she fell in with the skeletons of dead seamen of the past; the *Curlew* just another meal for the ship gobbler that Pa used to tell them stories about, raising Ma to a fury when they woke in the night, crying out in fear.

It took a week for Grace to recover from the chill she took in the storm. Winnie nursed her while Louisa went out selling the Laxtons' produce from the handcart. Billy returned to crewing the *Whimbrel* under a dark cloud, Jason apparently having warned him that one step out of line and he would be back onshore.

As for the *Curlew*, Louisa worked with Billy to restore her to some semblance of order during November and December, spending as many of the winter evenings on her as they could. When it wasn't raining, or freezing, or blowing a gale to extinguish the lanterns, they caulked her seams with cotton and oakum, tapping them gently in with a mallet, before sealing them with pine pitch.

'I'll 'ave a few shillin's by the end of the week, enow to pay Marlin what we owe for the rescue an' salvage. We've 'ad a bit o' luck out 'ovellin'. The master of the *Probity*, a merchant brig, paid us twenty-five guineas to tow her back into the Downs after she lost her rigging three leagues off from land. I've bought a new sail for the *Curlew*. I say new – it's been repaired, but it's perfectly usable. I'll go an' fetch it.'

'It's kind of you, Billy, but—' Louisa stirred the pitch.

'Don't cut off your nose to spite your face,' he said. 'I want to 'elp – it's to my advantage. I can't rely on 'avin' a place on the *Whimbrel* every time she goes out, and if this lady isn't seaworthy, then I don't 'ave any other way of earnin' my keep. Let me settle up with Marlin.'

'In that case, I'm very grateful. It will be one less weight off my mind at least.'

'It's me who should be thankin' you and your sisters. It 'asn't been easy after the tarrin' and featherin' the Rattlers gave me. It was one of the worst days of my life: bein' paraded through the town naked to the waist with that sign around my neck, and everybody joinin' in to throw feathers at me. Ever since, I've 'ad people tauntin' me to my face, and laughin' at me be'ind my back. Thanks to One Eye, some of my friends no longer believe I can be trusted. It's caused me much grief.'

'I'm sorry, but they will forget in time,' she said.

'I 'ope so. Louisa, it's too dark for this now – we should stop.'

'I want to finish this section. There's no need for you to wait for me.'

'I'm not leavin' you 'ere on your own.'

'I'd like to do another half an hour, while I still have feeling in my fingers.' She could hear men carousing at the Rattling Cat, and there were guests coming and going from the hotel. The *Whimbrel* had just been hauled up and her crew, whom she trusted, were still present, unloading their spoils from a salvaging trip.

'I'll run my errand then and come straight back.'

'Thank you, Billy.'

She was raking out the last of the old caulk from one of the seams when she heard the scrunch of footsteps on the shingle. A shadow fell across the boards. Catching her breath, she turned and looked up to find Jason staring down at her with a mast across his shoulder.

Slowly, she stood up, not knowing what to say. She'd been avoiding him since the incident on the Sands.

'Don't stop on my account,' he said gruffly. 'Here's a mast for the boat. My father says you can pay us back in a week or two – we'll add it to the rest the Lennickers owe us.'

'The rest? I didn't know …'

'Well, you do now. Righteous borrowed at least fifty guineas off my father – he said he had a temporary need for capital and then it kept slippin' his mind about givin' it back.'

She thought quickly. 'Keep the mast until I have the money in my pocket to pay you.'

'I'm not carryin' it back and forth. Besides, the boat's no use as she is.'

'I don't know how to thank you,' she stammered.

'It's nothin' to do with me – I wouldn't do anythin' to encourage you and Billy to take the *Curlew* out again.'

'I'm so sorry …' She hated that he thought badly of her.

'Sorry isn't enough. You risked your sisters' lives, and everyone else's for a few codlin's. Best thing to do is use some of your father's fortune to take on a proper crew, or have her rigged so Billy can take her out by himself with one or two of the boys – they're always hangin' around in the capstan grounds, hopin' for work.' He stopped abruptly and stared at her. She lowered her gaze, unable to meet his eye. 'She looks like she's almost ready. Tell me you aren't goin' back to crewin' her yourselves. Miss

Lennicker? Look me in the face and promise me you won't go out there again.'

'I can't do that, and you can't make me. You don't know my situation. You don't know anything about me. I won't risk going out in bad weather again – I've learned my lesson.'

'What about the shippin' in the Downs, and the privateers? You've heard how the crew of the *Cumberland* on their way back from Quebec, fired on the Frenchies recently off Folkestone, killin' sixty men? The last thing you want is to be caught up in the crossfire.'

'You and your crew take the *Whimbrel* out there with hardly a second thought.'

'Because I've been out to sea every day since I could walk – and my boat is armed, thanks to a generous donation from His Majesty's government. Billy is a fisherman, slow and ploddin' – it's clear he can't look after you, or make you see sense when the occasion demands. The sea is no place for a woman like you.'

'There are captains who take their wives on board with them,' she argued.

'That's different – they cook and sew, and tend to the sick, duties suited to the female temperament. They don't navigate or give orders,' Jason said in a tone of supreme confidence, which softened a little when he went on, 'There's plenty of opportunity to earn a bit extra, workin' landside, so there's no need for you and your sisters to take the *Curlew* out again. I'll tell my father that's what you've agreed so he can stop frettin' about your family.'

'I shan't agree to anything.' He had no right – he was not her brother or her husband – to impose his will on her. 'I shall do as I want, using my common sense—'

'A virtue that I've found sadly wantin' in you,' he cut in.

'I don't care what you think of me.' She stood with her hands on her hips, trying not to give herself away. Of course she cared. 'I'm very grateful that you found us and brought us to safety. Your bravery is admirable, but I find your character …' she struggled to find the words to describe him '… most disagreeable.'

'You judge me too harshly,' he said. 'You think I treat you badly, scoldin' you for what you did, but I find that I still have much regard for you, even though I don't think much of your stupidity.'

'How dare you call me stupid!' Hurt and affronted, Louisa turned away, her heart beating furiously, her cheeks hot. 'Go away!' she added, waiting until he had put down the mast, laying it across the *Curlew*'s stern before walking off.

Louisa returned to the caulking, jabbing the raking iron into one of the seams.

'It's me.' She was aware that Billy had come back, a roll of rust-red canvas at his feet, lit up by the flickering flame inside the lantern. 'What did you do to Marlin? He says you're a right hoity-toity madam.'

'He wanted me to promise that my sisters and I wouldn't crew the *Curlew* again, but I told him no.'

'Ah, then he's been most boldrumptious. In my experience, when a Lennicker's mind is made up, it cannot be altered,' Billy teased.

'He shouldn't have said anything to you about it. It's nothing to do with him.'

'That isn't 'ow it works around here – everybody knows everybody's business which leads me on to say that the other boat is languishin' in the yard. Awful Doins let slip that she's the *Pamela* and now nobody will touch 'er with a bargepole. Anyway, I 'ave the new sail – we're almost there.'

*

December turned to January, and taking advantage of a spell of settled weather, Louisa prepared for their first provisioning trip. She sent Winnie and Grace to collect the baskets of produce from the herring hang and line them up in the hall.

'How do we know what to take with us when we have no idea what will sell?' Winnie said.

'We'll sell anything and everything we can.' Louisa surveyed their cargo of beets, potatoes, some shrockled apples with woolly flesh, cheese, bacon, dried peas and fresh eggs, along with two buckets of fish they'd caught the day before.

'I don't think we'll get much for that lot,' Grace said.

'We're going to provide a few extras to make it worth our while.' Louisa slipped one of the last packs of tea they had left, beneath the apples.

'You mean, like Mrs Stickles does?' Winnie interrupted.

'I'm not talking about offering our services,' Louisa said, shocked by Winnie's comment. The idea of selling themselves to make money reminded her of her contract with the diabolical Mr Trice, making her feel sick to the stomach. 'I'm talking about free trade. The margins on tea and cognac are much greater than the profit on fruit and veg. We have a little of each left from the last run, along with some gloves and handkerchiefs – we'll try selling those.'

'What if we're found out?' Winnie frowned. 'The Revenue men are in the Downs most days, cruising back and forth, seeking out contraband.'

'It's a worry, that's true, but we have ways and means of dealing with them.'

'I'd rather we didn't take the risk,' Winnie said stubbornly. 'Why should we?'

'Because we are in debt.' Louisa went on to enlighten her and Grace about the money they owed the Witheralls in addition to paying off Mr Trice's loan. Soon, even Winnie was dreaming up ways of hiding the goods.

'We'll break into a loaf and hollow out the centre – that'll take at least two pairs of gloves,' she said. 'And I have an idea that we can line a basket with cloth, add a layer of the silk handkerchiefs, then another cloth before piling it up with potatoes.'

Louisa decided against using the bread, but they packed the baskets as Winnie suggested.

Early the next morning, the rays of the white winter sun broke through a gossamer mist, heralding a fine January day. Louisa put on extra layers for warmth, her shift, stays, two layers of petticoats, and stockings, held above the knee with garters, a woollen dress and coat.

When they were all ready, Billy and the Lennickers made their way to the beach, lugging the baskets with them.

'You're looking rather stout, ladies,' he said, amused. 'You've been indulgin' in too much belly timber, if you ask me.'

'That's most impertinent of you, young sir.' Grace put on the voice of a lady of the ton. 'One should never pass comment on a young lady's figure.'

'I can barely move,' Louisa chuckled, light-hearted as the bladder of cognac hidden beneath her petticoats bounced lightly against her leg.

'At least you'll float if you go overboard.' Billy grinned and blew on his hands to warm them up.

'Nobody's going overboard,' she said quickly, not wanting to be reminded of their experience on the Sands. Today was different – the weather was settled and there was no hint of an imminent storm. Each time the waves fell gently away, they left a fringe of lace across the shingle.

The *Whimbrel* and the Feaseys' lugger, the *Good Intent*, were about to launch, their crews making themselves busy. Louisa was aware that Jason was watching them, his expression inscrutable. Bareheaded, he wore a long coat over a loose white shirt, dark breeches and a black neckerchief, his attire similar to that of the other men.

She became aware that Black Dog, Lawless and Awful Doins were laughing and pointing in her direction. Feeling sick, she looked away.

'Let them think what they like,' Billy said. 'We 'ave to do what we can to get by. We'll be all right – the weather's set fair.'

'As it was last time,' Grace said quietly.

'Lightning doesn't strike twice,' Billy reassured her. 'That's what Mr Lennicker used to say.'

'Stop acting furtively, Grace. You have to look like you're going about your normal business,' Winnie warned her.

'I'm trying.' Grace waddled towards the *Curlew* with her feet wide apart, like a duck.

They let the luggers go before they fetched a tub of salted pork from the house to add to their cargo, then launched the *Curlew* into the waves. Louisa took the tiller and steered them into the Downs with Winnie on the look-out for other vessels: the naval provisioning boats and others like the *Curlew* whom the merchant shipping relied on for supplies. Billy looked after the sails while Grace, having apparently found her sea legs this time, waited to do her part.

There was a brig waiting for a pilot to show them into the Channel. The crew were already provisioned, but they were more than happy to purchase fresh food, the last they would see for many a moon, without too much haggling. Billy trimmed the canvas as they sent a rowboat up alongside the *Curlew*. They sold apples, bacon, some beets and a bladder of spirit, but as Louisa tucked the coins into the pouch at her waist and the rowboat returned to the brig, she spotted one of the Revenue cutters nearby. The *Guinevere* was painted black and carried gigs and galleys hoisted on her deck, astern and each side of her.

'What shall we do?' Winnie exclaimed.

'If we hurry away, it'll make them suspicious. I think we should sit tight and not panic,' Louisa said, but it was impossible not to feel nervous as the cutter lowered one of her white jollyboats with two officers on to the water. One took up the oars and rowed towards them. When they reached them, the second officer stood up and greeted them most affably. Louisa guessed he was no more than thirty years old and thought himself very much cock o' the walk.

'Good morning, ladies,' he said, taking no notice of Billy. 'I'm Officer Groves.'

'Why, he's a handsome one,' Louisa heard Grace say, before Winnie went on to rebuke her, at which the officer grinned like a cat going after a mouse.

'Compliments won't help you, if I find out that you're breaking the law.'

'Why do you pick on us when we're only out to make an honest living, sir?' Louisa had flutterbies in her belly, even though she knew he wasn't permitted to rummage a woman.

'I'll have to do a search, so I can make a report, otherwise my commander will be after me.' He stepped on to the *Curlew* while his fellow officer waited, resting his oars as the water slapped at the ship's sides. He rummaged Billy, patting him down from top to toe, finding only a small packet of baccy for his own use.

'What's in the barrel?' he asked.

'Salted pork, sir,' Louisa said, desperately trying to keep her voice steady, as he began poking about in one of the baskets, sending apples rolling across the deck.

'Oh, watch what you're doing, sir,' Grace exclaimed, falling to her knees and leaning across the basket. 'This is our bread and butter – who will buy spoiled fruit?' Sobbing, she began to pick them up. 'Look at them – they're all bruised.'

'I apologise unreservedly,' the officer said as Grace sat back on her heels. He paused and sniffed the air. 'I can smell brandy ...'

'I don't know how that can be,' Louisa said quickly, noticing the liquid spreading from beneath her sister's skirt. 'Unless you have a finely tuned nose for detecting wine and spirit. I can't smell anything, can you?' She turned to her sisters. 'Well, only the drink that's oozing from every pore of our skipper's body.' Glaring at Billy to keep silent, she went on, 'He's always in his cups.'

'I 'ad a few too many last night, and now I wish I 'adn't,' Billy sighed, then belched for good measure.

'Hm ...' The officer deliberated for a moment. 'You may continue on your way.'

As soon as he'd stepped back into the boat to join his fellow officer, Billy let out the canvas and Louisa turned the *Curlew* to catch the wind.

'I thought we'd had it then,' she said when they were out of earshot. 'You did well, Grace. And thank you, Billy, for lying on our behalf.'

'I wasn't lyin',' he said. 'I 'ad a right skinful last night.'

Grace giggled and soon they were all laughing, happy now that the Revenue cutter had gone, disappearing off among the ships in the Downs of which there must have been at least three hundred and fifty that day. By mid-afternoon, frozen to the bone and having nothing left to sell except for the lace wound around their waists, they returned to Deal. Louisa hid the money, pleased with their haul. Provisioning would be their lifeline, but the Lennickers needed to move into more lucrative operations, and soon. How they would go about it, she wasn't sure.

# Chapter Eight

## *United We Stand, Divided We Fall*

It was a cold and icy morning on the kind of day when the boatmen's noses dripped with congbells as they looked out to sea from the capstan grounds. Louisa had come to check on the *Curlew*, a habit she had acquired since they had lost the *Pamela*.

'Mornin', miss.' At the sound of a familiar voice, she looked up, shading her eyes. 'I heard about the Revenue officer from Billy.' Jason chuckled as he removed his hat. 'He said that you and your sisters had him eatin' out of your hands.'

'What does it have to do with you?' she said, recalling the howling wind and the waves swirling over the *Curlew*'s gunwales; Jason's strong arms as he helped her out of the boat on to dry land; his expression of pure fury; her consequent sense of shame and stupidity.

'Nothin', so it seems,' he said, his tone hardening.

Louisa felt suddenly ashamed for her rudeness. What would Ma have said if she'd been here to hear her? 'I apologise for my thoughtlessness. I haven't thanked you properly for what you did that day. If it hadn't been for you and the crew of the *Whimbrel*, I don't think ...' Her words caught in her throat. 'I don't think my sisters and I – and Billy – would be here to tell the tale.'

'I'm sorry too for sayin' things I shouldn't have.'

'No, you spoke your mind. Your accusations and censure were perfectly justified. It was all my fault – I was impatient to take the *Curlew* out.'

'You wanted to show her off.'

'Nothing like that – I needed to start making an income as quickly as possible.'

'I have to respect you for goin' out again after what you went through. You're either extraordinarily brave or extremely foolhardy, Miss Lennicker.'

'I'm not planning to make the same mistake again.'

'I'm glad I ran in to you,' Jason changed the subject. 'Billy mentioned on the quiet that the Lennickers have an interest in joinin' the next run, on the landside, of course. Righteous would have been part of it, meetin' at the rondy and formalisin' the arrangements, if he were still with us.'

It was perfectly true that Pa would have gone to the meeting along with everyone else – including the Rattlers – but Louisa hadn't faced up to the fact that she would have to do the same if she was to be involved in the run. 'But that means working with One Eye and the Rattlers. They're criminals – thieves, murderers!'

'It's always been the same. It's us boatmen and free traders against the Revenue. You don't have to get involved with One Eye, but you do have to cooperate with him. If we all work together, the Revenue can't do much – a handful of officers can't arrest a whole town.'

'Then I will take my father's place on the boat.'

'Oh no, that isn't possible – some of our fellow free traders are common ruffians and varmints who speak nothin' but profanities, while others aren't averse to committing acts of violence. A young lady like yourself would …'

'Swoon? Cry?' she suggested when he didn't seem able to find the right word. 'You underestimate me.'

He tipped his head slightly to one side. 'It wouldn't be good for a woman's reputation – I wouldn't allow my sisters, if I had any, to sit with those gentlemen.'

*Or Miss Hibben?* she wondered.

'I'll be your eyes and ears,' he continued seriously. 'I'll give you everythin' you need.' A strange yearning gripped her under the intensity of his gaze. It was tempting to think he might be a friend, on her side.

Could she trust him?

'The Lennickers have worked with the Witheralls for many a year – I'd like to think we can continue that relationship,' he said, as though reading her mind. 'It benefits all of us. Since the Kesbys and Startups joined them, the Rattlers have become too powerful by half. United we stand, divided we fall.'

She thought for a little longer – an association with Jason's family would be advantageous. There was safety in numbers.

'You will say yes?' he said.

'Yes, thank you.'

'My father will be delighted – the sooner you have money in your pocket, the sooner you can pay back what Righteous owed.'

She bit her lip, sensing she'd been a fool to think he'd made the offer out of friendship when it was business, pure and simple.

'Righteous used Mr Trice as his agent. Everyone around here does the same, and it's a cryin' shame there's no one else with his influence and contacts – and his negotiatin' skills – because he's a quick-tempered character who would just as likely knock you out as confuse you with legalese. I can introduce you to him … or I can deal with him on your behalf. Yes, I think the latter course of action is advisable, knowin' how he is.'

'Thank you, but I've already made his acquaintance. He's executor of my father's will, the one he drew up for him as it turns out.'

'He has a finger in every pie. That's how he makes his money.'

She refrained from mentioning the loan and Mr Trice's suggestion as to how she would pay it back. It made her no different from a piece of tawdry mutton like Mrs Stickles, and she was sure he wouldn't approve. Not that it should matter what he thought, she told herself.

'I have business with Mr Trice already,' she confessed. He had sent Mr Mellors to call on her at the end of each month with a reminder of what she owed, the interest mounting up, but it wasn't that that scared her. It was the thought that one day, it would be Mr Trice who turned up to claim his dues.

'You have made a deal with him? May I ask on what terms? Only I shouldn't like to see him take advantage of you and your sisters.'

'His terms were most agreeable,' was all she was willing to say. 'I do know how it works. The Lennickers have been in the free trade for generations. Our great-great-grandparents were owlers together, dealing in the export of wool.'

She let Jason explain Mr Trice's role, even though she understood it already. The attorney acted as intermediary for the foreign merchants in Flushing and Gravelines who arranged for their goods to be collected in small units, conveniently sized for the free traders to carry away. The boatmen collected the cargo and shipped it back to England for transport to Canterbury and London in return for a fee, a percentage of the profits made. When it had been sold, Mr Trice collected the money and forwarded it to the merchants, subtracting his commission first.

'He does the same round at the end of every month, sometimes with his clerk and bodyguard, depending on how much money he's expecting to carry. He travels up from Dover to Deal, then Sandwich and on to Ramsgate before returning to Dover again.

'He's tolerable if you keep on the right side of him. He allows us several months' credit, knowing we'll always pay up in the end. On occasion, he asks me to invest in contraband for his personal use, or on behalf of other contacts of his, a London draper for example, or a publican with space in his cellar, or sometimes …' Jason lowered his voice '… there are other, respectable gentlemen who like to be involved, people you would never imagine … but it's perfectly safe for them. They hand over their money to Mr Trice and he does the rest.' He paused before continuing, 'Be wary of him.'

'Thank you for the warning,' she said, regretting that she couldn't reveal the extent of her involvement, and that she already had an idea of the lengths Mr Trice would go to, to get what he wanted. It felt wrong to be lying to him when they had agreed that their relationship as free traders had to work on trust. She reassured herself, thinking that if the fusty weasel did reveal that he had loaned her money, he wouldn't go on to explain the terms of the repayment to anybody else.

'Do you have any idea how much he makes from it?' she asked.

'One per cent on every shipment. It doesn't sound much, but when you consider that he's dealing with huge volumes of goods on every run, it soon adds up to a tidy sum.'

She was indignant at the thought that Mr Trice was able to carry out his business with little or no hazard to himself or his fortune. 'He is a louse,' she exclaimed, 'living off men and women who risk their lives and liberty for the trade!'

'I detect a note of bitterness,' Jason said. 'I'm not sayin' I like the man – but he's sharp and quick-witted, and very persuasive. He has a reputation as a bit of a bully – in fact, rumour has it that he had to leave his home when he was but thirteen years old for fallin' into a rage and beating a friend to death. However, he's proved his worth, makin' many a free trader's fortune.'

'Is that what you're hoping for? A fortune?'

'Why not? The risks are high – there's more danger of bein' caught than there used to be – but the rewards can be phenomenal. Consider my cousin, Abel. His father had a bit of luck, importin' gold and silver watches. He made enough to sell his boat and buy the mill and the surrounding land ten years ago, although he likes to take part now and again, for old times' sake. Mind you, the free trader's responsible for any goods that are lost, and it does happen.'

'It does,' Louisa said. 'You know that it wasn't only the *Pamela* that went missing?'

He nodded. 'One Eye was braggin' about it afterwards – I told him he'd better stop, or he'd find himself on the wrong side of the rest of us: the Witheralls, the Brockmans, Terrier's lot, the Edwards men.'

'He's already on the wrong side of the Lennickers, and when I can find a way of wreaking revenge on him and the Rattlers for what they've done to us, I won't hesitate to carry it out.'

Jason chuckled.

'Why do you laugh at me like this?'

'You're very pretty when you're crossed.'

'How dare you say such a thing? I'm being serious about One Eye – he deserves to be punished. And as for you, you're ... you're walking out with Margaret. You're engaged, for goodness' sake.'

'I'm sorry – I don't know what came over me. You won't say anythin'? Oh, what am I doin'? I have no right to ask you that.'

'You haven't,' she said hotly. 'I thought you were mannerly, a gentleman like your father, but you're just like the rest of them.' Poor Margaret, she thought, annoyed that he had dropped her into a moral quandary. It wasn't her place to reveal it, but she didn't like to think of an innocent young woman being wronged.

'I said you were pretty ... I didn't say I wanted to marry you or anythin'. All I said was the truth. I swear it's harder to understand a young lady's heart than shoe a goose.'

He seemed so miserable, so abject, that she promised she would keep her mouth shut. Why would Margaret, whom she hardly knew, believe her anyway if she went to her with what he'd said?

'I'm very grateful,' he stammered, putting his hat back on. 'I'll keep you informed of developments. Good day, Miss Lennicker.' She watched his retreating back as he sauntered off towards the *Whimbrel*, noticing how he glanced over his shoulder, then turned away abruptly.

Her mind a tangled net of thoughts, she began to walk along the beach. Whatever Jason had said, whatever he meant by it, nothing could come of it – even if she wanted it to, which she didn't, she told herself – because he was taken. She wouldn't hurt Margaret by making something out of nothing, nor would she waste any time musing on what might have been, despite the fact she did find him handsome, and considerate in the way he was trying to help the Lennickers in their hour of need.

As she began to plan the run, she heard the soft clatter of a falling stone.

'Psst. Over 'ere.' Mrs Stickles stepped out from behind one of the boatmen's sheds. 'I'm sorry for waylayin' you like this, but I need to speak to you privately.'

'I don't think we can have anything to say to each other.' Louisa eyed her with distaste – she appeared to be wearing the same dress she'd worn on the day of Mr Lennicker's passing, with added signs of wear and tear, and a grey coat with a stained frontage. Still, that was no reason for bad manners on her part. 'I spoke out of turn – I didn't intend to be rude.'

'It's all right, ducky. Sticks and stones may break my bones ... Anyway, now that a decent time 'as elapsed since Robert – I mean, Mr Lennicker – passed away, I wanted to ask you if, by any chance, 'e 'appened to have left any of 'is fortune in my gen'ral direction.'

'You are telling me that you want paying for the hour you came and spent with him?' Louisa said, affronted.

'No, not that, but, if you was thinkin' of offerin' compensation for the wages Mr Feasey docked from me that day, I wouldn't offend you by declinin'.'

'I understand that my father paid you a retainer, but those days are over. My family is under no further obligation to you.'

'There was nothin' in his will? No mention of my name and situation?'

'This is most improper. What we did, inviting you to the house, was a favour to our dying father. Any association between my sisters and I, and yourself is over.' She thought Mrs Stickles might be about to cry. At first, she dismissed it as part of her ploy to extract money from the Lennickers, but as her' tears started to flow, she began to suspect that her sorrow was genuine. Not only had

Mr Lennicker passed away, he had neglected to provide for her as she might have expected. Louisa began to have a change of heart, sensing that Mrs Stickles was grieving for Pa as deeply as she and her sisters were.

'I can see that times are hard for you, and I think I may be able to be of some assistance. There's a run due soon and I need to know what goes on at the rondy. If you give me the details – times and places – I'll pay you.'

'You don't know what you're askin'.' Mrs Stickles frowned.

'I'm only too aware,' Louisa said gently.

'What about young Billy? 'E's often at the rondy – 'e can tell you what's said.'

'Does he go there often?' Louisa was surprised, considering how Billy felt about One Eye and the prospect of running into the Fey Lady.

'He turns up with the *Whimbrel*'s crew to play 'is part in the plannin'.'

'I see. His memory isn't the best, especially when he has a few drinks inside him. No, I need someone I can rely on.' It was all very well Jason saying he would report on the meetings, but Louisa wasn't sure she could rely on him either. She wasn't sure she could depend on anyone, but herself and her sisters. 'The truth is that our father left us in deep water, drowning in debt.'

'Well I never did,' Mrs Stickles said. ''E always made out 'e was a gen'leman of means.'

*You certainly did well out of him*, Louisa wanted to say, but she felt sorry for the woman. Since Ma had died, her father appeared to have kept Mrs Stickles hooked like a fish on a long line, pulling her in with promises of riches and respectability, then letting her go again, leaving her with nothing. She didn't believe he'd done it intentionally. He hadn't expected to die before he'd made provision for her.

'The only way my sisters and I can free ourselves of the debts we've inherited, is to join in with the next run. I need information.'

'I'll see what I can do, but I'm not promisin' anythin'.'

'I know,' Louisa said.

'I 'ave to get back to the inn – One Eye will ask questions if 'e notices I'm gone.' Mrs Stickles scurried away along the beach, like a crab in fear of being snatched up by a seagull.

Louisa and her sisters went on provisioning with Billy, going out on the *Curlew* to sell anything they could from fresh fish and bloaters, dried apple rings and pear halves, and salted pork, to cognac that they bought on the quiet from Mrs Witherall, and a few odds and ends of lace that they had left. The sailors on the merchant ships liked to spend their money on luxury items to take home to their wives and sweethearts, or exchange for other goods when they travelled to foreign ports.

During March when the winds blustered through the Downs, they began to spread their wings, going out to an East Indiaman in her distinctive livery: a black hull with yellow and cream trim; the deck painted black and red. They bought tea and cut it with dried rose leaves to sell on.

After a good day towards the end of April, when Louisa's purse was weighed down with coins and the baskets were empty, they beached the *Curlew* and the boys on the shore hauled her up with the capstan. Billy stayed behind to stow the mast and canvas while Winnie and Grace made their way home.

'I'll catch up with you later,' Louisa said, parting with them outside Compass Cottage.

'Why? What are you up to?' Grace asked.

'Nothing that concerns you.'

'You keep telling us we shouldn't go wandering about on our own,' Winnie said. 'Grace and I will come with you.'

'You have to trust me on this. Go and make a start on supper.'

'If you're sure,' Winnie said doubtfully.

'Is this about the next run?' Grace said. 'It is, isn't it? You should tell us who you're meeting, in case something goes wrong and we have to come looking for you.'

'Hold your tongue. You never know who's listening.'

Her sister fell silent, her cheeks flushing.

'You would tell us if you had a secret assignation?' Winnie began.

'No, because it would be just that – secret.' Louisa smiled. 'I have no time for courting. You're both making a mountain out of a molehill.' With that, she spun on her heels and hurried away to St George's where she waited in the churchyard at her parents' grave, clearing away a posy of dead flowers and replacing it with a handful of shells and a mermaid's purse, thinking that if Pa couldn't be on the beach, she would bring it to him.

'Miss Lennicker.' She looked up to find Mrs Stickles beside her, a veil over her face and a basket on her arm. 'Come with me. I'm afraid I'm bein' follered.'

Louisa straightened and hastened after her, catching a glimpse of a figure dressed in black in the gateway, as Mrs Stickles opened the extra door in the side of the church that had been installed for the boatmen's use. Louisa slipped inside as Mrs Stickles closed the door, then they ran along the aisle and into the vestry, Mrs Stickles locking the second door behind them.

'Isaiah must 'ave seen me leavin',' she panted. 'If 'e tells One Eye that I've met you – a Lennicker – One Eye will do for me.'

'Whist!' Louisa pressed her finger to her lips as she heard a shout, and a dog sniffing at a knothole in the door. *Go away*, she prayed.

'You've found somethin' of int'rest, my boy?' Isaiah said, and the dog whined.

Louisa glanced towards her companion, the whites of her eyes gleaming from the darkness, as they waited in what was little more than a cupboard with a few mothball-scented robes hanging up. How could Mrs Stickles, slumped against the wall out of petrification, be a reliable witness for what went on at the Rattling Cat?

As she heard the dog take one more sniff at the door, then turn and run after its master, she realised her mistake in asking for her help – she would never forgive herself if Mrs Stickles came to harm on her account.

'He's gone,' Louisa whispered as she heard the church door swing shut.

'Thank the Lord,' Mrs Stickles breathed. 'I 'ave the information you asked for. They've been plannin' the next big run – the Rattlers and the Witheralls, and everybody else. The men are takin' the luggers across the Channel on the eighth day of May. They'll spend four days loadin' then return on the evenin' of the fifth day.' She frowned as she counted on her fingers. 'That's what One Eye said, the evenin' of the fifth day. They're goin' to aim for the sand'ills for the landin'. If the gobblers get wind of it, they'll let everybody know where to be – and when – in the usual ways …'

Louisa knew what they were – the intricate methods of signalling used by the free traders involved sweeps' brushes poked up chimneys, the sounding of hunting horns and the setting of fires.

'Did they mention the Lennickers at all?'

'Not in so many words. It took me a while to work out who they were talkin' about – they 'ave their own language, you see. They think I don't understand what they're sayin'.' Mrs Stickles smiled briefly. 'They're callin' you "The Lace Maiden".'

Louisa wasn't sure if she should feel alarmed or flattered.

'Is there anything else?' she asked.

'Only that I wish you and your sisters weren't gettin' yourselves tied up in this enterprise.'

Louisa shrugged. 'I can't afford for us not to be. I have your money ...' She took three coins from her purse and dropped them into Mrs Stickles' palm.

'One last thing – don't trust nobody, miss,' she whispered before they parted, Louisa intending to leave the church a full half-hour behind her.

She waited, kneeling in one of the pews, praying for the safety of the Lennickers and Mrs Stickles, the well-being of the boatmen out at sea and the success of their venture, that she might pay off Mr Trice in full, settle her father's debts and live happily ever after with her sisters and Billy ... and ... She thought of Margaret and Beth and how they would soon be married, and for the first time, wondered if that was what she wanted for herself.

'Miss Lennicker, I'm glad that you're finding comfort and consolation in prayer.' Reverend North came walking towards her as she stood up.

'Yes, thank you,' she said.

'There's no need to hurry away.'

'I have to get back – my sisters are expecting me. I wish you good day, Reverend North.' She made her way out to the front of the church, turned right on to the High Street and walked home, reflecting on how close she and Mrs Stickles had come to being discovered.

*

'Where have you been? You said you wouldn't be long,' Winnie said crossly when she arrived back at the cottage.

'She's only annoyed because you weren't here to peel the potatoes,' Grace said.

'I was worried about you. You know, I don't feel the same since Pa died. I used to feel safe here in Deal, but Aunt Mary's right. It's a dismal, dangerous place where you have to watch your back all the time. Look at poor Billy – what with the Rattlers and the gangers, I'm surprised he doesn't want to head off to sea.'

'He won't,' Grace observed. 'He promised he'd look after us.'

'Did I 'ear somebody takin' my name in vain?' Billy came flying into the kitchen and divested himself of his boots, tipping out a tiny mound of sand from each one.

'I wish you'd take those off outside,' Winnie grumbled.

He apologised then turned to Louisa.

'I 'ave a message for you from Marlin – 'e wants to talk to you about the run. 'E says to meet 'im tomorrow afternoon – 'e'll be at the shutter station, unless 'e 'as to go out, of course.'

'What will Miss Hibben think of this?' Winnie said, wide-eyed. 'I wouldn't like it if I were her.'

Billy stared at her, his expression gently scathing. 'This is business. Why do young ladies always jump to the wrong conclusions? Marlin would never go back on 'is word – 'e isn't like that. Where's my supper? I'm starvin'.'

'It isn't much.' Winnie gave the pot a stir. 'I had a couple of cod heads left over, so I've made a stew.'

'I should 'ave bought one of Mrs Stickles' pies on the way 'ome – you can say what you like about 'er, but 'er pies are magnificent. Although not as good as yours, Winnie,' he added quickly. 'You make the best pies in Deal.'

Apparently mollified, Winnie served their supper and made plans to obtain the ingredients for Billy's favourite: beef pie with gravy.

'We can't afford such extravagances,' Louisa said. 'I'm sorry, but that's how it is.'

'We've sold everything that Mr Jansen delivered from the farm this week,' Winnie snapped back. 'You make out we're on our beam ends, but we can't be.'

'I'm not crying wolf, if that's what you're implying. I've paid Mr Jackson and Master Roper out of Mr Trice's loan, but I haven't settled the other outstanding debts.'

'Why not?' Winnie folded her arms across her chest.

'When I pay for the produce we sell, I have to give our uncle a percentage. We don't keep all the money. You know that, Winnie.'

'What about the cognac? That money's ours, along with anything you receive for the lace that you sell on the side.'

'It still isn't enough. If I don't pay him back, Mr Trice says he can sell the house—'

'Compass Cottage?' Grace said.

'Yes, our home.'

'Oh Louisa,' Winnie exclaimed.

'Everything – the roof over our heads, our livelihood, our self-respect – depends on the success of the next run. Let's be kind to one another and work together. Please.' Louisa bit back tears as Billy and her sisters nodded in agreement, and Winnie dished up more stew. She had to be strong for them, but inside she was in knots, not knowing how it would all end.

# Chapter Nine

## *The Smugglers' Code*

Louisa went to meet Jason the next day, walking to the shutter station on the seafront, where the glassmen watched day and night, ready to send signals all the way to the Admiralty in London via a series of similar towers.

He was standing at the foot of the wooden building which had six octagonal shutters that could be flipped upright and sideways, according to the code used by the glassmen.

'Ah, it's the Lace Maiden.' He smiled as she approached him. 'That's the nickname the men have chosen for you.'

'So I've heard. I'd rather have chosen one myself, but I do quite like it.'

'It could have been a lot worse, I suppose,' he said before changing the subject. 'As you're serious about takin' over from where your father left off, you need to be able to protect yourself, your sisters and your goods. Do you know how to use a pistol? Has Billy shown you?'

'My mother was going to give me a lesson in shooting, but she died before ...'

'I'll teach you then. Come with me.'

'You don't have to,' she said, hesitating.

'I want to,' he said firmly. 'I'd feel much happier knowin' you can defend yourself, should you need to.'

'I thought you were going to talk about the run.'

'We can do that at the same time. I thought we'd walk over to the mill – my cousin won't mind us shootin' in the woods there, as long as we don't scare the horses.'

'I'm not sure. It's very kind of you, but we shouldn't be alone together. People will talk.'

'Let them,' he said.

'What about Miss Hibben?' Louisa caught up with him as he began to walk away. 'I wouldn't like it if I were her.'

'Far be it from me to speak ill of anyone, but Margaret is nothin' but a trollop,' he said harshly.

'Forgive me, I thought you and—'

'She jilted me,' he cut in.

Louisa couldn't believe it – why would anyone let Jason go?

'I'd have dropped her,' he continued, 'but I decided to be a gentleman and let her have the satisfaction of sayin' that she had jilted me. Don't get me wrong, she's a clever one and she fair turned my head, but she's from a family of landlubbers, and even knowin' from the start that the sea is in my blood, she made it clear that she expected me to move inland with her to a house with roses around the door.'

'Did she want you to give up hovelling?'

'Yes, and any chance of winnin' a big prize. She told me I could take up a safer, more respectable line of work, like farmin' or breakin' horses like Abel does. Can you imagine me growin' peas and barley?'

'No,' she said, thinking of her uncle and his cowardly labourers.

'I couldn't marry a woman who didn't respect my way of life, and her opinions started to cause me great sorrow. In the end, the inevitable happened and we had to part over it. Any happiness we would have found in marryin' would soon have been drowned by her naggin' and my refusal to change.'

'I'm very sorry.'

'I couldn't get air into my bellows when we broke up, but then I found out that she'd been walkin' out with somebody else – one of the apprentices at the boatyard – behind my back. I didn't know what to think, except that despite all her declarations of love, I wasn't good enough. That really knocked me down ...' He shrugged. 'I don't know why I'm tellin' you all this.'

'I'll keep it to myself, I promise.'

'Thank you. I've been thinkin' about the run and I'm minded to leave the *Curlew* behind and have Billy on the *Whimbrel* with me. It makes sense – he's a good worker who gets on with all the men, and he'll be somewhere I can keep an eye on him.'

'I don't know about that,' she began.

'Don't run before you can walk. There's plenty of space on the *Whimbrel* for the Lennickers' goods. As I said before, I need you and your sisters landside to supervise the unloadin' and make sure the Rattlers don't make off with any of it. I can't have you out crewin' the *Curlew* for Billy.'

'We can do it – we've been out many times now.'

'Out of the question. I won't work with you, if you insist on carryin' the goods across the Channel yourselves.' He stopped and stared at her, then sighed as she stared back. 'I wish I hadn't listened to my father – I told him it was a stupid idea. You can't go around behavin' like a loose cannon.'

'All right. I don't like it, but I'll do as you say.'

'Very wise,' he said gruffly, and they walked on to the mill, slipping up through the side gate and along a well-trodden path past the ponies' meadow to the chestnut wood where the leaves were unfurling on the trees. A gust of wind came tumbling through, snapping off a twig. She paused as he went ahead.

'Are you comin' or not?' Suddenly, he grinned. 'Don't you trust me?'

It was hard to know who to rely on, but she felt safe with him. Whether she believed every word he uttered was another matter.

Having followed him into a small clearing where three targets stood in a row, she stepped aside as he took a pistol from his jacket.

'I don't suppose you know what happened to your father's piece?'

'One Eye will have had it. My mother used to have one, a lady's pistol, although she never used it. In fact, I can't recall what happened to that either.'

'A lady's firearm is no good – it wouldn't kill a mouse, let alone a man.'

'I wouldn't want to kill anyone,' she said, horrified.

'Then you shouldn't put yourself in a position where you might have to.'

'I have no choice, Master Witherall—'

'Enough of the formalities. Call me Marlin, or Jason like you used to do when we were littluns on the beach with our mothers.'

'You must address me as Louisa in return.'

'It doesn't feel right somehow,' he said. 'You and your sisters were always set above the rest of us, the way your mother taught you to speak and behave.'

'I don't want you calling me Miss Lennicker if I am to call you Jason.'

'All right.' He chuckled. 'Let's not argue, Louisa …'

She smiled back. 'The only way I can make enough money to pay off my father's debts is to take part in the honourable trade. I'll carry lace for the drapers in London as I have always done, and I'll keep selling it on the side for as long as the high-born ladies will buy it. And for good measure, I will avenge my father's death and ruin One Eye for what he's done to us.'

'I would counsel you against that.' Jason frowned as he fiddled with the pistol.

'You would have no scruples if it was your father who'd been murdered.'

'Everyone knows what happened, but you can't go around threatenin' to take One Eye down. He has friends in high places and low ones too.'

'I don't care,' she said stubbornly. 'He'll deserve his due reward when it comes. I'm not asking for your permission, or your support. This is something I have to do.'

'I'm not sayin' I won't help you. I'm advisin' you not to rush in. These things take time to plan – there's much truth in the sayin' that revenge is a dish best served cold. We all have our reasons for wantin' One Eye gone from Deal. He's a double-crossin', cheatin' brute, but a free trader doesn't let personal aggravation get between him – or her – and a profit.' A smile played on his lips, and she wondered suddenly what it would be like to kiss him. It was ridiculous when she had no idea whether or not he liked her in that way, and there was no chance she would lower herself to play second fiddle to Margaret, who had been engaged to him first.

He showed her how to load the pistol, pouring a little powder from a horn into the muzzle before wrapping a lead ball in a patch of cloth, and using the ramrod to push it down towards the powder.

'Don't pack it down tight, or it won't fire,' he said. 'Now you put a small amount of primer in the pan. When you pull the trigger, the flint hits the steel, making sparks. As the steel opens the pan, the sparks hit the primer. The primer catches and a flash travels into the muzzle to set the powder in the barrel alight. It's that which sends the ball out to hit the target, if you aim in the right direction. You won't get it straight away – it takes practice. I'll show you.'

She retreated a few steps as he placed one hand behind his back and held the pistol up with the other. He took aim and fired at a circle chalked on a piece of board that was attached to a tree trunk.

'Oh, well done,' she exclaimed as he hit it dead centre.

'Now you have a go.' He handed her the smoking gun and watched her load it. 'You'll need to be quicker than that,' he said impatiently. 'The enemy would have got you by now.'

She looked up. There was no malice in his comments – he was teasing her.

'Let me help you line it up.' He stood right behind her – she could feel his breath on the back of her neck, a not unpleasant experience, she thought, distracted. His hands were on her hips, gently directing her to stand square to the target. 'Hold the gun up and take aim. That's right. Make sure you hold it steady … fire when you're ready.'

She pulled the trigger and the shot rang out with a flash and a wisp of smoke. Her eyelids stung.

'Not bad for your first time,' she heard him say as he stepped back.

'Where did it go?' she asked. 'I didn't see …'

'Just to the left of the target. Have another go.'

He watched from a distance as she had three more attempts. On the fourth, she hit the target.

'You see.' Jason strode across to her. 'You can do it.'

'I'm very grateful for the lesson.' She tried to hand back the pistol, but he wouldn't let her.

'It's yours. I'll have no argy-bargy about it. I don't need it.'

'I'd better go home then – I've taken up more than enough of your time.'

'It's been a pleasure,' he said. 'I mean it. I'll walk with you into town – we can talk a little more about the run on the way. You're goin' to have to be as tough as nails if you're goin' to be a free trader in your own right. Are you absolutely sure you're up to it? Only it isn't too late to change your mind.'

'There's only one way I'll find out.'

He smiled again, and her heart turned over. Jason's presence, the scent of gunpowder, her sense of achievement and the warmth of the spring sunshine seemed to have cast their magic over what was turning out to be a memorable day.

As they walked back towards the sea – side by side, but with a respectable distance between them now they were no longer alone – they discussed the arrangements for running the goods, and by the time they parted, she felt more confident about restoring the family's fortunes.

She diverted into the town, heading to the market to buy milk and eggs to make a pudding. Spotting One Eye coming towards her, she held her course.

'If it isn't The Lace Maiden ... We are well met,' he said, stepping in front of her. 'I've 'eard that the Lennickers will be workin' alongside the Rattlers and the rest, against our enemy, just as they used to when Righteous was alive, accordin' to the smugglers' code.'

'There is no code,' she said coldly, noting the cutlass blade glinting at his side, 'and if there were, I wouldn't keep to it.'

'Don't think I'll treat you any different because you're a woman.'

'I don't want or need any special treatment,' she hissed.

His smile was one of mocking malice. 'I shouldn't get ideas above your station. As a member of the weaker sex, you're only useful for carryin' goods and lightin' fires, not much else … oh, apart from cookin', cleanin' and keepin' a man's bed warm.'

She didn't deign to reply, stepping aside and continuing along the street.

Having bought milk and forgotten the eggs, she returned to the cottage.

'You've been a long time,' Winnie said slyly when she arrived home to find her sisters lazing around, the dishes from the night before not yet put away.

She took the pistol from her pocket and placed it on the table. Grace's eyes widened.

'Jason's been teaching me how to use this.'

'Oh no, Louisa. I don't like it,' Winnie said.

'I don't like it any more than you do, but he gave it to me to keep us safe.'

'I don't mean that – it's good that we have a way of protecting ourselves. I mean that I don't like the idea of you going out with him, just the two of you.'

'Miss Hibben has broken off their engagement,' Louisa said.

'All the more reason for you not to spend time alone with him. Louisa, I don't understand. People will put two and two together and make five. It's much harder to keep one's reputation than lose it, and once lost, it's impossible to retrieve it again in one piece.'

'You sound like Aunt Mary,' Louisa said, but she was thinking of Mr Trice.

'She does have a point,' Winnie said. 'You're supposed to be setting a good example as the eldest.'

'If I can't talk to Jason, how else am I going to find out about the run?' Louisa said, slightly exasperated. 'If you ask me, keeping a roof over our heads is slightly more important than keeping my reputation.'

Winnie didn't respond.

'It's done now anyway,' Grace said. 'What did he say? What did you do?'

Louisa changed the subject quickly, not wanting to share the details of the time she'd spent with him, sensing that it would somehow break the spell.

It was the beginning of May and they were sailing the *Curlew* back from one of the fishing grounds, trying to escape the gulls that were terrorising them, intent on stealing their catch. Louisa was attempting to steer the straightest course possible through the shipping in the Downs, at least seven hundred vessels, including the boats from the navy's victualling yard, when she caught sight of a galley with twelve oarsmen, heading out rapidly towards France, skimming through the water faster than any cutter.

'That's one of the guinea boats,' Billy observed. 'Marlin's told me about them – they're laden with gold for old Boney.'

'That can't be right,' Grace said. 'Why should he have England's gold?'

'Like Wellington, 'e needs to fund 'is army, and the financiers don't 'ave any scruples as to whose side they're on, as long as they're making a profit. A bit like us,' he grinned. 'The government's banned imports of French brandy because of the war, but we still do a good trade in it. It isn't 'urtin' nobody.'

'But the guineas are going over to France to fund the men who are fighting against our soldiers,' Louisa pointed out.

'There is that,' Billy agreed eventually.

'It's a good start to shot-fare, even though it's early in the season. We've got a good catch today.' Winnie was counting the mackerel they'd hauled in with the net when they had risen like walms to the surface of the sea, silver against the green water.

Jason would be a good catch, Louisa mused. Handsome, clever, heroic ... She wrenched the tiller, narrowly avoiding a rowing boat that had strayed into her path.

'Louisa, will you concentrate on what's goin' on,' Billy shouted. 'You're in a daydream.'

'I know what she's dreaming about,' Winnie chuckled. 'A certain free trader. He confided in me the other day when Grace and I were bringing the handcart back from the market, saying he wished he could make himself more interesting, more intriguing to the opposite sex.'

'He has a fancy for you!' Louisa exclaimed with a sense of unreasonable disappointment.

'No, for you, silly. He was asking me about you.'

She thought of Miss Hibben and how she'd resented Jason's absences and irregular hours on the *Whimbrel*. She had no reason to suppose that it would be any different for anyone else – there were bound to be times when one would feel neglected and wonder if he cared more for the winning of prizes at sea than their company.

'Leave her alone,' Grace piped up. 'She isn't interested in him, only the plans for the run.'

'Thank you,' Louisa said. 'At least one of you can see how things stand.'

'Ah, but which one?' Winnie teased. 'There's no smoke without fire.'

Later, Louisa was dealing with the fish that they'd brought back from the fishing trip that morning, tipping the hundreds of slippery mackerel slithering into buckets of brine to let them soak until they were ready to split and hang in the smoke. It was the best catch they'd made so far, an omen of better times to come.

She was reciting the numbers Pa had taught her – four fish to a warp, thirty warp to a long hundred, one thousand to the cran basket, ten cran to the last – when Grace came bounding into the room, her eyes bright with excitement.

'There are two ladies here – the Misses Flinders wish to buy gloves and lace. Shall I show them into the parlour?'

'What a time to call when I am covered in scales!' Louisa wiped her hands and took off her apron. 'Yes, show them in. I'll be with you forthwith.' On her way, she collected her gloves and sprayed on a little violet-scented cologne.

'Good day and welcome,' she said, a little overwhelmed to find two young ladies of the ton, wearing white leghorn bonnets and delicate muslin gowns, in the Lennickers' humble cottage, and utterly horrified to discover that they were accompanied by an officer in his red coat. A flash of recognition crossed his eyes as he introduced himself and the Misses Flinders.

'It is a pleasure to meet you, Lieutenant Tempest,' Louisa said politely, praying that he wouldn't mention their previous encounter in the rose bed at Mundel Manor. 'Grace, have you offered refreshments?'

'It's very kind of you, Miss Lennicker, but we will soon be on our way,' the elder Miss Flinders said. 'You have been recommended to us by Mr Trice, our father's steward, who said it might be possible to purchase white kid gloves and French lace.'

'My sister is to be married at the end of July and we are looking for an adornment for her dress,' said Miss Marianne Flinders.

'Congratulations on your good fortune,' Louisa said, addressing the elder sister.

'I shall miss her – she'll be obliged to move away from Walmer to follow her husband.' Miss Marianne turned to Lieutenant Tempest and said, with petulance, 'I wish you wouldn't take her away from me, Harry.'

'I'll make sure Harry finds you a suitable husband from among his friends,' Miss Flinders smiled.

'You are not engaged, Miss Lennicker?' Marianne enquired. 'I'm sorry, that is impertinent of me. It is a fault of mine that my thoughts gush from my mouth unchecked, like water.'

'Suffice to say, I am not,' Louisa said, finding herself thinking of Jason. 'I realise that it's impolite to speak of financial matters, but I must warn you that the items that you wish to buy are unusually expensive, being both desirable and rare.'

'We understand that they are almost impossible to obtain, but money is no object,' Miss Flinders said, blushing.

'I think that Sir Flinders may have a different view on that,' the officer said lightly. 'Miss Lennicker, we are sorry for taking up your time with small talk. Have you any of these items for sale, or have we been misled?'

'Grace, will you fetch samples of the gloves, please?' Louisa said in reply. She laid a blue cloth across the table in the parlour and Grace returned with four pairs of fine kid gloves, placing them on top to show off their pristine whiteness.

'Your hands are very fine,' Louisa said when the Misses Flinders decided to try them on, forcing them so hard that she was afraid the seams would split. 'They will fit with a little help from some powder and a glove stretcher.'

'They are beautiful – we will be the envy of the county,' Miss Marianne said as Louisa held on to the fingertips to help her extricate her hands from the gloves.

'Don't you think they're a little small?' Miss Flinders mused aloud.

'Miss Lennicker is right – they will give,' Miss Marianne said, apparently determined to have them.

In the meantime, Grace had unwrapped three samples of lace and spread them across the tablecloth to show off the ornate patterns.

'It is all handmade?' Miss Flinders asked.

'I wouldn't sell anything else,' Louisa confirmed. 'It's of the highest quality, the most luxurious French bobbin lace – it drapes exceedingly well.'

'Is this all you have?' Miss Marianne said.

'There's—' Grace began, but Louisa cut her off with a quick stare.

'This is all I have at present – I shall have replenished my stock within the month, but as I've said, finding an amount of lace of this quality is like finding a hen's tooth.'

The ladies' frowns made her realise they'd led such sheltered lives that they had no idea that fowl didn't have teeth.

'It's very scarce, thanks to the Revolution,' she enlarged, and they nodded and smiled again. Louisa found it painful to think that many of the French lacemakers had gone to the guillotine because of their association with the aristocracy. She named a price for each piece of lace. The Misses Flinders wavered, and Louisa began to wonder if she'd pushed them too far. She glanced towards their companion, catching his eye. A ghost of a smile crossed his face.

'Allow me to buy these fripperies for you, my dears,' he offered.

'We can't let you do that, Harry,' Miss Flinders said.

'It would please me no end. Do say yes, before they turn to dust.'

'You are finding our shopping expedition dull,' Miss Marianne exclaimed.

'We do have other engagements to keep.'

Louisa studiously avoided any interaction with Grace, fearing that one or both of them would give themselves away. She could feel the laughter bubbling up in her throat. Lieutenant Tempest was bored stiff and scared to admit it.

'Then thank you,' Miss Flinders said, accepting his offer, but before he could arrange payment, she went on, 'Tell me, Miss Lennicker, is it possible to obtain human hair? I have a fancy for a hairpiece.'

'I'll see what I can do,' Louisa said, while Grace was wrapping their purchases in tissue paper.

'Here's my card,' Miss Flinders said, handing it over. 'I would appreciate your discretion in this matter.'

'Of course.'

Their visitors made their way out, leaving Grace speculating about the state of the elder sister's tresses.

'I couldn't see any curls peeking out from under her bonnet, and her eyebrows are painted on. I reckon she's as bald as a coot underneath.'

'It isn't right to laugh at a person's afflictions, if that is the case.'

'It's very odd that they should come here to buy goods when they could easily afford to go to a shop in London. Louisa, you did well, holding your nerve like that.'

'They thought they had a bargain and we made a tidy profit.' She smiled as she looked around her. It was their home and that was how it was going to stay, so long as she lived and breathed. She would do anything to keep the roof over their heads, even cut off her hair, if she had to.

To avoid being seen with Jason, Louisa exchanged messages with him through Billy, but when the run became imminent, he insisted on meeting her in person.

'I offered to go along with you, but 'e said not to,' Billy said.

'I'll go,' Grace said.

'I think somebody should,' Winnie confirmed. 'Mrs Edwards – you know what she's like – she told me one of her friends had seen you on your way back from the mill with him. She asked me if you were engaged and I said no, and that you must have fallen into his company by accident.'

Louisa wasn't sure she wanted Grace tagging along, relishing the idea of being alone with him once more, but she was uneasy that going without a chaperone would be overstepping the bounds of decency.

'If there's nothing in it, you won't mind me being there,' Grace said. 'I promise I'll be discreet – I'll take Ma's parasol and keep a few steps behind you, if that makes you feel better about it. You can speak to him privately, but if anyone says they've seen you consorting with him, I'll say I was there, which is the absolute truth. Please, Louisa. It will put Winnie's mind at rest.'

'I don't like the idea that you are spying on us, but yes, you can come with me, if you must.'

'Oh, I must.' Grinning, Grace fetched the parasol and returned to put on her boots.

The appearance of the sun and its fleeting warmth was suddenly extinguished by a clatter of hailstones and a chilly breeze. By the time Louisa reached the shutter station, her shawl was clinging to her arms and she was soaked through to the skin.

'Ah, there you are.' Jason came forward to greet her. 'You aren't dressed for this weather.'

'It was stupid of me,' she muttered, embarrassed by her lack of foresight.

'Allow me,' he went on, removing his oilskin.

'No, I couldn't.'

Ignoring her protest, he placed it across her shoulders, his fingers brushing against her arm, the light touch leaving a burning imprint. She leapt back then tried to laugh it off, but it was no laughing matter for he had noticed her reaction and was staring at her, a quizzical expression in his eyes.

'Walk with me,' he said.

Not *walk out with me*, she took care to notice. As they set off back towards the capstan grounds, the hail stopped, leaving the stones underfoot shining like jewels.

'What news do you have?' she asked as they strode along, side by side.

'You'll have to come closer,' he grinned. 'I don't want to shout out our plans to all and sundry, especially your sister. Why did she have to come with you, and carrying that ridiculous parasol that's no use in the rain?'

'She thought to disguise herself, hiding beneath it,' Louisa smiled. It was a pretty item in French grey with a black lace cover, but it appeared incongruous on the beach that was deserted but for a handful of the boatmen, the rest having taken shelter from the weather. 'I humoured her, allowing her to follow me.'

'I shouldn't be cross – I have great respect for the way you look after each other – but this is for your ears alone.'

'Is that better?' she said, moving nearer – within touching distance.

'Much better.' He went on to inform her that she would need to borrow at least three ponies from the Brockmans to carry the goods from the shore to the Three Kings, because he'd received word that the merchants had a larger consignment than usual of laces and silks. 'You'll have to contact Mr Trice's agent to arrange transport from there – or run it inland yourselves. I'll leave that with you.' He confirmed the details of the options for landing and how the landsmen would signal to the boatmen. 'Any questions?'

'Only ... do you think the Rattlers will try to cheat us this time?'

He shook his head. 'They wouldn't dare, not when we're all workin' together.'

'Ah, look who it is!' She heard Mr Witherall shouting from his perch on one of the upturned tubs. 'You've abandoned your post to go gallivantin' about the countryside with your sweetheart, my boy. Not that I blame you.'

'Does he not realise that it's a pretence?' Louisa frowned.

'What? That I'm courtin' you? Would it be such a terrible thing?'

Blushing, she turned away. She was falling for him, and it appeared that he had feelings for her, but she wasn't sure of him yet. It wasn't long since Margaret had jilted him, and if anything happened between them, her conscience would prick her to tell him of her obligation to Mr Trice, a detail she had deliberately withheld. Being a stickler for honesty, and already having been betrayed by Margaret, he would likely not take kindly to being lied to.

'I'll see you again in less than a sennight,' he added. 'We set out for France after dark.'

'I wish you well,' she said. 'God speed.'

Having watched him walk away, she waited for Grace to catch up, then went home. Winnie pounced as she took off her wet shawl and hung it on the hook in the hall.

'It's going ahead,' she said.

'What is? What are you talking about?' Winnie asked.

'I don't understand,' Grace said, joining in.

'How could you possibly not know?' Louisa frowned. 'The run. I've thought of nothing else for the past few weeks.'

'Oh, that?' Grace sighed wearily. 'We know, Louisa.'

'Then why were you making out that you didn't?' She stared at her sisters who suddenly broke into laughter.

'We were having you on,' Winnie giggled. 'Oh dear, you've been boring us to tears with it. It's run this, run that … every hour of every day.'

Feeling hurt, Louisa went into the kitchen and sat down by the fire to warm herself up.

'Have I really been going on about it that much?'

'Yes, you have,' Grace chuckled.

'I'm sorry – I don't want anything to go wrong.'

'We understand, but it's no different from any other run, except that Pa isn't here. It's a comfort to know that he and Ma will be watching over us,' Winnie said, blowing her nose. 'How I wish it was over and done with.'

Louisa felt the same, but for different reasons. Winnie hated the free trade for the danger and dishonesty, but Louisa wanted the money to get rid of the millstone of debt hanging around her neck. There was more to be made from selling lace than peddling beans and bloaters. She couldn't wait for the run to begin.

# Chapter Ten

## *The Call of the Seven Whistlers*

Deal was swarming with soldiers, waiting for ships to take them to join Wellington's army on the Peninsula. The officers were sleeping on carpets in the inns, and soldiers on their baggage on the beach. The slop sellers, ropemakers, taverns and bakeries were doing a roaring trade, and Louisa railed against their bad luck in choosing that day to bring the goods over. Even in the middle of the night, it would be impossible to work undetected. Even worse, the weather was quiet, a grey sky merging with a flat sea, the brigs and galleons becalmed in the Downs, a situation that would encourage the Revenue officers out of their comfortable beds after dark on a balmy May evening.

The curlews were singing during the day: the call of the seven whistlers, a bad omen, kept preying on her mind. Was the crew of the *Whimbrel* waiting, hovering in the Sands alongside the *Good Intent*, or were they still loading the consignment in Gravelines?

'The boats are set to come offshore at ten.' Louisa and her sisters were collecting up what they needed, as dusk began to fall. 'We'll fetch the ponies, take them to the sandhills, then signal when it's safe for the crews to make their move. Make sure you eat plenty, Grace. It's going to be a long night.' She ran through an inventory of their luggage. 'Pistol – I have that. Spout lantern?'

'It's in the hang,' Winnie said.

'Fetch it then – we can't afford to forget anything.' She continued down the list. 'Grace, where is the blacking?'

'It's in the oilskin bag. Louisa, we've checked all this before.'

They were ready before time, joining the tide of tub carriers and batsmen, the Lennickers' men – the labourers from Limepit Acres – the Witheralls' and Ropers' men, and the Edwards family, walking along the ancient highway along Sandwich Bay and entering the sandhills at the pre-planned mark, with three ponies, their stars and socks blacked out. Louisa felt sick with nerves.

Looking out to sea, she spotted the characteristic blue flash from a flint pistol and her heart began to beat faster. The spotsman – Mr Witherall, who'd been prevented from joining the *Whimbrel*'s crew by an attack of gout – returned the flash three times.

'Winnie, do you see anything amiss?' she whispered.

'No, I can't see anything unusual.'

'The numbers ... Where are the Rattlers? I'm afraid I smell a rat.' Louisa ran up to Mr Witherall, dragging her pony behind her. 'We can't let the boats come in,' she said urgently. 'Someone has set a trap.'

'What makes you think that?' he said, somewhat sceptically.

'There's no sign of any of One Eye's men. The women must light the fire, a beacon to warn them to sink the tubs and hide the rest of the goods.' She began to panic as she thought of the lace – it would all be ruined.

'Don't be too hasty – there's much at stake,' one of the batsmen interrupted.

'That's right – our lives and liberty,' she said. 'We can't take the risk. Trust me,' she added. 'One Eye has tipped off the Revenue that we're making a landing here so he can go and land elsewhere without interference.'

Earlier in the week, the women had collected a huge pile of wood and straw, covering it with an oilskin pegged down with stones. Louisa gave the pony to Grace and took the tinder box from their bag. All she had to do was light the fire, but the wood was damp, and she could barely raise a wisp of smoke as the crowd pressed in around her, their voices filled with complaint.

'You're makin' a mistake, missus. Put that out.'

'We can't risk being caught by the gobblers,' she said.

'They aren't here, are they? It's all right well for you, going about sellin' goods for a small fortune, but I rely on the few shillin's I get for carrying the tubs to feed my children.'

'You would stop the whole operation because we're a few men down? You confound me.' One of the other tub carriers turned to his wife. 'We won't be workin' with the Lennickers again.'

'I told you, we should 'ave joined in with One Eye like 'e asked us to,' the wife responded, but when she grabbed Louisa's arm and began to drag her away from the fire, it smouldered and burst into flame, and a commotion broke out further along the sandhills.

'Watch your backs!' came the sound of yelling and shouting, along with the thud of horses' hooves galloping on the sand. 'It's the gobblers.'

'And a band of militia, if I'm not mistaken.'

'Louisa, we must make ourselves scarce.' Over the noise, she heard Winnie and Grace screaming at her to hurry. She threw more wood on to the fire, praying that there would be enough flame – and enough time – for the boats to turn about.

'You should leave now,' Mr Witherall said, coming up to her as the enemy pulled up close by. 'There's nothing more we can do. The boys will 'ave to take their chance.'

'Our luck has changed,' she heard Officer Chase say as the crowd began to disperse, melting into the dark shadows of the dunes. 'Good evening, ladies and gentlemen.'

It was too late to pretend they'd been mending nets around the fire, Louisa thought. It was indeed time to make themselves scarce, but what of their menfolk?

'If they come in, we'll be ready to catch them. If they turn back, the cutter will be with them before they can dispose of the evidence,' the Riding officer said, puffed up with confidence. 'We'll have them this time for sure.'

'What about these people?' the captain of the militia asked, moving closer to the fire, the flames illuminating the brass buttons on his red coat. 'I'll have my men round them up and march them down to Deal – a night in gaol will give them time to think about what they'll say to the magistrate in the morning.'

'My orders are to arrest those responsible for importing the contraband,' Officer Chase said. 'The magistrates won't charge anyone unless they've been caught red-handed, and even then it's the luck of the draw. I know this town – much as it pains me to say so, many of those who are supposed to maintain law and order are in the pay of the smugglers.'

A shot reverberated from the distance, followed by a muffled boom.

The horses started, then settled again, but Louisa was gripped with fear. Was it the sound of an imminent battle between the free traders and the Revenue, or a warning shot across the bows?

'I told you we'd get them tonight,' Officer Chase bragged as more shots rang out, followed by a scream and shouting from offshore.

'It isn't often you have a reliable informant,' the captain observed.

Thanks to the Rattlers diverting the Revenue to the sandhills, it had been too late to head the *Whimbrel* off. A burning rage and resentment against One Eye and his men roiled in Louisa's breast as she thought of them unloading, unhindered, at Kingsdown or further south near Folkestone. How had the *Good Intent* managed to get away from Jason and his crew? Had she lost them somewhere inside the Sands? They had broken the smugglers' code, betraying the rest of the boatmen. One Eye was evil …

'Go 'ome with your sisters,' she heard Mr Witherall say. 'There's nothin' you can do.'

'I know who set this up,' she said, in a fury.

'We all do, my dear, but—'

'He must pay for it!'

'Not now – this isn't the time,' Mr Witherall said firmly. ''E'll 'ave 'is comeuppance in the end, though, I promise. If any 'arm has come to my boy and 'is men, I'll personally cut 'im into little pieces. Go 'ome,' he repeated. 'I'll send word to you when I 'ave any news.'

'You will let us know straight away?'

'Dreckly-minute,' he confirmed.

Louisa explained the situation to her sisters while they were making the long, lonely walk back to the mill to return the ponies.

'I'm not waiting all night to find out what's happened to Billy and Jason,' Winnie said as they stumbled back in the dark, the light in the spout lantern having gone out. 'I'm never doing this again, not for you, Louisa, not for anybody. As I've said before, I want to end my days in my own bed, not on the far side of the world, or hanging from the gibbet on Penenden Heath, which is exactly where you're heading. I will never forgive you if you take

Grace with you. I'll never forgive you either if Billy's been hurt … or …' Her voice faded as Louisa reached for her hand and held it tight as she'd done when they were little girls.

'All will be well,' she said forcefully.

'Promise me that it will be so,' Winnie said. After a long pause she added, 'You can't, can you?'

Louisa didn't answer, taking Grace's hand too as they walked back into Deal, following the soft glow of firelight and the sound of voices to the beach.

'It's the *Whimbrel,*' Louisa said, her breath catching in her throat as she noticed one of her sails shot through and her foremast drooping. She felt utterly despondent, knowing that Jason would be distraught.

'Oh, my Lord,' whispered Winnie.

'She's in a terrible state,' Grace said. 'I don't like the look of it.'

'Where are the men?' Winnie asked.

'They've been arrested and dragged off to gaol.' Mr Witherall came limping across the shingle to them, his eyes glistening.

'On what charge?' Louisa said, watching the tide surveyors rummaging the lugger.

'For sailin' too close to the wind, in effect.'

Another boat – the Revenue cutter, *Guinevere* – crept up close to the shore, dropped anchor and sent her jollyboats to the beach loaded with a few sodden bales of what Louisa guessed was her precious lace, and a dozen or so tubs that Mr Witherall said they had taken up, having found them floating in the *Whimbrel*'s wake. The soldiers escorted the cargo to the Customs House at the corner of Customs House Lane and Middle Street, followed by a trail of angry men and women.

'That's our goods – all paid for.'

'That's the honest truth,' they shouted.

'You're takin' the food from my littluns' mouths.' A woman wailed and sobbed, and beat her chest.

'This is all the Rattlers' doin',' a voice said, and the crowd slowed down and stopped, and began baying for One Eye's blood instead of berating the soldiers. ''Ow did the Ridin' officers know where the landing was to be? Why didn't the *Good Intent* come in with the *Whimbrel*? I assumed the Rattlers escaped when the Revenue fired their guns at 'em. But no, ol' One Eye 'ad a plan to put us out of business. 'E's been gettin' far too big for 'is boots.'

''E needs takin' down a peg or two,' somebody else said.

'He needs taking out altogether.' Louisa couldn't restrain herself from joining in.

'Ah, it's the Lace Maiden, Righteous's girl. Well said, miss.' She recognised Mrs Edwards and Mrs Witherall standing side by side.

'Our venture has gone asprawl,' Louisa continued. 'One Eye has betrayed us, effectively fleecing us of our goods. Even worse, he has had our menfolk taken away from us.' The crowd began to gather around her as she spoke.

'How will we manage? How can we get our fathers, sons and brothers back when they'll be charged in the mornin'? How will we eat if they're locked up and the boats are left to languish in the capstan grounds?' said one of the wives who peddled fish in the market.

'Your mother would 'ave known what to do, miss ...'

'Let's put our 'eads together.' Mr Witherall limped to her side. 'Go 'ome to your beds, one an' all. There's nothin' we can do until mornin' comes.'

Louisa glanced towards the horizon – it wouldn't be long before the halo of the sun began to turn the sea blood-red.

'I'll send for Mr Trice,' she decided.

'I'll find one of the boys to fetch Abel – he can ride to Dover with a message,' Mr Witherall said.

'What about the magistrate? Who will it be?'

'Reverend North or Sir Flinders.'

'Both of whom are involved in the free trade in one way or another, receiving illegally imported goods,' Louisa said.

'Not Sir Flinders, surely?' Mr Witherall raised one bushy eyebrow. 'No, you won't 'ave any joy with 'im. 'E 'as to keep 'is nose clean – 'e wants to run for parliament.'

'I have knowledge I can use against him – the Misses Flinders aren't averse to purchasing a little lace now and then.'

'In that case, do your best for the men. My biggest fear is that my boy will lose 'is mind if 'e's locked up for too long. 'E'll be like a caged bear.'

'I'll see what I can do.'

''E's rather fond of you, you know,' Mr Witherall said.

'Oh, you're making that up,' Louisa scolded him. 'I'll see you at the courthouse. There's no time to waste.'

'How are you going to persuade the vicar to use his influence to get the men off?' Winnie asked when the sisters found each other again as the crowd dispersed, some of the women determined to spend the hours of dawn holding a vigil outside the gaol.

At home, Louisa wrote two notes: one to Reverend North, and the other addressed to Sir Flinders, before finding one of the boys who was killing time on the beach and paying him handsomely to deliver them.

'It's very important that you take this one to the rectory and the other to Mundel Manor – and I shall know if you don't,' she added sternly. 'I will invoke the Fey Lady to haunt you till the end of your days.'

'It's all right, miss. I'll do it.' He squinted in the rays of the rising sun. 'They call you the Lace Maiden now, don't they?'

'Maybe they do. Maybe they don't,' she said, amused. 'Run along. I'm not paying you to stand around talking.'

'No, miss. Will you give me the pennies now?'

'When you return,' she said. 'You'll find me at home, or at the gaol.'

He ran off, and having picked at a piece of bread and drunk a little ale, Louisa and her sisters joined the throng on the way to the gaol where they waited outside, while gentlemen of importance – representatives of the Revenue, the Mayor of Deal, witnesses, including the captain of the militia, the vicar – entered the building.

'What are they doing in there?' Grace asked after an hour had passed. 'It isn't right that they keep us in suspense.'

'Why don't you go home and fetch a stool?' Louisa suggested. 'We can take it in turns to sit down.' When Grace had left on her errand, she turned to Winnie who was looking more despondent than ever. 'I don't think it will be much longer before they allow us in.'

Another four hours went by. Not long after noon, the boy who'd delivered the letters found Louisa among the crowd, and having given her the message that Sir Flinders was away, took his payment and disappeared, before Mr Roebuck, who ran the gaol, came to announce that the men arrested the previous night would appear in front of the magistrates for a preliminary hearing.

It seemed as if the whole of Deal was trying to squeeze into the courtroom: friends, family and the curious had turned up to find out what was going to happen to the notorious free traders. They were all there except for the Feaseys and their gang, who must be preoccupied with hiding their spoils, Louisa thought bitterly as she sat beside Mr Witherall, elbow to elbow on one of the benches arranged around the perimeter of the courtroom.

The witnesses were being processed in an adjoining room, corralled by one of the guards as they made their marks or signed their statements, and a reporter for the local newspaper waited nearby, hoping to rake up some scandal.

'It's come to a pretty pass when a man can't go about his daily tasks, 'ovellin' and salvagin' without bein' arrested,' Mr Witherall observed.

There were general murmurings of agreement.

'All they found on the *Whimbrel* was 'alf an anker of genever.'

'And the rest,' somebody cut in.

'My son and 'is crew 'ave saved 'undreds of souls from the Sands – if there's any justice in this world, they'll be found innocent.'

When the prisoners were led inside, Louisa sat up straight, looking for Jason who was there at the head of the line, his arms cuffed and chained behind his back, his head held high and his shoulders straight. As he took his place in front of the magistrates, acknowledging her with a small smile, she noticed the bruise on his chin. Billy had been injured too, a bloody mark clearly visible across his chest through a rent in his shirt.

'I don't think I can bear this,' Winnie said, burying her face in her hands.

'It's One Eye and 'is men who should be on trial for betrayin' their fellows,' Mr Witherall said, and Louisa thought of Mrs Stickles and the information she had given her. Had she known it was wrong, or had One Eye deliberately fed her the lie, knowing she would tell the

Lennickers? She wasn't sure, but she wouldn't use her as their spy in future.

Reverend North introduced his associate, a second magistrate drafted in to replace Sir Flinders on the Bench, and perhaps an attempt to bring some impartiality to the hearing.

'Mr George Norris of Sholden,' he announced, and the gentleman beamed and nodded, apparently oblivious to the seriousness of the situation, the freedom of the free traders balanced on a knife-edge.

Louisa felt a sharp pain in her ribs as Grace nudged her.

'Is that *the* Mr Norris?' she whispered. 'Our cousin's fiancé?'

'I think it must be,' Louisa said, in wonder. Like their uncle, he looked florid and well fed, dressed smartly in riding clothes.

'Beth was right – he is very old,' Grace went on.

Louisa didn't care about his age, only that she didn't know whose side he was on.

'Where is Mr Trice?' she muttered. 'I can't see him.'

'Order!' The vicar brought the crowd to silence with a tap of his gavel, then promptly suspended the hearing for another hour, for examination of the evidence and witness statements. The prisoners were led out, and back in again at three o'clock in the afternoon, by which time Mr Trice had made his presence felt, demanding a desk for his clerk, a soft cushion for his seat, and the windows to be closed for the sake of his chest.

Louisa felt for the pistol, safely tucked into the garter secured to her leg, knowing she would never use it in anger, yet sorely tempted. Why should these men – the likes of the vicar and Mr Norris – pass judgement on the boatmen's fate? She thought she could trust Mr Trice to defend them, and the Reverend North to make a fair judgement, but what about Mr Norris? Could he be swayed to give a favourable verdict?

# Chapter Eleven

## *A Merry Dance*

As the temperature rose in the courtroom and the ladies fluttered their fans, the vicar read the charges made against the crew of the *Whimbrel*.

'On the night of the thirteenth of May in the year of eighteen hundred and twelve, the crew of the *Whimbrel*, captained by Mr Jason Witherall, was intercepted by the cutter *Guinevere*. In response, they fired at her in a dangerous manner with intent to cause injury to life.' Reverend North raised one hand to suppress the raised voices from the crowd. When they fell silent again, he continued. 'They were found in possession of illegally imported goods and a quantity on which duty had not been paid. Furthermore, they were observed attempting to hide the aforesaid goods, and then put up considerable resistance to arrest, occasioning a broken arm to Second Lieutenant Fox.'

He went on to introduce Jason, volunteer member of the Sea Fencibles, then followed with the rest of the alleged free traders.

'Mr William Fleet, crewman and owner of a twenty-fourth share in the same vessel …'

Reverend North called witnesses, and Louisa began to wonder if this was less a preliminary hearing, and more a proper trial.

The officer who was in charge of the *Guinevere* gave his version of events.

'These men – they lend what some have described as a predatory succour to the shipping caught on the Sands. Although they say they make their living from salvaging or "hovelling" as they call it, it doesn't tie up with the amount of assets some of them have stashed away.'

Mr Trice had been lying low, but now he leapt to his feet.

'This is your opinion, sir. We are here to judge the facts alone. On the basis of observation and speculation, I would suggest that these prisoners haven't twopenn'orth to rub together. Look at how their ragged jackets have been patched and re-patched.'

'You've made your point,' Reverend North said. 'Officer, do go on.'

'We were given information that the *Whimbrel* was carrying a quantity of French brandy, held in half-ankers, the kind of barrels that are peculiar to this sort of people.'

'You will name your source,' Mr Trice interrupted.

The officer turned to the magistrates. 'I've promised them complete discretion.'

'This revelation raises doubts over your informant's reliability and honesty. Do go on.'

'The lugger turned tail and led our cutter a merry dance, firing several shots across our bows. Having warned her to desist, she ignored us and proceeded to fire a second volley – she is armed with eleven brass guns, the *Guinevere* with twelve. I gave the order to fire back – we hit her once through the foremast, crippling her speed. When we came alongside her, she was remarkably higher in the water than she had been before, a fact I put down to much of her ballast having been apparently discarded.'

'Oh dear, officer.' Mr Trice shook his head gravely. 'Your statement doesn't hold water. It's all speculation – you have no proof of what the ballast you mention consists of.'

'The proof of it is over fifty per cent,' some wag said.

The officer wasn't having any of Mr Trice's nonsense. 'I set a boat to guard the area until daylight when my men made a search and found several tubs hidden underwater.'

'And did these tubs have any means of identification on them, any way of linking them to the *Whimbrel* and her crew who stand accused in the dock?'

'No sir, of course they didn't,' the officer said wearily.

'I believe then, this is another assumption that you make without evidence. It is essential to prove that these men were in possession of illegal goods. So far, your version of events is circumstantial.'

'Yes, yes, yes, quite right,' the vicar said. 'Please keep to the facts.'

'I have nothing more to say.' The officer retreated to the corner of the room, flushed and angry, as the Reverend North called for the next witness.

'Mr Jackson? What's he doing here?' Louisa whispered.

'I went up to 'is place this mornin' to drag him out of retirement,' Mr Witherall replied under his breath.

'I think you may be able to assist us, Mr Jackson,' the vicar began. 'Is this gentleman – Mr Jason Witherall – involved in smuggling, sir?'

'I 'ave 'eard that 'e is and that 'e isn't, so I don't rightly know what to say about it,' Mr Jackson said, all seriousness, until he gazed towards the audience, his eyes glinting with humour.

'You think yourself a clown, Mr Jackson? An entertainer of the people?' Mr Trice said.

'I've been told I can tell a merry tale,' he grinned.

With an almost imperceptible shake of the attorney's head, he fell silent.

'Thank you, Mr Jackson,' the vicar said. 'Mr Trice, what do you have to say on the matter of Mr Jason Witherall's character?'

'Hey, this isn't right,' the captain cut in. 'That gentleman is in the pay of these criminals.'

'He's being paid to offer advice on the finer points of the law?' Reverend North said.

'It's preposterous.'

'What is preposterous is the way you continue to persecute these poor men, Captain,' Mr Trice said, turning to his clerk who was screeving away at nineteen to the dozen. 'Strike that out and let me speak. I have a record of my association with the Witheralls going back nine years. I have advised them on various financial and legal matters, none of which are relevant to these proceedings.' He continued in a slow, long-winded way until Louisa wondered if he would bore the magistrates into giving a verdict of 'not guilty'.

He went through the ins and outs of what had happened on the night in question, concentrating on the fact that no contraband had been discovered on the *Whimbrel*, that the presence of the spare mast on the lugger only went to confirm the crew's story that they had been on the Sands all day, salvaging items from a wreck which had come to the surface with the change of the tide and winds. The half-anker of spirit found on board was for the use of the crew in such times as they required it for reviving persons whom they rescued in distress, to warm them and restore them to sensibility. He could call on Doctor Audley to provide a medical opinion on this matter, if they wished. The magistrates clearly didn't.

Louisa guessed that they didn't want to waste any more of their time than was necessary. The outcome of the hearing was not a foregone conclusion – the gentlemen and clergy of Deal might choose to demonstrate their contempt of those who broke the law. On the other hand, she doubted they would opt for giving up the luxuries that came their way, thanks to the free traders. 'What about the tubs that were found sunken under the water in the vicinity?' the vicar asked.

'There is no evidence that those had anything to do with the crew of the *Whimbrel*,' Mr Trice replied. 'There was, of course, another Deal lugger in the area at the time – the *Good Intent*.'

The vicar ignored Mr Trice's suggestion that the latter boat was responsible for the sunken tubs.

'Mr Witherall, what do you have to say?' He addressed Jason in the dock. 'How do you answer this allegation that you – as they say – sowed the crop?'

'I have no knowledge of it.' Jason cocked his head to one side, and Louisa wanted to remind him of his precarious position, but a trial away from being committed for hanging or transportation. 'The only crops I 'ave ever seen sowed are those on my uncle's farm: wheat for bread, peas and barley.'

'Mr Witherall, please keep to the point.' Mr Norris had been silent up until now, but as he spoke a ripple of laughter spread through the audience and Jason bowed deeply in apology.

'You tell 'em, my boy,' Louisa heard his father say, and the guards stepped closer to the prisoners as if afraid that they might be sprung from the courtroom.

'I will continue,' Jason said, loud and clear. 'The cutter – we didn't identify her as belongin' to the Revenue in the dark – took us by surprise, aimin' her guns at the *Whimbrel*. Not wishin' to see any injury to my men, or damage to the boat, I instructed my crew to fire a warning shot, then turn tail, not wishin' to be sittin' ducks for some foreign privateer.'

'You categorically deny having anything to do with this crime against the country, a crime that drains the coffers of England?' Mr Trice said.

'I have never sent a shillin' out of this nation in my life.'

Jason wasn't lying, Louisa thought, hiding a smile behind her hands. The free traders dealt only in coins of higher denominations.

'I would suggest that these officers, knowing of the Deal boatmen's reputation for both compassion and criminality, were biased and overzealous, determined to arrest them whether or not a crime had been committed.' Mr Trice polished the end of his silver cane to allow time for the message to sink in. 'I declare the imprisonment of the crew of the *Whimbrel* unlawful. Reverend North, Mr Norris, I rest my case.'

There were murmurs of agreement and dissent in the crowd.

'Anybody would think 'e was Lord Chancellor, the way 'e carries on,' someone said.

'All he wants is to see justice done,' Louisa countered quietly.

'Then why doesn't 'e go after One Eye? 'E should 'ave been tried for Righteous's murder.'

'And for what 'e done last night—'

'Whist! The magistrates are givin' their verdict.'

'Silence in court!' Reverend North smacked the gavel down hard. The audience shuffled and coughed. 'I declare, having considered the evidence—'

'You haven't consulted with Mr Norris yet,' the captain shouted, his face now a shade of beetroot.

'This is an outrage,' Officer Chase joined in.

The vicar's gavel sent out a volley of taps, reminding Louisa of the shots fired the night before.

'There is no case to answer,' the vicar said stubbornly. He turned to Mr Norris. 'You are in agreement, are you not?'

Mr Norris nodded. 'For convenience' sake, because I have left the kennelman looking after my favourite bitch while she's in whelp, I shall say that I concur. A man of the cloth is eminently more qualified when it comes to matters of the law, than a gentleman whose occupations can best be described as hunting, shooting and fishing.'

'This gentleman is impostrous. 'E's no magistrate – it's 'im who should be strung up,' Louisa heard one of the wives complain.

'Remember whose side we're on, Mrs Edwards,' she whispered. 'We are relying on Mr Norris's impartiality, and Mr Trice's ability to spin a web of confusion around the whole affair.'

Reverend North took to his feet, apparently unable to take any more.

'Give me strength, oh Lord,' he said, holding his hands up in supplication. 'I can confirm that Mr Norris does indeed hold the office of magistrate.'

'It doesn't matter who's who,' Mr Witherall said. 'All we want to know is when our boys can come 'ome – they've been deprived of a day's fishin'—'

'Guards, unchain them. Release them from their bonds,' the vicar shouted out to a great roar of delight. A few men and women fell to crying.

'It's the relief,' Winnie sobbed, but Louisa hardly heard her. Jason caught her eye and grinned – it was a gesture for her only, and it melted her heart. Could she dare believe that she had captured the affections of the bravest, most handsome and eligible young man in Deal? She smiled back, revelling in her triumph. Thanks to her foresight in sending for Mr Trice, the captain and crew of the *Whimbrel* were free to continue with their activities, making a living and saving lives.

Jason disappeared briefly, swept up by a throng who lifted him and his crew on to their shoulders, and carried them on to the street to noisy celebration. Louisa and her sisters followed.

'All is well as I told you it would be, Winnie,' she shouted above the din.

'All right. You don't have to remind me – you're such a wiseacre.' Winnie was laughing, her mood transformed.

As for the Revenue, they could only look on while the crowd clapped and cheered, and the vicar smiled, knowing he would receive his just reward.

'Miss Lennicker, a moment of your time …'

'Mr Trice?' She turned, sensing the pressure of a hand on her arm, and the scent of stale musk.

'Excuse me, ladies. I wish to speak with your sister.' He bowed to Winnie and Grace, and Louisa followed him to the corner of the street where his driver and bodyguard stood waiting beside the phaeton for him.

'I'm very grateful for what you've done for the boatmen,' she began.

'I don't do it out of the goodness of my heart, but for the benefit of the trade that keeps so many in clover. My clients depend on these able gentlemen to carry on with their business. However, as I've said before, every second, every minute of my time must be charged for, and as you initiated the request for my services, I am obliged to invoice you.'

She hadn't thought too much about how she was going to raise the money – she would have given anything to get Jason and the crew freed – but now the implications of what she'd done by involving Mr Trice in the matter, started to sink in.

'I've heard that you failed to meet with my agent at the Three Kings last night.'

'You know why – the goods have gone missing. They've been lost or stolen.'

'It makes no difference to me – I shall have my dues, no matter what. Good day, Miss Lennicker. I trust we shall meet again soon.'

She could only nod, her mouth dry, her words of protest caught in the back of her throat, as she watched him spring into the phaeton and order his driver to proceed.

'Is everything all right, Louisa?' With a start, she turned to find Mrs Witherall at her side.

'All's well, thank you,' she replied. 'At least, we have our men back, if not our goods.'

'Our men?' Mrs Witherall tipped her head slightly to one side, her expression teasing.

'Billy, I mean, and the rest of the crew.' Louisa's attempt at deliberately misunderstanding Mrs Witherall's question was betrayed by the rush of heat spreading across her cheeks.

'And my son, Marlin?'

'Of course.'

'He's a good lad,' Mrs Witherall went on. ''E 'ad that little bit of trouble with … the other young lady, but it wasn't 'is fault. They weren't meant for each other, and it was for the best that they found out before it was too late.'

'I don't think it's any of my concern,' Louisa said.

'You may be right, but I don't like anybody thinkin' badly of 'im. You'll understand one day, when you're a mother. You always want the best for your children, no matter 'ow old they are.' Mrs Witherall looked past her. 'Where are you goin'? 'Aven't you 'ad enow trouble for one day?' she called after the men who were marching away, dishevelled after their night's imprisonment, but determined.

'They're going to 'ave it out with the Rattlers.' Mrs Roper, with one child in her arms and two at her feet, was following them as the crowd began to chant, 'Fight, fight, fight.'

'This is madness,' Louisa said. 'They'll be back in gaol before you can say Jack Robinson.'

'They'll be killed,' Winnie wailed.

'They can make just as good account of themselves as the Rattlers can,' Mrs Edwards said confidently from nearby. 'It should be quite a scrap.'

'Oh no, I can't watch,' Grace said. 'Somebody will get shot, like Pa ...'

'Oh dear, oh dear,' Mrs Roper said. 'I don't want to watch neither, but I 'ave to keep an eye on my 'usband and make sure 'e doesn't do nothin' stupid.'

Louisa didn't want any part of it, but she needed to know that Jason and Billy were safe. To that end, she hurried after them with her sisters and Mrs Witherall to the Rattling Cat where the commotion had brought One Eye and Isaiah outside. They stood side by side, arms folded, as the constable staggered up behind them. Louisa recognised him as the one who'd lied about the altercation between her father and One Eye.

'What do we 'ave 'ere then?' One Eye said. 'I thought you lot 'ad been taken off the streets ...'

'We're free men, no case to answer.' Jason stepped forward with Billy at his side. Mr Witherall joined them.

'Why did you do it, after all those years when we worked alongside each other without argument?' Mr Witherall asked.

'I've done nothin'.' One Eye shrugged.

'You've done us out of our goods. You set the Revenue on to us. Well, I'm warnin' you – we won't be gulled again.'

'What can you do, old man?' One Eye interrupted. 'You've never 'ad the guts to make a real go of the trade. You're too soft.' He caught sight of Louisa and stared, before continuing, 'You're weak, like a woman, and no good for anythin'.'

'Take that back.' Mr Witherall tried to move closer, but Jason barred his way.

'Leave it. He isn't worth it.'

'Oh, it's worth everything – I'll 'ave 'im. I'll tear his 'eart out of his chest and rip the flesh from 'is bones for what 'e's done to us, and for Righteous. We all know who done for 'im.' Mr Witherall spat at his adversary.

'Leave off 'im,' Isaiah shouted. 'Look at you, Marlin. Why are you always downwind of your father? Don't tell me. You're scared.'

'Fart catcher!' One Eye mocked.

'Leave this to me.' His eyes flashing with anger, Jason pushed his father aside, then turned on Isaiah, grabbing him by his shirt.

'You came here lookin' for a fight?' Isaiah growled. 'Well, you've got one, and you'd better watch yourself because you've really set up my bristles.'

The rapturous crowd shrieked and shouted for blood as the two men stepped apart and stripped to the waist. They glared at each other, sizing each other up. Louisa felt sick as Billy egged Jason on, and one of the boatmen, seeing an opportunity, went around with paper and pencil, taking bets on who would win.

'Fight, fight, fight!' The audience closed in, a circle of baying hounds waiting for the kill.

Isaiah feinted on his toes, then ducked back.

'Lily-livered coward!' somebody yelled. 'What do you think you're doin'? I've put good money on you.'

Jason charged towards his opponent, head down, but Isaiah dodged him, making the crowd roar with laughter and frustration, but the second time, Jason made contact, grabbing Isaiah around the waist and throwing him to the ground. They pummelled and kicked, wrestling for their reputations, if not their lives, Louisa thought, fearing that Jason would suffer a permanent injury.

'Agh! You bit me!' Jason swore aloud.

Louisa held her breath as his body tensed, his skin glistening with sweat, his muscles rippling. With a growl of anger, he twisted and turned on his opponent and caught him in a headlock, pulling him by the hair. Isaiah kicked wildly but to no avail.

'I could finish you right now,' Jason hissed.

'No. Stop this!' Mrs Witherall appeared from around the corner of the street with a bucket. Having pushed through the crowd, she threw the contents over the two men, who froze, then slowly disentangled themselves and stood up. Isaiah shook the water from his hair and a solitary sprat fell at his feet. Jason grimaced, as the stench of rotting fish mingled with the metallic scent of blood. He was bleeding from his nose, Isaiah from a cut on his temple.

Mrs Witherall wagged her finger at them.

'You scrap like two little boys on the beach, you pair of caper-wits. Move on, everyone. The show's over. There's nothin' to see.'

'What did you do that for?' Jason said.

'Go 'ome before you ruin your looks,' Mrs Witherall scolded.

One Eye started to laugh, a deep and raucous laugh from the depths of his belly.

'I'm not scared of you, or anyone,' she addressed him. 'You've destroyed any goodwill there used to be between us.'

'I don't want your goodwill,' One Eye sneered, 'just as many of your men who will join me in my free-tradin' operations.'

'Who will join you and your band of thieves and liars?' Jason stepped in. 'You're a cheater, an ivory tuner of the worst sort.'

'Ha ha. That's the pot calling the kettle black.'

'I told you to go 'ome, son,' Mrs Witherall said. 'One Eye, you are a disgrace! And you who stand there watchin' are no better, 'opin' to make a few bob out of it.'

'Well said!' Mrs Roper shouted, and the other wives began to murmur their support while the crowd drifted away. 'The power 'as gone to One Eye's head. Like a little Boneyparte, he thinks he's the Emperor of Deal.'

Jason put his shirt back on and the Rattlers retreated to the inn.

'Where do you think you're goin' now?' Mrs Witherall said, as Jason, Billy and the rest of the *Whimbrel*'s crew reassembled and began to swagger along the road.

'Louisa, come with us,' Winnie called. 'We're going to the Waterman's Arms.'

Allowing herself to be whisked away to join the celebrations, Louisa resolved to put her troubles to the back of her mind, at least until morning.

# Chapter Twelve

## *All Honour to the Brave*

'I thought we'd 'ad it back there in that courtroom.' Billy raised a tankard of ale as the three sisters sat with him and Jason in the room above the bar at the Waterman's Arms, where there was hardly space to move for the crowds that descended to join in the drinking, music and dancing. 'I'll be eternally grateful to that Trice fellow – 'e spoke like a charm. And you knew exactly 'ow to answer whatever was put to you, Marlin.' Billy gazed at Jason, a faithful dog to his master.

'I did what I 'ad to do.' There was a crust of blood at Jason's nostril and he smelled of brine and spice, his men having thrown several buckets of seawater over him and sprayed him with cologne to mask the aroma of fish.

''E's a mother's boy,' Master Roper said, overhearing their conversation.

'I'm honoured to have such a mother. Everybody needs somebody who has their back.' He looked at Louisa. 'Isn't that right, Miss Lennicker?'

She nodded.

'More ale?' Billy asked him.

'No, thank you. I want to keep a clear 'ead,' he smiled. 'You 'ave another, though, as long as you're fit for work in the mornin'. We're takin' a pilot out to the *Mullion*, weather and tide permittin'.'

'What about the Rattlers? What are we going to do about 'em? They can't be allowed to keep gettin' away with it.'

'They'll have their just deserts in time.' Jason glanced towards Louisa again. 'I'll make sure of it.'

'I can't 'elp thinkin' of the goods – our goods – stuck in the warehouse under lock and key. Do you think we could 'ave a go at retrievin' 'em?' Billy asked.

'I don't think it's wise,' Jason said. 'We've already had our heads above the parapet – we might not be so lucky if we get caught sailin' close to the wind for a second time.'

Billy sat back and continued drinking while Louisa and her sisters danced. He drank until he could barely stand.

'I don't like to see it,' Louisa said aside to Winnie and Grace. 'Pa would have boxed his ears.'

'Let him enjoy himself – there's no harm in it,' Winnie said, but Louisa wasn't convinced. Their father would have disapproved – he said that drink addled the head, and Billy was proof of that as Winnie and Grace helped him home later. Louisa walked back along the shore behind them with Jason at her side.

'I saw Mr Trice talking to you,' he said. 'What did he want?'

'He was passing the time of day, and reminding me that he'll soon be sending his clerk to collect his dues.' She didn't say which dues, not wanting to reveal the Lennickers' business and her private shame.

'That means he'll be after us as well.' Jason rubbed the back of his neck as he stopped on the shingle.

'You go ahead,' Louisa called, noticing how Winnie and Grace lingered with Billy, waiting for her to catch up.

'All right. We know when we aren't wanted.'

Louisa heard them giggling as they headed in the direction of Cockle Swamp Alley, then the sound of the stones shifting beneath Jason's feet. The carousing had stopped, and the waves were washing back and forth gently below them.

'I thought I'd never get you alone,' he murmured.

'I can't understand why you'd want to,' she said, trying to make light of it in case she was mistaken, her hopes about to be cruelly dashed.

'Because I like you.' His tone betrayed an awkwardness which she found touching, a contrast to his usual confidence. 'I like you very much. I didn't think I could fall for you … not after …' She knew what he was referring to – the incident with the *Curlew* when they almost lost their lives on the Sands. 'But I find that when I'm with you, I can't take my eyes off you, and when I'm not with you, I can't stop thinking about you …'

'Jason, that's …' She bit her lip.

'You're thinking this is too soon, after Margaret? Let me tell you, that was calf love. I don't feel anything for her now and I'm glad she jilted me, because I'm free to be with you, if you'd like that …' He blundered on. 'Are you already spoken for? If you are, forgive me.'

'No, I'm not,' she said quickly. 'And you can trust me – we aren't all the same.'

'You aren't a flibbertigibbet,' he smiled. 'I know that.'

They looked at each other in silence as the half-moon, lying in its navy hammock, shone down, reflected in Jason's eyes.

'I don't know what to say next,' he began. 'I would go and ask your father for his permission, if I could … I want to go about this the right way.'

'What is it that you're asking?' she said, trembling.

'For your hand. Louisa, would you do me the honour of becomin' my wife?' When she hesitated, he went on, 'A yes or a no will do. Of course, I'd much rather the former than the latter.'

'Then I will say yes, gladly.' More than gladly, she thought, as he took her hands and bowed his head towards her.

'Ah, no kissing. Not yet.'

With a wry smile, he released her. 'Next time, then?'

'Maybe.' She took a step back, not wanting to leave him, but knowing something of the principles of flirting from the gossips on the beach, and her sisters' chatter.

'We are promised to each other,' he confirmed. 'Now we can walk out together openly.'

'You haven't asked me to marry you merely to aid your pursuit of the free trade?' she said, suddenly plunged into doubt.

He smiled. 'No, Louisa. I proposed because ... not because I want to spend the rest of my life with you, but because I can't imagine spendin' even a moment without you.'

'Oh, Jason.' Her heart missed a beat and then another, until she wondered if she might faint.

'I promise you I'll be the best husband I can be. Whatever you want or need, I'll bring it home for you. Whenever I'm out on the boat, I'll be thinkin' of you.'

He seemed so happy, so carried away in the moment, that she didn't like to bring him back down to earth, but it had to be done. He appeared to have forgotten that there were difficulties.

'Will it be a long engagement? I am not yet twenty-one and I can't marry without a guardian's permission. Unfortunately, my father didn't foresee the need to appoint someone to take his place.' She already knew that her uncle wouldn't do, not having been given the required legal standing. Not that it mattered, because Mr Laxton would never approve the union of his niece and a Deal boatman.

'How old are you now?'

'I'm nineteen, but I will be twenty very soon. There, you will change your mind.'

'It doesn't make any difference to my feelin's – we will have to wait a full year and a bit, that's all. It won't be easy – I'm not known for my patience.' He grinned. 'You see, we both have our faults.'

As he walked her home, they agreed to keep their betrothal private for now, though Louisa thought she would have to tell her sisters.

'I'll call for you tomorrow,' he said, as she wished him goodnight and closed the door. She took a moment to revel in her good fortune before finding Winnie and Grace in the kitchen.

'Have you put Billy to bed?' she asked.

'He's fast asleep,' Winnie said. 'What happened with Jason? Billy said he was going to ask you something.'

'Are you going to get married?' Grace blurted out.

'My goodness, you are terribly mistaken,' Louisa said. 'He wanted to have a word with me about the Rattlers.'

'No?' Grace said, disappointed. 'That's a pity.'

'He's told me – in a roundabout way – that he has no interest in me.'

'I'm sorry,' Winnie exclaimed. 'We thought – never mind. Why are we Lennickers always down on our luck? What have we done to deserve all this?'

Louisa couldn't contain herself any longer.

'I'm giving you a taste of your own medicine, my dear sisters.' Her cheeks ached from smiling.

'What are you saying?' Grace said, jumping up and down.

'We are promised to each other.'

'You have set your cap at him,' Winnie laughed.

'No, he threw his handkerchief at me and I'm the happiest woman alive, knowing that the boldest and bravest of the boatmen is going to be my husband.'

'Do you love him? Tell me that you do,' Grace said.

'I don't know yet.' She could hardly admit to herself that she didn't understand what love was, having found out that the marriage between her mother and father had been based on the sands of deceit, not the solid rock of romantic affection. 'I think it's something I'll have to learn.'

'When is the wedding?' Winnie asked. 'Tell me that it's soon.'

'I shall marry him when I turn twenty-one.' It was a long time to wait, but it gave her time to restore the Lennickers' fortunes, undo her obligation to Mr Trice, and get used to the idea of becoming Mrs Jason Witherall.

Slipping out of bed the following morning, Louisa checked her appearance in the mirror on the dressing table. She looked well. For a fleeting moment, her heart welled up with joy, until she remembered that she had to face her customers to let them know that she couldn't fulfil their orders. If she didn't turn up, dangling the promise that she would bring the goods at a later date, they would soon find other suppliers to step into her shoes.

Grace and Winnie accompanied her, and they called on Mr Gigg who was more concerned with the recent announcement of the murder of the Prime Minister than the fact that she had no lace for him.

'He was shot in the chest in the lobby of the House of Commons by a merchant who had a grudge. That man will be hanged by the end of the week. I apologise for speaking of it, ladies, but it's in all the papers: the *Morning Herald* and *The Times*,' he went on.

Louisa decided not to call at Limepit Acres, her sisters having been traumatised enough by Mr Gigg's talk of murder.

'It's best to let sleeping dogs lie – Beth won't mind if she doesn't have lace for her dress, but Aunt Mary will be very upset,' Winnie conceded.

'It's a long walk in this heat too,' Grace observed.

'And I owe our uncle for the last few weeks' worth of provisions,' Louisa said glumly. 'I'm afraid that he'll stop supplying us soon.'

'Cheer up,' Winnie said. 'When you marry Jason, you'll never find yourself on the rocks. He was going to buy a house, but he didn't go ahead with it after Margaret … well, you know all about that.'

'I'm not marrying him for his money.'

'You must acknowledge that it adds to the attraction, though,' Grace teased.

'That's enough,' Louisa said sharply. 'I don't want to hear any more about it.'

'Leave her alone,' Winnie advised.

'I'm sorry,' Grace said.

Louisa wished that she hadn't spoken severely, but the realisation that she hadn't yet been completely honest with Jason about Mr Trice and the extent of the Lennickers' problems, had begun to prey on her mind. And the sight of the Misses Flinders arriving on foot at Compass Cottage just as they arrived home, did nothing to improve her mood.

She showed them into the parlour. Miss Flinders was wearing a walking dress in lavender with a coordinating velvet pelisse. Her younger sister was dressed in a riding habit and hat.

'I'm afraid you've had a wasted journey – the delivery of the lace you ordered has been delayed on its way from France.'

'Oh, that is a shame,' Miss Flinders said.

'It is a matter of deep regret to me.' Louisa bowed her head. 'However, it is a situation for which the remedy is out of my hands.'

'What will you do about your trousseau, Honora?' Miss Marianne said crossly, reminding Louisa of a spoilt child.

'Miss Lennicker has just explained that it can't be helped,' Miss Flinders said.

'How will you do without it?' Miss Marianne pouted.

'There will be another delivery in a while,' Louisa said.

'Then I will hope that it arrives in time for our wedding. I'm ashamed to admit that I've led rather a sheltered existence, but I'm beginning to see that there is more to life than lace and jewels. We can never be sure when my fiancé will be called away to serve our country overseas.'

'You must tell them, they can't have him,' her sister said.

'That would be an act of cowardice on all our parts.' Miss Flinders smiled. 'I hope we may continue our association in future, Miss Lennicker. We wish you good day.'

Optimistic that she hadn't lost all her customers, Louisa looked forward to seeing Jason that evening, but he didn't turn up, and neither did Billy.

'He'll be fair gut-founded by now,' Winnie said. 'He's always back in time for supper.'

'They must have gone out with the *Whimbrel*,' Louisa said, and they went down to the beach, finding a crowd waiting at the top of the slope. Mrs Witherall was sitting on a chair, knitting a sock, while her husband surveyed the sea through his spyglass.

'The *Whimbrel* still 'asn't come back,' Mrs Witherall said, looking up

'Don't fret, my darlin',' Mr Witherall said. 'There's nothin' to worry about – she's gone to the aid of the *Polestar*.

I don't know 'ow she's done it on such a fine day, but she's run on to the bank and broken 'er back, by all accounts.'

'On whose account, in particular?' Louisa asked, recalling with a shudder how quickly the tide could rise up and swallow a stranded ship.

'We should go home,' Grace said. 'We can't do anything here.'

'I'm going to wait a little longer,' Louisa said, praying that everyone would return safely.

'I'll stay too,' Winnie said. 'I won't sleep until I know they're back.'

Grace remained on the beach with them, sitting at the top of the slope, looking out to the horizon and the brown stain in the sea: the Sands shrinking as the tide came in and the water like beaten copper burnished by the setting sun.

Some of the women made a small fire: others went to fetch fresh mackerel and bread, and to buy ale. Sitting around the flames, they sang of the Valiant Sailor, longing to return to his Polly on the shore. When the last words, 'And here I lie a-bleeding all on the deck and it's all for her sweet safety I must die,' faded, a shout went up.

'She's on 'er way back!'

'Hooray!'

A lump caught in Louisa's throat as the *Whimbrel*, her canvas fully set, came riding across the waves.

The crew beached the lugger, and the men and boys hauled her up with the capstan. The sailors who disembarked seemed subdued, talking in Dutch, Louisa guessed from having heard a little of the language spoken around Deal.

Jason organised his crew to unload the cargo they'd salvaged from the wreck: sails, rolled up; two hefty anchors; the ship's wheel and bell; trunks and beckets.

'Ah, Louisa.' His eyes lit up when he saw her. 'What's everyone doin' here?'

'We were worried when Billy didn't come back for his supper.'

He raised one eyebrow. 'I have no idea why – we always come back safe and sound. Would you mind takin' an inventory for the Collector of Customs and his deputy? I want this all done before he sends his men down here.'

The collector who was responsible for the warehouse and communicating with the Board of Customs in London, would put tidesmen on board to check that all the salvaged items were unloaded.

'You are asking for a true account of what you've brought back?' she asked, to be clear.

'Of course.' He winked as he handed her some crumpled paper and a pencil.

Walking across to Billy, who was standing beside a trunk, she began to take notes.

'Is there anything in that one?' she asked him.

He opened it and picked up a bag.

'Coins,' he said with a grin, 'and a bottle of cologne of some kind. No, don't write that down. This box is empty.' He tipped the contents into a cask. 'Only write one anchor down – Marlin says that's 'ow you stop it looking suspicious. You'll 'ave to mention the mast – that's 'ard to 'ide.'

'Won't the collector come down to inspect?'

''E's more than 'appy to receive the odd gift now and then in exchange for turnin' a blind eye. It's only when the 'igh-ups in London put pressure on 'im that he starts causin' us trouble. It's our right to make a bit extra from sellin' the rest. We risk our lives out in the Sands while 'e and 'is staff sit warm and dry in their office.'

'Well said,' Jason commented, overhearing him. 'This is our insurance, a nest egg to support our families should we meet our Maker the next time we go out. It's our tradition.'

'I thought you said that you always came back safe and sound,' Louisa pointed out.

'There are exceptions,' he admitted. 'My grandfather died out in the roadstead, and we lost old Oakley overboard that time.'

'And Nip when 'e broke 'is 'ead,' Billy added.

'You can never be sure when your time is up – when you're onshore, you can be run over by a carriage, or thrown from a horse.'

'You aren't making me feel any better,' Louisa said, half smiling as she returned to the inventory. When she had completed it, she gave it back to Jason.

'I'm sorry about being late,' he said. 'I was goin' to call on you. How about tomorrow?'

'Tomorrow,' she agreed.

'Now, I have to trawl the town to find food and rooms for these men. They've offered to pay handsomely for their rescue.'

'Goodnight,' she said.

'Goodnight to you too, Louisa ...'

She made her way back to her sisters who were watching, all agog.

'What are you staring at?' she said lightly, before they made their way home.

It was Louisa's idea to take the *Curlew* out on a provisioning trip as cover for finding the crop that the crew of the *Whimbrel* had sown. Jason had agreed, offering them a percentage of whatever they managed to bring back. Billy went with them and they trawled the area north of the Sands in the hot June sunshine, but Louisa was more preoccupied with other concerns than looking out for marks.

She and Jason had met three times since his hovelling trip to rescue the crew of the *Polestar*. They had walked along the cliffs and he had given her a tiny stoppered glass bottle of perfume taken from the wreck. She had opened it and breathed in the delicate scent of what he told her was wild myrtle and neroli, then closed it again, unable to bring herself to wear it because she felt like a traitor, not telling him of the worries that tormented her. The longer she left it, the more of an obstacle it became. They talked affectionately to each other, made plans for the next run, and – when nobody was looking – even held hands and snatched a few kisses, but speaking of the problem of Mr Trice and the Lennickers' debts seemed insurmountable.

'I can't see anything but seaweed and rocks.' Winnie dragged the five-pronged creeping iron along behind the *Curlew*. Apart from snagging an old lobster pot, she had no luck until Louisa spotted a mark: a piece of wood, floating but seemingly fixed in the water.

'What do you think of that?' she asked, pointing.

'It looks promising.' Grace steered the boat in closer as Billy trimmed the canvas.

Winnie lengthened the rope on the creeping iron, and they did another trawl, dragging it along the bottom.

'Ah, I've caught a monster.' Winnie grinned as the rope tightened. 'Billy, give me a hand, will you?' They hauled their catch up together, bringing a half-anker to the surface, followed by a second and a third.

Not for the first time, Louisa noticed how close they seemed, how Billy reached past her sister and rested his hand on her arm. It was a fleeting gesture, but enough to arouse her suspicion. Billy was their lodger, not a prospective husband. He was especially fond of Winnie – he always had been – but she was sure it hadn't been Pa's intention for them to marry. She was fond of Billy herself – in fact, she thought of him as a brother – but he liked his drink too much for Louisa's liking, coming across as happy-go-lucky and irresponsible, while her sister was serious and caring. She wasn't sure they were suited.

Resolving to have a word with Winnie later, she continued looking for marks until Grace spotted the *Guinevere* slipping out from between an East Indiaman and a naval cruiser in the Downs as though she'd been lying in wait.

'What shall we do?' Billy said, panicking. 'You can't 'ide an 'alf-anker under your petticoats.'

'Much as it pains me to do it, we'll have to throw them back overboard,' Winnie said.

Louisa thought quickly. If the Revenue caught them with the tubs in their possession, they would have reason to arrest and charge them with smuggling. If they dropped them back in the sea, they would lose them anyway.

'Shoot one of the nets,' she said, and Winnie and Billy hurriedly rolled the tubs into it and lowered them over the side. They were only just in time.

'Good day, ladies. We meet again. I never forget a pretty face.'

'Officer Groves ...' Louisa searched inside the chest they kept aft of the mast for the paperwork, the documents registering ownership of the boat.

'Your name, miss?'

'Miss Lennicker.' The *Curlew* rocked as she handed over the papers.

'All seems to be in order,' the officer said, handing them back. 'What trades do you follow?'

She didn't like the way he stared at her through narrowed eyes.

'Fishing and provisioning – we make our living from the sea.'

'What do you fish for?' With a smirk, he looked down into the net. 'Tubs, I see.'

'What can I do? We can't help it if we catch them in our nets.'

'To whom do they belong?'

'I don't rightly know, sir,' she said, holding her nerve. 'We shot the net, hoping for herring and a few dabs, and there they were, floating up to the top.'

'That was a bit of luck.' He gazed at the creeping iron that Winnie had left lying on the boards. 'For me, anyway, because now I can relieve you of your unwanted catch.'

'Of course,' Louisa said smoothly, suppressing the urge to rant and curse like a man. After all their trouble, they'd gone and lost the crop for good.

'I wouldn't mind wagering on finding a few more of those around here,' the officer smiled. 'Haul them in.'

Red-faced, Winnie helped Billy drag the tubs and net on to the *Curlew*, before the officer helped himself and left them to it, but they couldn't carry on with the *Guinevere* hovering nearby, watching their every move.

'As soon as we leave, they'll come and seize the rest.' Louisa blinked hard – she could have cried.

'It's a terrible pity, but worse things 'appen at sea,' Billy said.

'There's nothing worse than this – we have to pay for the goods we lose.'

'The United States 'ave declared war on us – what do you think of that?' he countered. 'The press will be out and about with a vengeance, and there won't be any men left to carry on the free trade. I'd say that's a lot worse.'

'You're right – it's a dreadful thought,' she admitted, feeling contrite, but with the prospect of having to pay Mr Trice for the goods they'd missed out on, she could see how men might be persuaded to join the navy and run away to sea.

'We can't stay 'ere all day,' Billy said. 'What are my orders?'

'To go around the Downs and sell what we have left,' she answered, and they set sail again, slowly making their way amongst the shipping until the crew of a merchant brig hailed them over. Louisa assumed that it was the purser who spoke to them.

'What are you selling, ladies?'

'The finest Bohea tea,' Grace sang out. 'Handpicked from the mountainsides of China.'

'Didn't we buy some from you before?'

'I don't think so.'

'Oh yes, we did. The previous batch didn't last for more than a single brew – it was weak and full of dust,' the man complained.

'That's a mark of its superior quality,' Louisa said. 'It has the delicate aroma and pale coloration much sought after by the gentry of Dover and Sandwich.'

'I don't think you know what you're talking about.' The purser looked down his nose at them. 'The leaves had been cut with something else. It didn't look like tea, nor did it taste like it.'

'It is an acquired taste that suits a more sophisticated palate than yours, sir,' Grace said, and Louisa wondered where she'd conjured up her sales pitch from. She smiled to herself – her youngest sister could sell anything: tea to China, if she needed to, while poor Winnie was too honest. 'I should forgo a purchase this time,' Grace advised. 'Why waste your money on something you can't appreciate? We have a limited quantity of tea from souchong, if you would prefer that?'

Louisa gave Winnie a glance. Their aunt had had the last of the China tea in return for a discount on the produce they received from Limepit Acres.

'How do I know it isn't cut with anything else?'

'Because it came straight off an East Indiaman this very morning,' Grace said, keeping a straight face. 'It'll be gone by tomorrow.'

'I'd better have some then.'

'You won't regret it.' Having taken his money, Grace handed over a packet of tea, the remainder of the fresh bread they had on board, and a crate of greens, before moving on.

'I don't like cheating people – it goes against my nature,' Winnie said.

'Everyone does it,' Louisa pointed out. 'How can anyone make a living without stretching the truth from time to time?'

'We've done the purser a good turn. Tea made too strong is disadvantageous to the body – it stains the teeth and stops you sleeping.' Grace giggled as Winnie's frown deepened.

'If you really don't like it, you can stay at home,' Louisa suggested.

'Oh no,' Winnie said hastily. 'You need somebody to stop you getting yourselves into bother.'

Louisa only hoped that Winnie was equally fastidious about keeping herself out of trouble.

'There's another tub,' Billy hissed. 'Over there, bobbin' about.'

It was a wonder that none of the crews on the other boats had spotted it, and it wasn't long before it was safely stowed under a blanket beside Grace's feet, but when they reached the cottage, they were disappointed.

'Lemons! Hundreds of them!' Winnie exclaimed as Billy jemmied the lid off, being unable to knock the spile out of the barrel.

'What are we going to do with them?' Grace said.

'Sell what we can and pickle the rest for ourselves. There's always a demand.'

Louisa counted twelve lemons, rather battered and bruised, scraped them with a piece of broken glass then cut them part way into quarters. She poured in as much salt as each one would take, rubbed them and strewed more salt over the top before placing them in an earthenware dish.

'Those need turning every day for three days, Grace,' she said, putting them away on a shelf in the pantry.

'Why should I do it? I've got to go to the chandler's yet.'

'Don't waste money we haven't got on candles – buy tallow so we can make rushlights.' Louisa changed the subject. 'Have you noticed how close Winnie and Billy are?'

'I've seen how they are always laughing and giggling together, and how she keeps giving him the biggest piece of fish and the pick of the baby turnips? Yes, I have, but I think she's keeping him sweet, so he'll stay. We depend on him, Louisa. I'm not stupid – he pays rent, skippers the boat, fetches and carries …'

'He does make himself useful,' she agreed. 'But I wouldn't say we depend on him – we could do everything ourselves if we had to.'

'Billy's like part of the furniture – I can't imagine him not being around, and he's been good to Winnie, especially.' Grace paused. 'You don't think there's more to it?'

'No,' Louisa said quickly, too quickly for Grace not to notice.

'You do, don't you? Do you think he's going to marry her?'

'Of course he isn't. They're too young, and Billy's too ...' Irresponsible, she was going to say, but she bit her tongue. 'Don't say anything to Winnie – she'll be annoyed if she finds out we've been talking about her behind her back.'

Louisa did have a word with her, though, when Billy had gone out drinking and Grace was in the kitchen dipping the piths from a handful of rushes into molten tallow. Noticing that Winnie had rushed out to the privy for the third time that evening, she waited for her in the yard, idly pulling weeds from the patch of ground where Ma used to tease the earth into life, magicking up sweet peas, marigolds, runner beans and marrows.

'You aren't well?' she said as Winnie reappeared, her brow beaded with sweat. 'I heard you casting up your accounts.'

'I must have eaten a bad egg.'

'I'll fetch you some ale.'

'No, I couldn't. Thank you. Don't fuss, Louisa. A few minutes in the fresh air and I'll be as right as ninepins.'

Louisa looked around to check that nobody was listening. Their neighbours' windows were shut and all was quiet, apart from the sound of horses trotting along the nearby roads, and the shouts of the Sea Fencibles on drill on the beach.

'You know it isn't right that you encourage Billy,' she began.

'I don't know what you mean.' Winnie's eyes glittered. 'I miss Pa, that's all. And so does he.'

'As long as you remember that he's our lodger.' Giving her a long stare, Louisa recalled how Aunt Mary had spoken to their father and felt sorry that she was having to lecture her sister in a similar tone. 'It affects you, me and Grace—'

'You, you mean? I can't believe how selfish you're being.'

'Selfish?' Her brow tightened.

'You've changed since you and Jason got engaged. It's like you've forgotten that both our parents lie dead!'

'How dare you!'

'You go around with that silly smile on your face, and then you tell me I can't be friends with Billy, just because you're worried about what Jason will think. Jason this, Jason that. And it isn't even a proper engagement – you have to have your father's permission to marry when you're not yet twenty-one.'

'That's unfair!'

'It's the truth,' Winnie said stubbornly. 'Billy's one of us, an honorary Lennicker. Now, stop poking your nose into my business and leave me alone. Go away,' she added when Louisa hesitated.

Louisa returned indoors, cut to the quick, because she suspected that her sister was lying. Winnie had made a point of quoting Aunt Mary's advice that they needed to protect their reputations by making sure they had a chaperone present whenever they went out and about, and then used it as a cover to go out with Billy. It was clear that Winnie wasn't going to admit to anything. All she could do was keep a closer eye on her, making sure she sent Grace with her when she went to help Billy.

# Chapter Thirteen

## *A Man We Want and a Man We Must Have (Naval Cry)*

At the end of the month of July, Mr Trice called at Compass Cottage.

'I was expecting Mr Mellors,' Louisa said coldly, wishing she'd known in advance of his visit so she could have made herself scarce.

'I thought to come and inspect my assets in person. May I come in?' Without waiting for her answer, he pushed past her and went straight into the parlour. He stood in front of the chaise where she and Jason had sat up together the night before while Grace sewed, and Winnie – being worn out – was in bed.

'Will you take a seat?'

'Not at present, thank you. The merchants are impatient for their money – there's a limit to how far they are willing to extend their credit. However, I have received information that there will be another shipment coming your way, if you are intending to continue in the honourable trade.' Smiling disagreeably, he went on, 'Rumour has it that you are maintaining a close association with the free traders of Deal.

'I see that this observation has taken you by surprise, but you have to understand that it's my duty to discover every detail. A little knowledge is a dangerous thing, Miss Lennicker. One requires the whole picture, and to that end, I employ many sets of eyes and ears in the inns and capstan grounds, and at the dockside in Dunkirk and Gravelines. But I digress.' He looked at her expectantly.

'I can make a part payment.' Her voice quavered, betraying her nerves. Flustered and angry for showing weakness, she excused herself to fetch the money she'd collected a few days before in readiness for his clerk's arrival. It was nowhere near enough, but it was all that she could scrape together.

'Here you are, Mr Trice.' She handed it over to him in a small box; he counted it out on the table, then without asking, wrapped a chain around the box and padlocked it. The bodyguard who had been waiting outside, was called by Mr Trice and told to remove the box and take it to the phaeton.

Thinking that giving up the box in addition to the money was a fair exchange, she began to breathe a sigh of relief, but he hadn't finished.

'Are your sisters at home?' he asked. 'And your lodger?'

She was about to tell him the truth, but instead she said, 'My sisters are in the hang.'

'That's strange – the evidence would suggest not. I smell no smoke.' He smirked. 'I know you're lying – I saw them pushing a handcart towards the market when my man dropped me off at the corner. As for Master Fleet, he was on his way to the capstan grounds. It seems to me that this is the ideal opportunity for us to become more ... intimately acquainted.'

'Please, give me another few weeks and I'll make sure you receive your money, every penny.' A pulse began to throb at her temple as she watched Mr Trice close the curtains. 'You would take my honour and ruin me for a husband!' All the time, she was thinking of Jason, and what he would say when he found out she had lied to him, and had lost her maidenhead to the contemptible Mr Trice.

'It is not too high a price to pay, considering you will keep the house for yourself and your sisters.'

She took a step back, fearing that he was about to steal a kiss, then felt his hand on her arm, pulling her back towards him.

'No!' She fought to push him away as he tore at her gown and clamped his fingers to the sensitive flesh of her breast.

'Louisa? What's goin' on?'

'Jason!' she exclaimed, hot with shame and anger.

Mr Trice released her and took a step back, readjusting his dress.

'Who are you to enter a lady's parlour unannounced?' he said stiffly. 'I have private business with Miss Lennicker. I've come to collect what's owed.'

'What is the meaning of this? Louisa, say something – your silence is scaring me.'

She clutched the lace across her breast to hide the gaping rent in her bodice.

'It's nothing, just a misunderstanding,' she stammered.

'There's no confusion,' Mr Trice said. 'Miss Lennicker and I have an arrangement, a long-standing, mutual agreement.'

Her heart filled with pain when she saw the expression on Jason's face.

'What kind of arrangement? Tell me.'

'I'd prefer it to come from the dear lady's lips, which I have to tell you taste as sweet as any nectar.'

'You are lying, sir,' she interrupted.

'It's the truth … not that any of your sort would know the difference between the truth and a lie.'

'Louisa, tell me what's goin' on,' Jason said. 'What has he done to you?'

'How did you know he was here?'

'Billy told me.' His hand hovered at his waist, his fingers touching the butt of his pistol. 'By rights I should call you out,' he growled.

'I shouldn't.' Apparently unafraid, Mr Trice walked over to him and rested his hand on his shoulder. 'You're a young man. It would be a shame if you ended up on trial out of a misplaced sense of chivalry when the young woman in front of us is no better than a whore.'

'I'm sorry,' she said, having no doubt that Jason was ready to shoot the abominable old stoat straight between the eyes. 'Please, don't do something you'll regret.'

He turned to look at her. 'All that about being chaperoned to protect your honour!'

Mr Trice, seeing that his adversary was floundering in uncertainty, picked up his bag and made a quick exit.

'I'll be back,' he said, as he closed the parlour door swiftly behind him, leaving Louisa to face her beloved.

'I'm sorry,' she repeated.

'Not half as sorry as I am,' he said through gritted teeth.

'Nothing happened.'

'It would have done if I hadn't walked in. Don't play the innocent with me, standin' there with your bosom heavin' and tears in your eyes. When were you goin' to tell me of this cosy little arrangement you have with him? I knew somethin' wasn't right when I saw you talkin' to him after the hearin'. He said somethin' that upset you. Oh, I've been such a fool. Again!'

'This isn't my fault. My father got into debt with Mr Trice and I've been paying him back, but not fast enough for his liking. It was him who came up with the idea of …'

'Buying you?'

She nodded, deeply humiliated and frightened that she was about to lose Jason over it. 'I wouldn't have let him—'

'Oh, Louisa. You aren't that naïve. He was about to force himself on you. If I hadn't walked in when I did …' He swore. 'It makes me sick to think of it. How could you do this to me?'

'I didn't tell you about it because I didn't want to put you off – I thought I could deal with Mr Trice myself, pay him back and nobody would be any the wiser.'

'I trusted you … Why didn't you feel you could confide in me?' He paced the tiny room. 'To think I was plannin' to marry you …'

'Nothing's changed on my part,' Louisa said.

'I'm not stupid – I won't be cuckolded.' He made to leave, but she stood in his way.

'Don't go,' she begged. 'Let me explain.'

'Do you really think I'd waste any more time with you? I've had it with women. They're all the same – complicated, disloyal, manipulative …' Jason left, slamming the doors behind him one by one as he stormed out of the cottage.

Every fibre in her being was aching to run after him, but what good would that do? He had made up his mind – she had let him down in the worst way possible. She looked around the parlour, its four walls pressing in. The pressure of Mr Trice's hands was fresh in her memory, along with Jason's expression of pure disgust.

She had to get out.

Having put on her boots and bonnet, and collected her shawl, she made her way to the beach where she watched Jason and his men launch the *Whimbrel* and sail off into the Downs. Then, grateful for solitude, she waited at

Pa's old place in the capstan grounds, looking out to sea at the squalls snatching at the tops of the waves, and at the grey rags of cloud dripping rain as they dragged across the horizon. She had never felt so miserable. So bereft. Because Jason would never marry her now.

She didn't care about her own reputation – their promise to each other had been private. She had told her sisters of their engagement, and a few others had guessed or come to their own conclusions, but so what if people considered her flighty, a wanton, and a barque of frailty?

All she cared about was that she had wounded Jason deeply, because she knew he loved her – had loved her, she corrected herself. He wouldn't have risked his heart for a second time, if he hadn't been fully committed to spending the rest of his life with her. How would he be able to hold his head up in the presence of his associates and his crew, when they goaded him for his inability to judge a woman's character?

She touched the shawl that she'd wrapped around her throat and shoulders to hide the rent in her dress.

'Go away,' she muttered as a dog came bounding towards her. It stopped and sniffed the air as its master walked up beside it from behind one of the huts at the top of the slope.

'I'm glad to find you 'ere, miss,' Isaiah said. 'It saves me troublin' you at 'ome.'

'Call the dog off,' she said.

'Maybe I will, maybe I won't.'

'I said, call him off.'

'I will shortly. I'm just imaginin' the scars if 'e should jump up and bite your pretty face.'

'Leave me alone – I want nothing to do with your sort.'

Grinning, he dragged the dog back by the collar. 'If I cut you through with a knife, I reckon I'd find out that you're made of the same stuff as I am. Miss Lennicker – you can pretend to be the innocent young lady as much as you like. It doesn't wash with me. We are much of a kind, and because of that, my father's keen to borrer you some money, seein' you're in dire straits.'

'I wouldn't touch his money, not after what he's done. I don't need to remind you of the injury he has caused the Lennickers, but I won't let him destroy us. It's only made us stronger and more determined to survive, and you can tell him that.'

'Brave words. This isn't personal. It's business. You and your sisters 'ave a special understandin' of the market in fine lace and silks. You 'ave the contacts – the buyers – while we – the Rattlers – 'ave the goods. You 'ave the gift of the gab when it comes to sellin' while we 'ave the means to protect you. What do you say? My father's expectin' an answer – the right answer …' His grip tightened on the dog's collar. Its amber eyes narrowed, its stare sending a shiver down Louisa's spine.

'You've proved you won't get anywhere with the Witheralls and Ropers and the rest of them. Come and join the professionals – you won't regret it.'

'Never,' she snapped, and after a long silence, he let go of the dog, slapped his thigh to gain its attention, then turned and walked away, leaving her on the beach, not wanting to go home, not wanting to stay, Isaiah's presence having spoiled the peace she had sought.

When Winnie and Grace returned from the market later that morning, the produce sold and a few shillings in their pockets, they found Louisa crying in the kitchen as she peeled carrots and chopped onions to add to the pot of stew left over from the night before.

'Is it the onions making you cry?' Grace asked, putting her empty baskets on the table.

Louisa shook her head.

'Are you sad about Pa?'

'In part.'

'The lost goods? You know what Ma would have said – it's no use crying over spilt milk.'

'I'm not crying over them ...'

'What is it then?'

'I don't want to talk about it.'

'You can tell us, you know. We're your sisters and we look after each other.'

'Grace, it's sweet of you, but there's nothing you, or anyone else, can do.'

'You must say, or I'll worry,' Winnie interrupted.

'It's Jason,' she whispered.

'You've had a disagreement, a lovers' tiff,' Winnie said. 'Oh, don't worry – he'll be back.'

'He adores you – it's written all over his face,' Grace said.

'No, he's gone.' Louisa looked down at the chopping board where the onion was shredded into tiny pieces, while Winnie and Grace stared at her.

'Then he isn't the man I thought he was,' Winnie said eventually. 'He's treated you most cruelly.'

'It isn't possible,' Grace protested. 'A gentleman would never break an engagement.'

'It wasn't Jason's fault. I have only myself to blame, but that doesn't make it any easier to accept.'

'I'm heartily sorry then,' Grace said.

'We both are,' Winnie added. 'I was looking forward to the day when I could say he was my brother-in-law. Oh dear. The road to love and marriage is fraught with obstacles. I wish Ma was here to advise us.'

All Louisa could do was pray that the situation with Jason didn't affect her sisters' prospects. As for herself, she couldn't envisage marrying anyone else, even if they'd have her after what she'd done.

'What will we do about the next run?' Grace asked. 'Will we still be working with the Witheralls? Do you think Jason will include the Lennickers, or wash his hands of us?'

'I don't know, but we're going ahead with it. We're going to get back what we're owed from One Eye and the Rattlers, if it's the last thing I do.'

'Grace and I have been talking and we're of one mind,' Winnie said.

'I didn't say that exactly.' Grace raised one eyebrow, but Winnie went on anyway.

'I've said before that the Lennickers should bow out of the free trade. The Rattlers have become too dangerous, too clever, too powerful. We can't beat them, Louisa. You know that.'

'If there was any way of avoiding making another run, I'd jump at it, but circumstances compel us to carry on, at least until …'

'Until what?' Winnie said sharply.

'There are things you should know, that I should have told you before.' The weight of guilt dragged on her shoulders like an apron of lead as she finally confessed everything: the debt she had with Mr Trice and the deal she had made with him to repay it; the real reason Jason had broken up with her; the threat of losing the cottage, their home.

'Why? Why do you lie all the time? Oh, I know what you're going to say. Because you didn't want to worry me and Grace … I can tell you, it worries me a whole lot more when I don't know what's going on,' Winnie said.

'I'm not asking you to forgive me, because—' Louisa sensed that what she'd done was unforgivable, transgressing the unwritten code, not of the free traders, but of her sisters: that they shouldn't keep anything from each other.

'You kept all this from us?' Winnie was furious. 'We're in the devil's own scrape.'

'If you can see another way out, then tell me.' Louisa dropped the knife on to the chopping board and wiped her hands.

'Do you really believe we'll be able to keep our home if we continue with the free trade?' Winnie said eventually.

'It's the only way, and even then, there's a risk that something will go wrong again, or we won't make enough money in time.'

'But if it does work out,' Grace said, 'we'll be free of debt.'

'If so, we'll be able to make a fresh start,' Winnie mused.

'You are persuaded?' Louisa asked, surprised that it had taken so little to twist her sister's arm.

'If we lose the house, we'll be on the streets, or in the poorhouse. It's a certain path to a pauper's grave. We have to at least try to save ourselves.'

'How will we go about it?' Grace said.

'I'll have to pluck up the courage to speak to Jason – we'd already started on the planning with Terrier and Smoker, and their families.' There was a long way to go before they'd have any chance of digging themselves out of the hole they were in, and there was a risk that they could end up much deeper if Jason refused to deal with the Lennickers, or – if he did agree to continue their association – the next run ended as badly as the previous one.

A couple of days later, the boatmen and their families were on the beach, the women singing and mending nets, the men watching the horizon for ships in distress. Louisa and her sisters were with them, having returned from a fishing trip with Billy. All they had caught were a few whiting in the deeper water – Grace had cleaned them, split them and laid them out wet on the boards. The sun and wind had dried them, turning them golden on their way back.

Winnie squatted on the shingle, grilling the fish, as Louisa chased off the speckled young gulls that were stalking about, looking for food.

'At least we're still in on the run,' Winnie said in a low voice.

'It's all set for the fifteenth day of the month or thereabouts depending on the weather – that's when the boats will leave for France.' There wasn't much left for Louisa to do, except let the tub carriers know, and send word to the agent to notify him as to when to expect his delivery of lace to the Three Kings.

Billy had relayed a message from Jason to confirm the date while they'd been out on the *Curlew*. Louisa had tried to speak to him in person, but he had brushed her aside.

'I don't know the ins and outs of it, and I don't want to know,' Billy had said. 'But Marlin isn't 'imself. 'E doesn't smile, or 'ave a laugh with the men any more.'

'Hey, Louisa, you're supposed to be keeping the little varmints off!'

Winnie's squeals and a commotion between two of the young gulls brought her back to the present. They swooped up from the fire, squabbling in the air over a fish, which they dropped over the sea, before one dived and swallowed it whole.

'That had better be mine,' Louisa sighed.

'There's another one here for you,' Winnie said.

'It's all right. I'm not hungry.'

'You have to have something, or you'll fade away.'

'Winnie, please don't fuss.' She was sorry about losing the whiting – it was another small and unnecessary loss to add to all the other, more significant ones they'd suffered. She glanced along to the *Whimbrel* where Jason was talking to his father. Recalling the touch of his hand on her arm, the sweet kisses they'd snatched when her sisters hadn't been looking, and the sheer delight of knowing that they would one day be man and wife, she turned away, heartbroken.

Gradually, she became aware of the women's chatter growing more serious. 'There are rumours of a press officer and 'is gang going around Ramsgate. I've sent my 'usband to stay with 'is mother – she lives in Chartham 'atch, not far from Canterbury. I 'ope it's far enow away,' Mrs Roper said. 'Did you 'ear what 'appened to Mrs Ford?'

'Not exactly,' someone said. 'Only that she turned to higgling, but couldn't make a success of it, bein' in the family way and about to drop. She's 'ad to turn to the parish. It's terr'ble 'ard makin' ends meet at the best of times, let alone 'avin' to do it alone.'

'Count yourself lucky – my ol' man spends everythin' 'e earns if I don't get my 'ands on it first.'

Louisa wished they would stop whining about their nearest and dearest – they were fortunate to have husbands and children. She checked herself, wondering where that thought had come from as she sat down on an upturned tub, watching the blond-haired blue-eyed cherub toddling around at Mrs Roper's feet, and the babe in her arms.

'If they turn up 'ere, we'll send them straight back to where they came from,' Mrs Edwards said. 'It's a disgrace that they take our menfolk when they're already employed.'

'They won't impress those who can show their paperwork,' Mrs Roper said. 'Anyway, all they 'ave to do is tell them their age. They don't take the oldies or the young'uns. What do they say? When it comes to the press, no man is older than 'e looks, and no lad younger than 'e avows.'

'This is no ordinary press – it's an 'ot one where they can take whomsoever they like, no questions asked. It doesn't matter what documentation they're carrying – they don't accept any exemptions,' Mrs Witherall contributed.

'Some say it's a necessary evil in a time of war with Boneyparte on the other side of the Channel, waiting for 'is chance,' Mrs Roper observed.

'He can't do nothin' while the Frenchies are fightin' the war in Portugal.' When one of her children started to cry, Mrs Edwards swept him up and stuck her finger in his mouth to keep him quiet.

'It's the worst of times,' Mrs Roper said. 'You don't know what's goin' to 'appen next. Mr Cole got taken into the King's navy last spring and Mrs Cole 'asn't 'eard from 'im since. We're losin' our men to the army as well – look at all the families camped in the sand'ills, not knowin' what else to do.'

A breeze gusted across the capstan grounds as the shadows lengthened and the boats disappeared into the dusk. Having eaten but barely tasted the fish, Louisa pulled her shawl around her shoulders and began working with the netting needle and twine, making loops and square knots to repair the torn mesh in the *Curlew*'s net which had been damaged by a spiny crab. The rough twine shredded her skin and her fingers ached, but she felt she deserved the pain.

It wasn't until she heard the scrunching of the shingle that she stopped and looked up to see Abel Brockman riding along the beach.

'Ladies and gentlemen,' he bellowed as his mount, dark with sweat, tossed foam from its bit. 'There's a press officer and his gang about a mile north of here and headin' this way. It won't be long before they're in Deal where they'll take anyone, young or old, seafaring man or landlubber, with or without documents. I'll let you do with that information as you will. I'm not goin' to hang about.' He turned his horse and walked it up to the road where he spurred it into a gallop, its hooves drumming a beat of panic and uncertainty that echoed in the rhythm of Louisa's heart.

The Edwards child started to cry again, and the young gulls took flight, abandoning the shore. The *Good Intent* was out with the Rattlers' men, but they weren't safe from the press – there was bound to be a frigate out there waiting in the Downs with officers prepared to take men straight from their boats.

Louisa followed Winnie who'd gone across to the *Whimbrel* to check that Billy had heard Abel's warning.

'We heard,' Jason confirmed. 'I think that a fishin' trip is in order. We have more chance of gettin' away on the lugger than hidin' in town. If the Yellow Admiral's on the lookout, we'll disappear into the Sands and stay there for a while.'

'Who is this Yellow Admiral, Marlin?' Billy asked.

'It's what the navy call the senior press officer: a man let down by defects in his nature or condemned never to captain another ship because he's made an unforgivable mistake.' Jason glanced at Louisa, and the shame and regret came washing back.

'May God be with you,' she said.

'Thank you,' he replied abruptly. 'Billy, get ready to launch her as soon as everyone's here. Father, you're comin' with us.'

'I won't take the place of a younger man. What use can I be to 'is Majesty's cause? I'm old and riddled with gout.'

Jason almost picked him up by the scruff of the neck. 'Get yourself over there with Billy.'

'I'll 'ave none of your lip, my boy.'

'You will do as I tell you ... Think of your wife, my mother.'

Louisa noticed how tears sprang to Mr Witherall's eyes as he shuffled meekly towards the lugger, an old man who had realised that he was no longer king of the beach.

'It's for his own good,' Jason said aside to her. 'What are you waitin' for? Go into town and raise the alarm.'

She ran up and down the alleyways with Winnie and Grace, knocking on doors and shouting that the gangers were on their way, but as they left Oak Street, a boy interrupted them.

'It's too late – they've got 'em,' he gasped, and Louisa's heart sank to the soles of her boots.

Having thrust a ha'penny into his hand for his trouble, the sisters returned to the beach, where a throng of women and children were surging around the gangers who had clapped the men into cuffs and leg-irons and forced them into line. The women pushed and shoved, and the gangers shoved them back without respect or understanding.

'Please, don't take our men away!' they wailed.

'These men are Sea Fencibles. Who will be left to defend us and our shores?' Louisa joined in.

'My 'usband mends watches – what use will he be to the navy?'

One of the gangers drew his cutlass. 'Keep back, ladies. And you, old man. The Prince Regent's ships have greater need for them than you do. Without sailors, England cannot fight this war.'

The officer leading the gangers nodded towards Mr Witherall. 'Take him as well.'

'No! He's sick!' Jason shouted, receiving a punch in the mouth for arguing.

'A few weeks on naval rations and you won't recognise him.' The officer smiled as one of his men put Mr Witherall in an armlock.

'How can you treat us like this when our men have always gone beyond the call of duty for King and country?' Mrs Witherall said. 'There was a time when they rallied together, takin' one hundred luggers to Walcheren to land soldiers and guns. After the capture of Flushin', they 'elped move the wounded to the Naval Hospital here in Deal. Doesn't it count for nothin'?'

'Long may their generosity of spirit continue in the service of the navy,' the officer said bad-temperedly.

'This isn't fair,' Mrs Edwards retorted. 'I've 'eard there are plenty of seafarin' men loitering about in Dover and Folkestone with nothin' to occupy them.'

'I wish that were so, madam, but we're here now and we have our quota. Let the old one go – he'll only hold us up.' The officer's eyes latched on to Mr Witherall who had stumbled and fallen face down on the ground.

Louisa went to help his wife bring him to his feet.

'I want to go with my boy,' he muttered.

''E can look after 'imself – 'e's a grown man and you need to remember that,' Mrs Witherall said sadly.

'They will break 'is spirit.'

''Ow can they? 'E's a Witherall: unbreakable.' Her voice faded as they watched the gangers marching their men along the beach towards the barracks where they waited for a jollyboat to take them to the tender out in the Downs. Once on the tender, they would be guarded by men who had been chosen for their resistance to bribery, rum and petticoats, until the navy were ready for them. After that, they would be taken on to crew one of the men-o'-war.

As they pushed Billy into the jollyboat, Winnie ran at one of the gangers, her fists raised in anger.

'Let him go. I need him. We need him ...'

'I'm sorry, missus.' The ganger caught her by the wrists as Louisa rushed in to drag her back.

'Winnie, stop it,' she said, hauling her away by the waist.

'Whose side are you on?' Winnie spat, her ribs rising and falling with each breath. 'Let me go.'

'You're making a terrible scene – everybody's looking at you.' Louisa could understand her desperation, certain now that her sister was in love with Billy, whatever his intentions were towards her.

'I'm going after them …'

'How, when you can't swim?' Grace said, stepping up to help Louisa hold their sister back.

'I can't stand by and do nothing.'

'And we won't, I promise,' Louisa whispered into her ear as the gangers pushed off, the oars of the jollyboat gently splashing through the water as they set off for the tender where the men would be held for the night. She could see the back of Jason's head covered with a bandanna, and the breadth of his shoulders as he sat helpless in the bow. Her heart broke all over again. How she wished that their last exchange had been a happy one.

'They'll be back – they'll find a way,' Grace kept saying, but nobody believed her. They'd heard too many stories of how men were taken by force to the guardships where they were held until they agreed to volunteer for the King's shilling. If they refused, they were taken out to the men-o'-war and kept locked up until they were miles from land, when they had no option but to stay.

Louisa pictured Jason sitting trapped like a bird in a cage, fired up with anger and frustration. As for Billy, she had little doubt that he would be crying his eyes out, wondering if he'd ever set foot in Deal again.

It was a disaster. How would they carry on without the men?

'Why didn't Jason and Billy leave as soon as they heard that the gangers were on their way?' Winnie asked as they returned to the cottage.

'Jason wouldn't have left without knowing his crew were safe,' Grace said.

'I'm surprised you still have such a high opinion of him, considering how he's treated our sister.'

'He had his reasons,' Louisa said.

'We have to do something,' Winnie insisted. 'We can't just leave them to their fate.'

'I know – I'm thinking.'

'Well, think quicker, will you?'

At dawn the next day, Louisa and her sisters launched the *Curlew* into a calm sea with the help of Terrier Roper who had escaped the press, being out of town the day before.

'I know what you're doin', Miss Lennicker,' he said gruffly, 'but you won't 'ave any luck. They'll be guarded day and night and if they do make it off the tender, they'll come ashore with a price on their 'eads. I'd advise you against this course of action if I were your father – it's a dangerous situation.'

She couldn't stop, though. She wasn't trying to prove herself, or charm her way back into Jason's favour, although if there was any chance of that, she would take it. She was doing it out of love, whatever he thought of her.

Several other boats launched at the same time – fishing and rowing boats, loaded with the wives and children, mothers, sisters, cousins and aunts – and they set off together into the Downs in bright sunshine.

'We'd scare the wits out of the Frenchies if they turned up now.' Grace took the tiller while Louisa set the sails and Winnie stood in the bow armed with a bat. 'If old Boney and his army saw us, they'd soon turn about and flee for home.'

'There she is!' Winnie shouted, pointing aft towards a tender with her naval colours nailed to the mast.

The women shouted and wailed, begging for their menfolk's release as the flotilla surrounded her. The tender's crew, all smiles and waves at first, became weary of the intrusion and gestured at them to go away.

'We have no intention of leaving until we have them back,' Louisa called, at which one of the guards raised a pistol and fired, sending the ball whistling past her ear.

'Perhaps that'll change your mind, missus,' he bellowed as the sound of the shot died away.

'We should go home,' Grace said, pale-faced.

'Don't think you've beaten us. We'll be back tomorrow and the day after that,' Louisa shouted, as they dipped the lug and turned about, 'and every day until you let them go.'

The women returned with a great caterwauling of grief, having made no headway in retrieving their men.

'What am I going to do without him?' Tears streamed down Winnie's pinched features.

'Oh, pull yourself together,' Louisa said, angry at being thwarted. 'You're a Lennicker, not a milksop. We aren't giving up on them yet.'

# Chapter Fourteen

## *A Brown Bess and Blacking*

The navy called on the militia to send a detachment of soldiers to stand on the beach to prevent any further sorties, and when the Lennickers went back down to the shore late the same evening, they were intercepted and questioned.

'Ladies, this is a pleasant surprise. I wasn't sure we would meet again, knowing that the regiment will soon be moving abroad.'

'Lieutenant Tempest . . .' Louisa recognised him instantly. 'You can't prevent us from going about our business.'

'That depends on what kind of business it is. You are taking a walk?' he asked, looking at their bags, boxes and buckets.

'We're going fishing.'

'At night?'

'Everyone knows it's the best time to catch cod and flatfish – they come in closer to the shore in the dark,' she said scornfully.

He scrutinised her face, apparently disbelieving, yet too much of a gentleman to raise an argument with her.

'Since our father died, this is the only means we have of putting food on the table,' she went on. 'Please, don't delay us.'

'You have turned away from other methods of making your living?'

'I beg your pardon, I don't know what you mean, but maybe as you're standing around doing nothing, you could help us launch our boat – all you need to do is wait until we're aboard, before releasing her down the rollers.'

'I can't believe your nerve,' Winnie said when they were heading out into the swell, their blankets, provisions and a box containing Pa's musket – a Brown Bess – stowed in the bow.

Louisa smiled as she took the tiller and asked Grace to black out the boat's name using the pot of paint that they'd brought with them.

'We'll cast a long line, rather than shooting a net, then we'll pass the tender and wait for the men to appear on deck, under the pretence that we're fishing. We'll create some kind of disturbance to distract the guards, so they can make their escape.'

'I don't know how you think this will work – Billy can't swim,' Winnie said.

'I realise that, but we won't be far away. We'll be able to pick him up. Anyway, you're worrying unnecessarily. I'm sure Jason will steal one of the jollyboats if he gets the chance.'

'I don't like this plan of yours. It's flawed.'

'You'd better tell me if you have a better idea.' Taking Winnie's silence to mean that she hadn't, Louisa took the musket out of the box and checked that there were plenty of charges in the cartouche.

'Are you sure about using that?' Winnie said.

'No, but I've fired a pistol a few times. It's a flintlock so it works in the same way.'

'As long as you don't blow us all up.'

'I'll do my best not to,' she said dryly. She had no intention of harming anyone.

They stopped as close as they dared to the tender, keeping away from the light that shone from her mast. They took in the canvas, cast out the line and waited, the waves slapping gently against the hull and the stars shining in the vast sphere of the heavens. After a while, Grace yawned loudly.

'Whist,' Louisa hissed.

'There's nothing going on,' Grace grumbled. 'This is a waste of time.'

'The fish are biting,' Winnie observed. 'We'll have some to sell tomorrow.'

'What if they've retired for the night?' Grace asked. 'We'll have had a wasted journey.'

'I hear voices,' Louisa said urgently.

'That's them,' Winnie whispered as the men came up through the hatch, accompanied by two guards, one bearing a lantern, the other with the silhouette of a firearm slung over his shoulder.

Louisa nodded. Winnie pulled in the line and Grace set the canvas.

Her heart pounding, Louisa loaded the musket, taking the charge and biting off the musket ball, keeping it in her mouth while she poured a little gunpowder into the pan and the rest down the barrel. She spat the ball after it, then rammed the wad in next with the ramrod, before raising the hefty Brown Bess and aiming it across the tender's bow, but the *Curlew* was rocking in the water, rising and falling, and the figures on the tender's deck were moving around. She was scared witless that she was going to hit someone.

The wind began to fill the *Curlew*'s sails and set her off towards home.

Unable to hesitate any longer, Louisa pulled the trigger. The flash dazzled her and the recoil took her by surprise, the musket punching her shoulder as chaos broke out on the tender.

'What the—?' The guards started shouting and yelling, and one fired back in the general direction of the *Curlew*. 'Get the men back down in the hold. Launch the boat and get after them.'

'This isn't supposed to happen,' Winnie gasped. 'You didn't say they'd fire back.'

'It doesn't matter now.' Louisa heard splashing, more shouting and a series of shots. 'We have to get away from here.'

'We must turn about,' Winnie protested.

'We can't do that – we'll all be killed!' Grace cried.

'We have to pick them up – we can't leave them to drown,' Winnie went on.

'Stop firing!' Louisa stood up and bellowed at the top of her lungs. 'Stop, sir!'

'Who is that?' one of the guards said.

'It's a woman,' said another.

'I don't believe you – you wouldn't recognise a member of the fairer sex if she threw herself at you.'

'We're out doing a little night fishing,' Louisa called. 'I beg you not to fire on us, but to go after the lugger, the *Good Intent*. She almost ran us down.'

'The prisoners – keep your eyes on them. There's some in the water … they're in the jollyboat.'

'Which boat?'

'Our boat.' One of the guards swore above the sound of the oars in the rowlocks. 'Where's Officer Dent?'

'He's entertaining the ladies in Deal – he won't take kindly to being disturbed. The *Good Intent*, did you say, missus?'

'Yes, she's made off towards the Sands.'

'Then I thank you for the information.'

'It's a pleasure,' she shouted back as the wind picked up, carrying the *Curlew* away.

'I think you've just been gammoned,' she thought she heard one of the guards say as they cut through the water with Grace at the helm.

'Listen,' she whispered, but she couldn't hear the sound of men's voices or the splash of oars in the water.

'Louisa, what if they didn't make it on to the jollyboat?' Winnie said. 'I've told you, we have to go back and find them.'

'And I've told you why we can't. They must sink or swim.'

They waited, watching and listening until dawn brought the boys to the beach to bring the *Curlew* in and drag her up the shore. Mr Witherall was already there – perhaps he had been waiting all night. Louisa told him of their exploits.

'I don't know whether to scold you or give you a heroes' welcome,' he said. 'Do you think they all managed to escape un'armed?'

'I don't know,' she admitted. 'All we can do is pray and wait for news.'

The press gang moved south to Dover and the tender remained in sight for the rest of the day, while the Lennickers waited in vain for the knock that would tell them that Billy and Jason were back safely. The authorities put up posters, offering a reward for a missing boatman by the name of Isaiah Feasey, which caused much confusion, because the *Good Intent* had returned on the same day as the *Curlew* had, and Isaiah had been seen alive and kicking at the Rattling Cat until someone had warned him that he was wanted.

The next day, when Louisa looked out to sea through her father's spyglass, the tender had gone.

'I'm sorry,' Mr Witherall said. 'It isn't fair that they get away from the press while our men … my boy …'

'I did my best,' she observed.

'I know you did. You're a fighter, Louisa, just like your mother.'

'There must be something else we can do.'

He shook his head. 'We wait, watchin' out to sea as we've always done, in the 'ope that they'll come 'ome where they belong. Meanwhile, we'll 'ave to fall back on our contingencies. For the run,' he explained as Louisa's forehead tightened. 'We'll scratch a crew for the lugger and leave the galley punt be'ind. You and your sisters seem perfectly capable of crewin' the *Curlew*, the landside operatives are still available, and I can enlist Abel and his men from the mill to make up numbers.

'It's too late to back out now – the merchants will 'ave their stock waitin' in the warehouses. If we let them down, they'll find others willin' to move it soon enow. I want to be sure that there's somethin' for my boy to come back to.'

His boy, she mused. The man who could have become her husband, had she not been so stupid.

'You have lost your smile,' he went on.

'I have lost almost everything,' she said softly, a lump in her throat.

'We'll carry on, keepin' faith that they'll return one day soon.'

Their fight with the Rattlers and her desire for revenge against One Eye didn't seem that important any more, but she had no choice but to continue with the run if she was to have any chance of getting Mr Trice off her back. She had to get rid of him – he was like a leech sucking the life blood from her, yet she couldn't concentrate on how to do it, because she couldn't stop thinking of Jason, wishing he was back in Deal.

'Winnie, you have to pull yourself together,' she said later. 'We're all sad and sorry, but we have work to do. As Mr Witherall said, the run has to go ahead.'

'How can it? There aren't enough men left to crew the *Whimbrel* and the *Spindrift*.'

'I'm going to talk to a few people to see what can be done.'

'Do as you will.' Winnie shrugged and as Louisa left the house, she overheard Grace telling Winnie to be kind, that Louisa was only trying to help them.

Another day passed and there was no sign of the men, but the arrangements for the run gathered pace, even though Louisa's heart wasn't in it. She was desperately worried about Jason, and Winnie was hardly eating, a consequence of her anxiety over Billy's fate.

On her way back from paying their dues to her uncle and telling the labourers that they should expect to be needed one evening soon, a stranger came trotting up on a small pony, his legs dangling down, his feet almost touching the ground.

'I'm lookin' for a Miss Lennicker who lives in Cockle Swamp Alley. Do you know of her, miss?' His voice was muffled by the scarf he wore across his mouth and nose.

She gazed at him, unsure whether or not she should identify herself.

'She's also known as the Lace Maiden.'

Was this something to do with the Rattlers, or Mr Trice?

'I'm acquainted with her,' she said eventually.

'Then I'm relieved not to 'ave to go 'untin' any further. I 'ave a message for 'er.'

He leaned down. 'She is to go to Kingsdown Cliffs this evening, after dark ...'

'Pray, tell me who has sent you.' Please, let it be Jason, she breathed inwardly.

'I can't say, bein' that I'm sworn to secrecy. Suffice to say that lives will be in danger if anybody apart from the persons or person concerned is found out.'

It made sense that Jason and Billy – if they were on the run from the navy – would want to lie low, but what if it was a trick, a ruse to divert her into danger?

'These persons,' she said. 'Are they hurt?'

'I can't say no more. Tell Miss Lennicker to make 'er way to the cliffs without tellin' a soul.'

'May I ask your name?'

'You may ask, but I won't tell.' With that, the stranger turned his pony and trotted off along the street, disappearing towards the town, leaving her to hurry home where she paced up and down outside the cottage, unsure what to do. Was he a stranger, or was there something familiar about him? Was he one of the Rattlers' men? Should she go against his instructions and speak to her sisters? They would keep her secret, but she had no doubt that they would insist on accompanying her.

'I'm going out,' she said later, as dusk began to fall.

'Why? Have you received news?' Winnie's voice was filled with hope.

'There's no news – I have a meeting with Mr Witherall, that's all.'

'I don't understand why they haven't sent word, knowing how we're sitting here, waiting and worrying.'

Grace looked up from her sewing. 'They'd send word if they could.'

'That's what I'm afraid of,' Winnie sobbed. 'Why haven't they, if they're alive and well? I can only fear the worst.'

Grace stared at a drop of scarlet on her thumb. 'How can we do the run without them? We'll have to delay it.'

'There's no question of that – everything's been arranged,' Louisa said.

'You can ask Mr Witherall's advice about what we should do,' Grace suggested.

Louisa nodded, biting her lip until she could taste blood, hating that she had to lie to her sisters to keep their men safe. They wouldn't have to suffer for much longer, though. With luck, she would be bringing them home before dawn.

She went down to the beach in a dark cape and bonnet, the evening air cool against her skin. Abandoning her lantern beside the pile of lobster pots near the *Curlew*, she took advantage of the light of the full moon to make her way back to the road, taking the turn to Walmer and walking up the hill to the mill. Its sails were still, and the curtains were drawn in the house next door.

Having tiptoed around the back, she made her way to the meadow where the ponies were grazing. She took the bridle and rope from the hook on the gatepost and climbed over the gate. The ponies wandered across to her and she caught Gubbins – their favourite – and led him outside. He whinnied and fussed at being taken away, but it wasn't long before he settled and began to walk alongside her in a mannerly way. When they reached the well-worn path along the clifftop at Kingsdown, he dropped behind her, following in her footsteps.

Taking deep breaths of the salt-laden air, pungent with the scent of sea kale, she felt better, even optimistic.

The pony stopped and snorted.

'Jason?' she whispered as she heard a rustle in the scrub alongside her. An eerie silence descended, making her wonder if she'd imagined it. She tugged at the rope, but the pony refused to budge. 'Show yourself …'

'That's 'er, that's the one.' Turning sharply at the sound of a man's voice, she caught sight of two figures, wearing broad-brimmed hats, and scarves around their faces.

'Are you sure it isn't the Fey Lady?'

'It isn't a ghost. It's Miss Lennicker, I'm certain of it.'

'I don't know this lady of whom you speak,' she said quickly, her heart beating a fierce tattoo, and inwardly castigating herself for not having been prepared with the pistol which was sitting useless in her pocket.

'Oh, she isn't no lady, my dear.' She recognised his voice; it was the stranger who had given her the message to come to the cliffs. 'She's a varmint, a smuggler o' the first order, and one who would betray us without a second thought.'

Slowly, she backed away towards the startled pony, thinking that she would vault on to his back and gallop him home, but she was too late. The stranger pounced, grasping her by one shoulder as the other man grabbed her about the waist. She fought back, twisting and kicking out, but they were far too strong for her.

'Leave me alone. Let go of me!' She recalled her father's advice, and much as it pained her to do so, she aimed a kick at one of the strangers who released her like a shot, doubling up and howling.

'Aha, she got you,' the other man crowed as he held her with her arms behind her back. She swore and spat. 'Such pretty language, eh, Lawless?'

'And from a waterman's daughter ... Did you just call me by my name?'

'If I did, I don't recall,' the other man said sheepishly.

'Don't do it again ... You 'eard what One Eye said – we're supposed to be goin' about this incognito.'

'Mr Feasey put you up to this?' Louisa said as they rummaged her and snatched the pistol from her pocket.

'We aren't tellin',' Lawless said, examining the piece before dropping it into the bag slung from his shoulder.

''E said to do the deed and keep our mouths shut,' the other man said.

'What deed?' She was panicking. She had been a fool, thinking it was Jason in the first place. No matter what he thought of her, he would never have put her in danger.

''E said to bundle 'er up and throw 'er off the top, makin' it look like an accident.' Lawless had been partaking of a little too much Dutch courage, she guessed from the stench of his breath. 'All we've got to do is give 'er a little push, like this.' She stiffened as he shoved her in the belly, forcing her and her captor to take a step towards the cliff edge.

'Hey, watch what you're doin'!' the other man exclaimed, pushing her back on to the path.

'If you hurt me, you'll be hanged,' she said.

'Oh no, ol' One Eye looks after 'is own.'

'He thinks he got away with murdering my father, but it'll come back to haunt him one day,' she went on.

'Murder, you say?' the accomplice responded, looking towards Lawless.

'I don't know about that. I wasn't there,' Lawless said hurriedly.

'You kill me and he'll let you take the blame for it. He told me himself – he doesn't have a conscience.'

'I 'ave to confess I'm not keen on the idea of 'urtin' a woman .... I 'ave daughters ...'

Lawless laughed. 'That was a bit o' tomfoolery on my part. We aren't goin' to 'urt 'er, just keep 'er out of the way for a bit, like One Eye said. We'll tie 'er up and take 'er back with us – she can stay where she's put until the run's over and the goods are 'idden away.'

Louisa screamed, 'Help me!' at the top of her lungs, but the wind caught her words and cast them aside.

'Shut yer mouth,' Lawless said, and then she remembered the pony.

'Whoa!' she shouted. 'Whoa there!'

He turned tail, his hooves thudding at a full four-time gallop in the direction of home.

'What did you do that for? One of us could 'ave 'ad a ride back into town.'

She screamed again, the sound quickly stifled by a hand on her nose and mouth that stopped her breath until she lost consciousness.

When she awoke, she found her wrists bound tight behind her back and the smell of lanolin and sheep's treddles on her clothing.

'Get up, woman,' Lawless said roughly, and she struggled to her feet, hot tears running down her cheeks.

'Don't cry, dear. We won't let you come to no 'arm. Me and Lawless are genl'emen with good 'earts,' the accomplice said, at which Lawless punched him.

'Ow! You got me in the physog – what did you do that for?' He pulled down his scarf, revealing his face in the moonlight and confirming his identity: Awful Doins.

'Cos you did it again, you ruddy clodpole.'

'Did I?'

'You did, bone'ead.'

'It doesn't matter though, does it? She knows very well who we are.'

It appeared that Mr Feasey had sent two of his roughest, most unkempt clowns to catch her. All the time, Louisa was looking for a chance of escape, loosening the rope at her wrists and wondering how they could call themselves boatmen when they couldn't tie a knot to save their lives.

'Let's get 'er back to the rondy – One Eye can decide what to do with 'er,' Lawless said, and they marched her back to Deal. They were jostling her along the street in sight of the Rattling Cat when a bell tolled eleven.

'Please, help me. I'm being taken against my will, sirs,' she shouted when a pair of soldiers in uniform came sauntering towards them. For a moment, she thought they were going to cross the road, but they stopped.

'May we be of assistance?' one asked.

'These men have taken me against my will.'

'My dear, don't make a scene,' Lawless said. 'I'm sorry, my wife doesn't know what she's sayin'. She went missin' and my friend and I found 'er in a bit of a state. I'm takin' 'er 'ome now.'

'I'm not your wife,' she said, horrified. 'These men are strangers.'

'It's a terr'ble thing when you find out that the woman you married is a lunatic. With tonight's full moon, you find 'er at 'er worst.'

The soldiers glanced up at the great orb in the sky and nodded sagely, before wishing them well and moving on.

'That was the best bamboozle I've 'eard for a long time,' Awful Doins chuckled, and while Lawless was congratulating himself on his quick thinking, Louisa let the ropes drop from her wrists and made to run away. But there was no respite, as Awful Doins caught her around the waist and dragged her along, his hip grinding against hers, while Lawless, having knocked her hat off, grabbed her by the hair, yanking it tight until she feared she'd lose her scalp.

They took her into the inn via the rear door, sending the cats scattering as they marched her through to the bar.

'Where's One Eye? Where's the boss?' Lawless called as the men put their playing cards down next to their pistols and stared. Mrs Stickles looked on from behind the counter, beer pouring from the barrel into the tankard in her hand, foaming and spilling over the top.

One Eye swaggered across the floor.

'Don't forget you owe me for what you waste,' he growled.

Mrs Stickles shrank back.

One Eye turned and, with mocking laughter, he pointed at Awful Doins.

'You let a woman give you a split lip!'

'It was 'im – we 'ad a few fisticuffs on the way.' Awful Doins nodded towards Lawless. 'The Lace Maiden gave us a bit more trouble than we were expectin'.'

'Perhaps she isn't of the female persuasion,' someone called out. 'There have been rumours, the way she can fire a musket.'

'Make 'er take 'er clothes off,' someone else joined in. 'Off, off, off!'

Another stood on the table, raising his tankard. 'Let's see what she's made of.'

Encouraged by the circle of baying men, Lawless put his arms around her from behind. She felt him tugging at her lace, and in a fury of shame and anger, she stamped hard on his foot, making him shout out, at which One Eye fired his pistol towards the ceiling, sending down a shower of plaster amid a cloud of smoke.

So much for wreaking revenge on One Eye for what he'd done to the Lennickers, she thought.

She trembled as he walked up to her, blowing smoke into her face. 'I 'ear you're plannin' to do me out of what is unlawfully mine ...' Grinning, he sniffed at her shoulder as he reloaded the pistol. 'I can smell the fear on you, my darlin', which is 'ow it should be. I am the king of the smugglers, and I won't 'ave anybody changin' that.' He turned to Mrs Stickles. 'Take 'er and lock 'er up.'

'Foller me, miss,' she said.

'You can't do this,' Louisa protested. 'My sisters will be out looking for me.'

One Eye gestured at her, pistol in hand, and she gave in, dragging her feet as she went past the counter and into the back room with Mrs Stickles who closed the door behind them.

'Do as you're told, and you won't come to no 'arm,' she whispered, lifting the rug from the flagstones to reveal a wooden trapdoor beside the fireplace. She took a key from her bosom, unlocked the padlock and slid the latch. Having raised the panel, she pushed Louisa towards the dark hole in the floor.

'Go on,' she said, when Louisa hesitated. 'It isn't such a bad place to spend a few days.'

At the bottom of the stone steps, she felt along the roughened walls, finding herself in a damp passageway; the only light was the faintest strip from the trapdoor where two planks didn't quite meet. She heard the latch being slid across, the men talking in low voices in the tavern above, the chink of cutlery and china, and then a breath, a small sigh and a racking, bubbly cough. That, and the scent of rosewater, confirmed she was not alone. She didn't know whether to be thankful or petrified.

She cleared her throat and steadied her breathing.

'Who goes there?' she said gently.

She was answered by the rustle of petticoats, then silence.

'Don't be afraid – I won't hurt you,' Louisa went on urgently. 'I'm being held against my will. Can you help me get away from here?'

From along the tunnel, she saw the figure of a woman dressed in white, protecting the flickering flame of a candle with the palm of her hand. She stopped three feet from Louisa, her face obscured by a cap and veil.

'You are the Fey Lady?' Louisa said, trembling.

'I am her, on occasion, but mostly I'm Nancy Stickles … You are Miss Lennicker.'

'You know who I am?'

'Oh, I've longed to meet you. It seems that my prayers have been answered at last.'

'I'm sorry, but who are you? And why are you here?'

'I'm your 'alf-sister.'

'I beg your pardon?' Louisa exclaimed. Having been reassured that the mystery woman wasn't a ghost, she was horrified by her allegation that they were related by blood. 'No, I forbid you to repeat that – it's a lie.'

'We share the same father – we've suffered the same sad loss.'

'It can't be. You're making this up. What do you want from me?'

'Why would I take advantage of my sister? I 'ave everythin' I need, apart from my freedom.' She raised her veil and lifted the candle, illuminating her features. Louisa suppressed a gasp at the sight of the young woman's cratered skin – her nose was shrivelled by scars. 'God punished me for the circumstances of my birth with a visitation of the pox. It was many years ago, and because my appearance made me repellent to even the lowest in society, it was decided that I should remain invisible. Of course, it suited Mr Lennicker to 'ave me – the outcome of his infidelity – 'idden away, even though it meant leavin' me at the mercy of One Eye. That's one of the things they were arguin' about on the day he was injured – my mother let slip that One Eye had taken a stick to me for steppin' outside during daylight. I'm not allowed, you see.'

Recalling Pa's admission of his fleeting infidelity with Mrs Stickles during his marriage, Louisa began to wonder if there was some truth in her tale.

'How old are you?' she asked.

'I'm eighteen – I was born after you, and before Winnie.'

'How do you know this?'

'I watch and listen. Robert – that's what I used to call 'im when 'e used to come 'ere in the days when 'e was on good terms with One Eye – 'e told me about you, and I used to live through his stories, imaginin' what it would be like to be part of a proper family. I used to walk up and down indoors, pretendin' I was you.' She dropped her veil, covering her face again. 'You're beautiful, clever and successful. Why should I 'elp you get out of 'ere?' she spat resentfully. 'You 'ave everythin' I've always wanted.'

'Your situation is not of my making,' Louisa said. 'Please, don't punish me for it.'

'You must 'ave 'ad an inklin'.'

'I had no idea. My father –' she corrected herself '– our father never mentioned you, and if my mother knew, she didn't let on. I've never heard any gossip to the effect that he had another daughter.'

'It suited One Eye to spread the rumour that the tavern and 'is other hidin' 'oles were 'aunted, and it was convenient for Robert too. Those who caught a glimpse of me jumped to the conclusion that I was the Fey Lady – they weren't inclined to investigate further.'

'I'm very sorry that you've had to suffer like this. If I'd had any idea that you existed, I'd have helped you get away from here.'

'You're just sayin' that because you want me to show you the way out.'

'I'm saying it out of respect for my long-lost sister,' Louisa whispered. Whether she believed Nancy's tale or not, she needed to get away.

'I don't like the thought of what One Eye might do to you, if anythin' goes awry durin' the run. That's why you're 'ere – to keep you out of the way until it's over,'

Nancy said after a long pause. ''E's a nasty piece of work – when anythin' goes wrong, 'e takes it out on somebody else. 'E's 'eld my 'ands in the fire until I've swooned from the pain, and I've lost count of 'ow many times 'e's beaten me black and blue. For a while, 'e took pleasure in 'alf starvin' me to death. I can't 'ave it on my conscience to let 'im do that to you. I'll show you how to get out of 'ere …'

'What about One Eye, though?'

'It'll put 'im into a rage, but my account of your escape will be watertight. You must play your part, though – if 'e discovers the truth, 'e'll kill me.'

'Come with me then. I'll keep you safe.'

'I can't leave – I 'ave to think of my mother. I 'ave a pistol tucked away – I'll say you turned it on me and threatened me with my life if I didn't show you the way out. One Eye doesn't know I 'ave it – Mr Lennicker gave it to me a long time ago.'

'I can't see how I'll get out through the trapdoor alive,' Louisa said, her palms damp as she thought of trying to sneak out through the inn unnoticed while the Rattlers were playing All Fours, their pistols to hand. She knew One Eye would have no compunction about using his piece, and her own was in the hands of Lawless and Awful Doins.

It pleased her, though, to imagine the look on their faces when they discovered that she'd shot her way out, and One Eye turning on them for not rummaging her properly, assuming that she'd been in possession of two pistols at the beginning of the evening.

'There is another way out of 'ere,' Nancy said.

'Won't he have put a guard on it?'

'There's a padlock on the door, but I 'ave a key.' She guessed that Nancy was smiling as she went on, 'I think it's best that we make it look as if the lock has been forced, otherwise people will start to believe that I'm not the only being in Deal who can pass un'indered through walls and locked doors. Come this way.'

Louisa followed her along the passageway to a small door beside which stood a trunk and an iron bedstead. Nancy handed her the candle and dug about in the trunk, removing a pistol from the clothing inside and handing it over to her, along with a small powder bag. Louisa gave her the candle back and loaded the pistol.

It would be dark outside – she didn't relish the idea of not being able to see her way home.

Nancy unhooked the padlock and pushed the door open.

'Use the ladder to get over the wall into the neighbour's garden. Go left and through the gate, and you'll find yourself in the alley. Turn right or you'll end up in the dead end.'

*And dead, maybe* – the thought crossed Louisa's mind.

'Don't forget to fire a shot when you're outside – I'll start screamin' and hollerin' when I 'ear it. That'll buy you time. Good luck, my dear sister,' Nancy said.

'I'll see you again,' Louisa said, but she couldn't be sure.

Having made her way out, her eyes taking time to adjust to the darkness, she felt for the ladder and climbed up to the top, where she took aim into the sky with the pistol. On the first pull of the trigger, nothing happened. On the second, it sparked and fired, its sound mimicking the soft pop of a cork from a bottle, but it was enough to turn Nancy into a keening banshee. On hearing men's voices, Louisa dropped over the other side of the wall, landing in a small garden. Leaving her boot-prints in the veg patch, she made her way to the gate on the opposite side, but the latch was stuck fast.

'Who goes there? Show yourself!' A lantern came swinging along the path towards her. 'I've 'ad enough of people like you thinkin' you can use my property as a privy.'

Louisa had another go at the latch – this time it opened and she was able to get through the gate, closing it behind her and stumbling away in the dark. What had Nancy said? Turn left? Or was it right?

In her panic, she couldn't remember ...

'Whoever it was went that-away!' She heard shouting and heavy footsteps.

She turned left and ran. Wrong, she thought, finding herself trapped. There was no way out. As she prepared to meet her maker, she took a step back and found herself falling. She wasn't sure how far she fell before she landed in a heap of sawdust.

'I can't see 'er,' she heard Awful Doins shout from above.

'She can't 'ave got far,' Lawless responded.

'Where's One Eye?'

'He's organisin' a proper search. This is 'is fault – 'e knows she isn't just a pretty face. 'E should 'ave been more careful, especially after all the bother we've gone through to get 'er 'ere.'

''E's blamin' us for not finding the other weapon on 'er, but I'm sure she didn't 'ave it on 'er person. I checked 'er garters an' everythin'.'Ave you seen Black Dog recently?'

'He won't 'ave anythin' to do with 'er escape. He's been lyin' low since 'e saw the posters, but One Eye's sorted that out now – 'e paid Doctor Audley to confirm that Black Dog 'as been afflicted with a terrible sickness, a contagion that would wipe out all on board, if 'e were to volunteer for one of the navy's ships.'

'That's very convenient, isn't it?'

Their footsteps faded back into the distance, and suppressing the urge to sneeze, Louisa rolled over and waited.

# Chapter Fifteen

## *Tarred with the Same Brush*

Louisa rushed through the door and closed it behind her, gasping from lack of breath, as she slipped the bolt across.

'Where have you been all this time? We've been worried sick!' Grace exclaimed.

'Are you alone?' Winnie appeared from the kitchen, cloth in one hand, candlestick in the other.

'I'm hoping so – oh, I've had quite a night of it.' She brushed sawdust from her hair and shook it out of her skirt. 'I was running away from One Eye's men. It was dark and I couldn't see where I was going. The ground disappeared from under my feet and I found myself in a cellar full of sawdust – and spiders. As soon as dawn broke, I climbed out and came home.'

'We've just called on Mr Witherall, who knew nothing of this meeting you were supposed to be having with him,' Grace challenged, her eyes flashing with distress and anger and justifiably so, Louisa thought. 'The only meeting last night was the one at the Rattling Cat.'

'I'm very sorry for putting you to this bother.'

'Is that what you call it? Bother? It was torment not knowing where you were. We've been beside ourselves.'

'Grace, it doesn't matter now.' Winnie tucked the cloth and candlestick into her apron and stepped forward. She threw her arms around Louisa and hugged her. Grace joined in.

'We were planning to go up to Limepit Acres next, and then St Leonard's,' Grace went on.

'We thought you might have drowned or that some drunken Jacks had dragged you off the street, but then Abel rode down to tell us that the pony had come home. He wondered if we'd borrowed him and if we were all right. What could Grace and I say, except that we didn't have a clue?'

'Two of One Eye's men tricked me into meeting them – they captured me and took me to the Rattling Cat, hoping to put me out of the way for a while. That's the long and short of it. Are the doors locked?'

'We've taken precautions,' Grace said.

Louisa drank milk laced with a little brandy while Winnie prepared a meal of leftovers from supper the night before. Grace tried to keep their spirits up with her chatter.

'I have interesting news,' Louisa said after they had eaten. 'I haven't told you the story of the stranger I encountered at the inn. She is a woman a little older than you, Winnie, and younger than me, and the daughter of Mrs Stickles.'

'We'd have heard if she had a child,' Grace said scathingly. 'We know everything that goes on around here.'

'She's been kept hidden, being pitifully disfigured.'

'I'm going to take a guess,' Winnie said. 'This has something to do with our father.'

Louisa nodded. 'She's our half-sister.'

Grace paled. 'It isn't possible.'

'I didn't believe her at first, but it explains why Mrs Stickles approached me in the past, grubbing for money. When I went through Pa's accounts, I found regular payments for what I assumed were services rendered.

They were contributions to Nancy's keep. She can't work, you see.'

'Nancy?' Grace said.

'It's a pretty name,' Winnie said. 'What a shame – we've missed out on so much, all of us. Why did Pa keep her from us? I can see why he didn't say anything while Ma was alive, but he could have come out with it afterwards, after a decent length of time had elapsed.'

'It was for the same reason he didn't see fit to mention his friendship with Mrs Stickles. He was ashamed – even more so when his illegitimate daughter's looks were ruined by the scourge of smallpox,' Louisa responded.

'I won't have anything to do with this,' Grace said with vehemence. 'She's nothing to me.'

'She's our flesh and blood, and she helped me get away from One Eye, at great risk to herself.'

'She was born the other side of the blanket,' Grace said.

'The child of such a union doesn't deserve our condemnation,' Winnie said.

'You're right – it's the immorality of the mother for lying with the father when she isn't married,' Grace went on. 'Aunt Mary will be appalled at our disgrace – she'll disown us to make sure Beth's wedding goes ahead. This mustn't go any further. A half-sister, sprung from a whore's womb? Oh no, we must deny it, and in the strongest way possible.'

Louisa flinched. Her sister's words stung – there was still a risk that she'd have to sell herself to Mr Trice to pay off their debt, her plight being no different from the desperation Mrs Stickles must have suffered in the past.

'These things happen between a man and a woman. We shouldn't judge our father or Mrs Stickles because no matter how it looks, they were mightily fond of each other,' Winnie said sadly. 'They say that gin and hot baths can stop an infant coming, but I believe that's an old wives' tale.'

'I feel sorry for her anyway,' Louisa said. 'She's done me a good turn.'

'Oh, listen to you,' Winnie said suddenly, getting up from her chair. 'How can you be so cheerful when the men are still missing?'

'Because I'm happy to be alive. Last night, I thought I was staring death in the face.'

Grace reverted to the subject of their half-sister.

'I suppose it isn't this Nancy's fault.'

'Of course it isn't,' Louisa agreed.

They passed the rest of the day peacefully indoors, smoking a few mackerel that Mrs Witherall had given them, and sewing new bags to protect the next batch of run lace. However, when dusk fell, they heard a sharp rap at the front door.

'Who can that be at this time of night?' Winnie said.

'They've come for me. I knew One Eye wouldn't let it lie.'

'Hide,' Winnie urged her. 'I'll fend them off.'

'Don't let them in!'

'I won't … Go …' Louisa noticed the flash of scithers as Winnie slipped them into her pocket. 'Quickly!'

She ran up to their father's room with Grace close behind her.

'It's all right. The coast is clear,' Winnie shouted as they moved the wardrobe and slid the panel aside. 'It's Jason.'

Louisa's heart leapt.

'He's come back to us. You must hurry down to him.' Grace was beaming from ear to ear, but before Louisa could move, Jason – oblivious to propriety, and dressed in muddy boots and a coat that clearly didn't belong to him – had raced up the stairs to join them. Louisa stared at him, hardly able to believe her eyes.

'You look as if you've seen a ghost.' He gave her a weak smile.

'It's becoming a habit of mine,' she said dryly, thinking briefly of Nancy as she looked past him. 'Where's Billy? Isn't he with you?'

'I was hopin' to find him here, tucked up in bed,' he said as they made their way back down to the hall.

'We've seen neither hide nor hair of him,' Grace said, breaking off to console Winnie who had begun to sob in distress.

'We've been praying that he got away from the tender with you.'

'The last time I saw him was the day you came with the *Curlew* – it's one of the reasons I'm here: to thank you for what you did. The shot you fired distracted the crew who went into a panic, allowin' us to escape in their jolly-boat. There were several of us and we managed to get away from the guards, rowin' for our lives.

'Knowin' the coast like the back of my hand, I suggested we land somewhere in the marshes, but one of the naval frigates intercepted us. As they sent their boat to pick us up, Billy and I jumped and swam for it.'

'Billy can't swim,' Winnie cried out.

'It turns out that he can,' Jason told her. 'We made it to the rocks where we had a rest before scrambling up the cliff. Unfortunately, we came face-to-face with these two old biddies who were out takin' the air. We must have given them quite a fright: a pair of drowned rats poppin' their heads up from the scrub. I told them they needn't get into a funk, but it was too late … their screams attracted the attention of a passing detachment of soldiers. Seein' we were about to be caught, Billy went one way and I went the other.

'The soldiers were right on my tail, and the only way out was to take a tumble into some bushes below the cliff path where I lay quiet despite the prickles in my unmentionables.' He stopped short, blushing. 'I'm sorry. I should be more careful about pickin' my words in front of you.'

Louisa didn't care what he said – he was back, and that was all that mattered. She just wished Billy had come with him.

'I hitched a ride with a carter who took me to Dover where I stayed for three or four days, lookin' for Billy. I should have sent word, but you never know who you can trust.'

'Oh, he's dead and gone and there's nothing I can do about it,' Winnie sobbed.

'He'll be back – you know what Billy's like. He'll stroll in here with his hands in his pockets and a grin on his face like he always does.' Grace tried to soothe her, stroking her back, but Winnie was inconsolable.

'Grace, give her a tot of brandy.' A thought occurred to Louisa. 'Jason, does your father know you're back? Poor Mr Witherall has been beside himself.'

'I was comin' straight here when I ran into my mother. I said I'd see her later.' He rubbed his stubbly beard. 'Louisa, I need to talk to you in private – about the run.'

'Go and wait in the parlour,' she said softly. 'I'll bring you something to eat.'

He finished off their fish stew, three rolls and a large slice of fruit cake while Louisa had Grace fetch hot water, soap and Pa's razor, and dig out some of their father's slops, before she closed the door behind her, noting the astonishment on Grace's face.

'Are you sure you don't want me to stay?' she demanded from the other side of the door.

'No, thank you,' Louisa said as Jason looked up from his empty plate.

'I didn't just come here to say thank you. I had to see you.'

She didn't dare ask why, afraid that his answer would shatter the glorious illusion that he was here to tell her that he still loved her …

'I'm sorry for what I said about you and Mr Trice,' he went on. 'I know you wouldn't have agreed to give him what he wanted if you weren't desperate.'

'I didn't give him what he wanted,' she interrupted. 'I haven't seen him since the day …' Her cheeks burned at the memory of his judgement and condemnation when he'd found her and the attorney together.

'On my way here, I saw the sign for the auction at the Three Kings.'

'What auction?'

'You don't know? Oh, I expect your neighbours haven't said anythin' because they think you know all about it. Compass Cottage – your home – is for sale by order of the executors of Mr Lennicker's will on the thirty-first, the last day of this month.'

'The end is nigh then.' Louisa took a seat opposite him, exhausted. 'Mr Trice said he would have to sell it if he didn't get his money. I've paid some back, but it's never enough. The bill keeps going up, what with interest and—'

'You paid him to represent us at the hearin'. I assumed it was my father who received the bill, but it was you. He told me that he'd sent Abel to fetch Mr Trice on your instruction. Why didn't you say?'

'I was too ashamed to admit the depth of my obligation to that man. Oh Jason, when I thought we were going to be married, I had never felt so happy. I didn't want anything to break the spell, least of all Mr Trice.'

'But he did anyway,' Jason said quietly. 'I was upset that you lied to me about your involvement with him, and when I saw him with his greasy hands all over you, I was livid – at him and at you for deceivin' me. It reminded me of how Margaret had been seein' somebody behind my back.'

'You don't know that for certain.'

'She took up with him with indecent haste after she jilted me, but that's in the past and the past can't be altered. Louisa, I had time to reflect when I was locked up in that tender and I realised that I've done and said a lot of things that I didn't mean, out of anger and a young man's arrogance. I misjudged you when it came to Mr Trice, and I'm sorry, because I know from your bravery and strength of character that you'd never throw yourself away on the likes of him. If he had forced himself on you, I don't know what I'd have done to him.'

'I'm sorry too.' She stood up. 'This won't do – the water's getting cold.' She closed the curtains and lit a candle, an act of wastefulness, but a necessary one. She poured the hot water from the ewer into the basin that Grace had left on the table, then watched him out of the corner of her eye as he took off his coat and waistcoat, before stripping off his shirt. As the crumpled linen slipped from his shoulders, revealing his well-muscled chest, he turned away slightly.

'What happened?' she asked, noting the criss-cross pattern of angry welts across his back. 'You can't tell me that the brambles did that to you.'

'Billy and I had a go at escapin' before you turned up with the *Curlew*,' he said. 'Billy spoke to one of the men on the tender who was guardin' the scuttle, offerin' him a guinea to be paid at a later date if he'd let us go up for a breath of fresh air. We were workin' out if we could steal one of the jollyboats, when the other guard grew suspicious. I said it was all my doin', and they chucked Billy back down into the hold and gave me a whippin' for it.' He picked up the washcloth and dipped it in the water.

'Let me do it.' Their fingers touched as she took the cloth and wrung it out, then pressed it gently against his wounds.

He winced.

'You'll have to bear it,' she smiled, trying again. She worked back and forth along each welt until he began to relax, and when she was done, he washed his hair and let her comb out the nits.

'After they took us off the street, they rowed us across to the tender, took our details and locked us in the hold to give us time to decide if we wanted to volunteer for the King's shillin'.' Jason smiled wryly as he picked up the razor to shave, the cut-throat blade scraping roughly across his skin.

'It's no choice, of course. If you object, they sign you up anyway. Billy didn't have his papers on him, not that they'd have counted this time. When I showed them my paperwork, it only made them more determined to have me.'

'One seafarer is worth at least two landlubbers, if not three.'

'That's right – a trained seaman already knows the ropes, so to speak. I understand that impressment is a necessary evil, but I had no intention of volunteerin' for the navy. I told them they were makin' a mistake in takin' me off my usual duties as a Cinque Ports man, already loyal and working for His Majesty, but all I got was a fat lip for my trouble. Before last year, they would have paid me as a man in lieu to impress men for them. I'd have got eighteen pence a day and a penny a mile road money for the return home.' He paused for a moment to put down the razor and wipe his face.

'How do I look?'

'Very well, as always,' she admitted.

'You can't imagine what it's like to be shut away with the stench and dirt of thirty or forty men cryin' for their wives and children. It put me into a right passion, I can tell you.'

'Won't you always be looking over your shoulder now you have a price on your head?'

'Ah, I took the precaution of smearing my face with dirt to darken my complexion, rubbing soot into my hair and swapping hats with one of the other men. Then I showed the press officer another man's indenture, a forgery I had made up some time ago for just such an eventuality. I told the press officer I was a boatman by the name of Isaiah Feasey. Of course, it made no difference when it came to bein' deprived of my liberty, but it's his name that will be marked with an R for run, not mine.'

'Unfortunately, he is unmarked now, thanks to an arrangement that One Eye made with Doctor Audley,' Louisa said, falling silent.

Jason cleared his throat. 'Why did you do it? Why did you risk your life for us?'

'I did it for you,' she whispered, biting back tears. 'Out of love, whether or not it's reciprocated. Because I realised, a little too late, what true love is.'

'Are you saying that you love me?'

She nodded, hardly able to breathe as she gazed into his eyes, his pupils dilated with passion.

'Then our feelings are mutual. Oh, I missed you. Locked away in the dark, I couldn't stop thinking of you and how I ached to hold you. Will you say that we can start again, that we are engaged?'

'Of course I will.'

'My love …' He reached out and grasped her hand, their fingers intertwining as he pressed his lips to her wrist, working up to the crook of her elbow.

'Jason, please ...' she said.

'Are you sayin' please go on, or stop?' Behind his quizzical expression, she detected a glint of amusement.

'I'm saying stop,' she said sternly, then added, 'for the present.'

'You almost had me there.' He chuckled as she took a small step back.

'I've had rather an adventure of my own while you've been away.' And she went on to tell him of the kidnap and her escape, aided by Nancy Stickles.

'I should have been here to protect you.'

'It was One Eye's doing, and he's going to get his comeuppance one day soon, so don't go rushing in. Our priority is this next run. We can't afford to jeopardise it, not if I'm going to keep the roof over my sisters' heads.'

'You're right. This young lady you speak of – I've always thought there was something odd about the tale of the Fey Lady.'

'She and Nancy are one and the same,' Louisa said. 'She claims that she's related to my family by blood. We share a father.'

'Do you believe her?'

She nodded. 'I didn't want to but, having had time to reflect, it makes sense. Pa kept Nancy's existence secret out of respect for our feelings, but it's caused great harm, depriving us of our sister's company, and Nancy of a comfortable life. It grieves me even more to think that Pa might still be alive if we'd known about our half-sister.' She recalled how Billy had told her that Pa's argument with One Eye on the evening he was shot had escalated because of One Eye's threat to reveal his scandalous secret. Having met Nancy, she now knew what that secret had been.

'I'm sure Righteous had the best of intentions,' Jason said. 'He didn't intend any harm to come from it.'

'How could he have left his child to suffer from One Eye's cruelty?'

'If you look at it from your father's point of view, he was safe in the knowledge that the child remained with her mother. He would have assumed that Mrs Stickles would keep their daughter from harm, and that One Eye's story of the Fey Lady would keep their secret safe. What's done is done, Louisa. You can't change it.'

'I know,' she sighed.

Jason got dressed and Louisa saw him out. He hesitated on the doorstep, then turned and leaned towards her, planting the softest of kisses on her cheek.

'I'll call on you tomorrow. Good day.'

'Good day,' she echoed, her instincts screaming at her not to let him out of her sight, but he was an adventurer who thrived on danger and excitement. If she wished to be with him, she had to accept that she couldn't change him.

She watched him stride away along the street, then closed the door. Her joy that he felt the same about her as she did about him, was soon tempered by the sound of Winnie crying, reminding her that Billy was still missing.

Hurrying up to their room, she found Winnie sitting on the edge of her bed, her body racked with sobs.

'My dear sister.' She sat beside her with her arm around her waist. 'You're in love with him. I understand.'

'There's more to it than that, Louisa. I'm with child.'

'No! How?'

'I couldn't help it,' Winnie cried. 'Billy promised we'd get married as soon as possible. I need him back before I start to show.'

'Does he know about—?'

'No, I didn't get to tell him.'

'Calm down,' Louisa said, trying to soothe her.

'What will everyone think of me? Of us?'

'Let's cross that bridge if we come to it.' Louisa felt a little sick as Winnie's sobbing began to subside, wondering if Jason would assume that all the Lennicker sisters were tarred with the same brush.

She woke at dawn the following day with pins and needles where she had been lying with her arms around Winnie. Not wanting to disturb her, she gazed up at the ceiling, listening to the familiar sounds of home: the floorboards creaking as Grace went downstairs; the cries of the gulls echoing down the chimney; the chatter and laughter as their neighbours swept the pavements outside their houses.

Where would she and her sisters be in two months' time, if they lost Compass Cottage? There was nothing she could do but carry on with the next run and sell the goods before the auction – their lives, their prospects and the future of Winnie's unborn child depended on it.

# Chapter Sixteen

## *A Baker's Dozen*

Jason called that evening.

'Shall we go out for a walk?' he said, smiling as he hovered on the step. 'Will your sisters be persuaded to accompany us?'

'I'll ask them,' she said gaily, hoping they would refuse the offer. It was all very well being patient and chaste when they had the rest of their lives ahead of them, but who knew how long that would be? Then she recalled Winnie's situation. The last thing she wanted was to end up holding Jason to ransom over an unborn child. She wanted him to want her for who she was, not marry her because he had to.

'I'm not interrupting anything, am I?' Grace said brightly, appearing at the foot of the staircase. 'Of course I am. I'm afraid Winnie and I can't join you. She's sleeping – I gave her a dose of what's left of the laudanum that Doctor Audley prescribed for Pa. I thought it a good idea and she didn't object, but now I wish I hadn't because I can't rouse her.'

'How much did you give her?'

'Only what she told me. She was in a dreadful state, sobbing and shaking. I didn't know what else to do.'

'Did she take anything else?' Louisa felt a sense of trepidation.

'Only some gin, I think. Just a little. Oh, do you think she was trying to harm herself?'

'Grace, not in front of …' She nodded towards Jason who was frowning.

'Too late, I reckon,' he said softly. 'You'd better go to her, Louisa. I'll wait.'

She didn't argue, hurrying up to the bedroom with Grace close behind her.

'Shall I send for the doctor?'

Louisa leaned over the bed and spoke into Winnie's ear.

'Wake up, my dear sister.' Winnie didn't stir. 'What have you done?' She pinched her cheek and gave her a prod in the arm.

'Has she gone?' Grace whispered.

'She's still breathing.' Louisa shook her shoulder. Winnie uttered a small moan. 'Open your eyes!' Louisa found herself staring into a pair of eyes, the pupils like liquorice. There was a flicker of recognition before they closed again.

'Do you think she's going to be all right?' Grace asked.

'I reckon so. We should watch over her until she wakes.'

'I'll sit with her. You go out with Jason.'

'I can't leave her.'

'Sit up with him, then. I'll let you know if anything changes, I promise.'

'All right. Thank you, Grace.' She kissed Winnie's forehead, then went downstairs, downhearted. She found Jason in the parlour, his back to the fireplace.

'How is she?'

'I fear she has overdosed on laudanum.'

'It was a mistake, I expect. My father had a right telling-off from the apothecary when he took more than advised of the medicine for his gout – double the dose doesn't give twice the effect.'

'Winnie knew what she was doing.' Louisa sat down at the table and rested her head in her hands.

'You'll have to explain.' Sensing the pressure of his palm on her back, she looked up into his eyes, into his very soul. 'It's Billy, isn't it?'

'For Grace and I, it's like a brother has gone missing, but for Winnie, it's more than that,' she confided. 'I promised I wouldn't keep any more secrets from you, so I'll tell you now – in the strictest confidence ...' she paused, and he nodded, '... Winnie and Billy are sweethearts.'

'I guessed so.'

'Did you? When?'

'A while ago now. It's the way they look at each other, the small gestures of affection: a look, a brief caress. It's tough for women when their menfolk are impressed. Poor Winnie – all I can say is it's a godsend that there are no children involved.'

'She's with child,' Louisa said flatly. 'Jason, did Billy seem any different? Could he have guessed?'

'He was still the same old Billy: light-hearted; playin' pranks on the other crew; drinkin' a bit too much.' Jason shrugged. 'He didn't give the impression he was about to settle down to become a husband and father. I'm sure he'd have mentioned it when we were packed into the hold of that tender. We did a lot of talkin'. Come to think of it, he went on about Winnie an awful lot, but I was only half listenin', bein' preoccupied with thoughts of another young lady.'

'I'm afraid you'll change your mind about us after what Winnie's gone and done,' she said sadly. 'You'll think we are all moonstruck. I wish I'd seen what was going on under my nose—'

'This isn't your fault. She isn't the first unmarried woman to sprain her ankle, and she won't be the last. I'm sure everyone will look after her and the infant when it comes – as Billy would expect – until he returns, which he will do, as sure as eggs are eggs.'

'How can you be so certain?'

'I can't ... I only know that Billy will do his utmost to get back to where he belongs here in Deal with his own people. In fact, I hope he's back in time for the run – I know I grumble about him, but he's fit and strong, and he means well. I rely on him to keep our spirits up when there's no wind, or we've missed out on a hovel because one of the other luggers has beaten us to it.'

'He wants to be a boatman like you.'

'He wasn't born into it, but he is one of us,' Jason said.

'He'd be very proud to hear that.'

'I'll tell him when he gets back.'

'If,' she said.

'Anyway, Mr Witherall and I have been puttin' our heads together over the finer points of this run, there bein' little time left to prepare. He's scratched a crew, a few extra hands chosen from men loyal to our cause, but he hasn't yet found out about the Rattlers' operation.'

'We've already set the date,' Louisa said.

'I know, but it isn't set in stone – I'd like to travel a couple of days ahead of the *Good Intent*, having an idea about how we can salvage some honour – and profit – from what they did to us last time.'

'I can't ask Mrs Stickles again – it wasn't her fault, but she spun us quite a yarn.'

'What about Nancy? She's on our side?'

'Yes, she is – and she hears everything at the Rattling Cat. But she's worried that One Eye would take it out on her mother, if he found out that somebody had blabbed.'

'Talk to her anyway,' Jason said.

'I can't unless we can offer her protection.'

He sighed wryly. 'How can you call yourself a free trader with a conscience like yours?'

'I'll ask her, but only if we can spirit her and Mrs Stickles away and out of danger should it become necessary.'

He nodded, and went on, 'We'll load in Gravelines and when the *Good Intent* turns up, we'll head for the Sands where we'll wait for you and the crews of the smaller boats to collect the goods and bring them ashore in small quantities so there's less chance of attractin' attention.

'Then, when the *Good Intent* is on her way back, fully loaded, we'll intercept her and do our worst. The Rattlers won't know what's hit them.' He raised her hand to his lips and kissed it tenderly until she could barely concentrate. 'Don't worry, my love. I have no intention of riskin' my life and those of my men.

'The *Good Intent* will signal to their spotsman, who'll be waiting to signal back to let her know when it's safe for her to land, so if our plan is to succeed, we must find out who the spotsman is and prevent him sendin' out a signal. The Rattlers will know something is amiss, and I hope it will create enough confusion and delay to allow us to pounce. The icin' on the cake would be to have a little fun with the Revenue, especially Officer Chase, who seems determined to catch us out, even against the orders of his Superintendent.' Jason grinned. 'We're wastin' precious time …' He took her into his arms and kissed her, not leaving until well after midnight.

In the morning, Louisa asked Winnie if she was trying to get rid of the baby.

'Not deliberately. Oh, I don't know. I don't know what to do. I'd never hurt it – I couldn't – but I do think life would be much simpler, much better for everyone if it wasn't here. What if I don't love it, Louisa? What if I resent it because my Billy is gone?'

'Oh, Winnie,' she sighed.

'What if he's staying away because he knew somehow? Because he guessed and didn't want to be with me any longer? His father abandoned him soon after he was born. It's like history repeating itself.'

'You can't mean that. Billy, whatever I think of him, is a kind lad. He wouldn't abandon you because you were with child.' Louisa paused, then came to a decision. She needed to be honest with Winnie. 'I've told Jason.'

'Oh no. You didn't. I'm mortified. I wish I had ended it now.'

'No, you don't. I trust him not to say anything. Winnie, you have to stay strong – for yourself and the infant, and for Billy.'

'I'm tired,' she said, 'so very tired.'

'Then go back to bed. I'll come and wake you in an hour or two. In the meantime, Grace and I will go down to the market.'

'You're making me feel guilty for not helping you.'

'Get some rest.'

'I'll see you later,' Winnie sighed as she tramped up the stairs, her back bowed like a tub carrier's, as if she bore the weight of two half-ankers.

Mr Jansen arrived with the horse and cart from Limepit Acres and unloaded three baskets of fruit and veg on to the doorstep.

'I wish you good day, misses.' He jumped back on to the cart and picked up the reins.

'Is that all you have for us?' Louisa asked, noticing that there was no salted pork.

'Ah yes. I pointed it out to Mr Laxton who said you'd have more when you'd paid him for the last lot … and the one before that. I'll see you next week.'

'Yes, of course. Thank you.' Louisa and Grace sorted the produce and arranged it on the handcart, the ripest and shiniest fruit on the top, the questionable items underneath.

'You have the change with you?' Grace asked.

She'd forgotten, being swept up in Winnie's troubles. 'I haven't.'

'I'll fetch it.' Grace returned soon after with Louisa's purse.

Louisa pushed the squeaky handcart along to the market where it was so busy they couldn't use their usual pitch, and even though she protested to Mr Jones who allocated spaces to the traders, they ended up on one of the side streets because the road from the well by the chapel to Five Bell Lane was blocked with market carts.

'Penny a lot – fine berries,' she cried out.

'Hi ho, come and have a look – you've never tasted peas and beans like these, fresh from the field,' Grace joined in.

Louisa shouted until she was hoarse, yet they made very little, just a few pence here and there, because almost every passer-by had already spent their money.

'We can buy a penny roll and a ha'porth of sprats, if you like. And some beer is good for raising the spirits,' Grace suggested hopefully.

It seemed that as soon as they had any money, it trickled out like water between their fingers, Louisa thought as Mrs Stickles appeared, looking for a bargain.

'I'd like a dozen of those apples, thank you,' she said. 'I'll pick the ones I like the look of, if you don't mind.'

Louisa took a step back, keeping an eye on her, watching out for any sleight of hand. Mrs Stickles counted thirteen apples into her basket. 'You did say a baker's dozen, didn't you?'

'I didn't –' she held out her hand for the money '– but as it's you …'

'I'm glad my daughter could be of assistance,' Mrs Stickles said quietly as she dropped the coins into Louisa's palm. 'I assume there's a reward – she was taking a terr'ble risk going against Mr Feasey.'

'That's between me and Nancy.'

'You're just like Robert – 'e could be a parsimonious, penny-pinchin'—' She stopped abruptly.

'My sisters are keen to meet our half-sister – I wonder if you might ask her to call on us, if she can get away from the inn.'

'I expect she can drop by one evenin' after dark – as long as it's to 'er benefit.'

Louisa didn't want to discuss any reward. 'Send her tonight after seven. It's caused us much distress to think that our father kept her from us.'

'We did what we thought was right at the time. When I was a young woman, I 'ad a soft spot for Robert. 'E paid me a fair amount of attention and one thing led to another. Afterwards, filled with remorse, 'e went back to your mother. When she passed away, 'e came in to the Rattlin' Cat, cryin' 'is eyes out. Well, although 'e'd done me wrong in the past, 'is tears touched my 'eart, and we reconciled upon 'is promise that one day, 'e would marry me and set me up with a pot 'ouse. As you know, it didn't 'appen. Oh, I'd better get back to work – pies don't make themselves, more's the pity.'

Louisa had been fearful of her sisters' reaction, knowing how hard it was for them to accept they had a half-sibling, but it had to be worse for Nancy, an only child unused to society, Louisa thought later that evening when Nancy arrived at the cottage.

'Come in,' she said.

'That's very kind.'

Louisa showed their visitor to the parlour.

'This is a pretty place.' Nancy kept away from the window as though exposure to the light would make her wither like some rare fern and die. 'You're very lucky, but I 'ear that Compass Cottage is to be sold. I 'ear things. They say women gossip, but men are worse. Once they 'ave a couple of pints inside them, they don't stop talkin'.

'My mother told me to come – she said my sisters wanted to meet me, but perhaps they don't at all ...' Nancy's voice trailed off behind the veil.

'I'll go and find them shortly,' Louisa said. 'Was there much trouble when One Eye found me gone?'

''E flew off the 'andle all right, but 'e accepted my version of events. 'E sent Awful Doins and Lawless after you, but they didn't have any enthusiasm for the task – I watched them lurking in the alleyway, waiting for a reasonable time to elapse before returning inside to tell One Eye you'd given them the slip.'

'I have your pistol – you must have it back.' Louisa slid the secret drawer in the table open and gave it to her.

Nancy tucked it into her basket.

'I 'ave more freedom than you might imagine, comin' and goin' unremarked, because to many, I am no more than a ghost, an apparition of One Eye's invention. 'Is gang, not being blessed with much intelligence between them, 'ave never guessed that the Fey Lady is made of flesh and blood. I want to 'elp you.'

'In return, I will get you away from the Rattling Cat – it isn't right that you live in that den of thieves and murderers.'

'I've dreamt of movin' away with my mother, but it's impossible. The only money I 'ave is the few coins that

One Eye throws in my direction from time to time – for 'is own amusement. Louisa, I don't expect any reward, only the pleasure of seein' One Eye get 'is comeuppance. I was there when our father was fatally injured and when One Eye punched my mother in the face. I 'ear 'im gloating about what 'e's done, and I 'ate 'im for it.

'I've 'eard about Billy Fleet and 'ow 'e's missin'. 'E isn't the only one gone – the Rattlers are a few men down too. They didn't all get away in time.'

'They knew of the press in advance?' Louisa said.

'One Eye knows everythin' before anyone else does.'

And he didn't warn the other men, Louisa thought, but then, why would he?

'Anyway, 'e's plannin' another run for the Rattlers soon. I can let you know where and when. Forewarned is forearmed.'

'How?' Louisa asked. 'Will you send a note? It won't be safe for you to keep turning up here in person.'

'I'll find a way,' Nancy said.

'Just promise me you'll be careful.'

'I promise.' Nancy changed the subject. 'I see that my sisters don't wish to meet me,' she went on sadly.

'I'll winkle them out of their hiding places,' Louisa said, annoyed that they had both disappeared. She called for them, but only Grace appeared, looking a little sheepish for hiding away.

'At last,' Louisa said.

'I would have joined you earlier, but Winnie called for me. Louisa, she is indisposed. Nancy, it's . . .' Grace hesitated, then smiled. 'This is a miracle. To find out completely out of the blue that we have another sister.'

'It's lovely to meet you,' Nancy said. 'I 'ope we may 'ave a long acquaintance. I should go, or I shall be missed.'

'Wait.' Grace went out of the room and came back with a folded handkerchief. 'This is made from silk. Pa gave it to me – I'd like you to have it, from one sister to another.'

'Oh no, it's yours. You must keep it.'

'Take it.' Grace pressed it into Nancy's hand before dashing away. 'We'll see you again very soon.'

'There's nothing I wish for more.'

They bade each other farewell and Louisa showed Nancy out before joining Winnie who was sitting up in bed with Grace fussing over her.

'What's wrong?'

'The infant has gone ...' Winnie was crying. 'My courses have started.'

'Grace, did you know about the child?' Louisa asked.

'I guessed when Winnie was sick – Mrs Roper was dreadfully ill the last time she was in the family way.'

Louisa wished that Grace would express a little shock at the thought that her sister had conceived a child out of wedlock. As for her, her feelings were mixed: sorrow for the lost soul of an innocent child and her sister who was terribly upset, and guilt for thinking that it was one less problem for them to worry about.

Nancy kept her word and the next morning when Louisa went outside to sweep the pavement, there was a loaf of bread on the doorstep with a crock over the top.

Having taken it into the kitchen, she noticed the crust had been cut. She lifted the top of the loaf away to reveal a roll of paper in the hollowed-out centre. She pulled it out, unfurled it and began to read.

*Run – second to last day of this month, X.*

She told Jason when he called later, having been out all day with the *Whimbrel*.

'Who is your spy?' he asked, perusing the note.

'Nancy.'

'It doesn't tie in with the rumours going around the capstan grounds or at the Waterman's Arms. We should take that information with a pinch of salt – and destroy the evidence with a little cheese, perhaps.'

She sniffed the loaf – it smelled all right. She found some cheese – minted with mites – and served it up with slices of bread.

'I have no reason to doubt Nancy's word – she wants revenge on One Eye as much as I do.' She thought of how she'd spent her life in the dark, invisible and scared of what One Eye might do to her next. 'Probably more.'

'If this is correct, we have more time to prepare. Assumin' that the Rattlers would go to France in the next two weeks, I'd confirmed my father's arrangements with the merchants to have the goods ready and waitin' in the warehouse.' Jason wiped the crumbs from his jacket. 'Louisa, I'm really not sure about this – there's somethin' fishy about it.'

Louisa brooded over it – she had thought she could trust her half-sister, but Jason had planted a seed of doubt in her mind. With the run coming up, she felt she was sailing an uncertain course: riding the crest of a wave one moment, then being driven dangerously close to the rocks where her enterprise might crash, ruining any hope of keeping her family's fortunes afloat.

## Chapter Seventeen

## *The Calm Before the Storm*

On the Sunday evening, a year to the day that One Eye had shot their father, Winnie lit the candle on the sill in the parlour. The flame flickered, spewing dark smoke, and the wind whistled through the rafters. The rumble of the barrels across the roof was replaced by a drumroll of thunder, as a flash of lightning announced the arrival of the storm that had been brewing all day, the anvil clouds hovering like giant ships on the horizon.

'How are you?' Louisa asked her.

'Hush,' Grace said quickly, almost at the same time, but it was too late.

'That's the tenth time you've asked me that,' Winnie said testily. 'I'm grateful that you care, but I really can't be doing with it. I feel bad, dreadfully bad for Billy, not knowing where he is on a night like this. I can't eat. I can't sleep.'

Louisa couldn't sleep either – for the heat and feverish anticipation, wondering about the imminent run and when she and Jason would next be able to snatch a few hours together.

'The giants are playing skittles tonight,' Grace said as the thunder rattled the windows and a seagull screamed down the chimney.

'I hope the men don't have to go out in this,' Winnie said quietly.

'I hope not too,' Louisa said, the reality of being a Deal boatman's sweetheart beginning to sink in as she began to pray for the ships out at sea.

'There's bound to be at least one gobbled up by the Sands tonight,' Grace said as someone tapped on the window.

Louisa looked out to find Mrs Witherall hurrying away along the alley towards the beach with a group of their neighbours, their lanterns swinging as they walked.

'Quickly, grab your oilskins. Something's happened,' she said. 'Winnie, do you think you should stay here?'

'No, I'm coming with you.'

'So am I,' said Grace.

As they followed the clanging of a bell down to the shore, Louisa hoped that Winnie wasn't going to be disappointed again. Had Billy and the remaining pressed men been returned to them, or was a vessel stranded on the Sands?

The *Whimbrel* and *Good Intent* were side by side on the shingle, the boatmen assembling near one of the capstans where Mr Witherall was ringing the bell. A wind blasted across the beach, raising an enormous swell, the like of which Louisa hadn't seen before. Jason – she knew it was him, even though he was dressed in an oilskin, boots and sou'wester – was taking charge, looking out to sea with his spyglass and shouting orders. Isaiah was organising his crew, ready to launch.

Jason waved her over.

'Go on – he's asking for you,' Grace said, giving her a nudge when she hesitated. 'You're engaged – everyone knows. We'll wait.'

'I'll wish him God speed.' Having arrived at his side, she gave him a brief smile, the gale threatening to blow her teeth down her throat.

'We have to go out. There's a schooner, the *White Hind*. She's been torn from her moorings and blown on to the Sands.' He pointed towards the horizon across a sea that was white with spindrift. 'That's her, flashin' lights and firin' blanks.'

Louisa hung on to her hat as Isaiah came marching across.

'You will agree that neither one of us goes out tonight,' he said. 'Everyone avows that those waves will 'ave us and smash us straight back on to the beach.'

'There are women and children on that vessel – of course we're goin'. Oh, I see.' Jason brushed the raindrops from his nose. 'You're runnin' scared and you're afraid we'll get there first and take the spoils.'

'Not at all,' Isaiah said, but Louisa knew he was lying.

'I don't care what you and your crew decide to do. This is my calling – I'm not going to stand by and let them perish.'

'Then you're even more stupid than I thought.' Isaiah glowered at Jason, then shook his head. 'You can't possibly launch a lugger in this. Everybody's sayin' it's the worst storm in livin' memory.'

'We're comin' with you, Marlin,' Mr Edwards said, and the rest of the *Whimbrel*'s crew cheered.

'No man will be forced to risk his life,' Jason announced as Isaiah looked on, his face dark with anger and resentment.

'It's more of a breeze than a hurricane,' Mr Roper called.

'I'll be accompanyin' my boy,' Mr Witherall said, stepping up. 'You could use somebody of my experience.'

Louisa noticed the flicker of doubt cross Jason's face.

'I might come to regret this decision, but yes, the more hands, the better.'

'I'm coming with you.' She would rather be drowned than live without him.

'Oh no. That's impossible—'

'You need me. The women and children will be terrified – my presence will reassure them.'

'The Lace Maiden's comin' with us – she'll look after the passengers,' Jason shouted to his men.

The sea flared as the lightning flashed. Tiles were flying off the houses along the beach, and one became completely unroofed. The crew began to mutiny against their captain's decision, talking amongst themselves.

'It's bad luck to 'ave a woman on the boat.'

'That's an old wives' tale. There are more than a few of the gentler sex who've taken to life on the ocean wave.'

'Are you sayin' she should be allowed, then?'

'She's no ordinary woman. She's Righteous's daughter – that 'as to count for something. 'E was a storm warrior and master of the sea, like Marlin 'ere.'

Jason's voice rang out across their argument.

'Anyone who disagrees can stay ashore. There's no time to waste. Prepare to launch.'

Louisa felt Winnie tugging against her sleeve.

'I won't let you go. I can't bear it, not after Billy.'

'They need me,' Louisa said.

'We need you too,' Grace responded, her eyes gleaming with fear.

'I know. I'll be back. Don't worry.' Louisa was swept up by the crew – nineteen or twenty men – rushing to embark. They took their places and showed her where she should sit, out of their way in the cabin.

'Let her go!'

A giant wave came ashore as the *Whimbrel* flew down the beach. The roller burst into a towering mass of foam, enveloping the lugger completely as she crashed into the water with an ear-splitting bang.

'She's lost – the *Whimbrel*'s gorn,' the crowd screamed from the beach.

Fighting for breath, and to see her way through the spume, Louisa held on tight, waiting for the boat to rise again on the crest of the following wave. After what seemed like an eternity, the *Whimbrel* bobbed up to cheering and crying.

'Get bailin'!' she heard Jason shout as some of the crew used oars and poles to keep the lugger away from the beach, and others battled with the sodden canvas while Mr Witherall took the helm. 'Keep her steady!'

The lugger began to thrash through the seething water, making her way slowly but surely towards the deadly Sands. Louisa turned her gaze away from Deal, the town shrouded by low cloud and sea spray, the figures small and receding on the shore. There was no telling if they would make it back in one piece, but the screams of the men and women in the distance drove them on.

The waves broke over their bow, sending washes of water across the boards. The crew's voices became almost inaudible in the wind, and the lanterns dimmed.

Louisa checked the supplies in the cabin: a half-anker of spirit; cloth for bandages; a knife and scithers; a vinaigrette and a box of snuff; blankets, some of which were already wet; ship's bisket. Then she ventured on deck with a bucket, and despite the frowns of disapproval from the men, started bailing, a thankless task, because each time she emptied the bucket over the gunwales, the water continued to rise up her calves, soaking her skirts beneath her oilskin cape.

She kept moving, trying to keep warm, reminded of how cold the summer sea could be.

'Has anyone seen the *Good Intent*?' Mr Roper called.

'There's no sign of 'er,' Mr Witherall called back.

'Keep your eyes peeled!' Jason shouted urgently as a cruiser at anchor loomed out of the murk. 'Stop frettin' about the Rattlers – they won't be on our tail in these conditions. They are nothin' but pigeon-hearted poltroons.'

A fork of lightning lit up the skies as the *Whimbrel* turned aft of the cruiser and passed her. The rumble of the thunder rolling around them became mingled with another more deadly noise, a constant roar.

'It's the breakers hittin' the sandbank, miss,' Mr Edwards said, apparently having noticed her pause. 'It's nothin' to worry about.' His gaping grin did little to allay her fear as the wind and waves took them inching closer to the Sands. The sea tossed the lugger about like a formless monster, tasting and swallowing its prey, then spitting it out again as though teasing the last living frights out of it.

'Keep her well trimmed,' Jason yelled. 'The *White Hind*! She's straight ahead of us, her sails flying, her foremast gone.'

Louisa could hear the pitiful cries of the crew and passengers, and the mournful tolling of the ship's bell, as the stricken schooner hove into view. She could make out the dark figures lashed to the main rigging as the sea surged around them.

''Er bowsprit's gone, washed away. What are we goin' to do, Marlin?' Mr Roper bellowed.

'We've got to get the men, women and children off,' Jason responded. 'She's too far gone to try re-floatin' her with all on board. Bring her closer!'

'It's too dangerous,' his father called from the stem. 'If we 'it 'er, we'll go down with her.'

'Bring her closer!' Jason repeated. 'That's an order. Who's captain here?'

'You, my boy. I mean, Marlin. But on your 'ead be it.'

Louisa turned to Jason – he'd lost his sou'wester, his hair streaming back in the wind and rain; the muscle in his cheek taut; the vessel in his neck pulsing as he yelled out more orders, loud and clear and without panic. He held their lives in his hands, and whatever happened, she adored him, and would always love him, heart and soul.

'Rope me to the lugger and I'll jump.' He glanced briefly towards Louisa. Pressing her fingers to her lips, she nodded, and with the ghost of a smile, he looked away. He was brave but knew the risks, and although her instinct told her that they should turn away while they were still able to, she wouldn't hold him back.

The ribbon-like strips of the *White Hind*'s sails cracked like whips.

Forcing herself to watch, she held her breath as Jason and one of the younger men leapt across the foaming chasm between the two boats. Jason caught hold of the *White Hind*'s drooping sail and clung on while the sea rose up, hiding him behind drapes of spray and green water, before falling away again to reveal his figure further along the schooner's deck.

'Make sure you're ready for 'em, Louisa,' she heard Mr Witherall shout, as Jason returned with the first of the *White Hind*'s passengers, having made the *Whimbrel* fast to the schooner with ropes.

'There are two women and this child,' Jason said, handing her a shivering boy who couldn't have been more than three years old. 'They are all scared out of their wits. One has hit her head on the mast. Do what you can.'

'Mama?' the boy said as she carried him into the cabin and wrapped him in a blanket.

'She'll be here soon.' Peering out into the gloom, she could make out the soft haloes around the lanterns on the ships. There was more shouting and screaming, and a massive splash.

'Man overboard!' someone shouted, and her heart stopped.

Jason?

'The captain of the *White Hind* ... He lost his footing. Shine a light. This way!'

While some of the crew searched the waves, Jason and the others continued to work swiftly, bringing the passengers across safely to the *Whimbrel*, and reuniting the mother with her son. The second woman arrived, making her own way into the cabin. Her fine clothes were drenched, and blood was trickling from a cut at her temple.

'Miss Lennicker?' she exclaimed. 'I can hardly believe my eyes. I didn't expect to meet with you out here and on such a day as this.'

'Miss Flinders?' Louisa said tentatively.

'Mrs Harry Tempest.' She held out a gloved hand, then withdrew it. 'Oh dear, this is neither the time nor place for formalities. How is the child?'

'He's blue with cold,' the mother said.

'Do I need to ask if you have any brandy, Miss Lennicker?' Mrs Tempest asked.

Louisa gave out more blankets, along with some brandy and ship's bisket, as the boat pitched about in the water.

'That cut of yours needs some attention,' she said.

'It's merely a flesh wound,' Mrs Tempest asserted, but Louisa wasn't convinced. Her charges required medical assistance, a visit from Doctor Audley, but the crew of the *Whimbrel* were still battling against the elements. She left the cabin to find that Jason had rigged the *Whimbrel*'s mainmast on the *White Hind* as a foresail and attached a hawser.

As they started to drag the schooner off the sandbank, the rope took up the strain and the boats' timbers creaked.

'Keep goin'!' Jason shouted, his face tense and pale.

There was another creak, followed by a sharp crack.

'Slip her,' Jason yelled. 'She's caught on the bank. If you don't slip her, I will.' She recognised the barely suppressed panic in his voice as he went on. 'The *White Hind*'s broken her back. She won't make it off the Sands. We'll have to take the crew off and salvage whatever we can. Slip her ...'

The rope dropped in an arc into the wild smother, and the *Whimbrel*'s crew manoeuvred the lugger back in broadside to the stricken ship.

'How long will we be, Marlin?' Louisa shouted.

'It could be another two or three hours – we can't go back to Deal until the storm dies down and the tide turns. We can't beach in this – the swell's too much.'

She had no choice but to look after the passengers as best she could while the crew of the *White Hind* came aboard – ten men, three of them with broken arms and legs. At the same time, Jason and his men carried off whatever they could from the wreck: the bell; provisions; wine; rum; sails. They towed the remains of the schooner's masts behind them then took shelter in one of the channels inside the Sands, listening to the wind howling around them.

Mrs Tempest, the mother and child were huddled together in the cabin, the former holding a handkerchief soaked in brandy to her wound while the boy lay in his mother's arms, clutching a bisket.

'He has a little colour back in his cheeks,' Louisa said. 'That's a good sign.'

The mother gave a small smile. 'I wish I'd never agreed to it. I knew something terrible was going to happen. I'll never set foot on a boat again.'

'Mrs Ellwood and I are supposed to be following our husbands – fellow officers – to the Continent,' Mrs Tempest explained. 'I shall continue my journey – I can't bear to be too far from my dear Harry's side, but I understand Mrs Ellwood's reluctance to travel.'

'I'll never forgive myself if he ...' A tear trickled down Mrs Ellwood's face.

'He'll be all right,' Louisa said, praying that the boy would make a full recovery from his ordeal.

'I'm sure I speak for Mrs Ellwood when I say that words cannot express the extent of our gratitude for our rescue,' Mrs Tempest said. 'I feel that we will forever be in debt to you and the brave captain and crew who have saved us from the very jaws of death.'

'I wish we had managed to bring everyone to safety,' Louisa said softly before returning to the open deck.

The men supped brandy out of respect for the dead captain, Mr Roper took out his fiddle, and they sang of sailors returning dank-eyed to let their lovers know they had drowned in the lowland sea, of Nelson's victory, and of mermaids. Although their voices soothed her as they headed back through calmer seas to Deal, she had never felt so happy to be back on dry land, the ground still and serene beneath her feet.

She took a deep breath as her sisters came running, skidding and sliding along the shingle.

'We've been praying all night,' Grace said, throwing her arms around her neck.

'We didn't think you'd come back,' Winnie added wanly.

'We have news for you – Nancy didn't want to speak to me last night, but I insisted on taking a message. She came knocking on our door after midnight – she said to say that the ...' Grace lowered her voice before continuing,

'They've set the date for the run – they are takin' the *Good Intent* to France on Wednesday, that's in two days' time.'

'That can't be right.' Louisa frowned. 'What about the note in the loaf?'

'This came straight from the horse's mouth. She'd come straight from the Rattling Cat where she'd overheard the men talking. I asked her why she hadn't sent a note this time, thinking it would have been safer for her, but she shrugged and said she'd never been taught to do anything more than make her mark.'

'So the note was a ruse ... Thank you for telling me. Keep it to yourselves, won't you?'

'What do you think we are? Traitors?' Winnie joined in.

'I'm just being careful – Nancy has put herself in danger for our cause.'

'Oh, look at you – you're wet through,' Winnie said. 'We should get you home.'

'Not yet. I want to know what happened,' Grace said.

'And I'd like to be sure that my charges are safe,' Louisa added. 'Jason and his crew were heroes, the most courageous men you'll ever meet. You can't possibly imagine what it was like out there, yet only one life was lost, that of the captain of the schooner.' Louisa wished she had bitten her tongue – Winnie had a tear in her eye, having been reminded of Billy and not knowing his fate. 'Miss Flinders, now Mrs Harry Tempest, was on board.'

'We heard about that – Sir Flinders sent his carriage to wait at the Three Kings.'

'There is a mother and child – the boy is excessively chilled.'

'They're takin' him to the hotel to await Doctor Audley,' Mr Witherall cut in from beside them as the news of their return spread, bringing the wives and children, and the boatmen who'd chosen to stay at home, down to the beach.

'There's to be a celebration for the bold and gallant crew of the *Whimbrel* – there'll be milk and brandy, and music. I can't think of a better excuse for merrymakin'. My boy and 'is men will make themselves a small fortune out of what they've salvaged.' He turned suddenly, flinging out his arms to embrace his wife. 'Ah, Mrs Witherall, you find us in one piece.'

'Oh, my dear,' she sobbed as he held her tight. 'I thought I'd lost you.'

'There's life in the old dog yet,' he reassured her as Jason strode up to Louisa and her sisters.

'Good mornin', ladies,' he smiled. 'May I have a word with my fiancée, in private?'

'I'm not sure you should be alone together when you aren't yet married,' Grace said.

'Are you flirting with my intended?' Louisa had to ask, laughter bubbling in her throat.

'No.' Grace blushed. 'You may have her to yourself, Jason. She is unbearable.'

'I'll have you know that she's the bravest of the brave,' he said.

'I'm sorry for exposing you to our sisterly spat,' Louisa said as he drew her aside. 'What's happened with Isaiah and his crew?'

'Apparently, they retreated to the Rattling Cat and haven't been seen since.'

'They're preparing for the run,' she whispered. 'You were right about the note – somebody was feeding us false information. I have it on good authority that the Rattlers are leaving for France on Wednesday.'

'That doesn't give us much time. My men are exhausted ...' He deliberated for a while. 'We'll have to carry on as usual, otherwise the Rattlers will smell a rat. And we have to get Nancy and her mother out of there. The items that we salvaged from the *White Hind* must be taken to Customs and the boats prepared. The beach party will go ahead, and we'll set sail at midnight. The rest of the plans remain in place.'

'Will I see you before you go?' she asked.

'Of course – I'll forgo the drink, but I'm not missin' out on the dancin', not when I can be dancin' with you,' he added. 'Take care, Louisa.'

# Chapter Eighteen

## *The Third Run*

'Dance with me.' Jason took Louisa's hand, and at dusk on a balmy August night with the sea rolling calmly back and forth across the stones below, collecting up the ribbons of seaweed washed up from the deep by the storm the night before, they joined in with the dancing. Skipping and turning with the rhythms of the music, Louisa had eyes only for her partner, while the rest of the dancers became merely a blur. As the pipers and fiddlers broke for refreshments, Jason pulled her close.

'All is set,' he whispered into her ear. 'You know what to do?'

With mixed feelings of desire and regret, she nodded. They walked hand in hand to where Grace and Winnie were giving out tankards of milk and brandy, and Jason took one and turned to face their fellow revellers.

'I wish to say something,' he shouted. 'I won't interrupt the celebrations for long.'

'Silence for Marlin! Silence for the captain,' somebody yelled.

'A toast to my loyal friends and family – without you, none of these ventures would be possible,' Jason said, and the crowd erupted in cheers. 'And I'd like to say thank you with all my heart to the lovely lady at my side, who has agreed to become my wife.'

'If there's anyone I'd want to be shackled to by the leg, it's the Lace Maiden,' she heard one of the boatmen say.

'If you're expectin' a peaceful life with 'er waitin' about for you with your dinner ready, you'd better do a runner now,' said another.

'I want to marry her,' Jason said. 'I don't think of wedlock as a prison.'

'Oh, you will, my boy,' Mr Witherall joined in with the teasing, his face beaming. 'Give it a year or two, when you 'ave a couple of squallin' babes in the 'ouse.'

'She's a stubborn one, and clever. There isn't much she won't turn 'er 'and to,' said another.

'More fool 'er,' somebody joked.

'Is the Lace Maiden comin' over to France?'

'No,' Jason smiled. 'She's needed here.'

'She didn't do too bad for a woman yesterday,' Mr Roper admitted. 'In fact, she did better than poor Billy would 'ave – do you remember the time 'e caulked himself, lying down for a nap on the deck? When 'e got up 'is slops were covered in stripes from the tar between the boards. You pointed it out to 'im, Marlin, and the chucklehead only went and tried to deny it when the evidence was plain for all to see.'

'I do,' Jason said, sobering up. 'I wish he was here. A toast to Billy and those who haven't yet come back to us.'

It was a sombre and heartfelt cheer that went up, but the mood soon reverted, the musicians playing with renewed fervour as the blanket of darkness fell over the beach.

As Louisa watched Jason and the men walk across to the boats, Mrs Witherall hastened towards her, arms outstretched.

'Oh, my dear,' she exclaimed, embracing her. 'What wonderful news! I 'ad no idea …' Her eyes sparkled as she released Louisa and took a step back. 'To be honest, I 'ad an inklin'. Our boy's never been 'appier, thanks to you. You make a lovely couple.'

'I'm glad you think so,' Louisa acknowledged, blushing.

'I know so,' Mrs Witherall said emphatically. 'I can't stop now – Mrs Roper wants me to 'elp 'er fetch and carry dreckly-minute.' With that, she excused herself and made off towards the top of the slope where Mrs Roper was waiting with some of her littluns.

Smiling, Louisa turned away, grateful that her future mother-in-law approved of her son's choice.

Anyone who saw the Deal boatmen that evening would assume that their lives were one breathless whirl of drinking and revelry, she thought. Not only did they work hard when the occasion required it, but they knew how to enjoy themselves. It was late on the Monday night when the sailmakers, slop sellers and boatwrights would be abed, ahead of an early rise for work the next morning, while the boatmen didn't care for regular hours, being guided by the tides and weather, and the requests from the masters of the ships in the Downs.

The fiddlers and pipers played, and the men and women danced by firelight, but when Louisa looked closely, she saw figures darting in and out of the shadows, carrying trunks and equipment to the lugger and galley punt that lay side by side on the shore. She had doubted that Jason would find enough men to crew both vessels, but there were plenty willing to declare themselves loyal to the Witheralls when there was the prospect of a fortune to be made.

As she tried to make out Jason's silhouette amongst the men, she drank the rest of her tankard of milk, the brandy leaving a slight sting at the back of her throat and warming her cheeks. She called Winnie to help her bring the baskets of bread, pickled onions and cheese that Mrs Witherall and Mrs Roper had carried down to the beach, and leave them beside the *Whimbrel*.

Jason darted across and kissed her cheek.

'I'll be back, my love,' he whispered, his breath a warm caress against her skin.

'I'll be waiting for you,' she said, unable to tear her eyes from his face as she took in every contour and shadow illuminated by the lantern in Winnie's hand, imprinting them on her memory so she wouldn't forget if by any mischance he failed to return.

'Don't mind me,' Winnie muttered.

Reluctantly, Louisa turned and walked away, her chest tight and her limbs like lead.

'Wait.' She felt Winnie catch hold of her hand. 'They're launching the boats.'

They stopped and listened for the grating sound as the *Spindrift* began to move down the rollers, picking up speed until she hit the sea with a tremendous thump. The *Whimbrel* followed suit a few minutes afterwards, landing in the sea with a crash loud enough to wake the dead. Silence ensued until Louisa caught the soft splash of blades dropping into the water above the whisper of the waves. The rowlocks on the galley punt had been wrapped with cloth to deaden the clunk of the oars.

With their names painted out, and carrying their black canvas, the *Whimbrel* and *Spindrift* soon vanished, invisible to those on the shore, and – Louisa prayed – to any Revenue vessel, privateer or man-o'-war with an interest in acquiring men or goods.

'They'll be back. Don't you worry.' Winnie squeezed her fingers. 'Shall we go home? I'm not in the mood for dancing.'

Louisa didn't have to ask if she was thinking of Billy again.

Most of the men had left on the boats, but a handful remained to assist on the landside, one piping a mournful tune while the wives looked out to sea.

'I have an errand to run,' Louisa said.

'At this time of night?'

'I'm going to get Nancy and Mrs Stickles away from the Rattling Cat before One Eye notices the boats have gone. I can't risk letting them stay there any longer. When he knows that Jason's gone to Calais ahead of time, he'll guess that one of them has snitched.'

'I've been selfish, thinking only of myself,' Winnie said ruefully. 'It would be a great sorrow to lose our sister when we've only recently found her. How are we going to go about it?'

When all was quiet, apart from occasional unrestrained bursts of laughter from a group of Jacks who were lying around like seals near the lobster pots, and the bitter wrangling of words between husband and wife carrying from an open window, Louisa and her sisters made their way to the rear entrance of the Rattling Cat. There was light coming from the kitchen and the door was wide open.

Grace placed the dishes of fish they'd brought with them on the ground, and they waited a little way away, next to a figure slumped against the fence. At first Louisa thought that the man was dead, but he was snoring, a pistol at his side.

'Ugh,' Winnie complained. 'He has cast up his accounts.' But Louisa wasn't put off. She took an old beanpole from the overgrown vegetable bed in the yard, bent down and hooked it through the pistol, drawing it slowly towards her.

The man shuddered. She stopped, hardly daring to breathe, but it wasn't long before he was snoring again, and the pistol was tucked into her garter.

'They're coming,' Winnie whispered.

'Who?' Louisa tensed.

'The cats,' Grace said as a line of five felines came stalking outside. Four went straight to the dishes. The fifth came trotting up to Grace, mewing softly.

'Go away!' Louisa whispered.

'He's all right,' Grace said. 'He's my favourite.'

'If he makes a noise, we'll be discovered.' Louisa hadn't wasted several perfectly good dabs for nothing.

Grace picked the cat up and plonked him down beside one of the dishes. The bones on his collar rattled as he ate.

'You two go around to the front and listen. If you hear me yelling, make a lot of noise. Fire the pistol. With luck, the distraction will buy me time to get Nancy and her mother away.' Her fear had gone, replaced by a rush of excitement.

Her sisters disappeared, leaving her free to creep towards the door where she hesitated, listening for sounds of life: the splash of water; the chinking of crockery and pans. Glancing through the runnels of condensation on the window, she could just make out Nancy and her mother at the sink.

There was no sign of One Eye, or Isaiah and the dog.

Louisa stepped inside and pushed the kitchen door open, making Mrs Stickles start.

'Oh my, it's ...' She clutched at the lace at her bosom, as Louisa pressed her finger to her lips.

'Come with me,' she mouthed.

'I can't just walk out,' Mrs Stickles whispered. 'I 'ave to pack my clothes.'

'This is your one chance – it's up to you.'

'Our lives are worth more than possessions,' Nancy said in a low voice as she took off her apron and dried her pockmarked hands.

'Follow me,' Louisa urged.

She thought she heard a dog bark when they were hurrying along the street, having reunited with Winnie and Grace, and she wished that Mrs Stickles didn't make such heavy footsteps, because when they reached Compass Cottage, she noticed the candle moving behind the Witheralls' window. Having locked the door behind them, she showed them the hiding hole behind her father's wardrobe in case of an emergency.

'I'll never fit in there,' Mrs Stickles opined.

'It'll be a squeeze, but you mustn't complain when I've 'ad to live most of my life in darkness,' Nancy said. 'Thank you, my sisters. I promise you that we'll be as quiet as mice.'

'When One Eye finds out that you're missing and that Jason has already left for France, I fear there will be hell to pay. Come this way. You can share Billy's room.'

They were safe – for now – but Louisa didn't sleep well. Her dreams of Jason's kisses were interspersed with nightmares of One Eye and his cats circling her on the beach, waiting to pounce and tear her to shreds for what she'd done …

The next morning, Nancy and her mother slept in, apparently accustomed to keeping late hours. Feeling unsettled, Louisa left Winnie and Grace on watch, with strict orders to keep the doors locked while she went to the capstan grounds in search of news.

When she saw Isaiah and his dog, and the Rattlers assembling around the *Good Intent*, she wished that she'd stayed at home. As she joined Mr Witherall who was looking out to sea with a couple of other fellows, she spotted something gleaming from between two stones. She picked it up: a shilling that must have fallen from one of the sailor's pockets the night before.

'What's that, miss?' Mr Witherall asked.

'Money,' she said.

'Mrs Witherall has this sayin': find a penny and pick it up, all the day you'll 'ave good luck.'

'It's a shilling,' she said, tucking it inside the hem of her sleeve where the stitches had come undone.

'Then it is to be your day,' he smiled, but the smile fell from his face when Isaiah, who had been yelling orders at his crew, came striding over.

'You know what's going on, Miss Lennicker,' he said. 'Tell me.'

'How do I know what Marlin's doing? I'm not his keeper.'

'A little bird told me that you will be very soon.' He turned to Mr Witherall. 'Come on, what does the old man say?'

'I 'ave no idea of 'is whereabouts,' he responded. 'As you say, I'm of an age when your memories start to fade. Nothing I say can be relied on.'

'Where's 'e gone?' The dog growled as Isaiah leaned towards Mr Witherall.

'He's gone out hovelling,' Louisa said.

'A likely story.' He turned to her, his brow glistening with sweat. 'Other's might believe you – I don't. Don't just stand there,' he bellowed suddenly. 'I said, prepare to launch!'

Isaiah called one of the boys across and waved a coin in front of him.

'Go and tell my father there's been a change of plan.' Holding the boy's ear, he bent down and whispered instructions before dropping the coin in his palm. 'Run along then.'

The boy headed off in the direction of the inn, his face pained as he walked barefoot across the stones back to the road.

'Faster than that, or I'll set the dog on you!' Isaiah yelled.

The boy scarpered and one of the *Good Intent*'s crew, who had been sent to argue with their captain, received a fist in his belly for his trouble.

'We're goin' out, whether you like it or not,' Isaiah told the man who limped away, bent over double.

Within the hour, the *Good Intent* made off at speed towards the Downs with every stitch of her canvas set, and the boy came back from the Rattling Cat, the tracks of his tears like slug trails down his cheeks.

'What's wrong?' Louisa asked him and he showed her his neck. 'These are finger-marks,' she said, tracing the purple flares on his skin.

'Ol' One Eye nearly done for me,' he gasped. ''E was mad already because Mrs Stickles 'as vanished into thin air, and now 'e's mad at Black Dog for goin' against 'im. 'E says 'e'll kill 'im when 'e gets back.'

'From Gravelines?'

'Oh no, they aren't goin' to France. They're goin' to lie in wait in the Sands.'

'Are you sure about that?' It hadn't occurred to Louisa that that might be a possibility and she was sure that Jason wouldn't have thought of it.

'When the *Whimbrel* and *Spindrift* are on their way back, they'll ambush them and take the goods.' He bit his lip until the blood drained from it. 'I shouldn't 'ave said.'

'You've done the right thing,' Louisa said gently. 'Do you know where they're planning to land the goods?'

'Either Kingsdown Beach or the Sand'ills, depends on the Revenue and the weather. The spotsmen are to go and wait on the cliffs tomorrow night – that's when Black Dog thinks they'll be ready to land the goods.' He looked up at her, his eyes wide and blue. 'You won't tell 'im I told you, will you, miss?'

'No, but I'm going to give you a shilling for your trouble.'

'A whole shillin'?'

'On condition that you make yourself scarce for a couple of days. Keep away from the beach, and most importantly, avoid the Rattling Cat and One Eye's men. Do you understand?'

He nodded, and she gave him the coin from her sleeve, at which he ran away, much cheered.

'That's very gen'rous of you,' Mr Witherall said. 'I don't think that little tyke's ever seen a shillin' before, let alone 'eld one in 'is 'and. I didn't get a chance to congratulate you yesterday on your engagement to my boy. Mrs Witherall and I are very taken with the idea of 'avin' a Lennicker for a daughter-in-law. It's a terr'ble pity that Righteous and your mother aren't 'ere to see it.'

She thanked him and stood quietly, watching the *Good Intent* grow smaller as she headed into the Downs.

'What can we do, Mr Witherall?' she said eventually. 'How can we send a message to Jason?'

'It's too late,' he murmured. 'A guinea boat might catch up with 'im before 'e's ready to leave Calais, but even if we did get word of Black Dog's plan to ambush 'im, all Jason can do is play for time. 'E could hover out at sea until Black Dog's fed up with waitin', but the longer 'e's out there, the more likelihood there is of the Revenue catchin' 'im.'

'He could avoid the Sands ...?'

'Again, the boats would be out in the open and vulnerable to attack. We must remain optimistic – my boy knows what 'e's doin'. The *Whimbrel* and *Spindrift* are armed. It's two against one. When you think about it, the Rattlers are fools, imaginin' they can take on both vessels at the same time.'

'We still have to collect the goods and run them inland,' she said. 'I have an idea about how we can cause some confusion to delay the *Good Intent*. The Rattlers won't start a fight until they're ready to transfer the goods. Aware that a single shot will alert the Revenue, they'll want to move the goods from our boats to their lugger and bring them ashore before the Revenue can get to them.'

Mr Witherall nodded in agreement when she told him of her plan.

However, she was filled with unease as she returned home. The disagreements between the free traders – the slights, thefts and her father's murder – had been brewing for a while, fermenting like yeast in a barrel of ale, the pressure threatening to burst the hoops apart.

The sun rose higher and the day grew hotter, until it was almost unbearable. The flies and dumbledores couldn't be bothered to take flight. They crawled around the cottage, dropped into the butter that was melting in the pantry, and infested the windowsills. The bedbugs multiplied. As Louisa and her sisters scrubbed the beds, pouring water into the joints to kill them, she couldn't stop thinking of Jason and the battle royal that would begin when he came face-to-face with Isaiah and his men.

On the Wednesday night, the four sisters left Mrs Stickles at the cottage and trudged up to the top of the cliffs in the dark, guided by the moon shining on the chalk path, and the narrow cone of light cast by the spout of the lantern. Grace chattered nineteen to the dozen, while Nancy remained silent, seemingly overwhelmed by the sudden change in her circumstances: freedom and the onslaught of sisterhood.

'Grace, be quiet now,' Louisa warned. 'You never know who'll be abroad at this time of night.'

'It can only be those who are up to no good.' Winnie had been persuaded to join them in the faint hope that they might find Billy, but she was right, Louisa thought. One might come across the military, or the Revenue, or an escaped prisoner of war, or other members of the free trade. Whether or not they were friend or foe depended on whose side you were on.

'Mind you, I'll speak to anybody – any loose screw, bounder or rake – to find out if they've seen or heard anything,' Winnie went on. 'Billy could be anywhere by now: on the other side of the world on one of His Majesty's ships or—' Louisa heard a sob catch in Winnie's throat as she went on, 'Maybe I'll never find out.'

The smell of pipe-smoke caught in her nostrils.

Holding up her hand, she stopped, bringing her sisters to a halt behind her. As she struggled to hear over the sound of blood rushing in her ears, she recalled another time when she'd been out in the open, alone and afraid.

'I think we 'ad the best of it,' a man said, apparently unconcerned about keeping his voice down. 'I've never seen One Eye lose 'is dobbin like that – and that's sayin' somethin'. When I realised Mrs Stickles 'ad gone, I thought 'e'd done away with 'er, but it's them Lennicker women who's got 'er by all accounts.'

'What accounts?' the other man – Lawless, Louisa could tell from the voice – sneered. 'It's all rumour and 'earsay.'

'Hey, did you see that? There was a flash – a blue one – from over there.'

'How many times do I 'ave to remind you that I can't see in the dark, you fool?'

'Have a bit more baccy an' calm yourself down.'

'Was it the *Good Intent* or not?' Lawless went on, irritated.

'I don't know. It was only one flash,' said Awful Doins.

'Then it can't be – you know the code. Sit back and keep your eyes peeled.'

'I will, I will. Don't keep naggin' me.' There was a long silence. 'Tell the truth, I don't like what's 'appenin'. I want a quiet life – to do things as we used to, 'avin' a bit of a chuckle, workin' alongside the rest of them – the Witheralls, the Lennickers and the like. We used to respect one another. We'd never 'ave cheated anyone out of what was rightfully theirs.'

'You're right there – I've always prided myself in bein' as honest as the day is long. 'Ave a nip of brandy – it's from that keg I found sunk in Sandwich Bay.'

Louisa glanced at her sisters. The Rattlers' men were in their way, precisely at the mark that she and Jason had chosen for their exchange of communications, and they deserved special treatment for scaring the living daylights out of her. She took several steps back into the darkness, taking care not to miss her footing on the narrow path on top of the cliff. There was a ledge three feet below to catch you if you fell, but below that was a sheer drop of one hundred feet or more – on to rocks.

'We're going to catch them and tie them up,' she said.

'Two grown men?' Winnie whispered back.

'Nancy will distract them.'

'But they suspect that I'm not really a ghost,' Nancy protested.

'We'll have to rely on the element of surprise,' Louisa said, 'taking advantage of the fact that they wouldn't expect to find you here in a month of Sundays. Winnie and I will take Lawless. Grace and Nancy, you can deal with Awful Doins, the little one. We have two pistols between us, bandannas for blindfolds, snuff if we need to use it, and rope. Nancy, are you ready?'

Nancy removed the cloak Louisa had loaned her, revealing her pale gown and white gloves. She whisked ahead of her sisters and moved noiselessly towards the two men who had lit a small fire in the hollow where they were waiting. Awful Doins was fiddling with a spyglass.

'Did you 'ear somethin'?' he said. 'I 'ave that sense …'

'Ha ha, you 'ave no sense, my friend. None at all.' Lawless slapped his thigh and guffawed at his own joke.

'Stop it! I'm bein' serious – you know 'ow the 'airs on the back of your neck stand on end when you're bein' watched?'

'It'll be rabbits – I wish I'd brought my piece.'

'No, look! Over there! It's the Fey Lady. The Lord save us!'

Nancy rose from the undergrowth. She swayed, waving her arms above her head in what Louisa considered an overly theatrical manner, but it did the trick. The men leapt up. Awful Doins jumped on to Lawless, clinging to him with his arms around his neck and his legs around his waist.

'Let go of me!' Lawless barked.

'Go!' Louisa pounced, blindfolding Lawless as he was hindered by Awful Doins, while Winnie stuck the muzzle of a pistol between his shoulder blades.

'One false move and I'll fire,' Winnie hissed as Grace threw snuff into Awful Doins' eyes. With a cry, he let go of Lawless and fell back, rubbing his face. Nancy and Grace grappled with him, wrenching his arms around his back and tying him firmly and securely with rope before blindfolding them both with the bandannas. With the spotsmen out of action, Louisa took a breath.

'What are we going to do with them?' Grace asked as the men stood trembling like jellies.

'We'll drop them over the edge,' Louisa said lightly, recalling how they had threatened her in the past.

'Not that, missus,' Lawless said, alarmed.

'I 'ave a wife and children at 'ome,' Awful Doins whined.

'Out of compassion for your families, we're going to leave you here for the night, out of our way while we carry on with our work,' Louisa went on. 'Grace, more rope, please.'

'Oh, it's the Misses Lennicker,' Awful Doins said. 'You're bein' very polite. I appreciate your kindness.'

'Why don't you let us go and we'll say nothin' more about what's 'appened?' Lawless said.

'I wasn't born yesterday,' Louisa chuckled as she and her sisters tied the men's ankles together, making a blind, three-legged creature with two heads. They pushed and shoved them and turned them about until they could barely stand, then told them to lie down.

'I don't know which way is what any more,' Awful Doins complained as Lawless staggered and tripped, pulling him down.

'Stay where you are,' Louisa said, seeing how close to the edge they'd fallen.

'One false move in the dark and you'll be over the edge, your heads splatted like marrows across the rocks.' Louisa didn't relish the bloodthirsty tone of Grace's voice, although it seemed to have the desired effect.

The men froze.

'My legs are danglin' in thin air,' Awful Doins muttered. 'I don't want to die.'

'This is nothin',' Lawless said. 'What's One Eye goin' to do to us when 'e finds out we've been stitched up?'

'I beg you not to leave us like this, Miss Lennicker,' Awful Doins pleaded. 'I'm mightily sorry for what we did to you, but it was One Eye's orders.'

'I'm not listening,' Louisa responded, and the sisters left them, walking a few hundred paces further along the cliff where they settled down to look out for signals from the Sands.

'How will we recognise the *Whimbrel* and *Spindrift* out of all those ships?' Grace whispered as they surveyed the shipping in the Downs: a fleet of lanterns punctuating a backdrop of Prussian blue, the sky being almost indistinguishable from the sea, apart from a few stars breaking through the cloud.

'We have a code.' Louisa had made a note and memorised it, then destroyed it in the hearth.

'The Rattlers 'ave somethin' similar: three long, then three short flashes,' Nancy said.

'The *Whimbrel* will send alternating long and short – and there she is.' Louisa squinted through the spyglass. 'Grace, you're in charge of the lantern – you know what to do.'

Grace arranged the lantern with its long spout facing out to sea. She returned the flashes, alternately covering and uncovering the beam, signalling to Jason and his crew that it was safe for the little boats that were waiting to the north to come in and unload the goods.

The *Whimbrel* signalled back once more: message received.

'It's time for us to leave,' Louisa said, and they headed back along the cliffs and past the groaning spotsmen to the road where Abel was waiting with a horse and cart, his figure shrouded in black and the horse's hooves wrapped in cloth.

'There are four of you?' he enquired as she helped her sisters into the back where they sat on sacks filled with straw, little comfort for the rickety ride down into Deal.

'This is Nancy, our sister,' Louisa explained.

'Half-sister, actually,' Grace said, and Louisa aimed a soft kick at her ankles.

'There is such a thing as being too blunt,' she whispered. 'Abel doesn't need to know the details.'

'He's on our side, though?'

'I'm like everybody else,' Abel piped up. 'I'm on the side of those who pay me the best price for my services. My cousin says this is the biggest run the boatmen 'ave ever undertaken. Where am I takin' you?'

'The sandhills, north of town,' Louisa said.

'We'd better get a move on, then. Whoa!' he said, touching his whip to the horse's rump and making it stride out at a brisker pace.

When they reached the sandhills, they bade farewell to Abel and made their way through the dunes in the dark to the tideline where Grace sent three flashes from the lantern out to sea.

Three flashes came back, and not long afterwards, Louisa caught sight of the dark hull and sail of a small boat hovering close to the shore.

'That's her,' she whispered, and holding hands, they waded into the water.

Grace uttered a yelp.

'Whist!' Louisa hissed.

'I'm sorry, but it's gone over the top of my boots. My feet are wet through ... and it's colder than it looks.'

'We are well met,' Mr Witherall said as he leaned over the side of the *Curlew* to help them scramble in, weighed down by their sodden petticoats. He had insisted on playing his part, promising to enlist the aid of one of the boys from the capstan grounds, and Louisa hadn't been able to deny an old man the pleasure of feeling needed. 'There are four of you? Oh well, the more the merrier.'

Louisa stared out to sea, where she could just make out the lanterns on a flotilla of little boats bobbing up and down on the waves. The Rattlers were out there somewhere. When would they make their move?

Mr Witherall and the boy turned the boat about.

'Let's get this over with,' Mr Witherall said gruffly. 'The sooner we're done, the better. I'm afraid that there'll be more than a few fisticuffs tonight.'

# Chapter Nineteen

## *A Blood-red Sky*

They had delayed Isaiah and his crew by tying up their spotsmen, but how much grace did they have? Gazing at the dark figures of her sisters who seemed deep in thought, Louisa understood a little of how Nelson must have felt sailing into battle, as they sailed the *Curlew* towards the north end of the Sands, the south end being illuminated by the lightship.

Mr Witherall was helmsman, being familiar with the banks and swatches in the Goodwins. The tide was falling. She could hear the waves breaking across the sand on either side of them, and the growl of the undertow, as they traversed deep water, following the flashes sent out by the *Whimbrel*.

She heard Winnie mumble a prayer for their salvation before the *Curlew* entered Trinity Bay, a great bay in the heart of the Sands where the calm surface of the water cradled the reflection of the moon. There, waiting for them, were the *Whimbrel* and *Spindrift*.

The flotilla of little boats followed in the *Curlew*'s wake.

There was no sign of the *Good Intent*, but Louisa didn't like it.

Mr Witherall took the *Curlew* in close to the lugger where Jason looked down, a big grin on his face.

'What took you so long?' he jested.

'This is no laughing matter,' she called back. 'The *Good Intent* is lurking in the Sands. Isaiah's planning to intercept the boats, take the goods by force and run them to Kingsdown or the sandhills. I've disabled the spotsmen so they can't communicate with their landside men, but I don't know how long you've got before they find you.'

'Thank you. We must make haste. It's a great haul – there are four hundred half-ankers of brandy, one hundred of rum, over ninety bags of baccy and enough gloves to put the English glovers out of business. There's about half that amount again on the *Spindrift*.' He gave the order to his men to begin unloading the goods. The plan was to empty the *Whimbrel* completely, freeing her to act as decoy for the Revenue if they should make an appearance, allowing the *Spindrift* to disappear further up the coast until it was safe for her to land. 'The Rattlers will be expectin' the lugger to be weighed down – they'll have a bit of a shock when they find out how fast and agile she is. That's if they do take us on … I'm not sure Black Dog will dare.'

'He has a point to prove – One Eye's furious with him for going against him. Take care, my love.' She caught hold of the bale of material that he passed down to her and lowered it into the *Curlew* where it nestled with three baskets, a trunk of silks and a small coffin that Jason had taken to France and filled with lace.

'Are the Revenue allowed to rummage the dead?' she asked.

'I don't think they have a rule against it, but I trust that even the gentlemen of the Revenue would be reluctant to disturb the mortal remains of the recently deceased – a child, no less.'

'I see,' she said, smiling at his ruse.

'That's all for now,' he said. 'Be careful how you go. Mr Witherall, I'm glad to see that your gout isn't gettin' in the way of gallantry. Get goin' quickly, before the tide falls any further – the last thing you want is to be stranded like a fox in a foxhole. Go! I can hear voices. Things are about to turn sour …'

Winnie and Grace dipped the lugsail and they were beginning to head back, some of the little boats already on their way, some a distance behind, when a great shout went up and a shot rang out, followed by a splash as the ball missed its mark.

Louisa looked back. Dawn was breaking, the red orb of the sun rising into a crimson-streaked sky behind the *Whimbrel* and *Spindrift*, and … her heart skipped a beat … the charcoal silhouette of the *Good Intent*.

The bay became an amphitheatre, the sandbanks with the heavens arching above them, a backdrop for the action, as the Rattlers' lugger sailed in and the *Spindrift* stood back, turning broadside, her guns glinting. The *Whimbrel*, higher in the water than she had been before, set out across the bay as though her crew were running scared, but then she turned and came towards the *Good Intent*.

Louisa heard a shout and the Rattlers fired their cannon; twelve guns in all. A man screamed, and a fracas broke out on the *Good Intent* with yells of, ''E's blowed 'is 'and off.' But she didn't care about them, her eyes on the *Whimbrel*'s black sails as she gracefully turned further along the bay, apparently having avoided injury.

On her return, the lugger sandwiched the *Good Intent* between her and the galley punt. On Jason's orders, the *Whimbrel* and *Spindrift* released volleys of cannon fire as the *Good Intent* fired back. Flashes and smoke rose into the sky, obscuring the outlines of the boats. Sharp cracks and booms, and the sound of splintering wood, pained Louisa's ears and filled her heart with terror.

She could hardly watch as the smoke dispersed to reveal the *Spindrift* still in one piece and the *Whimbrel* on the perimeter of the bay. The *Good Intent*, her lugsail shredded and dangling from a broken mast, was a sitting target, but like a wounded stag, she wasn't going to lie down and die.

Isaiah was bellowing orders to his men to reload the guns.

'We should leave,' Mr Witherall said. 'Louisa, did you 'ear me? There's nothin' we can do – and if we stay 'ere, we're liable to get caught in the crossfire. The tide 'as turned.'

'As long as it's turned in favour of our men.' As the sharp scent of gunpowder drifted into her nostrils, she noticed the other little boats making a rapid retreat, full sail, out of the bay. The *Whimbrel* was bearing down on the *Good Intent* for a third time.

'Let's go,' she decided quickly, and they moved off into the channel where the water was rising fast, covering the hazardous sandbanks on either side. Beyond them, a row of seals basked on the exposed sand, completely unconcerned.

Another volley of gunfire echoed around the bay behind them and when she looked back, all she could see were the tips of the boats' masts and shadows of the hulls emerging from the smoke, set against a blood-red sea.

Glancing towards Winnie, who was covering her ears against the screaming and shouting of the men they'd left behind, she felt sick.

'She's 'oled! There's water comin' in.'

'Keep bailin'! I said, keep bailin'.'

'They have destroyed each other,' Grace said quietly as the battlefield fell eerily silent, but there was no peace.

'Those poor creatures,' Winnie sighed.

'Shouldn't we go back, Mr Witherall?' Louisa asked.

'My boy will look after 'is own,' he muttered. 'No, we 'ave to get away, ladies.' He looked at the boy who was huddled in the bow under a blanket, his face whiter than a kid glove. 'We are obliged to carry out our orders – anythin' else would be a dereliction of duty.'

'We must keep praying,' Grace said, putting her palms together and raising her eyes towards the sky. Nancy followed suit.

'There's no time for that,' Louisa said, eyeing the run goods on the *Curlew*'s boards. 'Our fortune lies there – we can't let it slip through our hands. It would be a travesty after all we've gone through, and the sacrifices the men have made.' Inwardly, she prayed that none of them had gone so far as to give up their lives for barrels of cognac and bales of silk.

'Master Appleton, get up and do what you're bein' paid for,' Mr Witherall said, and the boy scrambled up, casting the blanket aside and revealing a row of bruises on his skinny ankles. His scruffy blue trousers ended midway down his shins and his shirtsleeves stopped just below his elbows. He could have been no more than eleven years old, and Louisa felt sorry for him, trapped in a situation he had no control over, his eyes like those of a hare caught in lantern light.

The *Curlew* emerged from the channel into the open sea, the wind picking up and carrying them into choppier waters, and there waiting for her with their bowsprits arrowed towards her, were a naval cruiser and a Revenue cutter, their attention attracted by the earlier sound of gunfire.

Mr Witherall uttered a few choice curses, followed by a fervent prayer for divine intervention while Louisa and her sisters hastily covered the goods and sat on them.

'Try not to worry,' she said. 'We have nothing to hide.'

'Nothing that isn't already hidden.' Grace flashed her a quick smile.

'We've painted out the *Curlew*'s name – it makes us an obvious target for the Revenue,' Winnie pointed out.

'We can't stand inside the Sands all day, waitin' for them to disappear,' Mr Witherall said. 'We'll 'ave to keep movin', and 'opin' for the best.'

They sailed on past. The navy and Revenue left them alone – they had bigger fish to catch – but there were other hazards awaiting them: a freshening wind from the west slowing their progress as they wended their way between the vessels in the crowded Downs. It was broad daylight now, and the provisioning boats were out and about, along with fishing boats, several men-o'-war and an East Indiaman showing acres of sail. In the distance, the white cliffs looked as if they'd been freshly laundered with ashes and lye.

'I wonder how our blindfolded friends are,' Louisa said, recalling what they'd done to Awful Doins and Lawless.

'Somebody will 'ave found them by now,' Nancy said.

'I don't know why you're worrying about them – they hadn't got far to fall,' Winnie said crossly. 'We have troubles of our own.'

'I suggest you get on and do what you 'ave to do, ladies,' Mr Witherall said.

In the burgeoning heat and glare of the sun, Louisa jemmied the trunk open to reveal layer upon layer of colourful silks. She passed them in batches to Grace, who wrapped some of them in oilcloths and returned them to the trunk. Before Louisa closed it up again, she added an old gansey and some knotted pieces of rope.

They tucked the remaining silks inside their bodices, then opened the bale of lace.

'Is it all right?' Grace asked.

'There doesn't seem to be any damage,' Louisa said, removing the first piece and surreptitiously holding it up to the light. The pristine white thread formed a delicate pattern of fruits and flowers. 'The ladies are going to love this. Winnie, help me ...'

'I'll avert my eyes – and you'll do the same, laddie,' Mr Witherall said, and with the aid of a blanket and some discreet removal and replacement of items of clothing, the sisters wrapped the lace around their torsos.

'I wish I'd worn another dress,' Grace observed. 'I can hardly breathe.'

'Never mind, it won't be for long,' Louisa reassured her. 'Leave the rest, Winnie. Nancy, I'm very grateful for your help, but I think you've overdone it.' She refrained from adding that she looked as stout as her mother.

'Oh, you have.' Grace stepped back as the *Curlew* rocked from side to side on a bumpy swell. Winnie caught her arm as she lost her balance, bringing her back from the brink of falling overboard.

'Have a care!' Louisa exclaimed. 'The lace!'

'Is that all that matters to you?' Winnie rounded on her.

'It came out wrong ...' She loved her sisters, even Winnie when she was out of sorts.

'What are we supposed to do with that?' Apparently unperturbed, Grace pointed to where the coffin lay under a blanket, a bad omen of times to come, perhaps.

'Nothing – we have to deliver it to Mr Trice's agent at the Three Kings.' Louisa glanced towards the north – they still had some way to go across open water to reach the sandhills. She looked behind them, her spirits lifting at the sight of the silhouette of a giant lugger emerging slowly, all sails set, from the northernmost point of the Goodwins. 'It's the *Whimbrel*! Where is the spyglass?'

Mr Witherall handed it to her, saying, 'Tell us what you see.'

'She's heavily laden ... and I can see men on board ... and there are other vessels ... I'm afraid to say that the Revenue and navy are following in her wake.'

'Ah, then they are in deep water.' Mr Witherall's brow reminded Louisa of deeply rippled sand. 'It can't be 'elped – they'll 'ave to talk their way out of it.'

'Where is the *Spindrift*? And the *Good Intent*?' Nancy asked.

'We'll find out soon enough,' Mr Witherall responded.

It would never be soon enough for her, Louisa thought, desperate to find out how Jason had fared. As the *Curlew* continued on her course with the gulls crying and swooping above, she glanced across at Winnie who was staring into the emerald depths, her mouth curved down at the corners – a reminder of how it felt, not knowing if your beloved was alive or dead.

They took the *Curlew* up a small creek into the dunes where Abel was waiting for them with the cart, the horse munching contentedly on the contents of a nosebag.

'Have you any news from Deal?' Louisa asked him as they transferred the goods, leaving the boy to guard the boat.

'About the gunfire? I 'ave no idea – I've been stuck 'ere waitin' for you. Uncle, what took you so long?'

'The Misses Lennicker will tell you on your way to Deal – it's quite a yarn.' Mr Witherall returned to the boat to take her home, while Louisa and her sisters rode back on the cart with the trunk and baskets covered with hessian sacks, and the coffin on top. Grace fell asleep, her head heavy against Louisa's shoulder, ringlets of hair curling across her cheek: a picture of innocence that wouldn't be much help against the Revenue if they should make an appearance. Were they taking too much of a risk, running the goods in plain sight?

'There's trouble ahead,' Abel said when they were a few hundred yards shy of the Three Kings, and close to the capstan grounds. Louisa caught a glimpse of a large crowd on the shore, looking out at the cutter, cruiser and the *Whimbrel* anchored in deep water off the beach. Noticing Officer Chase nearby, she nudged Grace from her slumber.

'Wake up.'

'What is it?'

'It's our favourite Riding officer,' she hissed. 'If he should ask, we're a sorrowing family, taking a child to the chapel for a Christian burial.'

'Whose child?' Nancy asked.

'Let me do the talking.'

As Abel pulled in off the road, Officer Chase came trotting up to them on a sway-backed nag that whinnied and fidgeted when he pulled up alongside the cart.

'Good morning, ladies. I see you are out and about.'

'That's very astute of you, officer,' Louisa said. 'Pray, tell us what is going on – I have never seen so many people.'

'I can't help thinking that you know very well what's happening,' he said as Grace uttered a huge sob and covered her face with a brightly coloured silk bandanna. 'I'm sorry. Is there something wrong?'

'We are carrying the body of a child – our orphaned cousin – to St George's,' Louisa explained, wiping a pretend tear from her eye, but the more she thought about it, the more distressed she became, thinking of Jason and how she didn't know what state she would find him in, or if the sea had become his winding sheet.

Officer Chase appeared torn between carrying out his duty and upsetting the Lennickers and the small number of onlookers who had stopped to see what was going on.

'Out of respect for the dead, I will refrain from rummaging this cart today,' he announced.

'Thank you, sir,' Grace sighed.

'On your way then – and don't think you'll get away with gammoning me again, if this turns out to be one of your tricks.'

'As if we'd make light of such a tragedy,' Louisa said indignantly as Abel made a clicking sound in his throat, sending the horse on, jolting the cart and everyone in it.

'I must congratulate you on an excellent performance,' Grace remarked.

'It was real – I was thinking of … oh, it doesn't matter now. Where is Mr Trice's agent?' She hoped that the message about the timing of the run had reached him – she had sent it by hand to the attorney's offices in Dover.

To her relief, she found the agent reading the newspapers in one of the public rooms at the hotel, and it wasn't long before they had transferred the coffin – with some ceremony, assisted by the agent's man and two post boys dressed in beaver hats, brass-buttoned jackets and white leather breeches – to the post-chaise where they strapped it to the roof. With the trunk secured to the platform between the front springs, Mr Trice's agent left for London.

Abel continued on through town on his way back to the mill, and the sisters ran on to the beach where Mrs Witherall called them to her.

'When did you last see my 'usband?'

'Not so long ago,' Louisa said. 'He and Master Appleton are safe and bringing the *Curlew* home from their fishing trip.'

'Was it a success?'

Louisa nodded, as Mrs Witherall smiled and went on, 'Our men 'ave 'ad the luck of the devil today – all accounted for and only an 'andful injured. One 'as broke 'is foot – 'e's 'ad to be dragged, kickin' and screamin' to the bonesetter.'

'Jason?' Louisa asked.

Mrs Witherall grinned. 'Oh, 'e's fine, quite the hero apparently. 'E was out doing a bit of 'ovellin', and about to come back empty – 'anded, when the *Good Intent* came along and took a shot at the *Whimbrel*.'

'Did they say why?' Louisa carried on the pretence, aware that they were within earshot of the Revenue.

'It was over a quarrel they'd 'ad – the Rattlers and the rest of them. Black Dog assumed – mistakenly – that Marlin was running goods across from France. Thinkin' 'e could make a fortune out of it, 'e attacked them, but 'e started a battle for nothin', and 'e's lost the *Good Intent* for good measure. Marlin and 'is crew are still on the lugger with Black Dog and 'is men. The Revenue won't let anybody except the wounded come in until she's been thoroughly rummaged.

'Anyway, I'm glad to see you – you're all lookin' well, more buxom than ever.' Mrs Witherall winked as if she had something in her eye. 'Come and wait with us.' She nodded to where the other wives and their children were gossiping further along the beach. 'I 'ave some sliced beef and rolls, and plenty of porter.'

Weary and aching, Louisa ate while keeping her eyes on the *Whimbrel*.

'Why are the gobblers taking so long?' Grace asked. 'They've been searching her for hours.'

'I 'eard that Marlin had to step in to stop them cutting her masts in 'alf,' Mrs Edwards commented. 'They're determined to find somethin' they can pin on 'em.'

'I've found a cask,' one of the officers shouted.

'Open it then,' ordered his superior. 'What is it?'

'Water ...'

'Keep searching!'

'Sir, we've taken her apart – there's nothing here.'

'I find it impossible to believe that these men have turned over a new leaf. They must have spirited the goods away before we picked them up.'

At last, the men were allowed to bring the lugger in. When they disembarked, the jubilant families of the crew of the *Whimbrel* cheered, while the wives and children of the *Good Intent*'s crew stood silent and stony-faced. Jason, his shirt torn to shreds and his cheek bloodied, strode up the beach to talk to the officer from the Revenue cutter.

'You are satisfied with your search?'

'I would not put it like that. I am satisfied that there are no run goods on board the lugger, but I must enquire as to the whereabouts of the galley punt that was reported as having been seen travelling heavily laden, earlier today. You have shares in another vessel, do you not?'

'I'll take your word for it,' Jason said coolly.

'We will find her, mark my words. We have every reason to believe that you have recently returned from Gravelines. And there is only one reason for a Deal boatman to visit Napoleon's shores, and that is for profit. I have the measure of you. We would have had you and your men last time, if it hadn't been for that corrupt hearing. You won't get away with it again. I intend to request a full trial well away from this town, this den of liars and thieves.'

'You should perhaps loosen your collar – you appear to be throttlin' yourself.'

'And you should show some respect!'

'Have you finished? Only I am a busy man.'

'Go,' the officer blustered. 'But I'll be watching you, and as soon as you step out of line, I'll have you seized by the withers.'

'Thank you for your interest.' Jason turned away as a whisper of alarm ran through the crowd, and Nancy made herself scarce, hiding behind the *Whimbrel*'s hull.

'One Eye is 'ere. I don't like it. 'E 'as a murderous look about 'im.'

He walked across to the Feaseys' hut and stood outside it, the brim of his black hat shading his face.

Jason strode towards him and offered his hand.

One Eye looked down and spat at his boots.

'Do your worst, sir,' Jason said loudly so everyone could hear him. 'I'll be takin' what we've salvaged from the *Good Intent* to the Lord Warden's depot where the commissioners will assess the items and make a reasonable reward for our services.'

'Where is she? Where is my boat?'

'Her captain took it upon himself to turn her guns on the *Whimbrel*, and we were havin' a right royal battle when one of our cannonballs put a hole in the *Good Intent*'s side.'

'She is sunk? Gone?'

'No amount of bailin' could stop her fillin' with water. She tipped, beaching her stern on the sand, but when she reached a critical weight, she slipped right off into deep water.'

'I blame you for this ...' One Eye swore and cursed, and some of the women put their hands over their children's ears.

'It was self-defence. I gave your captain a choice: stop firin' and strike her colours, or carry on and go down with her. We took him and the crew off, but there wasn't much we could salvage and there's no point in goin' back – she'll be a good few fathoms below by now. What was your son thinkin' of, openin' fire on his fellow boatmen, men who've always worked together, savin' ships and savin' lives?'

Isaiah stood well back – he appeared to have lost his boots and was shifting his feet on the stones. Behind him were his battered and crestfallen men, a raggle-taggle crew in torn slops, reunited with their womenfolk who wept and wailed with relief that they had returned safely.

'Where is it? Where's what you promised us?' one of the women said, prodding her husband with a walking stick. She was wearing an oversized black bonnet as though she had been expecting bad news.

'I don't know. I don't know what you're talkin' about.'

'You're lyin' to me again. You know very well—'

'Shut your mouth,' he growled, and everyone stared as she stormed off up the beach, the ruffles of her bonnet flouncing with every step.

'Ah, what have we here?' Mrs Witherall said, and all eyes turned to where one of the Rattlers' landsmen was walking down the beach, marching Awful Doins and Lawless ahead of him.

'Look what I found,' the landsman said, poking them with a hazel twig.

'Explain yourselves,' One Eye snapped. 'Where was you last night? Out drinkin'? I can't trust you as far as I can throw you.'

'I found them blindfolded and trussed up, with their legs danglin' over a ledge with no more than a couple of feet to fall, yet they swear they were too afraid to move in the dark, having been left on the edge of the cliff.' The landsman grinned. 'Better than that, they say they were sprung by three young ladies and a ghost.'

'We were,' Awful Doins protested. 'It's no word of a lie.'

'You mean, the Lennickers got you?' One Eye guffawed and a ripple of laughter ran through the onlookers. 'Oh, I'd 'ave liked to 'ave seen it.'

Awful Doins forced a smile, and Lawless uttered a hollow laugh, not out of good humour, but to pacify his leader.

One Eye suddenly soured. ''Ow 'ave I ended up in charge of such a band of incompetents? Get them out of my sight. Take them back to the inn and lock them up – I'll deal with them later. And I'll give Nancy and her whorin' mother a good 'idin' when I get my 'ands on them. I don't know why they've turned against me after all I've done for them.' Hands on hips and a scowl on his face, he addressed the crowd. 'If there's anyone else who wants to change sides, say so now. I won't 'ave turncoats disruptin' the Rattlers' operations.'

A couple of the men shuffled forward. Another joined them, his wife shoving him in the back.

'I want to go back to 'ow it was,' he croaked. 'I've 'ad enow of 'avin' to watch my back every time I step outside my door. I don't want no more to do with your operations, One Eye.'

Incandescent with rage, One Eye leaned close to him, eyeball to eyeball.

'You ungrateful—!' He ranted at the quivering man, punching the air with every syllable. 'You've broke the code! You'll never run goods again. I'll make sure everyone – the merchants, buyers, lawmen – know who you are. You're a liar and a cheat – I've watched you slippin' cards up your sleeves when you're suppin' my ale!' He paused, gasping for breath.

Expressing disloyalty was one of the greatest insults his men could have paid him, Louisa guessed as One Eye stumbled towards Black Dog, stopping a few feet in front of him.

'What kind of son goes against 'is father?' he roared. 'You are no son of mine.'

'I did what you said to do.' Isaiah's hands balled into fists. 'When I saw the *Whimbrel* 'ad gone out, I used my initiative.'

'You should 'ave waited. Spoken to me first. You're like your mother. Weak in the 'ead.'

'She wasn't so stupid as to stay with you, though. I remember 'ow you used to beat 'er till she was beggin' for mercy. You are a ...' Isaiah seemed to be struggling to find the right words '... a bilge rat, the lowest of the low.'

With a roar of anguish, One Eye charged at him. Isaiah turned one shoulder and barged him. One Eye lost his footing and fell backwards. An awful cracking sound cleaved the air as he landed, his head hitting the stones. His body lay perfectly still, then started to twitch.

Isaiah fell to his knees at his father's side.

'I didn't mean it!' he cried. 'We'll buy another boat, and ...' He slapped his father's cheek. 'Speak to me. Say something, you stupid old goat.'

It was Louisa and her sisters who went to help. There was foam on One Eye's lips and blood creeping across the stones from the back of his head. His eye stared heavenwards with an expression of hopelessness, as if he understood that the angels were never coming for him.

Nancy emerged from behind the *Whimbrel* and stood staring in disbelief.

'He's gone,' Winnie whispered.

'He's as dead as a doornail,' Grace said in wonderment.

'I'm sorry, Isaiah,' Louisa said, but she didn't think he heard her. He sat back on his heels, raised his eyes to the sky and howled like an animal.

# Chapter Twenty

## *The Tide is on the Turn*

'I'm sorry you had to see that.' Jason touched Louisa's shoulder as she sat back on the shingle, hugging her knees. 'May I help you up?'

'Thank you,' she said, holding out her hands. He pulled her to her feet, then released her. They stood facing each other while she drank in every detail: his eyes that matched the blue depths of the sea; the graze on his cheek; the contours of his collarbone and chest, exposed by the rent in his shirt.

'I'm glad to see you,' she murmured.

'As I am to see you. It was a bloody battle.'

'The *Spindrift*?'

'She got away – the *Whimbrel* provided the diversion, attractin' both the navy and the Revenue.' He smiled suddenly. 'They were sure they had us this time, but it wasn't to be.'

'You look well,' she said, yearning to be alone with him.

'And you look more beautiful than ever. I wish I could stay, but I have much to do.'

'I know.' Her heart ached, but it had to be this way – Jason had to make repairs to the *Whimbrel*, make sure the salvaged goods were taken to the Customs House, and attend to unloading the run goods from the *Spindrift*. She watched him go, disappearing behind the great lugger and into the crowd.

'How must it feel, knowing that you've killed your own father?' Grace sipped the milk and brandy that Mrs Witherall had provided to restore their spirits while they watched Black Dog and the Rattlers carry One Eye's body away.

'He didn't mean to kill him,' Louisa said. 'I'm not standing up for Isaiah in any way because he's a bully, but all he did was push him away. It wasn't his fault that One Eye hit his head like that.'

'I'm glad 'e's gone. I don't 'ave to do his bidding any more or worry about what 'e'll do to my mother,' Nancy said quietly.

'It's divine retribution for what he did to Pa,' Winnie said. 'He's got what he deserved, and this town will be a whole lot better off without him.'

'You aren't in fear of Isaiah?' Louisa asked Nancy.

'It may surprise you to 'ear that 'e is capable of performin' acts of kindness. There 'ave been occasions when 'e's slipped me an extra candle or 'andful of rush-lights, or a piece of pie. One Eye liked to control everybody – 'e was brutal. I've 'eard 'im beating the livin' daylights out of 'is son. I've seen men disappear, never to return.'

A shiver ran down Louisa's spine as she thought of how her father must have felt when One Eye had aimed the pistol at him.

''E knew I 'ated goin' out 'auntin', yet 'e made me do it, sayin' 'e'd throw my mother down the well if I didn't. These scars –' she pointed towards her veil '– they aren't all from the pox. Some of them are where 'e burned me – 'e'd 'old a flame to my face until I gave in and agreed to do what 'e asked.'

'I'm very sorry,' Grace gasped, aghast.

'I didn't realise you'd suffered so badly,' Louisa said, thinking of One Eye slowly burning in Hell. Was it punishment enough for what he had done?

The women remained on the beach when the men went off to continue their work, quietly celebrating the loss of the Rattlers' hated leader, as the sun dried the shingle, removing its sheen.

'I expect Black Dog will step into 'is father's shoes,' Mrs Witherall said.

'Oh no, One Eye's shoes what 'e left be'ind are far too big for 'im. I can't see the Rattlers returnin' to their former glory,' Mrs Edwards observed.

'That man always petrified the life out of me.' Mrs Roper untied the knot at her littlun's neck and laid the bandanna over his head to protect him from the afternoon sun.

'I don't know why the likes of Awful Doins and Lawless stayed loyal to 'im,' Mrs Witherall said.

''E threatened them,' Mrs Roper replied.

'And 'e wrote off their tick at the inn every so often, so they'd feel obliged to 'im.' Mrs Edwards frowned. 'I won't miss 'im.'

'The Rattlers will 'ave a go at fallin' in with the rest of us, I reckon,' Mrs Witherall said. 'But we won't let them. They can't be relied on.'

The waves were retreating further down the slope, the air was growing close and still.

'Winnie, Grace, Nancy, we should go home. I feel the need to divest myself of some layers,' Louisa whispered, fanning her face.

Under protest from Grace who was afraid of missing something if they left the beach, they returned to the cottage with Nancy hurrying along, eager to give her mother the news of One Eye's demise. Louisa felt a pang of regret as she opened the door: Ma had had it painted green, and

Pa had attached the brass knocker in the shape of a lion's head. It wouldn't belong to them for much longer.

'Mother, where are you?' Nancy called as they went inside, only to be greeted with silence. 'It's me, and my sisters. We are back.'

Nancy checked the kitchen while Louisa looked in the parlour.

'You don't think One Eye did something to her while we were out?' Winnie whispered.

'Don't! I wish we'd asked her to come with us now,' Louisa said as Grace crept up the stairs.

'It's all right – I've found her.' There was a yelp and a chuckle from overhead. 'She's in the hiding hole ...'

'Mother, what 'appened to you?' Nancy asked as Mrs Stickles hobbled down the stairs, her hair dishevelled and her dress crumpled.

'I was in the middle of choppin' up the cold beef I found in the pantry when I 'eard a rat-a-tat. Thinkin' at first that it was you, I made towards the door before rememberin' what you said about makin' myself scarce. It was One Eye, sayin' 'e'd 'ave the door down if nobody answered. I didn't know what to do. My feet were frozen to the floor, my 'eart was 'ammerin'. And then 'e left. Walked away. I didn't know why, and I didn't care. I was in such a terror that I went and 'id myself away, and then it was so cosy and dark in there that I fell asleep. Oh, thank the Lord we are all safe.'

'Except One Eye.' Nancy lifted her veil, revealing her scars and crooked smile.

''E 'as met 'is nemesis?'

Nancy nodded, and they all helped Mrs Stickles into the parlour where she collapsed into a chair, faint with delight and relief at the news of One Eye's demise. She shed a few tears too, for the wasted years she'd spent slaving at the Rattling Cat, waiting for something better for her and Nancy.

Although One Eye was gone, they couldn't be too careful when it came to protecting themselves and the run goods. Louisa made sure the doors were locked, and Winnie closed the curtains, before they undressed in the parlour by candlelight.

Grace stood in her chemise and petticoat with a long section of lace wrapped around her middle.

'Winnie, take the end,' she begged, half laughing. 'Unwind me.'

Winnie did as she was bid, and as she tugged at the lace, Grace held out her arms like a dancer and spun, her waist growing thinner and thinner.

Winnie laid the lace out on the table for Louisa to measure and catalogue.

'I don't know why you're doing that,' Winnie said. 'Won't those records incriminate us if they fall into the wrong hands?'

'I'm writing it in code – it'll be useful as proof against deception.' Mr Trice had taught her one lesson at least: document everything.

They had kept back a good amount of lace. They hid some in the space behind the panel in their father's old room, some in the secret drawer in the table, and the remainder in the hiding hole in the parlour, having sprayed it with a little perfume to remove the musty odour it had acquired on its journey. There were one or two marks on it, much to Louisa's chagrin.

She was looking forward to selling it, but there wouldn't be enough profit in it to buy the cottage as well as pay off Mr Trice. Lace was expensive, property even more so.

*

During the next sennight, Louisa saw Jason no more than a handful of times. She busied herself selling the run goods to the draper.

'I see that you've brought me the usual,' Mr Gigg said, but as she unfurled the first piece of lace, he fell silent. 'Not bad,' he murmured.

'It's perfect.' She'd steamed out the marks – it looked pristine.

'Before you insult me, offering me a silly price, let me tell you that I have ladies of the ton queueing up to buy lace of this quality.'

'Miss Lennicker,' he said gravely, 'may we omit the patter. I have customers waiting.'

'Of course. Make me an offer I can't possibly refuse and I'll be gone. Although there is more.'

'Show me,' he said, and he bought all of her remaining stock.

'I'd like to show you something before you leave. Do you read the newspapers? I doubt you have the opportunity,' he added when she hesitated, 'although you must be able to afford to buy a weekly edition, if not a daily one.'

'What is this about, Mr Gigg?'

Having removed his gloves, he took a paper from the side table and held it up to show her. 'You are front page news: "The Darlings of Deal".' He snatched it back before reading, '"Notorious smugglers, Mr Jason Witherall and Miss Lennicker ..."'

'I beg your pardon.' Blood rushed to her face, and she wondered if she had imagined it, or if he had added the description, intending to humiliate or amuse her. It was the first time she had heard him use her name.

'"And the noble crew of the lugger, the *Whimbrel*",' he went on. '"Sir Flinders of Mundel Manor has provided a reward for the brave rescue of his daughter who was travelling to—" no matter. That is the gist of it. It appears that you are in the money, but I digress. You are expecting payment.'

Mr Gigg counted out the money. Louisa wrapped it and placed it in two small leather bags with drawstrings that she attached to each wrist and tucked inside the capacious sleeves she had worn that day for the exact purpose.

It wasn't enough to save the Lennickers from eviction.

Louisa had dreamt of attending the auction on the last day of August, standing with her head held high as she placed the winning bid and turned to her sisters, all smiles, but it wasn't to be. By the time the fateful day dawned, her optimism had been completely dashed.

She and Grace returned from a provisioning trip with Mr Witherall as a sea fret rolled in, obscuring the sun. Winnie had spent the day running errands and wasn't yet home. Back at the cottage, Louisa put the baskets away, ready for Mr Jansen's next delivery.

'Shall we go out?' Grace asked. 'I thought we could walk up to Hawksdown.'

'Haven't you had enough fresh air for one day?' Louisa sighed. 'I'm not in the mood for walking—'

'It's good for the constitution, and it will take our minds off … well, you know what I'm talking about.' Louisa nodded as Grace continued, jutting her chin. 'Winnie's worried that Billy won't know where to find us, but I'm looking at this as an adventure and a chance to sail from the past towards a brighter horizon,' she said bravely. 'Although I shall miss our home more than I can say, we will still have the *Curlew*, and our provisioning. We can carry on very much the same.'

'I feel so guilty for putting you and Winnie through these uncertain times.' After the auction, they would have one month's grace, time to pack their belongings and find a new place to call home. 'I've made mistakes – borrowing from Mr Trice, for example – and although I've tried, I haven't succeeded in putting them right.'

'Nobody could have worked harder than you,' Grace reassured her. 'Compass Cottage would rightfully have belonged to us for ever, if Pa had been more careful with the Lennickers' money.'

It was the first time Louisa had heard her criticise their father.

'I've learned that nothing stays the same. But whatever we've lost, we still have each other. That's all that matters.' Recent events had changed Grace: she was no longer a young girl, caring only about how she was going to obtain a new gown. She had grown into a young woman, albeit with the weight of the world on her shoulders.

Grace darted past her, answering a knock at the door.

'I thought you were Winnie coming back from the beach.' Louisa heard her giggle as she let Jason in.

'I'm not sure where the resemblance begins, let alone ends,' he teased. 'I shall have to buy you a quizzing glass.'

'What are you doing here at this time of day?' Louisa asked, delighted to see him as he took her hand and kissed her on the wrist.

'I've been collectin' the money for the items we managed to salvage from the *Good Intent* and dividin' it amongst the men.' He grinned. 'We've made an excellent profit on the run goods as well. I'm feelin' fairly flush in the pocket.'

They had spirited away a good haul on the *Spindrift*. She and her crew had had to stay out for a week to avoid the Revenue, coming in on a dark and rainy night for the landside men to unload her.

'What's more, I have your share of the reward from Sir Flinders.'

Louisa showed him into the parlour, shutting the door firmly in Grace's face.

'What are we going to do with it?' Jason said, resting his hands on the curve of her waist. 'What do you think? Hide it under the mattress? Spend it on high livin'?'

Would he lend it to her to buy Compass Cottage? she wondered, before reminding herself that she had yet to pay off Mr Trice. Having reviewed her account the previous night, she had worked out that if she offered the attorney a percentage of his dues, she could afford to pay rent for a few weeks.

'I have some ideas,' he went on with a twinkle in his eye, 'if you'll let me be your knight in armour.'

'Oh, I don't know about that.'

'We are still promised to each other?' he asked gently. 'You haven't had a change of heart?'

'No ... What is this?'

'I just wanted to be sure.'

He needed reassurance after Margaret, she thought. Her fiancé wasn't always the brave, indefatigable hero that he liked to portray; the handsomest boatman on the beach; the cleverest, most wily smuggler; a villain without a conscience. Jason had flaws and vulnerabilities: that's why she loved him.

Stretching up, she kissed him on the lips.

'Will you come to the auction with me?' he asked, taking a small step back.

'I can't go – it will grieve me too much.'

'Hey, don't cry.' He reached out and wiped away a tear from her cheek. 'All will end well. Let me look after you, my love.'

She smiled ruefully. 'That's very kind of you.'

'Kind? It's my duty and honour. What if I buy the cottage for you? For us? And your sisters? It makes perfect sense.'

'I don't know,' she stammered. 'It's the answer to my prayers, but—'

'Much water has passed under the bridge since I asked you to marry me, but my heart and mind, despite everything, are unchanged. We'll soon be man and wife – did you really expect that we'd live apart?'

'It's another year before we can legally wed, and I was under the impression that you were planning to buy a house on Dolphin Street.'

'That was before I fell for you ... If you want to stay in Cockle Swamp Alley, then I'll do what I can to make it happen, but if you prefer to live elsewhere ...'

She thought of her mother aspiring to live in a house like Mundel Manor, and her aunt seeming dissatisfied by the farmhouse at Limepit Acres. A large establishment didn't necessarily make one happy. Here in Deal, the Lennickers had everything they could wish for.

'We have good neighbours here, the salt of the earth,' she said, as children's laughter echoed along the street outside. 'The cottage is cool in summer and cosy in winter.'

'And it's benefitted from some rather intriguing alterations, according to my mother,' Jason added, with a grin. 'If we are to have any chance of making it ours, we should make haste.'

Louisa told Winnie, who had arrived back home, and Grace that she and Jason were going out, but she didn't say where, not wanting to raise their hopes. There was many a slip twixt cup and lip.

'Ah, it's the Lace Maiden and Marlin, neither of whom can be trusted.' His face dark with anger, Isaiah approached them as they arrived at the Three Kings. 'She comes 'opin' to stop the sale of 'er father's 'ouse. Well, Miss Lennicker, who've you robbed recently for the means to buy it?'

'Leave us alone.' Jason took her arm and guided her past him. 'We have nothin' to say to you.'

'You did the dirty on me,' Isaiah hissed.

'That's the pot callin' the kettle black,' Constable Pocket interrupted. 'I'm 'ere to make sure law and order is maintained. Take your argument outside.'

Isaiah glared at Jason then turned away.

'He's bound to be sore – he's only recently lost his father,' Jason murmured. 'You got what you wanted, Louisa: revenge.'

She took little satisfaction in it, she thought, watching Isaiah retreat. Having imagined that it would taste sweet, she was bitterly disappointed. It had made no difference: nothing could bring their beloved father back.

'I have to register my interest and proof of assets with the auctioneer's clerk. Let me find you a seat first.' Jason showed her to one of the benches that had been placed in rows in a public room at the hotel, and she waited for him to fill in the required forms, listening to snippets of conversation from the assembled crowd.

'There aren't enow 'ouses in Deal – it'll go for well over the estimate.'

'How can a low-born boatman's daughter afford to buy a house?'

'Because they aren't so poor as they like to make out. Mr and Mrs Lennicker were very comfortable before she passed away. I've heard that the family's fortunes have gone to pot since then, though.'

Louisa gave the gossips a long stare. They looked away.

Jason joined her, and the auctioneer took the stand, having been delayed by a last-minute flurry of potential buyers. Louisa could have cried, wishing that she hadn't let Jason persuade her to come.

'Welcome to today's sale of the property known as Compass Cottage on Cockle Swamp Alley, Deal. This will be followed by further lots, including various maritime effects salvaged from the *White Hind* that are being sold on behalf of the Commissioners. Regarding Compass Cottage, possession of the whole may be had on the thirtieth of September next, and, if it helps, part of the purchase money may remain on mortgage.

'Let's start the bidding. Where shall we begin, ladies and gentlemen? What will you offer me for this most attractive family residence, adaptable for many purposes? A lodgings-house? A pot-house?'

'A smuggler's 'ide, being convenient for the beach,' someone contributed, sending a wave of laughter through the audience.

A gentleman offered fifty pounds, to further amusement.

The auctioneer sighed and shook his head. 'Is there any advance on fifty pounds?'

The bids came in thick and fast. The price doubled, then trebled. The atmosphere in the room grew close and stuffy, filling with the scent of cologne, dirty clothes and sweat. One of Deal's landlords, intent on adding to his stock, dropped out of the bidding.

'Ah, a fresh bidder!'

It took Louisa a moment to realise that it was Jason.

'Mr Anthony, are you in or out?' The gentleman whom the auctioneer had addressed, conferred with his companion.

The gentleman's brow twitched. Jason bid again, while Louisa kept very still, neither blinking nor moving her fan as the bidding continued. The gentleman conferred with his client for a second time, then shook his head.

'Then I am selling, make no mistake. Going, going, gone.' The auctioneer brought down his gavel with a snap. 'See my clerk before you leave, sir.'

Louisa waited while Jason dealt with the paperwork. There had been a time when her pride would have taken the shine off her opinion of his gallantry, but they were bound together by their promise to each other, and one day, they would be man and wife. The only fly in the ointment on her journey to happiness was Mr Trice – she could picture him at his desk in his office, rubbing his paws together with glee at the price he'd received for Compass Cottage, and revelling in her misfortune. She suppressed a shudder of revulsion at the thought of him turning up on the doorstep with his scallion-laced breath and threats to claim her.

'I reckon I paid a little over the odds,' Jason said, returning to her side. 'It will be worth it, though, to see your sisters' faces. I'm going to offer Mrs Stickles a loan for her and Nancy to set up the pot-house that they've always wanted.'

Grace and Winnie were over the moon at the thought of keeping Compass Cottage, while Mrs Stickles and Nancy were delighted at the idea of making their own income from baking puddings and pies.

'You are a hero, Marlin,' Mrs Stickles said. 'You will have fresh pies every day.'

'You mustn't give away all the profits.' He grinned, touching Louisa's hand. 'Louisa will explain how to run a successful enterprise.'

'May I go and unpack?' Grace asked. 'I'd started putting my clothes in boxes, on the assumption that we'd be moving out soon. Are you sure you want to live with us, Jason? My sisters say I can be quite annoying at times.'

'I'm certain we'll rub along very well,' he reassured her. 'We're bound to have some choppy waters to navigate, but if I do fall into a bad humour, I go out on the boat and fight the elements – it never fails to improve my mood.'

They celebrated with cake and a strong porter, after which Jason and Louisa escaped for a walk to check on the final repairs to the *Whimbrel*. Out of habit, they stopped at the top of the slope and looked out to sea. The Sands were a golden line beyond the masts and pennants of the ships anchored in the channel.

'There won't be any hovellin' today,' Jason observed.

'You are disappointed?'

He looked at her, one eyebrow raised. 'Why should I be? Do you really think that badly of me? That I would prefer to be out there than here with you? Oh no. Louisa, I want you to know that I hold you above everythin' else. You are more precious to me than … even than the *Whimbrel*. That might not mean much to a landlubber, but you understand. That lugger and I have lived in the wildest of seas – we've worked together, each dependin' on the other's strengths and allowin' for their weaknesses.'

She nodded, smiling as he went on, 'What I'm tryin' to say is that I love you more than the boat, more than anythin' in the world. And I'm goin' to be the best husband anybody could have, I promise. There, your presence has roused me to a passion.' He grinned ruefully. 'I'm used to strugglin' to find the right words in some situations, but when I'm with you, they come easily.'

'It's a sign that this is right, that we're meant to be together,' Louisa said, her heart soaring like a ship on the crest of a wave. 'All I want is for us to be man and wife, but we must wait.'

'There is another way …'

'Are you suggesting that we should marry over a broomstick?'

'I'm saying there's another way it can be done legally.'

'If there is, I haven't heard of it. Unless you are talking about applying for a special licence from the Archbishop of Canterbury, but I thought that was out of reach for the likes of us.'

'I'm talking of marrying over the anvil, eloping to Gretna Green in Scotland.'

The name stirred a distant memory.

'I think my mother might have mentioned it – she and my father considered it when her father threatened to withhold his permission for their betrothal.'

'What do you think?' He gazed at her, his eyes alight with hope.

'Let's make the arrangements forthwith,' she smiled. She didn't want to wait a moment longer than they had to.

# Chapter Twenty-one

## *Over the Anvil*

Winnie and Grace altered one of their mother's gowns for her, adding a trim of French lace. They made a posy of sea lavender and dried honesty, and Louisa bought a pair of satin slippers, her single extravagance.

'I wish we could come with you,' Grace said hopefully.

'We want to keep our wedding as quiet as we can. Anyway, you'd hate travelling all that way in a carriage. Remember how seasick you were when we took the *Curlew* out for the first time?'

'I'm sure I'd get used to it.' Grace's forehead crinkled. 'Why the secrecy? Are you not proud to be seen on Jason's arm?'

'I have my reasons – one day you'll come to understand.'

'Your husband is going to move in with us on your return. People are bound to notice – and talk.'

'Humour me, my dear sister, and promise that you won't say a word.'

'Don't stare at me like that – I'm perfectly capable of keeping a secret. Jason is most fortunate – to think he almost married Margaret Hibben,' Grace babbled on.

'I'm sure he'll make me very happy – and also as cross as crabs on occasion.' Louisa had no illusions when it came to marriage.

Grace chuckled. 'And vice versa – you are both passionate creatures.'

'You will live in bliss as long as your husband has sufficient funds,' Mrs Witherall put in, having invited herself to take part in the bride's preparations, 'and you make up at the end of each day.'

She would find great joy in that, Louisa thought, but she did have some regrets: that she wasn't to be married at St George's; that her father wasn't alive to present her to her groom; that Mrs Witherall, not her mother, was packing her boxes for the journey to Scotland.

She and Jason travelled by post-chaise and four, with two postilions, Jason having left the *Whimbrel* and *Spindrift* in his father's charge, and Louisa having given Winnie and Grace strict instructions to stay out of trouble.

'It's only another three hundred miles or so,' Jason said when they left London, having been delayed waiting for a replacement when the chaise lost a wheel. 'Do you think we'll be able to stand the sight of each other by the time we get to Gretna?' he teased as he placed his arm around her and kissed her hair.

She nestled against him, revelling in the prospect of time alone together. 'I'm going to enjoy the next few days. It will be a luxury knowing that you won't suddenly disappear on a hovelling trip, and I won't be worrying about whether or not you'll come back to me in one piece.'

'You aren't asking me if I'll anchor ashore?' he said, his voice laced with suspicion.

'No,' she sighed, looking up to meet his gaze. 'I'd never do that – I know you too well.'

They continued along the rutted roads, changing the horses every ten to fifteen miles.

'Perhaps we should have waited to marry in the ordinary way,' she said, when Jason had paid an extra tip to the ostler at one of the inns to change the horses quickly.

'I don't care what it costs,' he smiled. 'When we're married, you won't have to worry about financial matters – that's what a husband's for, to provide for his wife and family.' He paused. 'That doesn't please you?'

The chaise jolted forward as the postilions urged the horses to a faster pace.

'Oh Louisa, what is it?'

'It pleases me greatly, not having the worry of it, but—'

'There is always a "but" with you,' he said, amused. 'With good reason, I'm sure.'

'My father kept me in the dark about the debts he racked up after Ma passed away. You know how I've had to suffer the consequences.'

'With Mr Trice? Yes.'

'All I'm asking is that you'll keep me informed about our financial position when we're married. For my peace of mind.'

'Of course. Just as you have no intention of keepin' me away from old briny, I have no intention of hidin' anythin' from you. I don't think I could – you can read me like a book.'

'Then I am reassured.'

'I'll do anythin' for you.'

'Anything?' she said coquettishly.

'My wish is your command.'

'Kiss me then,' she whispered, and the hours before the next change of horses passed almost unnoticed.

After three full days on the road, they reached Longtown, the last village on the English side, before the road crossed the river that marked the border into Scotland.

'Welcome to Gretna Green,' Jason said as the horses pulled up outside the blacksmith's shop at the Headless Cross. He helped her down from the post-chaise, and they took adjoining rooms at the inn where they rested and had some refreshment.

She put up her hair and revived her posy, then dressed in her gown and slippers. She was ready, she thought, studying herself in the mirror on the dressing table. Her cheeks were glowing with health and happiness – she looked well, yet she felt that she hadn't yet matched the air of sophistication demonstrated by the likes of Beth and Mrs Tempest.

She turned at the sound of a knock at the door.

'Louisa, are you ready? The landlord says that Mr Elliot and the witnesses are waitin' for us.'

She took one last look at herself in the mirror, the last time she would see the reflection of Miss Lennicker gazing back at her.

'You may come in,' she said lightly, and the door opened to reveal her fiancé, dressed in a white linen shirt and cravat, a dark cutaway coat, a waistcoat, knee breeches like a second skin, and black stockings and pumps. His hair glinted gold and his face was clean-shaven.

'I hardly recognise you,' she teased.

'I'd feel more comfortable in my oilskins,' he grinned, his eyes flashing like the sun dancing on the waves. 'Here, take my arm and I'll walk you to the blacksmith's shop.'

She slipped her gloves on – a white pair made from kid leather – and they walked down the rickety staircase and through the inn, the landlord pointing out the view of the Cumberland hills and wishing them a good day.

The anvil priest and two of his neighbours greeted them at the forge.

'Welcome to Gretna Green,' he said. 'Pray, tell me if you are expecting any kind of interruption, if we are to proceed with haste, or at a more leisurely manner.'

'We are in a hurry to marry – for selfish reasons, none other,' Jason answered.

'I understand, having been only recently introduced to the joys of matrimony myself. We will begin then, without further ado.'

Mr Elliot led them across to the anvil where Louisa and Jason took their places, standing side by side.

Mr Elliot asked them their names and addresses.

'Are you both single persons?' he went on. 'And did you come here of your own free will and accord?'

When they had answered his questions in the affirmative, he completed the certificate.

'Now we may carry on,' he said. 'Mr Witherall, do you take this woman to be your lawful wedded wife, forsaking all others, kept to her as long as you both shall live?'

'I will,' he said, glancing shyly at her.

The anvil priest asked her the same question.

'I will,' she said softly.

'The ring? You do have a ring?' The priest addressed her, and she began to panic.

'I have it,' Jason smiled as he fumbled in his pocket.

'Then give it to the lady,' the priest said, 'then the lady gives it to you, who gives it to me.'

The priest then returned the ring to Jason, and suddenly Louisa wished her sisters could have been here to see her get wed. She could picture Grace trying to suppress a chuckle at the sight of Mr Elliot's face, all seriousness, as the ring made its way to the tip of the fourth finger of her left hand.

'Repeat after me – with this ring I thee wed, with my body I thee worship, with all my worldly goods I thee endow in the name of the Father, Son and Holy Ghost, Amen.'

Their hands trembled as Jason uttered the words, tripping on them only once, substituting 'run' for 'worldly', before he slipped the ring on to her finger. Louisa didn't think that Mr Elliot noticed because he continued smoothly, 'Now take hold of each other's right hands. The lady repeats after me – what God joins together, let no man put asunder.'

She echoed his words as Jason gave her hand a gentle squeeze.

'Forasmuch as this man and this woman have consented to go together by giving and receiving a ring, I therefore declare them to be man and wife before God and these witnesses in the name of the Father, Son and Holy Ghost, Amen.'

'Amen,' she whispered, as the sunlight slanted through the door into the shop, glancing off the anvil and the tools of the blacksmith's trade that were hanging from hooks on the wall: knives; hammers; pritchels and tongs.

Mr Elliot picked up a hammer and struck the anvil, the sound ringing out to confirm that their marriage was sealed. Louisa thought she could feel her father's presence, looking on in approval, and her mother saying, *'I'm proud of you. Your husband is a good man who will cherish you for ever. You couldn't have chosen better.'*

'Mrs Witherall, it is done. Louisa?'

The sound of Jason's voice – her husband's voice – brought her to her senses.

'I'm sorry,' she said, turning to him. 'I was just thinking of those who couldn't be here ...'

'There's no need to explain,' he said softly, as though he understood. 'I thank you for officiatin', Mr Elliot.'

'I'm delighted to be of assistance. I used to work in farming and horses, and I've only recently joined the family business. You have links with the free trade? I couldn't help noticing the slip of the tongue. Coincidentally, my grandfather-in-law turned from smuggling and fishing to marrying couples over the anvil. He's quite a character – he's the only man of my acquaintance who will drink a Scotch pint of cognac a day.'

'I should have liked to have met him,' Jason said, refusing to allow himself to be drawn on the subject of his occupation, but Louisa guessed that Mr Elliot was convinced. How else would a couple like them have found the money to marry at Gretna Green, and – she looked down at her hand – with a gold ring, not brass?

They stayed for one night at the inn before making the long journey back to Kent.

'I can't wait to get home,' Louisa said when they had finally reached Deal and passed through the tollgate on Queen Street.

'You are fed up with me already?' he said with a chuckle.

'I want to show you off – all right, I know. We must lie low while we decide how we deal with Mr Trice.'

'It won't be for long.'

The post-chaise delivered them to the Three Kings where they dined before walking to Compass Cottage. Grace was waiting for them, throwing the door open even as they reached the corner of Cockle Swamp Alley.

'Welcome home, Mr and Mrs Witherall.' She ran out on to the pavement with a bowl filled with dried rose petals, closely followed by Winnie, Nancy and Mrs Stickles, who, with peals of laughter, took handfuls of petals and threw them at the newlyweds. The petals floated down then swirled, taken up on a gust of wind. More doors opened, their neighbours spilling out on to the street, cheering and offering their congratulations.

'So much for lying low,' Louisa said wryly, but she couldn't stop smiling as the fluttering petals settled on her bonnet and shawl, and Jason's coat. Her brave hero of a husband looked anxious, as though overwhelmed by the rowdy expressions of affection and support.

'What are you waitin' for, my boy?' Mr Witherall said, limping up to them with his wife at his side, beaming from ear to ear. 'Carry 'er over the threshold.'

'Yes. Yes, of course,' Jason said. Louisa put her arms around his neck and he lifted her carefully into his arms, as if she was a piece of the best china one could buy. 'Hold on tight.'

'You must make sure she doesn't touch the ground,' Winnie said.

'I know what I'm doin'. You don't really think I'd drop my wife, do you?' Jason said, amused, as he carried her into the house, the sinews in his neck straining slightly when he made sure that she didn't bump her head on the doorframe. He lowered her to the floor, kissing her as he did so. He turned to address her sisters and Mrs Stickles, and his mother and father, and Mrs Edwards, and Mrs Roper and some of her children who had followed them into the cottage.

'I'm sure you'll understand, but we've had a very long and tiring journey, and I'd like to take my wife straight to bed,' he said, a smile playing on his lips. 'To rest,' he added sternly as a blush began to creep across Louisa's cheeks.

'You won't be gettin' much rest, my boy,' Mr Witherall commented.

'Leave them alone,' Mrs Witherall scolded. 'They must be worn out with all that … travellin'.' With a wink, she turned and began to shoo everybody out.

The following day, life began to return to some semblance of normality, apart from the arrival of an invitation for

Miss Lennicker to dine at Mundel Manor in recognition of the services she had rendered to the Flinders. A pony and trap would be sent to collect her and deliver her back to Deal, when she would be in the company of one of their trusted maids. At dinner, Mrs Tempest would take her under her wing, as she had taken Mrs Tempest under hers when they were out in the storm.

'You're going up in the world,' Winnie said, reading it over her shoulder.

'I'm not going,' Louisa said.

'Why not? You must!' Grace said, joining in.

'I'm a married woman – it would be wrong to go without my husband. And Mrs Tempest and I have nothing in common.'

'Except for a love of lace.' Grace grinned.

'I suppose so.' But there was something else that bothered her about attending a function at the manor, something she preferred not to have to explain to her sisters. What if Mr Trice had been invited too? It wouldn't be unexpected – she recalled seeing him there before when she and Grace had been caught hiding in the rose bed.

'Don't be too hasty. Speak to Jason before you send a reply.'

'I'll think about it,' she said, knowing that she had plenty of time. Her husband had kissed her cheek, said that he loved her, then gone out early with the *Whimbrel* and her crew, saying he would be back in a day or two.

While Mrs Stickles and Nancy began to search for suitable premises to rent, the three sisters went to call on their uncle to settle the debt they owed him.

'Mr Laxton, your nieces have come to settle up with you. I've sent them around the back.' Louisa heard her aunt's shrill voice from the depths of the house at Limepit

Acres, haranguing him as she went on to disparage the kindness that he'd shown them.

They waited for him to turn up at the door that led into the scullery and kitchen.

'I would ask Mr Jansen to take payment when he calls at your home to avoid upsetting my wife, but it isn't unknown for him to stop at one of the inns on the way back. I can't trust him with even a penny.' Their uncle gazed at Louisa and continued with a note of challenge in his voice. 'Do you wish to terminate our arrangement now that you are a married woman?'

'Married?' She feigned surprise, but it was clear that he didn't believe her.

'Mr Jansen had an interesting conversation with your sister when he was out on his rounds the other day.' He turned to Grace who was staring at the ground, moving a small stone around in the dust with the toe of her boot. 'Mrs Laxton and I are very upset that we appear to be the last to have heard your news, when we should have been the first. You would have been best advised to have sent Mr Witherall to introduce himself to me and ask my permission for this ill-considered union.'

'There is nothing ill about it, Uncle,' Louisa said, infuriated with him, and Grace. 'It is a love match.'

'I see. Then you are as foolish as your mother, misinterpreting the first flush of—' He stopped abruptly, his cheeks turning scarlet, before going on, 'Mistaking an initial attraction for everlasting affection. She rushed into marriage without thinking and without consulting her family, just as you have done. It wasn't until it was too late that she realised that Mr Lennicker hadn't the means to support her. I assume that, having made a similar discovery, you are here because you're going to have to continue providing for your household.'

'You are my uncle, not my legal guardian. You have no say in whom I marry,' she said. 'As for wealth, I would rather be poor and happy than rich and miserable. Yes, I wish to continue provisioning with my sisters, using the produce from the market garden, because I like working. I'm not ashamed to get my hands dirty, nor do I wish to sit around idling all day. Do you want to continue with our arrangement or not?'

'I suppose your money is as good as anyone else's,' he acknowledged, 'and I can rely on the interest as a reliable extra.'

'We will be paying in full every month from now on.'

'At least you have your mother's head for financial matters.' She thought she detected the glimmer of a smile on her uncle's lips when he turned away and began to put on his boots. 'Is there anything else? Only I think I can hear Mrs Laxton calling for me. If I don't make my escape soon, she'll have me back indoors looking at schemes for decorating your cousin's bedroom now that she has flown the nest.'

'Only that you don't give us any more rubbish, thank you,' Louisa said. 'No more rancid bacon or bruised apples. The beetroot you sent was hardly fit for pigs and we had to pick the bruts off the potatoes before we could sell them.'

'I'll have a word with Mr Jansen. Good day.' He took a hat from the hook inside the door and made his way past them and out into the fields.

'Mr Laxton? Where are you?' Aunt Mary appeared, her cap awry. 'How are you still here? Where is my husband?'

'He went that way,' Grace said helpfully.

'Oh, he is insufferable. I don't know why he bothers with your sort.'

'Because whether we like it or not, we're family,' Louisa said sharply, but from her aunt's expression of disgust, she realised that it didn't count for anything with her. 'Good day, Aunt Mary,' she added.

On their way home, Louisa tackled Grace.

'I asked you especially not to say a word about my wedding.'

'I'm truly sorry about that. Mr Jansen asked after you, seeing that you weren't at home, and I mentioned that you had gone away, and he said where to and why? I told him the truth without thinking. If I could take it back, I would.'

'Oh dear, Grace. What are we going to do with you?'

They hurried on back. Louisa missed Beth, but she didn't care for her aunt. It was Jason and her sisters, Mrs Stickles and the other boatmen, their wives and children: they were her family. And, she thought sadly, Billy was too.

'I don't want you to feel uncomfortable or out of place, but I think we should accept,' Jason said when she discussed her dilemma with him on his return. He was eating his supper in the kitchen while her sisters and Mrs Stickles were in the parlour, shrieking with laughter as they re-enacted some argument that they had overheard between their neighbours earlier that day, when Jason's mother had dropped round with an invitation to the manor addressed to him.

Jason rolled his eyes at the noise.

'Sometimes a man yearns for a little peace and quiet when he gets home,' he sighed. 'Oh dear, I'm soundin' like my father.'

'I'm sorry,' she said. 'I can go and tell them to keep their voices down.'

'No, it's all right. I don't want to cause any bad blood.' He poured more apple sauce on to the pork she'd put aside for him. 'Meetin' the great and good of the county – and I use that description advisedly, knowin' that many of them disguise their true motives behind veneers of respectability and philanthropy – could very well turn out to be to our advantage. Knowledge and contacts are essential when it comes to the honourable trade. This could be a steppin' stone to a more lucrative business.'

'What about Mr Trice? What if he should be present?'

'We have been invited separately. Why should anyone at the manor know that we are married?'

'I see what you mean.'

'I'll be there, if he should try anythin'.'

'He wouldn't, I don't think, not when others are present.' She picked up one of her satin wedding slippers from the floor, having not wanted to put it on the table in case it brought bad luck. 'It's when he gets me alone …'

'We will stop this,' Jason said. 'I promise.'

Taking a pen and ink from where she kept her father's ledger, and the records she had added, she began to write on the sole of her slipper.

'What are you doing, my dear wife?'

'I'm making a record of our wedding day, then one day, when I'm old and grey, I'll be able to look back and be reminded of the happiest day of my life.'

'Are you going to write the bit about the "run goods"?' he laughed.

'Maybe …'

As she walked up the steps into the manor at five o'clock sharp on a bright September evening, the Flinders' maid at her heels, Louisa felt a sense of trepidation. Her wedding gown matched with a pair of gloves, a beaded reticule that they'd found among their mother's possessions, and a simple turban of silk pinned with a brooch, didn't look out of place, but she was nervous, not knowing what to say, and half expecting to come face-to-face with Mr Trice.

At the foot of the sweeping staircase beneath the gilded frames that held the portraits of gentlemen dressed in military uniforms and ladies who bore a resemblance to the daughters of the house, Mrs Tempest and Miss Marianne Flinders stepped forward to greet her, while a servant – the butler, she guessed – announced her arrival.

'I hope you are not overwhelmed by our welcome,' Mrs Tempest said, smiling. She wore a grey satin slip under a sarsnet overdress and her headdress was embellished with pearls and ostrich feathers. 'Ah, here is the hero of the hour, Mr Witherall.'

All eyes turned to Jason who handed his coat to one of the footmen and walked across to greet Sir Flinders and his wife, then Mrs Tempest and her sister, and finally, Louisa.

'This is a pleasant surprise, Miss Lennicker,' he said with a glint in his eye. 'I had no idea …'

'Let us show you to the drawing room,' Mrs Tempest said. 'Marianne, you walk with Mr Witherall. I shall stay with Miss Lennicker, as promised.'

The room soon filled with guests: Beth and Mr Norris; the Mayor of Deal; ladies and gentlemen from Dover and Sandwich.

'My sister is quite taken with Mr Witherall,' Mrs Tempest said, flicking her fan, a delicate creation made from hand-painted silk and mother-of-pearl, towards them. Louisa smiled to herself, secure in the knowledge that no matter how determinedly Marianne flirted with him, she would get nowhere. 'Ah, watch out for this one – he has a presumptuous air, if you know what I mean.'

'Mr Trice?' she said, spotting him in conversation with the mayor and his wife.

'You know him?'

'He acted as attorney for my father.' She was relieved when dinner was announced, and the ladies went into the dining room in order of precedence. Seeing that Louisa was unsure about where she should place herself, Mrs Tempest asked her to walk in with her. The gentlemen followed after the ladies. Lady Flinders sat at the upper end of the table, her husband at the lower end. Jason was seated between Lady Flinders and Louisa. Mrs Tempest and her sister were opposite them.

Sir Flinders said grace, and the first course was served: white soup and fish on a white tablecloth.

'Miss Lennicker,' Lady Flinders began, having sipped at her glass of wine. 'Much as I am grateful for your bravery in assisting Mrs Tempest when the *White Hind* foundered on the Sands, I have been asking myself who would allow their daughter to venture out to sea in such a storm. I would have forbidden Mrs Tempest to embark, had I been able to forecast the weather. Why did your mother not intervene?'

'She is dead, Lady Flinders.'

'Your father?'

'He passed away a year ago now.'

'Oh dear. Your guardian then?'

'I'm thankful that I'm free to make my own decisions,' Louisa said, noticing her interrogator's fingers tightening on her cup.

'You must allow that you are bound by social convention, even living on the beach as you do.'

'Lady Flinders,' Mrs Tempest interjected, frowning at her mother. 'You are inadvertently causing offence to our guest. I can assure you that Miss Lennicker lives in a house.'

'I can confirm that,' Jason added as Louisa swallowed her spleen, not wanting to upset Mrs Tempest.

'This soup is delicious, Lady Flinders,' she said, changing the subject. 'I have never tasted its like before.'

'It must be a welcome change from herring,' her hostess said, her attitude softening slightly.

When the dishes had been cleared, the footmen removed the white tablecloth to reveal a green one underneath, ready for the second course of meats: Romney marsh lamb; beef; pork cutlets; a ragout of pullet and sweetbreads.

'You are a humble fisherman, Mr Witherall?' Lady Flinders asked.

'I am a Cinque Ports man and volunteer Sea Fencible. My boats are armed, ready to protect our shores if Napoleon should attempt an invasion.'

Lady Flinders seemed impressed, but keen to point out that her husband held far more privileged positions in society, being an insurer of ships. He had also dined with General Wellesley and conferred with William Pitt the Younger on various financial matters.

After the meat course, the footmen folded the green tablecloth and left the table bare for desserts: floating islands; blancmange; trifle; bowls of sugar plums. Grace would have been amused at the changing of the cloths, Louisa thought, glancing along the table. Mr Norris was nodding off, his head jerking now and then. He had taken too much wine, she guessed, his complexion having turned an unhealthy shade of madeira. Aware that Mr Trice's eyes were on her, she was relieved when dinner was over and the ladies retired to the drawing room, leaving the gentlemen to smoke and drink port.

While Mrs Tempest and her sister played a duet on the pianoforte, Beth took Louisa aside.

'Do tell me what's going on. There has been no announcement of your nuptials – I read the newspapers every day from beginning to end, Mr Norris's eyesight not being as keen as it used to be. And you aren't wearing a ring, yet my father insists that you are married.'

'We are married,' she said quietly.

'You and the boatman? The hero of Deal?'

'That's right – we didn't want any fuss, so we –' she lowered her voice '– eloped to Gretna Green.'

Beth's mouth formed an O. 'Why did you run away? Why didn't you wait until you came of age?'

'Why should we have to delay our union because the law in England says so?'

I envy you marrying for love, but I will have security while you will always be living on the edge of danger, unless you mend your ways. Louisa, I don't care about your reputation – it's up to you how you present yourself. I worry about your safety.' She smiled. 'I don't know why I'm wasting my breath because you won't listen to me. I must return to my husband.'

'You won't tell him yet, will you?'

'I've mentioned it, but he won't remember. I shouldn't say it, but he's more interested in the liaisons that go on between his hounds than those of society.'

'I take it that you're disappointed in him.'

'He is as I expected, but no worse. It's all right, Louisa. I can please myself all day and every day, apart from Sundays when we spend time together, going to church and dining at Limepit Acres.' She stopped to applaud the young ladies as the music came to an end and excused herself when Marianne called her over to take her sister's place.

'Miss Lennicker, will you take the air with me?' Mrs Tempest asked.

'Will it not seem impolite?' Louisa said, hesitating.

'We don't have to stay out long. I thought you might like to see the gardens.' She gave her a knowing smile. 'I'd heard that you have an interest in roses. I know it's late in the season, but there are still a few flowers to be seen.'

Flushing, Louisa averted her gaze.

'I sincerely apologise for my mother's prejudice,' Mrs Tempest said as they walked together along the gravelled path that led down to the grounds at the rear of the house. 'My father insisted on inviting you and Mr Witherall to thank you for your trouble ... for risking your lives to save me. Miss Lennicker, I can't forget that terrible day – I thought we were all going to die.'

'I'm glad that it turned out as it did.'

'My mother is grateful too – in her own inimitable way. Anyway, I trust this goes no further, but I have an acquaintance who has expressed a wish to be put in contact with you. When we first came to call on you, we might have mentioned that we had tried to purchase lace from another seller, but there was a problem with his supply. It was a strange situation which he only divulged much later: he had attempted various methods of transporting the run goods – isn't that what you call them?'

Louisa nodded.

'He – oh, this is shocking to me – he paid to have the lace delivered in the coffin of some poor gentleman who'd passed away quite unexpectedly. His family wished to have his body repatriated to England, but what they didn't realise was that all but his head had been left behind, the rest of him replaced with the finest French lace.

'Unfortunately, Customs caught him out. The lace was confiscated, and the head allowed to continue its journey to the shires where it was laid to rest.'

Louisa refrained from commenting, thinking that interfering with the dead was a step too far when it came to smuggling goods and how they wouldn't be able to use coffins to carry lace again now that Customs were on to them.

'Anyway, I digress,' Mrs Tempest went on. 'Will you permit me to give my acquaintance your name and address?'

'I'd be most grateful.'

'Not as grateful as I am. My father has gone some way in rewarding you for your bravery, but I will forever be indebted to you, as is my husband. He has gone ahead of me with his regiment to the Continent where I believe he is to face the French with Wellesley in Portugal.' She smiled. 'My sister is still of the opinion that I should remain at home with her, but she will soon have a husband of her own – if one can be found. These are impoverished times for women of marriageable age when so many eligible men have been lost.' She changed the subject. 'Apparently, Mrs Ellwood's son is making good progress.'

'That is excellent news. Will you be attempting the journey again?'

'It takes more than the small matter of a shipwreck to keep me apart from my new husband. I'm sure that you wouldn't hesitate to return to the water, whatever the weather.' Mrs Tempest glanced back towards the house where the gentlemen's low voices and fragrant wisps of smoke drifted from the open window. 'It might appear that we live worlds apart,' she went on softly, 'but we have more in common than one might imagine.'

'We are all flesh and blood,' Louisa agreed, looking across the lawns and flower beds containing a few straggling summer blooms: lilies, pinks and blue love-in-the-mist. Beyond, lay the woods and farms that brought in some of the income that the Flinders depended on to maintain their comfortable lives. This was what her mother had aspired to, and she was proud to have been invited, but despite being at ease with Mrs Tempest, she felt like a fish out of water in the company of the rest of the society guests.

She would rather be singing and dancing on the beach with Jason and her sisters, drinking milk and brandy as the sun went down.

# Chapter Twenty-two

## *Nothing Ventured, Nothing Regained*

The days shortened and the cooler weather brought the first of the larger cod and whiting to the Kent coast, along with dab and flounder. Towards the end of September, Louisa found herself beginning to fret about Mr Trice's imminent visit. He had sent word to remind her that he would arrive on the last Friday of the month, not only to claim his dues, but to check that the Lennickers were preparing to move out of Compass Cottage ready for the new owner to move in.

'You aren't yourself, Mrs Witherall. You're usually very chatsome,' Jason observed, when she was stoking the fire in the kitchen that morning. She straightened, pulling her shawl across her shoulders against the autumn chill. He smiled suddenly as he helped himself to bread and bacon from the table. 'You don't think …?'

'Oh, it's far too soon for that,' she smiled back, delighted by his enthusiasm for having children. 'You will make a wonderful father, but not yet.'

'I can be patient. Louisa, is there something wrong? Is this about Mr Trice?'

She nodded. 'I'm expecting him to call today.'

'There's no need to worry – we have his money, and I'll be here by your side.'

'And if you are called away?'

'My father will come to the house. It's all arranged.'

'I'm looking forward to giving him a taste of his own medicine.' The memory of his paws chafing at her skin and the look he'd given her when they had been dining at the manor, gave her renewed courage. 'Are you ready for this?'

'I enjoy a little sport. The paint is dry on the boxes?'

She nodded. Two days beforehand, she had painted the initials R.L. after her father on a pair of identical boxes, appropriated from the salvage of the *Polestar* and perfect for transporting coins.

'Winnie has collected some ballast? And Grace has bought padlocks and chain?'

'It's all done – you don't think I'd leave anything to chance?'

'No, my dear wife.'

'It is I who is supposed to nag you,' she chuckled, as he leaned in for a kiss. 'You are ready to disappear at the sound of his carriage?'

'I'll make myself scarce. Will he be alone, do you think?'

'He usually has one man driving the phaeton and if he's expecting to collect large sums of money, he'll bring a bodyguard who rides behind him, and his clerk, Mr Mellors. They won't accompany him into the parlour, though – he always deals with me in private, calling Mr Mellors in to record the payment in his ledger and carry it out to his carriage. I predict he will follow his usual routine – he is a creature of habit who, despite the dangers, keeps to a strict round, calling on the boatmen of Deal, then going on to Sandwich and Ramsgate before returning to Dover.'

When Mr Trice arrived shortly before eleven, she showed him into the parlour.

'It's a pleasure to see you again,' she said, gritting her teeth.

'The pleasure is all mine, but … you are alone in the house?'

'My sisters are here. They understand that we are not to be disturbed,' she replied, which seemed to please him further.

'I'm glad we are back on good terms.' He placed his hat on the table.

'You have received the money for Compass Cottage?' she said, noticing how he had lost more of his hair.

'A tidy sum, minus auction fees. The deeds will be transferred to the new owner on Monday: Master Witherall, but you must know that as he is a neighbour of yours.'

'I was aware that that was the case – it has driven quite a wedge between us.'

'Ah, that is why you barely spoke to him – I noticed when we were dining with the Flinders. You left early, before we had a chance to renew our acquaintance, Miss Lennicker. You disappointed me.'

'I'm sorry. It was unintentional.' The words caught in her craw. 'The Flinders had kindly offered me the use of their pony and trap. When their maid gave word that it was ready, I left promptly, not wanting to hold anyone up.'

He squinted at her as he polished the ferrule on his cane.

'You are obliged to move out by midnight on Sunday, or you will be evicted. Forcibly.'

'Oh, Mr Trice!'

'The property has been sold, but there remains a large amount outstanding,' he said with a lecherous smirk.

'I have it here,' she cut in.

'All of it?'

'Every penny.' She took the box, already chained and padlocked, along with the key from the mantel and put them beside his hat. As she turned, he pressed himself upon her, placing his hands on her waist and pushing her against the table.

'You think you're so clever,' he hissed.

'The deal is done.'

'I will take goods in kind, Miss Lennicker. Please don't play the innocent with me. You know exactly what I'm referring to.'

'You will not have my maidenhead, sir.'

'I shall indeed.'

Aware of his hand tugging at her skirt, she slapped his face to bring him to his senses, but it only infuriated him more. His face moved closer to hers, his eyes wild with anger and lust, pearls of spittle on his lips.

'What you seek is already lost,' she yelled at him. 'I am a married woman!'

As if struck by lightning, he straightened and stared at her.

'You're making this up, sly woman that you are, but if you think you will put me off, you are wrong. I will have you, and I will have you now.'

'Take your hands off her.' The wall beside the fireplace slid aside and Jason stepped into the room. 'Mr Trice, allow me to introduce you to my wife.'

The attorney stood stock-still, white to the gills.

'Take your money and go. The debt is settled in full,' Jason said. 'In future, the Witheralls will be takin' their business elsewhere – there are other agents, plenty of gentlemen keen to have a slice of the cake when it comes to the free trade. What are you waitin' for?' He picked up the box and tried to hand it to him. 'Go! I will not have you under my roof again.'

'I will count it first.'

'I find the implication that you don't trust my wife rather insultin'.'

'I will count it with my clerk as is my custom,' he insisted, calling Mr Mellors in from the street.

Mr Mellors stood watching with a ledger under his arm, as his employer took a seat at the table. Mr Trice removed the padlock and chain, emptied the box and counted the coins, but he wasn't satisfied until he had counted them thrice and Mr Mellors had recorded the amount and denominations in the ledger. Only then did he return the coins to the box and close the lid.

He wound the chain back around the box and padlocked it securely, slipping the key into his pocket.

'Shall I write a receipt, sir?' Mr Mellors asked.

'Of course.' Mr Trice gave him a withering look. 'In triplicate. This transaction must be done by the book. There must be no room for accusations of duplicity.' Still smouldering with anger at not having had his way, he stared pointedly at Louisa. 'Mr Mellors, pick up the box and take it out to the phaeton. Do not let it out of your sight.'

As the clerk collected the box and ledger, Jason began to speak.

'Mr Trice, I trust that you will forgive the misunderstandin' that arose between you and my wife earlier on.'

The attorney turned to face him as Louisa stepped across to close the door behind Mr Mellors.

'You set me up, Mr Witherall. I should have guessed there was something going on between you when you walked in on us before, but I made the assumption that you were calling as a neighbour for some other purpose.

It was ungallant of you to wind me in. You are no gentleman, and your wife is no lady.'

'You will apologise,' Jason said, squaring up to him.

'Never!'

A fracas broke out in the hall. There was a thud, and after what felt like an interminable pause, Winnie cried out, 'She has swooned.'

'I must go to her,' Louisa said urgently, and the three of them – Louisa, Jason and Mr Trice – left the parlour to find Grace sitting on the floor, resting her forehead on the back of one hand, her eyes half closed, the image of feminine weakness.

'I don't know what came over me,' she mumbled as Mr Mellors knelt beside her, holding her wrist like a doctor, checking her pulse.

'It's all right – Mr Mellors is kindly helping us.' Winnie looked up, rearranging her skirts as she squatted between her sister and the stairs. 'Here are the smelling salts.' She handed him a vinaigrette – not something they'd planned, Louisa realised, but Winnie's idea of a prop to add realism to the scene.

Mr Mellors opened the vinaigrette and held it under Grace's nose. She sneezed.

'That is a remarkably effective treatment for an attack of the vapours,' he marvelled. 'It's a miracle. Can you believe it, Mr Trice?'

'The money?' Mr Trice said. 'Where is it?'

'Right here,' Mr Mellors responded, pointing to the box that he'd dropped on the floor in his haste to assist Grace.

If the clerk had had his hand on Louisa's wrist instead, he would have noticed the rapid acceleration in the rate of her pulse. For one unnerving moment, she wondered if they had been rumbled, but Mr Trice turned away, leaving Mr Mellors to stop attending to Grace, pick up the box and carry it outside. Soon afterwards, they heard the clip-clop of horses' hooves and the rattle of the phaeton's wheels as Mr Trice and his entourage left Cockle Swamp Alley.

'Thank goodness for that – I can breathe again,' Louisa sighed. 'You did manage to—?'

'Hey presto,' Winnie interrupted, jumping up and stepping aside. 'Look what I have conjured up from under my petticoats: one box of coins.'

'You are sure?' Jason asked.

'Of course I am. I didn't take pleasure in doing it, but I did it for you, Louisa. It isn't right that awful man can go around taking liberties, under cover of being a gentleman.' Winnie helped Grace up. 'You did quite a turn there.'

'It was worth it – I only wish we could see Mr Trice's face when he tries to open the box and finds that his key doesn't fit the padlock.'

'He'll have to break it,' Winnie observed as Louisa picked the box up and carried it back into the parlour.

'And then he won't be able to believe his eyes when he finds it full of stones. But Louisa, aren't you worried that he'll come back to confront us?'

'If he does, I have a copy of the receipt. There is one thing Mr Trice has taught me, and that is the importance of having evidence: the right evidence.' She stared at the box – there was something not quite right about it, and she wasn't sure what it was.

'Winnie, give me the key,' she said quickly.

'This one?' She touched the key that was dangling from a string around her neck. 'Oh no, it won't fit – it's the wrong one.'

'Don't argue. Just give it to me.'

Frowning, Winnie took it off and handed it over. Louisa slid it into the padlock and gave it a jiggle. It turned and the padlock fell open. Winnie's mouth fell open too.

'It is a coincidence,' she said. 'Two padlocks with the same key …'

'I believe that we have been double-crossed,' Jason said harshly, as with trembling fingers, Louisa tore the chain off and opened the lid to reveal the stones they had intended Mr Trice to have as souvenirs of Deal.

'How did he do it?' she exclaimed. 'Winnie, what happened? How did our plan go awry?'

Winnie began to weep.

'Oh, that's enough of the crocodile tears.'

'I'm not shamming them. I'm very upset.' Winnie ran out of the parlour and upstairs to her room, where she slammed the door.

'I'm not sure exactly what happened because I had my eyes closed,' Grace said. 'Mr Mellors put the box down on the floor and knelt beside me. Winnie had the other box – this one – hidden under her petticoats. She swapped the boxes, but while he was looking after me, he suggested that Winnie fetch the smelling salts. I didn't want her to, but I couldn't say anything because I was supposed to be in a faint.'

'I can guess what went on next,' Louisa sighed. 'Winnie left the room, forgetting about the box. Mr Mellors saw it and, knowing a little of the tricks of the trade from Mr Trice, took the opportunity to swap them back.'

'I think that must be what he did,' Grace agreed.

Louisa felt sick. Mr Trice had won. And they had lost.

'I don't blame Winnie – we took a risk, set it all up and then our bamboozlement went wrong. Anybody can make a mistake,' Jason said. 'However, there's no way I'm going to let him get away with stealin' our money.'

'It wasn't really ours, was it?' Louisa said quietly.

'Possession is nine tenths of the law. We get it back, and it's ours again.' He took her by the shoulders and gazed into her eyes. 'He owes you for what he's done to you. He's made your life a misery, comin' around here and threatenin' to take you by force, and fleecin' you out of hundreds of pounds, claimin' that it's interest. We've said before how he takes advantage of our good nature, insistin' on havin' his commission for doin' very little. He doesn't risk his life or liberty.'

'I'm not sure.'

'Go on,' Grace said. 'We don't want to be below hatches for the rest of our lives.'

'Don't you want to be there when he receives the greatest shock of his life?' Jason was smiling, apparently unafraid.

'I don't see how we can do it,' Louisa said, dispirited by the failure of their plan.

'We must hurry if we are to catch him by the tail. Louisa and Grace, take Winnie and alert my father to rally the boatmen. Then signal to the landside men, tellin' as many as you can to make their way to the sandhills, armed with staves. They must hide themselves in the dunes on the ancient highway just beyond the Chequers Inn and wait until I give the order.' He smiled briefly. 'Explain that they'll be paid the usual rate for a few hours' work. Louisa, we can't give up now.'

She was paralysed with doubt.

'It is a recipe for disaster. I'm afraid that somebody will be killed or arrested for this.'

'We aren't going to hurt him, just give him a scare. Come on, Louisa. Nothin' ventured, nothin' regained. We can't let the likes of Mr Trice ride roughshod over us – he'll only come back to have another go. We must unite and make it clear to him that he's finished when it comes to makin' money out of the French merchants and free traders. This is about takin' our very last stand against him.'

'I had thought it was the Rattlers who were our enemy,' she sighed.

'One Eye's death seems to have torn the heart out of them. My dear wife, am I to understand that we are havin' our first marital spat?'

'I'd describe it as a disagreement, Mr Witherall,' she said.

'A wife should respect her husband's opinion.'

'And a husband should listen to his wife ...'

'I am listenin',' he said seriously, 'but I think you'll live to regret it, if you give up now. Where is your fight, Louisa?'

The memory of Mr Trice's stinking breath and his hand groping at her breast came flooding back. He had influence throughout Kent. What was to stop him using it against the boatmen and their families in future, unless they taught him a lesson he would never forget?

'We will do it,' she decided.

Grinning, Jason kissed her and let her go.

'I'll see you in the sandhills,' he called as he headed out.

'Grace, fetch Winnie,' Louisa said. 'Tell her this is her chance to redeem herself. I'll put a few things together.'

She knew as they headed past the Three Kings and north to the fringes of the sandhills, that they were taking an enormous risk, preparing to ambush Mr Trice's entourage in broad daylight, but the ancient highway between Deal and Sandwich wasn't frequented by many travellers and the area was desolate, inhabited mainly by flocks of dunlin, sanderling and turnstone, and criss-crossed by channels of brackish water.

Having given Jason's father his orders, they were ready to alert the landside men. With any luck, they would be able to raise a small army to overwhelm Mr Trice, give him the frights and retrieve the money.

Under a cloudy sky, they dragged the wood and hay from beneath the broken hull of an upturned boat that had been left by some of the boatmen's wives ready for their next foray into the free trade. Louisa used the flint from the Lennickers' tinder box to light some kindling, but although they were in a hollow, a wicked gust of wind blew the first flame out.

'Let me do it,' Winnie said.

'Go on then,' Louisa said, a little disgruntled to see how quickly her sister managed to raise a fire. 'I'll go and fetch some water.'

'Hurry then,' Grace said. 'We can't have much time.'

Louisa took the empty bucket from beside the boat and filled it with sea water. Winnie poured it on top of the hay and the fire began to smoke.

'I'm glad it isn't raining. Although –' Winnie looked at her sisters '– I'm sorry.'

'It's all right,' Louisa said. 'I forgive you.'

'Thank you. I've been a little scatter-witted since Billy disappeared, but I won't do anything like that again. I wasn't thinking. I just wish I knew where he was.'

'So do we,' Grace said as Winnie threw another armful of hay on to the fire. Louisa added a splash more water. Smoke billowed into the sky.

'If they are labouring in the fields, they won't come,' she observed.

'They will,' Grace said. 'Mr Jansen told me that he's always looking out for ways of making extra money.'

'Did you hear that?' Winnie asked.

'Voices? Yes. The boatmen are on their way along the beach.' Louisa could just make them out, a group of about twenty men marching along the shore.

'No. Listen.'

Straining her ears, she heard the staccato notes of a hunting horn, repeated several times in the distance.

'They are doubling the horn,' Winnie said, 'the signal from the huntsman to his hounds that he wants them available in a hurry. We can put this out – they have seen our smoke.'

Louisa fetched more water and they extinguished the fire, stamping on the remaining embers and covering the ashes with sand. The boatmen had passed them, turning on to the rutted track, but Louisa decided that she and her sisters should keep to the sandhills as they continued in the direction of Sandwich with the great expanse of beach and sea to the east.

The clouds swarmed in, obscuring the sky, and a chill breeze swept across the low-lying land. There were few buildings, only the looker's cottage where the shepherd lived, and further on, the Chequers Inn. Louisa made sure that they skirted Mary Bax's stone, a memorial to a young woman who'd been murdered thirty years before, not wanting to be reminded of the peril that they and the men were about to face.

After they had been walking for another half an hour, figures began to appear from the west, men dressed in dark clothing, moving swiftly through the landscape, some walking, some riding. Once past the inn, Louisa and her sisters joined a crowd of boatmen and batsmen who were milling around on the highway, awaiting further instructions. On tenterhooks, she stared along the track, looking for Jason, praying that he would arrive before Mr Trice.

'There 'e is. There's Marlin and 'is cousin,' Mr Roper said, as two men on horseback came galloping along the track, their mounts' feet throwing up billows of sand.

They pulled up alongside them: two men dressed in black, apart from the brightly patterned bandannas around their necks, and riding matching black horses. The boatmen, carrying a variety of weapons from pistols to chains wrapped around their fists, and the batsmen armed with hefty staves, gathered to hear Jason's orders.

'What about us? What are we supposed to do?' Grace complained quietly.

'Ladies,' Jason said, turning to address them. 'Keep well out of the way for your own safety. Retreat to the looker's cottage – there's a haystack nearby where you can hide. Men, take your places.'

'What if 'e doesn't turn up?' Mr Roper asked.

'Will we still be paid?' Mr Jansen added.

'You will be paid,' Jason said impatiently. 'And if he doesn't make an appearance in the next few hours, we'll set a spy on him and waylay him the next time he passes this way.'

'I'm not going anywhere,' Louisa muttered as she and her sisters slid down behind a mound of sand and lay on their bellies in the rough, spiky grass, watching the men disperse. 'Jason has forgotten that he may have need of us ...' *To help with the injured,* she almost added. She wouldn't allow herself to feel guilty for going against her husband, certain that the anvil priest hadn't incorporated a promise to obey him in their wedding vows.

'You have the pistol?' Grace asked.

'Yes,' she whispered, removing it from her garter.

'That's all right then.' Grace smiled ruefully. 'I am being scratched and stung to bits.'

'You'll have to put up with a little discomfort,' Winnie said, apparently determined to see that her earlier mistake was put right.

An hour, two hours went by and Louisa was on the verge of giving up when she heard a dog bark three times.

'That's one of our men,' Winnie whispered.

Holding her cloak over her mouth and nose, Louisa crawled forward on her elbows and peered through the vegetation at the top of the sandhill. Her sisters joined her.

Mr Trice's bodyguard was a few yards in front of the phaeton, ambling along on his horse, while the pair of greys pulling the phaeton struggled along the ruts before reaching smoother ground when the driver whipped them to a faster pace. Mr Trice and Mr Mellors were beneath the hood, raised deliberately to hide their identities rather than for the onset of bad weather, Louisa guessed.

From her vantage point, she could see the boatmen and batsmen further along the road, waiting in the sandhills, and Jason and Abel walking their horses towards the oncoming entourage, talking and laughing as though they were two gentlemen on a leisurely day out. Sitting back, she loaded the pistol.

'No, Louisa,' Winnie whispered.

'It's just a precaution,' she murmured, her heart beginning to race as the bodyguard halted and glanced behind him.

Jason and Abel spurred their horses to a sudden gallop, pulling up beside the bodyguard, their pistols raised. The driver stopped and held his hands up, the bodyguard fumbled for his pistol and dropped it. It went off, sending the draught horses into a frenzy. As the boatmen and batsmen emerged on to the road, fore and aft, the horses dragged the phaeton off into the sandhills, tipping it on to its side and throwing the driver and one of the passengers clear. When it became lodged in a dip in the ground some distance away, having lost the rear axle, the horses were forced to stop. They stood stock-still, their heads down, breathing hard.

'I reckon the wheels have come off Mr Trice's enterprise at last,' Louisa said, 'but where is the old blackguard and who has the money?'

Jason and Abel had left the bodyguard to the mercy of the batsmen who surrounded him while he held his hands over his head, his horse having apparently thrown him and bolted. The driver was on his feet, dusting himself down, when Mr Witherall and Mr Roper took him by the shoulders and rummaged him, supervised by some of the other boatmen, one of whom relieved him of what appeared to be a hip flask.

In the meantime, Jason was cantering ahead of his cousin up and down through the sandhills in pursuit of a figure that Louisa recognised as Mr Mellors.

'Where's Mr Trice?' Grace said.

'I don't know,' Winnie responded.

'He's in the carriage,' Louisa said, standing up and shaking out the cramp from her arm. She hitched up her skirts and set off towards the phaeton.

'Where are you going?' Winnie hissed.

'To find him – before he tries to make his escape.'

'No, Louisa. We must wait for the men.'

'There's no time to waste.'

'Then we'll come with you.'

'No, Winnie. You stay here with Grace. Don't put yourselves in any danger, and don't worry about me – I can look after myself.' Louisa scrambled through the dunes, pistol at the ready. When she reached the phaeton, one of the horses looked up and whickered in anticipation of being rescued from its predicament, the other nibbled on the tips of some nearby grass. She stopped and listened. All she could hear was the distant sound of shouting and her heartbeat. Keeping the pistol raised, she stepped around the overturned carriage and looked inside, expecting to see Mr Trice caught up in the mangled wreckage.

'Help … me …' came a half-strangulated groan from somewhere behind her. She started to turn her head, but it was too late. One of his arms was tight around her neck and his wiry body was pressed against her back.

'Give me that,' he said, his breath hot and damp against her ear. 'Slowly pass it into my left hand.'

As her blood turned to ice, she did as she was bid. What choice did she have? She thought of Pa's instructions on how to disable a person of the masculine sex, but she was in no position to carry them out.

'Thank you, my dear.'

'What are you going to do?' she asked, trembling as the muzzle of the pistol dug into her back. 'There are men out looking for you.'

'Ah, did I ever enlighten you as to the importance of insurance? You are my surety.' Her skin crawled as he nipped at her ear. 'Don't scream. Don't do anything to attract attention. Now, pick up the box over there.'

Having spotted the box that was lying on the ground, she bent down and picked it up, hugging it to her chest.

'That's good. Keep your head down and start walking. That way.' He drove her ahead of him, sending her seawards where they could move across the sand without being seen from the highway.

'You will never get away – they'll be coming for you at any moment,' she argued.

'Not if we hurry. Make haste!'

'There'll be a hue and cry when they realise that I'm missing. Everyone from Dover to Sandwich will be searching for us.'

'Do you really imagine that your friends, the Deal boatmen, the scum of the earth, the lowest of the low, would risk raising a hue and cry for you? They would not want to attract the attention of a constable to their role in the creation of this fracas. Who do you think those in a position of authority would believe? A gang of liars and cheats, or a reputable attorney?'

'They'd believe me when they caught up with us – I'd make them,' she said, stumbling along.

'Ah, but it would be your word against mine. Who would listen to you? All I'd need to do is explain how you fled from the scene of the crime, the ambush of my carriage, and attempted theft of money that's rightfully mine. Being a gentleman and seeing that you were putting yourself in danger, a young woman in distress and alone in a place overrun with villains, I'd say that I chased after you to offer my protection, but you misunderstood my intention.'

Tears of frustration, anger and fear began to run down her cheeks as he went on. 'We can find a place to hide, and then after dusk, we'll make our way to Sandwich. I have associates there, and I'm sure the magistrate will be keen to hear my allegations against you and your fellows: robbery; violence; deception. You will all hang.'

The shouting began to fade as did Louisa's hopes of being found, not that she was sure what anyone could do while her captor was holding a firearm against her back. The box of coins grew heavier in her arms, and her legs began to tire as he pushed and shoved her across the dunes. Mr Trice said nothing, and Louisa couldn't help thinking that he was lost. They had doubled back to avoid traversing a channel of water, an inlet from the sea, and she had noticed that their tracks had crossed more than once. An hour or more passed, and they had made little progress towards their destination when she heard the faintest sound of men's voices through the whisper of the breaking waves and the mournful cries of the curlew.

'Stop,' Mr Trice hissed suddenly as they reached a hollow in the sand, hidden from the landside by steep banks topped with marram grass, and open to the beach and the sea beyond. There was the hulk of a small rowing boat abandoned near the tideline, one of many scattered about the sandhills, and a pile of firewood. 'This will do. Lie down and don't move.'

Louisa knelt and placed the box on the ground, playing for time, because she was certain now that she could hear the gradual crescendo of a hue and cry approaching from the distance. Despite Mr Trice's opinions to the contrary, Jason and her sisters had raised the alarm, but would anybody find her in time?

'I said, lie down.'

She glanced up, finding herself staring straight up the muzzle of the pistol.

'Lie down on your back, because I will have you. It would be a travesty to waste this opportunity.' He reached out with his free hand and wiped her cheek roughly with his thumb. 'Such pretty tears ...'

'Please, don't. They are coming for me. Can't you hear them?'

He paused to listen, and a flicker of fear crossed his face.

'I will not be thwarted again,' he snarled. 'By the time they reach us, it'll be too late. I shall tell them that despite my attempts to look after you, you ran away. When I caught up with you, I found you distraught and bruised, having been violated by another man.'

'I've told you, I'm married,' she entreated.

'You are still a maiden of sorts,' he crowed, fumbling with his breeches, as she lay on her back. 'They still call you the Lace Maiden, do they not?' Tossing the pistol aside, he knelt over her, tugging at her skirts.

She fought and struggled as he pinned her down, his hands like vices around her forearms, his expression voracious. She couldn't escape, couldn't breathe, her ribcage crushed by the weight of his body. The pistol and money box were out of reach and there was nothing she could use as a weapon to distract him from his relentless assault, but she continued to wriggle and twist beneath him. She would not let him have her as long as there was air in her bellows.

Gradually though, her strength began to fail. As she took her last gasps, she turned her eyes heavenwards and stared past Mr Trice's shoulder, determined that the last thing she saw in her earthly life wouldn't be her assailant's face.

'We've found them. They're over here!' came a loud yell.

With a growl of rage, Mr Trice reached for the pistol. He leapt up and snatched the box of money. All Louisa could do was drink in great gulps of fresh salt-laden air, and watch him turn and run towards the sea, his breeches around his thighs and pistol in hand, as a figure leapt down from the top of the bank, scattering sand.

Jason? Yes, Jason. Mr Trice was armed. She wanted to warn Jason and the men who followed behind him, but she couldn't utter a word.

'He has kidnapped my wife.' Jason fell to his knees beside her. 'He's taken her against her will, and—'

'I can see very well what's 'appened 'ere,' Constable Pocket interrupted.

'Go after him then while I attend to Mrs Witherall,' Jason said. 'What are you waitin' for?'

Louisa sat up slowly, becoming aware of a large crowd of people, including the constable, Reverend North, shopkeepers and boatyard workers from Deal, and the boatmen and batsmen, looking out to where Mr Trice was dragging the abandoned boat into the breakers. As it floated away from the shallows, he clambered in, rocking it so violently that it took on water.

Jason leaned closer and took her in his arms.

'Thank goodness we found you. He's hurt you though?' His tone hardened. 'I'm goin' to kill him.'

'Please don't harm him,' Louisa said, suddenly afraid for her husband if he should try. She didn't care about Mr Trice – he was beneath contempt.

'I don't see why I should grant the likes of him any mercy. Look what he's done to you. The bruises ...'

'I'll be all right.' She rubbed her arms to bring the blood back into them. 'You turned up just in time. Jason, kill him and you'll end up dangling by the neck from the gallows.'

'What do you want me to do then? Stand by and watch the coward get away when he's put you through hell?'

'I'd like to see him brought to justice according to the law of the land,' she said quietly.

'Arrest him.' Jason addressed Constable Pocket. 'The lady wants him arrested.'

'I can't swim,' he responded as they continued to watch while Mr Trice battled to keep the boat steady. The current had caught his leaky vessel, whisking it away from the shore.

''E's 'avin' to bail 'er out,' Mr Roper said, unable to disguise his delight.

Mr Trice was frantically scooping water out of the boat with his cupped hands, but as his figure shrank into the distance, he stopped and began yelling for help.

'We must go to his aid,' Jason decided. 'Men, we'll go back to Deal and launch the *Whimbrel*.'

'It'll be too late.' Mr Roper took his spyglass from his pocket and squinted out to sea. 'The boat is sinkin'.'

'We have to try,' Jason said. 'How would it look if we left him to die out there? And there'll be a fair reward if we do manage to rescue him, alive and well. Furthermore, I happen to know that he has a goodly amount of money onboard.'

'Then we have nothin' to lose and much to gain,' Mr Roper said.

'You go ahead. I'll catch you up,' Jason said, standing up and giving Louisa his hand. 'I must deliver my wife into the care of her sisters first.'

'Go now, my love,' Louisa said as he helped her up. 'Don't delay on my account.'

'Are you sure?'

'I'll walk with Constable Pocket. I'll be perfectly safe.'

'I don't like to leave you ...'

'Go!' she repeated, and he leaned down to kiss her before going on his way.

'Louisa! There she is.' On hearing Grace's shriek of joy, she turned to find her sisters hurrying up to her, their eyes filled with concern.

'Abel said we should wait for news, but we couldn't,' Winnie said. 'Are you all right? Oh no, you aren't. You've been crying.'

'Mr Trice attacked me, but he's gone now.' She glanced towards the spot where she'd last seen the boat and its occupant – they had disappeared. She felt a strange sense of compassion for him, knowing that he had almost certainly drowned, but also relief that he wouldn't be able to torment her any more.

'Let's go home,' she said, and she walked hand in hand with her sisters, back to Deal to await the *Whimbrel*'s return.

There were great celebrations on the beach that day when the *Whimbrel* grazed her keel on the shingle and the men hauled her up the beach with the news that they had used a creeping iron to find and haul Mr Trice's body from the bottom of the sea, not far from where his boat had sunk. The undertaker was sent for and the attorney's remains carried to the Waterman's Arms to await the coroner.

'It's good riddance to 'im,' Mrs Witherall said as the women and children waited for the men to join them.

''E deserved it. 'E was always takin' advantage of us,' Mrs Edwards added. ''E took a large cut out of what we earned, yet 'e didn't 'ave to go to sea or risk bein' caught by the gobblers.'

Although everybody seemed convinced that the free-traders wouldn't have to answer to the law over Mr Trice's death, Louisa felt uneasy. She sought out Jason as he was stowing the *Whimbrel*'s canvas.

He smiled when he saw her.

'I'm glad we found him,' he said. 'I hope it gives you peace of mind, knowin' that he can't come back to bother you.'

'I'm grateful, but I can't help worrying. What if Mr Mellors, his bodyguard and the driver should put all their horses together and say something to get us into trouble?'

'We've made sure that they'll hold their tongues. Mr Mellors was no match for the horses – Abel and I hadn't chased him very far when he fell flat on his face. We dusted him down and offered him a half anker of cognac – which he had no hesitation in acceptin' – to keep his silence about our part in the ambush. The bodyguard is a good man –

he joined the hue and cry when he knew you were missin', and he's agreed to act as a batsman when we need him. As for Mr Trice's driver, my father says that he claims to have no memory of the events that led to his horses boltin'.' He reached for her hand and squeezed her fingers. 'Have I reassured you?'

She nodded.

'The only downside is that we didn't find the box,' he said ruefully. 'Never mind.' She read the change in his expression as he gazed into her eyes, and heard the sob catching in his throat. 'Louisa, I was afraid I was goin' to find you dead, and I don't know what I'd have done without you.'

'Jason, don't be upset,' she murmured.

'I want you to know that I would rather have you, my darlin', than all the money in the world.'

'You don't need to tell me – I feel the same about you,' she said as the pipers and fiddlers began to play.

'Let's dance,' she said, and she led him across the beach to where the men were singing 'Nelson's Blood' and the mothers were bouncing their children on their knees. Louisa danced with Jason. Winnie danced with Grace. And as the men sang the chorus, they formed a line with Jason at the head, snaking along the shingle.

*So we'll roll the golden chariot along,*
*And we'll all 'old on be'ind.*

As the singers added an eighth and then a ninth verse, Louisa tugged on the tails of Jason's shirt.

'Stop,' she said, laughing. 'It's too much.'

Jason came to a halt and the line fell apart.

'You will wear them all out,' Mrs Witherall admonished the musicians.

''Ot pies,' came Mrs Stickles' shrill voice. 'Three different kinds, just as you ordered.'

Louisa looked up to see Mrs Stickles and Nancy carrying trays draped with striped gingham down from Molly's Pot-House.

'Wonderful,' Jason shouted, taking Louisa's hand and leading the charge towards the food. 'I'm starvin'.'

As they arrived to collect a slice of pie, some wag among the musicians began to sing again.

*Oh, a comely fat cook wouldn't do us any 'arm.*
*Oh, a comely fat cook wouldn't do us any 'arm –*

The men joined in and Mrs Stickles, far from being offended, nodded and smiled.

'I wonder who she has the eye for,' Jason whispered.

'As long as it isn't you, I don't mind,' Louisa chuckled. 'She and Nancy seem to be making a success of their new venture, thanks to you.'

'As long as they pay me back,' he said with a wink. 'I'm glad we could help them. We can give others a helpin' hand now that we are swimmin' in lard. It's always better to work for yourself than for others.'

They retired to sit further along the slope between the *Curlew* and *Whimbrel*, with pie and tankards of milk and brandy. As they gazed out to sea, watching the water turning gold in the late afternoon sunshine, a man came shuffling towards them.

'Good day to you,' he said, stopping beside them.

'Awful Doins? To what do we owe this pleasure?' Jason said sarcastically. 'I would have thought you would have known better than to approach me and my wife.'

'I've come in the spirit of reconciliation. I 'ave somethin' that will be of advantage to you.' He pulled his hand from his pocket, then opened his palm to reveal several teeth of different colours.

'Ugh,' Louisa said. 'Those are not animal teeth.'

Awful Doins kept his voice low. 'These are rare an' valuable souvenirs of Deal's most infamous smuggler, One Eye Feasey …'

'It is a sham,' Louisa said.

'These are the genuine article. Isaiah 'ad me take the plates out of his dead father's mouth, not likin' to see anythin' go to waste. I bought them off 'im for a knock-down price. You can 'ave one to keep for posterity for the sum of—'

'No, thank you,' Louisa and Jason said at the same time.

'There's nothin' I can say to change your mind, Marlin?'

'You're right. There's nothin' you can say or do. Take those ugly pearls and throw them to the waves.'

Awful Doins dropped them straight back into his pocket and walked along the beach to try selling them to somebody else. Louisa noticed how Winnie and Grace ignored him as he passed by where they were standing together, waiting for the next dance, Grace leaning her head against Winnie's shoulder.

'I think my sister will always be pining for Billy,' Louisa said.

'We mustn't give up hope, not yet. He could return at any time.'

'I know, but the more time that passes without us hearing from him, the less likely it becomes. She's lost the child, which some might say is a blessing, but I can't help feeling sad for her. It might have provided her with some consolation.'

'Or prolonged her agony. Oh Louisa, we have no idea of the depths of her sufferin', but whatever happens, we'll make sure she's all right.'

She glanced from her left hand where the ring was glinting on her finger, to her husband's handsome face. Her love for him was deeper than the ocean and wider than any sea.

'I'm sorry for going against you today,' she said.

'Let it be a lesson to you. Perhaps you'll be a dutiful wife and listen to me in future.'

'Maybe,' she teased.

He grinned, then grew serious. 'I like a woman who has a mind of her own. I love you, my darlin'. I realise there'll be stormy times ahead, but it makes me happy knowin' that we'll be sailin' through life together, you and me.'

A shout disturbed them. Some of the boys were pointing out to the horizon where a giant lugger with her dark sails unfurled was making her way along the Downs, half hidden by the other vessels anchored in the deep water.

'Who is she?' Louisa asked. 'I don't recognise her.'

'It's the Rattlers' replacement for the *Good Intent*. Black Dog is determined to continue in the free trade, takin' his father's place.' Jason took her hand, linking his fingers through hers. 'What do you think about making another run?'

She turned to him, smiling.

She should stop, she thought, but something drove her on. Smuggling came easy to her. Like breathing, laughing and loving, it was part of life, and she never wanted it to end.

Welcome to

# Penny Street

where your favourite authors and stories live.

Meet casts of characters you'll never forget, create memories you'll treasure forever, and discover places that will stay with you long after the last page.

Turn the page to step into the home of

# EVIE GRACE

and discover more about

## *The Lace Maiden*

Dear Reader,

It was a tiny snippet of information that I found while researching the history of East Kent that led me to write *The Lace Maiden*, Louisa's story set in the early nineteenth century when Britain was at war with France.

The Aldington Gang – also known as the 'Blues' because they wore blue smocks – were a gang of smugglers working along the stretch of coast to the south of Deal around that time. The reports of their dastardly deeds inspired me to delve further into the history of the town, but the Deal I found myself reading about was a far cry from my childhood memories of the place.

I first visited while on holiday with my grandparents, and I remember taking delight in throwing pebbles into the sea from the endless shingle beach and enjoying the special treat of a 99 ice-cream. I had no idea of the town's rich and varied maritime history, and the daring Deal boatmen who would go out in the fiercest of storms to rescue sailors and passengers from stricken sailing ships. While they were heroes, many of them were also involved in the free trade, smuggling gold and escaped French prisoners to France and illegally importing goods such as cognac and lace.

Prompted by my research, I returned to Deal to look at it with fresh eyes, staying at The Royal Hotel. Louisa and her sisters would have known it as The Three Kings and would have been children when Admiral Nelson and Lady Hamilton stayed there. They would have looked across the same stretch of water when the *Victory* came sailing past with his body after the Battle of Trafalgar.

I hope you enjoy getting to know the close-knit community of the boatmen and the families who lived in the houses in the narrow alleyways of Deal as much as I did.

*Evie x*

# The Allure of Lace

Why would smugglers risk their lives carrying French lace across the Channel to England? What was it about lace that made it such a valuable commodity? These are two of the questions I asked myself when looking into the history of smuggling in East Kent, in preparation for writing Louisa's story in *The Lace Maiden*.

I like to think of research as a long road with twists and turns, crossroads and alleyways, some being shortcuts to useful information, others being dead ends, and as I set out on my route, I discovered there was a lot more to lace than I'd imagined.

The demand for lace has always been driven by fashion. Before machinery was introduced, needle and bobbin lace were costly and time-consuming to make by hand, and only the gentry and clergy could afford to buy it. People cherished delicate pieces of lace, using and reusing them as collars, cuffs and trimmings to embellish their outfits.

Although lace was being made in England in the late eighteenth and early nineteenth centuries, French lace was still considered very desirable, but it was hard to obtain for two reasons, the first being that many of the French lacemakers had lost their lives during the French Revolution, due to their association with the aristocracy. For example, Chantilly lace made from black silk was favoured by Marie Antoinette. After she went to the guillotine in 1793, the Chantilly lacemakers lost their lives too, and the production of Chantilly lace stopped.

The second reason for the scarcity of French lace in England was that imports from France were banned during the Napoleonic Wars when *The Lace Maiden* is set.

I had found the answers to my questions. There was an impressive profit to be made from smuggling lace to sell to the drapers of London and the landed gentry, enough to make it worth endangering your life for. There were risks for the men who sailed the luggers – boats built for speed to evade capture by the Revenue and privateers – between Dunkirk and Gravelines, and the East Kent coast. It was the same for the shore-based smugglers, the men and women who helped to unload the goods, then carry them inland to hide or sell. If caught, they could be sent for trial at the assizes, convicted and sentenced to death by hanging.

Lace was so expensive that a smuggling gang wouldn't normally have the means to finance the purchase from the French merchants. Instead, wealthy businessmen used agents to buy the goods on their behalf, taking a share of the profits when they were sold. They would also have had to accept the risk that the Revenue might seize their goods, or that they would be lost at sea. Although I couldn't find any evidence, I would imagine that lace would have been easily spoiled by immersion in sea water, or mud, even when it was wrapped in oilskin.

Lace, unlike cognac, was lightweight and easy to carry. A society lady might smuggle a little back from a trip to the Continent inside a fur muff or wrapped around her waist. Others used more imaginative and rather appalling methods for hiding the goods. There are records of lace having been stuffed inside geese apparently intended for the table, and a tale of a small dog being wrapped in lace that was then covered with the skin of another, larger dog.

There were other methods of carrying lace and keeping it hidden from the Revenue and you can find them in Louisa's story.

Happy reading.

*Evie x*

Read on for an exclusive extract from *The Golden Maid*, the second novel in The Smuggler's Daughters trilogy.

Coming July 2020

**Available to pre-order in paperback and ebook now**

# CHAPTER ONE

## *Every Herring Must Hang by its Own Gill*

## *Deal, December 1812*

'Miss Winifred Lennicker of Compass Cottage, Cockle Swamp Alley, Deal. You are charged that on the eighth day of December eighteen hundred and twelve, you were found in possession of goods illegally imported from France, namely a half anker of cognac hidden in a handcart. Furthermore, you obstructed a Riding officer whilst he was carrying out his duties in accordance with the law.'

Trembling, Winnie stood listening from the dock as Reverend North, a well-fed gentleman in his fifties wearing a cassock, gazed at her from the Bench in the crowded courtroom. She glanced from the vicar to his fellow magistrates, Mr Norris, a portly figure with a florid complexion who had placed his whip and gold watch on the table in front of him, and Mr Causton, landlord of the Waterman's Arms. Standing to their left was Officer Chase who was bringing the case against her on behalf of the Revenue, watched by an audience that included Winnie's family, and many of the townspeople of Deal, both friends and strangers.

The stench of sweat and filthy clothes cut through the perfume of rosewater and herbs that had been scattered across the floor, making her retch. She was in deep trouble and it wasn't her fault.

'How do you plead?' the vicar went on, strands of powdered hair dangling from his Canterbury cap.

'Stop!' interrupted Officer Chase. 'There is another charge to be included.'

Reverend North gave a weary sigh.

'I understand that you are keen to obtain a conviction and hold this young woman up as an example to those who are involved in the free trade, sir, but may I suggest that your enthusiasm has as much to do with your desire for pecuniary reward as it does for your wish to see justice carried out.'

'You may suggest no such thing,' Officer Chase protested as a ripple of laughter spread through the courtroom. Everybody knew that the officer would receive a bonus if the case that he'd brought against Winnie was proven.

'These are summary offences that can be dealt with here quickly and quietly by the Bench,' Reverend North said haughtily.

'The prisoner—' Winnie didn't like the way the officer lingered on the word '– tried to deceive me by pretending to be somebody else. Impersonation is a capital offence. Miss Lennicker must go to trial at the assizes in front of a judge and jury. I am determined on this course – I will not be gammoned by the villains of Deal any longer. They have led the Revenue a merry dance for long enough.' Officer Chase was a young man, of not more than five and twenty, who stood tall and straight-backed in his riding clothes, his spurs flashing at his ankles. 'Of course, we all know why you won't consider this latter charge, Reverend …'

'Are you questioning my impartiality?'

''E's a man of the cloth, and as honest as the day is long,' somebody shouted.

'What am I to think when it's always the same? My orders are to arrest those responsible for importing contraband, yet no matter how many times I bring prisoners in front of the magistrates in this godforsaken town, they get away with their crimes. I've been a Riding officer for over a year now, employed along the coast to intercept the free traders as they carry goods inland, having dodged the Revenue cruisers looking out for them at sea. I'm no longer wet behind the ears. I've seen how this works.'

'What do you expect? You'll catch anybody who's goin' around mindin' their own business, then plant evidence on 'em,' called another heckler.

'You have no proof,' Officer Chase said, his face pink with annoyance.

'Quiet please.' The vicar raised an eyebrow. 'Let the officer speak. We haven't got all day.'

'I object to Mr Norris being present on the Bench.'

'On what grounds?'

'The accused is known to him. He is married to the prisoner's cousin.'

'I see. Why did you not mention this, George?'

Mr Norris leaned forwards, squinting in Winnie's direction.

'I apologise for not making the connection. I am barely acquainted with my wife's cousin,' he said awkwardly. 'I hardly recognise her – she has grown quite paunchy, like a bitch in whelp.'

'She is in whelp, I reckon.' Winnie heard Mrs Roper muttering to one of the other boatmen's wives as Officer Chase was asking Reverend North what he was intending to do about Mr Norris. The crowd, impatient with the delay for a point of order, began to talk amongst themselves.

Winnie noticed her brother-in-law, a Deal boatman, standing shoulder to shoulder with his crew, having decided to attend the hearing, rather than launch their giant three-masted lugger, the *Whimbrel*, that day. Usually, they would be out cruising, delivering pilots, anchors and letters for the merchant ships and men-'o-war that were anchored in the Downs, the stretch of deep water that lay between Deal beach and the Goodwin Sands. Or they would be rescuing sailors and cargoes from vessels in distress for salvage money, cover for their more profitable activities.

She was touched by their support. They often fought each other, but when they were running prohibited goods – gin, silks and lace – from Gravelines and Dunkirk, unloading them and carrying them inland to hide or sell, they worked together in harmony against the Revenue. However, Winnie couldn't help wondering if their presence – along with that of the other families who were involved in the free trade – all staring at her when she hated attention of any sort even at the best of times, was more of a hindrance than a help.

The vicar brought his gavel down thrice, calling everyone to silence.

'Mr Causton and I have come to a decision. Mr Norris will remain in his place, but he will not make a judgement on this particular case. Contrary to your opinion that we are biased against the Revenue, Officer Chase, we have also decided to hear your charge that the prisoner took on another person's identity with intent to deceive.' The vicar's words turned the blood in Winnie's veins to ice.

Gasps of shock and cries of horror echoed around the courtroom and some of the men started to argue that it wasn't right or fair.

Winnie searched the crowd for her sisters, catching sight of them as they pushed their way to the front. Louisa who was twenty, two years older than Winnie, and married, was leading their younger sister, fifteen-year-old Grace, by the hand. Both were dressed modestly in their Sunday best, Louisa in a navy gown and redingcote, and Grace in one of Winnie's hand-me-downs, a dark brown dress adorned with black ribbon.

'My sister has done nothing wrong,' Louisa said, addressing the magistrates. 'It's me who should be on trial, not her. We were out all day yesterday, selling provisions to the ships in the Downs. When we returned, I left the handcart unattended outside the house for a while. Somebody must have placed the cask inside it then.'

Winnie was grateful to her for trying, but her sister's intervention would make no difference. Nothing would. She didn't care about the minor charges – the Deal magistrates were notorious for making sure that the punishment fitted the crime. For being found in possession of some cognac and obstructing a riding officer, she might get a fine and a spell in gaol, but if indicted on the charge of lying about her identity, she would be on her way to the assizes.

Her throat tightened as though the noose was already around her neck.

She squeezed her eyes shut and pressed her hands to her ears as the courtroom descended into uproar. How had she come to this?

The previous morning, she woke with a sense of unease which intensified when she noticed the pennants of grey cloud streaming across a fiery sky as she was sweeping the pavement outside the cottage. Blowing on her fingers, she returned inside to find Louisa and Grace lining up baskets of pies and apples, and packets of salted pork in the hallway.

'Red sky in the morning, sailors' warning,' she said.

'I hope you aren't suggesting that we stay at home,' Louisa scolded lightly. 'The weather's set fair, according to Jason, who left hours ago by the way. The herring have been swimming up in walms for the past few days - I thought we'd do a little fishing at the same time.

'Don't be such a meaker,' Louisa went on, smiling. 'My husband will rush to our rescue if anything should go wrong, which it won't.'

Offended at being called a mouse, Winnie waited for Grace to fetch the net that she had repaired using fresh twine and wooden shuttles the evening before, straining her eyes in the flickering flame of a tallow candle. Grace had rinsed and dried the pigs' bladders that their uncle had sent from Limepit Acres. Louisa had sewn up the holes and filled them with cognac, watered down and caramelised to suit the English preference.

The bladders were sitting in string bags in a bucket in the hall. Winnie eyed them with distaste.

'There are two each,' Louisa said. 'Two for you, two for me.'

'What about Grace?' Winnie asked.

'Louisa says I'm too much of a clumsy clodpole to carry cognac – I've burst one too many bladders in the past.' Grace chuckled. 'I'm going to bring some lace in case I can persuade a jolly Jack Tar to buy a piece for his sweetheart.'

'Take this.' Louisa handed Grace a length of white galloon. 'It isn't the best and it's a little grubby, so I can't sell it to our more discerning customers.'

She meant the ladies of the ton, Winnie thought as Grace wrapped it around her waist over her dress, then put her cape over the top.

'I wish I had a figure like yours.' Winnie envied her younger sister's elegance and narrow waist. A head taller than Winnie and almost the same height as Louisa, Grace had recently shot up like a runner bean.

'Some ladies can't help being stout,' she said gently.

She was being kind, refraining from giving Winnie the truth. She wasn't merely stout – she freely admitted that she was beginning to look like one of their uncle's fat pigs.

'We are both jealous of your hair,' Louisa joined in. 'God blessed you with the golden locks while I take after Ma, God rest her soul.'

Winnie felt slightly mollified – Louisa's hair was dark brown, and Grace had thick ebony tresses. However, her sisters' attempts to cheer her up couldn't pull her out of the megrims. Louisa considered herself the luckiest woman alive, being married to Jason Witherall, or Marlin – short for marlinspike – as he was known among the men, while Grace was always happy and smiling, with hardly a care in the world.

Winnie helped load the handcart, a painful reminder of Billy who was supposed to have oiled its squeaky wheels but had never got around to it. She didn't enjoy feeling sorry for herself – she considered that she'd been hard done by. Since her beloved Billy had been taken by the gangers back in August and 'volunteered' for service in the King's navy, threads of sorrow and anxiety had woven themselves inextricably into the fabric of her daily life. She thought of him every day, and each night, she lit a candle for him to light his way in case he should find his way home.

As she walked with her sisters along Cockle Swamp Alley and crossed Beach Street to the shore, two bladders of cognac hidden under her petticoats, Winnie refused to consider that Billy might not be alive.

Master Appleton was waiting for them at the capstan grounds, his nose dripping congbells in the cold air. He was twelve years old and small for his age, yet his skinny frame belied his strength.

'Mornin' ladies,' he grinned, relieving Grace of the handcart and trying to shove it across the shingle to their boat, the *Curlew*, one of a handful left at the top of the steeply sloping shore among the makeshift huts and piles of lobster pots.

'Good morning, Cromwell,' Grace said.

Shivering, even though she was wearing extra clothing, including two pairs of stockings, a felt hat and gloves, Winnie gazed from the small fishing boat and her single mast to the three hundred or so merchant ships, East Indiamen, men-o'-war and Revenue cruisers assembled in the Downs beneath a flat grey sky. There was barely a ripple to be seen across the surface of the sea. Where was Billy? Was he out there somewhere?

She winced as Louisa pinched her arm.

'What was that for?' she said, affronted.

'You're supposed to be helping us.'

'I'm sorry,' she muttered.

'I'm sorry too. We're all thinking of him,' Louisa said gently, her eyes filled with compassion.

'Thank you.' Overwhelmed, Winnie turned away, hiding fresh tears as she picked up a basket.

It wasn't long before they had loaded the *Curlew* and were ready to launch, Winnie and her sisters sitting in the boat with Cromwell, holding tight to the gunwales and looking down at the sea thirty yards below, while another of the shore boys prepared to release the rope attached to the *Curlew*'s bow.

'Let her go,' Louisa shouted, and the shore boy let go of the rope.

The *Curlew* began to move stern-first, accelerating over the rollers that were laid in a row down the beach, until she flew into the water, hitting it with an enormous bang. As she settled, Cromwell used an oar to push them clear of the beach. Winnie took the helm while Louisa and Grace rigged the lugsail and Cromwell bailed out a couple of buckets of water from the *Curlew*'s hull, and they set out across the water, joining the other small boats competing to provision the large vessels that stood in the roadstead.

Later, they cast out the net and fished for a while at a mark to the south. Looking back, Winnie could see the white cliffs of Dover and then the town of Deal with its muddle of houses – some with red Dutch roofs, some tiled, some thatched – built along the beach.

'Winnie, you are in a world of your own,' she heard Louisa say. 'I said, it's time we were going home.'

'It's turned out to be a good day, despite your doubts to the contrary,' Grace said cheerfully, looking at their empty baskets and buckets spilling over with herring. 'We've sold everything except the lace, and the Revenue didn't come over to bother us.'

Winnie had to admit that it had been better than she'd expected.

Having left the herring to rouse in salt for a few hours the same evening, it was after dark by the time Winnie went back into the hang, a small extension attached to the rear of the cottage. She took one of the sticks that they used as a spit and hooked the silver fish by the gills along its length. Then she clambered up the ladder to hang it in the dark chamber above her head where the timbers were tarred with oil and smoke from years of use. After climbing down again, she fetched a candle and touched its flame to the pile of oak shavings, coaxing them into a quiet smoulder.

She watched a curl of smoke rise into the air and snake its way around the deeply forked tails of the row of fish, transforming them into bloaters. By morning, the skins would have turned to gold and their flesh grown soft, gamey and ready to eat – just as Billy liked them.

Winnie dashed a hot tear from her cheek as she remembered their neighbour's son who was the same age as Louisa. He had been a boy with dirty knees and a cheeky smile, whose father had gone away to sea a few weeks after he was born and had never been heard of again. They'd called him 'carrot top' and 'big ears' and teased him mercilessly about his freckles and the holes in his shoes until Ma had given them a stern telling-off. Mrs Fleet, his mother, struggled to get by, and Ma used to give her their broken bloaters while Pa took Billy out fishing. Mr and Mrs Lennicker had taken Billy in when he was orphaned at fourteen by his mother's untimely death.

At first Winnie had been jealous of the time he'd spent with her father, but her feelings had changed as he turned into a young man, and she had fallen for him.

'Winnie! Are you avoiding us?' On hearing Louisa's voice, she checked that the shavings were still burning, and reluctantly left the hang.

'Oh, there you are,' Grace said as she entered the kitchen.

'What is it you want?' Winnie asked, addressing Louisa who was tucking a small packet inside her bodice.

'A stranger called,' Grace said.

'I didn't hear anyone.'

'That's because you were hiding like Pa used to.' Louisa smiled wryly and Winnie smiled back, recalling how their father would disappear into the hang with his pipe.

'Who was it?'

'A stranger – I told you.'

'There's no need for us to know his identity. In fact, the less we know, the better. Suffice to say, I have some papers and cognac to deliver to a gentleman who's waiting at the Five Bells at Ringwould and you're coming with me.' Louisa looked from Winnie to Grace and back. 'I would ask Jason, but he isn't home yet.'

'I'm not going,' Winnie said quickly. 'It's terrible cold and dark and the only people about are those who are up to no good.'

'You can't mean Old Boneyparte and his Grande Armée,' Louisa said. 'The news is that he's in retreat from Russia.'

'How do you know that's true? It could be a rumour to put us off our guard.' Winnie could hardly remember a time when they hadn't been at war with Napoleon. Since she was a child, she'd seen him as the bogeyman, waiting on the other side of the Channel for his chance to invade England.

'I'm not worried about the Frenchies,' Louisa went on. 'It's the drunkards and thieves, and men who would take advantage of a lone woman.'

They were living in dangerous times. The Great War against the self-appointed Emperor of France, and Mr Madison's War, the conflict against America, had brought an influx of foreigners to Deal. People came to work in trades such as ship's chandlery and ropemaking, while the wives of the men sent to reinforce the Marquess of Wellington's army on the Peninsula, brought their children to wait for their return. There were soldiers, sailors, naval officers, builders, provisioners and sailmakers. And then there were the rest: the pickpockets, robbers and ruffians.

Winnie's reflection scowled from the polished copper pan that hung from a hook beside the fire. She was tired out, having been on her feet all day. Where would she find the strength to walk the three miles or more to Ringwould?

'I can't afford to turn work away. I'm doing this for us, our family.'

Winnie felt a little uncomfortable because Louisa had always done her best for her and Grace, and she was too kind to remind them that they depended on her husband's goodwill for their keep and the roof over their heads. Jason had bought Compass Cottage when it was auctioned off to pay some of their father's debts after he died.

'The three of us will keep each other company,' Louisa added in a tone that brooked no argument.

Why did she always let her sister twist her arm? Winnie grumbled to herself when they were walking along the alley, wrapped up against the cold. Following Louisa and Grace, she pushed the handcart along towards Lower Street, its wheels squeaking with every turn, and the contents of the cask that was hidden beneath a sheet inside it, sloshing about.

As they travelled further, making the most of the light from the crescent moon and stars, the great stone walls of Deal Castle loomed from the shadows.

'Listen,' Grace whispered, slowing down. 'There are men on horseback … they're coming this way.'

'It's the gobblers, Riding officers. Don't stop,' Louisa muttered.

'Who goes there?' a voice rang out.

'There's no answer – perhaps it is a very large meaker.'

There was laughter as Louisa and Grace's figures melted into the gloom, leaving Winnie with the handcart. As the pair of mounted officers approached her, her heart missed a beat, and then another until she was afraid it was going to stop altogether.

'Show yourself, missus.'

Almost blinded by lanternlight and scared witless, Winnie had no choice but to step forward when she recognised the two men from past confrontations: Officers Chase and Lawrence.

'Your name?' Officer Chase said.

'Mrs Fleet,' she replied after a moment's hesitation.

'I didn't know Billy had got wed before he left. Tell me your name truthfully.'

'I've told you – I'm Mrs Fleet.' She went on to fill the silence, remembering to speak roughly like a peasant woman, not a lady as her mother had always insisted upon. 'I've been nursin' my sister-in-law since she fell bodily ill last week,' she elaborated. 'We buried her yesterday.'

'Then I'm sorry for your loss,' he said with mock gravity. 'Do convey my commiserations to your brother-in-law.'

'My brother—' she began to doubt herself.

'It's very strange, considering that you have no brothers, apart from Billy himself.' He had caught her in a lie, and she had gotten herself into a tangle. She tried to think of an explanation, her mind frozen like her fingers and toes. Louisa would have known what to say and how to put it in the best light, but she'd gone and left her in the lurch.

'Don't treat me like a fool, Miss Winnie Lennicker. I'm not going to let you, or your sisters pull the wool over my eyes again.'

'You cannot rummage me,' she said, alarmed at the thought of anyone except her Billy touching her.

'That's true as you are a member of the fairer sex, but there's nothing to stop us examining the handcart for contraband.' Officer Chase jumped down from his horse, looped the ribbons over his arm and stepped closer.

Winnie couldn't bear it, knowing that her part in a crime was about to be discovered.

She shoved herself between the officer and the handcart, planted her palms on his chest and pushed him away.

'Oh dear,' he smirked. 'You aren't helping yourself, are you? I'm going to have to arrest you for obstructing a Riding officer in the course of his duty.'

In her panic, she made to run, but he grabbed her by the arm and hissed in her ear, 'You would be wise not to add to your tally of misdemeanours. Understood?'

'Yes, sir,' she said.

'Good.' He drew a cutlass and used the tip of the blade to lift the corner of the sheet, revealing the cask. 'Aha, it's as I suspected.'

'Something to keep our spirits up on a long cold night?'

'We will take it to the Customs House in the morning—'

'After we have tested the contents,' Officer Lawrence chuckled. 'Let me take the seized goods and your horse while you see this young woman to gaol.'

'No,' Winnie gasped, looking around wildly for her sisters. 'I want to go home.'

'The magistrates will decide in the morning what will happen to you,' Officer Chase said. 'I anticipate that justice will be served.'

She cried as he led her along the streets to the gaol where a miserable old hag with no teeth locked her in a room with three other women who had been arrested for whoring and theft. The privations of the gaol – the cold, hard floor, the thin blanket crawling with bugs, and the congealing mass of cold porridge – were sickening, but she barely noticed, being consumed by fear and regret, and resentment that her sisters had abandoned her to her fate.

The vicar's voice and the rat-a-tat-tat of his gavel brought her back to the present.

'Pray silence, ladies and gentlemen.' The audience settled and Reverend North turned to address Officer Chase. 'Did you see the prisoner place the cask in the handcart?'

The officer frowned. 'No, I can't say that I did.'

'Then you cannot confirm that Miss Lennicker was aware that she was transporting illegally imported goods?'

'No, but her unwomanly behaviour in trying to prevent my search has to give weight to my view that she is guilty of the charge.'

'The law relies on evidence, supported by witness statements, not your perceptions,' Reverend North said. 'The allegation of possession cannot be proved beyond reasonable doubt. However, I find the prisoner guilty of obstruction.'

Winnie struggled to breathe as she awaited the decision on the third and final charge.

'I have read Officer Lawrence's statement regarding your charge that the prisoner attempted to mislead you by taking on another person's identity. Miss Lennicker was pretending to be married, that's all. She was in effect, impersonating herself. That is not a capital offence.'

'What you are saying is fustian nonsense,' Officer Chase exploded, losing his temper as well he might, Winnie thought, knowing he had come within an ames-ace of sending one of his adversaries to the assizes. 'It's a bag of moonshine and slum.'

'How do you respond, Miss Lennicker?' the vicar asked her directly. 'Why did you tell the officer that you were Mrs Fleet?'

Winnie was torn. Reverend North was giving her a way out. In truth, she had pretended to be somebody else, hoping that the Riding officers wouldn't recognise her as one of the Lennickers, but it appeared that if she gave her secret away, she would avoid the gallows.

Suddenly, she found her voice. Burning with shame, she confessed.

'I am with child,' she said. 'I didn't want anyone to think badly of me.'

'She gave a false name to protect her reputation, not to evade justice. The charge is dismissed.' The vicar raised his hand as the officer opened his mouth to argue, then closed it again. 'Officer Chase, have no fear – you will receive your bonus. I sentence the prisoner to one hour in the stocks as an example to others. That is all.' He turned to the guard. 'Mr Stripe, take her down and bring the next prisoner in front of the Bench.'

As Winnie was being led away, she looked for her sisters. Louisa was smiling with relief while Grace appeared dumbfounded – as well she might, having found out that the sister she looked up to was carrying a child out of wedlock. She had made a fine mess of things. Not only had she been humiliated in the courtroom, she was about to be disgraced in the stocks.

It was her own fault – she had set out on the wrong course, bringing her misfortunes upon herself: lying with Billy before they were married; failing to stand up to Louisa. She recalled a saying their Ma used to use: every herring must hang by its own gill. From now on, she vowed to stand up for herself and – she stroked her belly – her unborn child.